THE SAINT

AMELIA SHEA

Amelia Shea

This book is a work of fiction. The names, characters, places and incidents are products of the writer's imagination, or have been used fictitiously and are not to be construed as real. Any resemblance to real persons, living or dead, actual events or organizations is entirely coincidental.

Copyright © 2020 by Amelia Shea
All rights reserved.

The unauthorized reproduction or distribution of this copyright work is illegal. No part of this book may be distributed, reproduced, or stored in a retrieval system, or transmitted in any form or by any means, electronic, mechanical, photocopying, recording, or otherwise, without express written permission of the publisher.

Dedication

For Ann-Marie, my forever friend.

Chapter 1

"Somebody shoot me and put me out of my goddamn misery."

Bailey tightened her lips, resisting the urge to smile when Gerry quietly muttered his request.

As mayor, her professionalism was required. She side glanced Gerry, one of the councilmen seated next to her at the head table of the town hall. She couldn't fault him. She was having similar thoughts. Hers hadn't been nearly as violent. She was leaning more toward a meteor hitting the abandoned field behind the building. Enough of a disruption that they'd have to evacuate, but safe enough no one would get hurt. A meteor would definitely put their small town on the map. She'd given it a good amount of thought. She had the time—this meeting was well into its second hour.

In between her natural disaster daydream and listening to the local complainer, she spared a few glances toward the back of the room. Discretely, of course, or so she had hoped.

Several members of the Ghosttown Riders Motorcycle Club had taken up the last row in the town hall. It wasn't their first time attending a meeting. In fact, since they had officially moved in four months prior, at least two members had attended each meeting. They mostly listened and remained silent. A few times, she caught their amusement when a new topic was brought up. She couldn't blame them. Installing video cameras on Main Street to identify the pet owner who didn't clean up after their dog was humorous. *Welcome to Ghosttown.*

She peeked past the shield of her auburn hair, intently focused on one member in particular. He was seated between Kase, the president, and Gage. She wasn't sure if Gage had a title amongst the club. Had it been club flirt, it would have been accurate. She dropped her gaze to the table then glanced up again. She couldn't resist.

Saint. There was something about the man centered between the others. Besides the obvious draw of him being stunningly sexy with his dark hair and violet eyes, there was a quiet, mysterious edge she couldn't help find appealing. Even with his guarded stature of crossed arms and stern scowl, he was handsome. Actually, it may have made him even more appealing in her eyes. He wore his cut over a long-sleeved dark gray shirt. *It's a shame.* She'd seen Saint enough times in short sleeves to know what was hiding underneath. Sculpted muscular arms covered in an array of multi-colored tattoos.

She crossed her legs and shifted in her seat.

She hadn't spoken to him often, but she took every opportunity presented to her. When she didn't have one, she settled for staring at him. The corner of her mouth curled as her gaze traveled over his body—from his dark, worn boots, up his legs covered in black pants, to his leather vest fitted tightly around his chest, and making her way to his clean-shaven chiseled jaw and his smirking lips.

Smirking lips. What?

She blinked and inched her gaze up to find his eyes staring back at her. Her heart did a funny jump, or maybe a skip. *Oh hell, did it stop?* She should have looked away. *I can't.* She was frozen in a trance. He had the most magnificent eyes. From a distance, they could be confused with hazel, or possibly blue. Up close, they were violet. His dark long lashes and thick brows only enhanced their beauty. The knot in her throat tightened. *Look away.* A small shift in his jaw seemed to break her daze. He raised his brows and the corner of his eyes crinkled.

She flinched when she felt a poke in her side. She whipped her head toward Gerry, who seemed to be holding back a laugh. He lifted his chin, gesturing to the room. It wasn't until then that she realized the whole room was staring back at her.

Oh my God. She tried to swallow, but the lump in her throat prevented even a deep breath. A quick scan was an indication she had missed something. She cleared her throat and smiled.

"I'm sorry, what were you saying?" Her palms were clammy as she rubbed her hands together, trying her best to beat down the blush she knew was invading her cheeks. She focused solely on the man standing in the center of the room and ignored the stares from everyone else.

Arnett Collins, Ghosttown's resident pain in the ass, was standing a few feet away with an aggravated scowl penetrating his brows. He had been speaking for fifteen minutes when she zoned out and set her sights on more interesting things. Mainly the hot biker in the back. *Big mistake.*

He sighed dramatically, waving his hand over his head, fisting a stack of papers. "I said, I got evidence right here. It's her cat." Arnett whipped around and glared back at Mary, who seemed unaffected by his accusations. She pursed her lips, glancing up at Bailey, then rolled her eyes.

"It's not Murray." Raising her voice was out of character for the usually sweet older woman. Then again, everyone seemed to take the same tone when dealing with Arnett. The man had a way of wearing people down. Bailey included, though she never lost her temper.

"It is," Arnett shouted, his face turning as bright as a tomato. For those who didn't know him, it may have been cause for concern. As a local who had the unfortunate luck of dealing with Arnett on a weekly basis, she knew this was the norm for him.

Mary, God love her, snorted and shook her head. "Nope, it's not."

Bailey leaned forward on the table, catching Arnett's attention. "Can I please see the pictures?"

He scoffed and stormed up to the desk. Instead of handing her the photos, he slammed them down on the table. He remained bitter from three years ago when he ran for mayor, and she won. No one was more surprised when they made the announcement. She hadn't even been in the race. It seemed the townspeople had gotten together and decided she was the best person for the position, unbeknownst to her until they announced it. She initially pleaded her case with reasons why she should not be mayor. The town disagreed, and she settled in as mayor of Ghosttown. She may not have wanted the position, but felt an obligation to do her best. Most people seemed pleased with her. *Not everyone.* She eyed Arnett and smiled.

"Thank you." She slid the pictures in front of her and peered down. Gerry and Bert, the other councilmen, leaned closer on either side. They all gave it the proper attention. In the end, there was no denying it. As mayor, she had to break the news.

"It's not Murray."

"I told ya," Mary said, then smiled at her. "Thanks, Bailey."

"The hell it isn't. This is her damn cat. I have proof right there."

Bailey held up her hand. "It's not her cat in the pictures, Mr. Collins. Murray has a thicker tail and a shinier coat. This cat has speckled feet, and Murray's are all white."

She watched Arnett, waiting on his rebuttal. He'd have one, he always did. Gerry leaned closer. "Do the gavel thing before he starts up again."

"Please, Bailey, end this," Bert pleaded.

She grabbed the gavel and hit the desk. "Meeting's over, thanks so much to everyone who came out." She pushed back her chair and averted her gaze from Arnett. He'd back down, until next month when he'd be back again with something else.

She remained seated, gathering up the paperwork from the table. A quick glance around the room showed most people had darted out as soon as the gavel hit the table. Except a few. She bowed her head and peered through her hair, catching the club members filing out through the side entrance.

They stood out in the small town, and while people were curious, most residents kept their distance. It was the persona, she assumed. Even Bailey could admit their presence was intimidating. But they had shown only good intentions since their arrival, and Bailey was determined to make them feel as welcome as possible.

Saint was last in line, and as he breached the door, he turned his head and aimed his gaze directly at her. *Maybe he felt my stare?* She shifted in her seat. It was mortifying enough to get caught ogling him in front of half the town. She wasn't looking to extend her embarrassment. However, he'd obviously caught her staring. She couldn't just look away. She smiled and lifted her hand in an awkward wave.

He dipped his chin. She noticed he did it a lot in acknowledgment. He kept his eyes on her until he walked through the door. She inhaled a breath, settling into her seat.

"Night, Bailey," Gerry said, halfway through the room with Bert following close behind.

"Bye. Have a nice night, guys, and thank you." She always felt compelled to thank them. While they were paid for holding their positions, the money was mediocre at best. Both Gerry and Bert held full times jobs aside from their positions in the town.

They usually offered to help clean up. Not tonight. She couldn't fault them, they were both married, and Gerry had kids. They needed to get home to their families. The hall cleared out in record time. Most meetings, there were a few stragglers who settled in with a refill of coffee and pastry, to talk to a neighbor. However, with the meeting going longer than usual, it seemed everyone was eager to leave.

She walked over to the closet and grabbed a garbage bag.

When she turned, she was surprised to see Coop at the entrance. He was leaning up against the doorframe peering outside. Bailey made her way to the snack table.

"What are you still doing here?" she asked as she opened the bag.

Coop turned his head, facing her. He shrugged. "Figured I'd help ya clean up."

Bailey smiled. He and his wife had always been very friendly to her. She didn't know their exact ages. If she had to guess she would say early thirties. They had her over a few times for dinner at their place. They were currently in the process of trying to have a baby. And struggling.

"You should go home. I got this."

His shoulders tensed, and he glanced outside again. "I'll wait."

"Okay." She wouldn't argue. She glanced down at the table. "You want me to pack up some of this for you and Marley?"

Coop eyed the table, and she caught the gleam in his eye right before he shook his head. "No, you take it."

Bailey laughed and raised her brows. "No way am I going to be able to eat all this, Coop." There had been less of a showing at tonight's meeting than usual. The snack table, however, had been in full supply. "How about we split it?"

Coop smiled and nodded. Bailey divvied up the leftovers giving his plate more than hers. When he moved to argue, Bailey beat him to it.

"You have two people. Besides, Marley loves those cheese stick things Mary makes."

Coop laughed and took the plate from her hand. She expected him to leave. He remained. When she cleared the table, she moved forward with the garbage bag. They had a dumpster out back. Coop shifted in front of her, taking the bag out of her hands.

"I'll take it. You get your stuff and close up."

"Okay, thanks."

She watched him walk out and twisted her lips. Coop was a

sweet guy and helped her out with a few things. His offering wasn't out of the ordinary. Though, he seemed on edge for some reason. She grabbed her bag and switched off the lights. She did a quick scan of the hall and locked the doors behind her.

Their town hall was a restored barn from the sixties. A few years ago, with the surplus in taxes, they were able to redo the interior and add a new roof. She was quite proud of the project. A few residents had argued they should remodel with more of a modern appeal. Arnett and the longtime residents had protested. They won.

When she turned, Coop was standing a foot away.

She jumped back and grabbed her chest. "Oh my God, you scared me."

"Sorry."

Bailey laughed. "No, it's fine. Well, tell Marley I said hi. I'm due to have you guys over soon, so pick a day and have Marley call me."

"Okay." He didn't move.

She furrowed her brows. "Are you alright?"

He glanced over to the edge of the building. "Yeah, I'm fine. C'mon, I'll walk you to your car."

She glanced over his shoulder. His pickup truck was parked out front while hers was on the side.

"Don't be silly, Coop, you're parked right there." She pointed over his shoulder and noticed his jaw lock. "I'll be fine." She smiled, which did nothing to ease his tension. "Go home to your wife."

"Promised my wife, I'd make sure I saw you to your car."

She furrowed her brows. *Why?* She angled her head, and then it clicked.

She tightened her lips, holding back a muttered curse. Small towns held no secrets. Especially Bailey's. She rarely shared her past with any of her new friends. It was a hard rule she usually followed. Her story drew pity, which Bailey didn't want. However, her story could easily be found on the internet and drew attention in the town once she was elected mayor. She couldn't be sure of the source who outed her, but she had her suspicions. An angry, bitter ex-mayoral candidate was top on her list. Most residents had the decency and respect for her privacy to not ask any questions. A few of the older women and men had taken a protective stance with her. While it was appreciated, Bailey viewed it as unnecessary. She was safe in Ghosttown. *For now.*

Coop dug his hands in his pockets and stared back at her silently. She drew in a breath. *I should have kept my mouth shut.*

While she had always remained tight-lipped about her past, as her connections to a select few grew, she shared, at the suggestion of her therapist. It was supposed to openly help her heal, especially at a time when her memories were being brought back to the surface by Adam's upcoming release.

Upon the advice of her doctor, she spoke at a support meeting and shared with Marissa and her friend Trista. She hadn't expected to share with Marley, however, when her friend spoke about their very personal struggle with getting pregnant, and opened up about her previous miscarriages, Bailey felt compelled to give something of herself to Marley. She hadn't gone into extreme detail. She gave the PG version of the incident. Not many people could stomach the whole truth. She mentioned her ex-boyfriend and his impending release from prison. She hadn't made it a big deal. If anything, she downplayed her concern as to not cause panic with her friend. Marley's face was easy to read. Bailey was able to gauge her uneasy worry once she mentioned Adam getting out soon. Marley had even gone as far as offering Bailey her spare room if she felt unsafe staying at her house. At the time, Bailey was touched by the gesture. She hadn't considered it being anything more than a passing concern. She'd underestimated the effect it had on Marley. And now, Coop.

Bailey forced a smile and reached out, grasping his forearm with a reassuring squeeze.

"I'm fine, Coop. And I am so very thankful to have friends like you and Marley who care about me." Her heart grew with her statement. She'd found good people to surround herself with in the small town. "I'm good. You guys don't need to worry about me. It's unnecessary."

He shook his head slowly, as though he was trying to make an important point. "I don't think it is, and neither does my wife."

Bailey drew in a deep breath and smiled. It was her only defense mechanism.

"He hasn't gotten out yet, Coop. They'll notify me when he is released." She forced a smile she had hoped came off as genuine. "And while I appreciate your concern, I'm fine. Really, I'm not worried." Her voice shook, and she quickly cleared her throat. Hiding emotion was never something she'd been gifted with. She averted her eyes in hopes he wouldn't see past her lie.

It is a lie. Possibly one of the biggest she'd ever told. Adam would get out of jail, free to roam wherever, including Ghosttown if he chose. The idea of ever coming face to face with him again stirred an unfathomable fear in her. For all the steps she'd taken to heal and move on, his impending release was setting her back to a time when fear ruled her existence. *I'm not that girl anymore.*

"After what he did to you?" He shook his head, his lip curling in disgust. "The bastard should rot in prison, Bailey. He doesn't deserve to see the light of day."

Coop's words had been muttered a million times over by her mother and father, her brothers, countless friends. Even from her own mouth in the early days of her recovery. It seemed easier for Bailey to forgive and push on than it was for the others. *If I don't forgive him, I'll never move forward.*

Coop flattened his lips and tugged his ball cap over his eyes. "You mean a lot to Marley and me." He sighed. "This town. You're one of us, and we take care of our own."

Bailey smiled and fought against the tears pooling in her eyes. She'd felt at home the second she moved to Ghosttown. Hearing Coop's words only confirmed it. She was exactly where she was supposed to be.

"You need to let us take care of you, Bailey. A few of us will make a schedule. We'll stay on the nights you close up the meetings and walk you to your car. We'll even follow you home if you want."

She shook her head. She swallowed the knot in her throat. It was all too much. "He's not going to come here and…"

Coop stepped closer and narrowed his gaze. "You don't know that, Bailey."

She gasped and a cold chill spread over her skin like frost. He was right. No matter how much she'd played it off to her friends, her family, and even herself. She didn't know where Adam's head was at, or what he was thinking or potentially planning and plotting.

"Every meeting, one of us will walk you to your car." It was a statement, not a question. He glanced at the empty edge of the building. "He may not be out yet, but there are other threats around, and ya shouldn't be out here alone at night. We should have been doing this since you became mayor." He nodded. "I'm walking you to your car, Bailey." His tone was firm and a bit out of character for the easygoing Coop. But he was a good guy, doing a good guy thing.

Among the fear and anxiousness of the situation, her belly warmed, and an ease rolled through her. *I'm one of theirs. One of Ghosttown's.*

Bailey smiled. "Okay, then walk to my car." They started down the steps and through the empty lot. She eyed him carefully. His focus was straight ahead, and he seemed on high alert. He remained quiet while she tried to gauge where his tension was stemming from. Maybe it was residual from their conversation. Or was it something else?

They rounded the side of the building where she had parked. Immediately, her eyes widened. Next to her car were four motorcycles and their riders standing in a circle.

Why are they still here? They had headed out as soon as the meeting ended, and she assumed they had taken off. They didn't usually linger afterward. The town as a whole hadn't quite warmed up to the club moving in just yet. It would be a process. She had done her best to assure those who were skeptical that the Ghosttown Riders weren't interested in taking over their town, they just wanted to be a part of it. She had swayed a few. Others were harder to convince.

She noticed Kase, the president, glance up and eye her, then shift his gaze to Coop. One by the one, the members turned. She recognized them all. Rourke. Gage. Her heart sped up and her face heated when Saint turned and his violet eyes landed on her.

Ahhh...this man. It figured. The first guy to pique her interest since the incident would be a man completely beyond her reach. Her attraction to Saint was possibly ruining her chances for any man to come into her life. *Talk about setting the bar high.*

She smiled, but it wasn't returned. Saint's attention had shifted to Coop as his gaze narrowed.

Coop shifted closer to her and angled his body, so he was standing almost in front of her. *Ohhhhhhhh.* Now it all made sense. She chuckled, and Coop glanced down at her with a scowl.

"I'm assuming they are what you meant by other threats?" she whispered.

Coop shifted his gaze. "We don't know them, and until we do? I don't trust them."

"Are you playing bodyguard?"

"If I have to."

She flattened her lips and nodded slowly. It shouldn't have surprised her. Coop was truly a gentleman, and if it had been a group of strange men, she may have been thankful for his protective stance. It wasn't necessary, though. Not with the club.

This was where the true divide between the club and the townspeople stemmed from. Fear of the unknown.

They moved closer to her car, and in turn, closer to the guys. They watched as she and Coop approached. If she didn't know better, she'd think they had been waiting on her.

Bailey lifted her hand in a short wave. "Hey."

She noticed the chin lifts and nods, but none of them said a word. They all seemed to be eyeing Coop with suspicion. Introductions were necessary to bridge the town as a whole. She was up for the challenge.

"Have you guys met Coop?" She glanced up to see him returning their glares. "He and his wife Marley, live down the street from Trax and Cheyenne."

No one said a word, and the men seemed to be in an odd stare-down. Bailey pushed her way in front of Coop. "So, Coop, this is Gage, Kase, Rourke, and..." Her breath hitched, and all eyes darted down to her. *Why the hell did I pause?* Her cheeks heated and she turned to Coop, who was eyeing her suspiciously. "And Saint."

"Nice to meet ya, man," Gage said, reaching out.

Bailey refused to glance in Saint's direction until the blush was gone, which might be never.

She was happily surprised when Coop shook his hand. It may not have been much, but it was something. Coop returned to his position next to Bailey in a protective stance.

It'll take more than an introduction, I guess.

Bailey smiled up at Kase. "Is there something I can do for you?"

He remained silent, eyeing the distance between her and Coop. His brows furrowed, and he side glanced to his left. She followed the direction and landed on Saint who was staring at her through hooded eyes. She smiled and the corner of his mouth curled. The man had perfected the half-smile.

"Wanted to invite ya to a party this Saturday."

Bailey whipped her head to Gage, who was grinning. She wasn't sure if he was happy or thoroughly amused by what she assumed was her shocked reaction.

Me? She gulped. *At their party?*

HER REACTION WAS PRICELESS.

He almost hadn't made it to the meeting with his schedule. Thank fuck he did. He wouldn't have wanted to miss her face when Gage invited her to the party.

He was a master at the poker face in most situations. Bailey changed the game for him. Her wide eyes and jaw-dropping pouty lip had his control wavering. *So damn sweet.* He objected to the invite when Kase brought it up a few days ago. His plan with Bailey had been a year in the making. If she was going to be at the clubhouse, he wanted to be the one to bring her in with his claim fully known to the club. He'd waited long enough, but there were still a few loose ends he needed to clear up before he was a permanent resident in Ghosttown. When it was all secured, he'd finally make his long-awaited move.

He'd been shot down. Kase stressed the importance of having Bailey show some sort of solidarity with the club. The townspeople had yet to warm up to their presence. He figured if Bailey showed at the party, the residents would feel more comfortable around them. The club had plans of expanding the town, and the last thing they needed was having to go head to head with Ghosttown to make it happen. Saint had no doubt they'd prevail either way. At his suggestion, Kase was taking the diplomatic route.

"A party?" Her voice cracked as she stammered out the two words.

Gage chuckled, and her face instantly paled. He knitted his brows. Was she scared? Bailey had never shown any fear from the club. There was no mistaking the signs of stress lining her face. He balled his fists.

When Kase stepped forward, she didn't back away. It was a good sign.

"Just a barbeque. It's a family thing. Riss and Caden are coming up. Figured you come by, check it out, then report back to the fine people of Ghosttown," Kase's gaze slowly turned on Coop. "Tell em' we're not the fucking degenerate criminals their small minds fucking think we are." Kase sneered, making him appear almost sinister. "Not burying bodies in the yard." He paused and smiled with his stare remaining on Coop. "At least, not this weekend."

Saint drew in a breath, remaining silent. It was not how he would have handled it. Kase lacked the finesse. Saint had to give Coop credit, he didn't shy away, though Saint read the uncertainty in his eyes. He'd be smart to fear them. They could be civil members of society. Or they could be Ghosttown's worst fucking nightmare.

A sharp movement from the corner had Saint jerking his stare to Bailey, who seemed caught off guard by the tension. *Shit!* It was not how they intended it to go down.

"I'd, um, love to come." Bailey forced a smile, and her lower lip trembled. He was making a mental note for the future. Bailey was not a fan of confrontation. He'd watched her handle her own against a few angry residents with grace and patience. Something about male against male was making her tense and uneasy. He reached out, gripping Kase's arm. When Kase looked over, Saint merely stared. Kase sighed and stepped back, taking his non-verbal cue to back off.

"What can I bring?"

Saint glanced over at Bailey, and his lips twitched. *So fucking adorable.* If he had to wait much longer for her, it would be impossible. Gage stepped closer, and he noticed she didn't back away. *Good.*

"Whatever ya want. Starts at three."

Bailey smiled. "Great, I'll be there." She turned to Coop. "Thanks for walking me out." She walked to her car, opening the door. "Don't forget to tell Marley about dinner at my place."

Coop smiled, and his shoulders seemed to relax. "I will. Drive safe, Bails." He stepped back slowly. Saint had the feeling Coop wouldn't leave until Bailey was out of the lot. The act alone had earned him Saint's respect.

Bailey settled into her seat and reversed the car. As she rolled backward, she glanced up at them again, her eyes were solely on him. When she pulled out of the lot, he noticed Coop halfway to his pickup.

"I thought we were supposed to play nice with the people, Kase," Gage said with a laugh.

"Ya wanna look at me hard, motherfucker better be able to back that shit up," Kase said with a smirk. "Just proving a point."

"Yeah, you're a fucking charmer, Prez," Rourke said as he took a drag from his cigarette.

Saint sighed. It could have been worse. He made his way to his bike parked between Kase and Gage. He mounted the motorcycle and grabbed his helmet when he felt the stares. He glanced up to see all three brothers watching him.

"My guess is you'll be there Saturday?" Kase asked.

Saint remained silent. His appearances at parties were rare. However, he'd definitely be there this weekend.

Gage chuckled and shook his head. "It's becoming clear now." He walked over, smirking at Saint. "Bailey is off-limits to the club unless you're the VP." He snickered. "Not fair, man. Using your power to snatch up the mayor."

Saint ignored the teasing. It had become clear to quite a few members of his interest in Bailey, and while she was off-limits as per Kase, it didn't apply to Saint.

He turned back, staring at the empty road where her taillights were no longer in sight. It was a five-minute drive to her house. He'd take a quick ride and let her settle in before doing a drive by. He'd kept tabs on Bailey for the past three months. He had also dug into her past when Caden, Kase's brother, shared some unsettling news.

Bailey didn't know it, but she had an entire motorcycle club watching her back.

"Got Decker watching. He'll let us know," Kase said, and Saint glanced over his shoulder.

Decker was a friend of the club. He was linked as the go-to guy for both Kase's MC and Ghosttown East. Saint had made the call personally to find out about Bailey's ex a few months ago.

Decker called in to Kase a week ago informing them his release had been approved. His time in prison was ending.

Rourke leaned forward. "Not one fucking guy in with him?"

Saint sighed, jerking his chin. "No."

Their contacts ran far and wide, including prisons. Unfortunately, they had no one on the inside with Bailey's ex. Not even an extended contact they could call in a favor with to help with their issue. If they had, the only way the bastard would be getting out would have been in a body bag.

Chapter 2

"The MC is classing up, I see."

Bailey smiled at the man approaching her table. The very handsome and impossibly irresistible club flirt. She'd been on the receiving end a few times. Not a bad place to be when it came to Dobbs. He wasn't necessarily her type, a little too sexually aggressive for her, but who didn't like being flirted with? He stopped behind Meg and rested his hands on her shoulders. She shook her head and looked up.

"Yeah, we're trying to keep it classy, so behave."

He furrowed his brows and scanned all the women at the table. "Behave? Me? You're asking too much, Meg." He gazed over to Bailey, giving her a wink.

Cheyenne and Macy giggled and began teasing Dobbs. Bailey turned to Marissa. She seemed amused also, watching and listening to the banter from Dobbs and the ladies. Of all the women seated, Bailey and Meg were the only single women. Meg was Mick's old lady. He had died a short time ago. Bailey found it odd she still gathered with the MC, until Meg explained, they were family for life.

She couldn't have predicted in all her twenty-five years she would ever be sitting at a motorcycle club party. Strange how life threw curves. A path she never saw for herself, and there she was, a town mayor at a club party.

This wasn't the first time she'd been at the Ghosttown Riders' clubhouse. A few months ago, when Marissa and Caden got married, she was invited to the reception held at the clubhouse. However, she'd never been invited to one of their club barbeques. Until today.

When the invitation was extended last week she was surprised, but she saw the motive behind it. It was smart on the club's end. She didn't take offense to be invited for a purpose. She shared the same agenda. Her attendance was a good faith effort on her part to unify the residents. The town had resisted the acceptance of the club. Bailey figured if they saw her attending the party, they might be more inclined to give this group a chance. Most residents were older and enjoyed their quiet, tranquil existence in Ghosttown. They missed the bigger picture. If the town developed, it would be lucrative in business and real estate. It was a win for all of them.

She had shared her views with the locals. Giving them her perspective of the potential of growth had swayed some to give them a chance. *Some, not all.*

"So, Bailey, what do ya think of our little barbeque" Dobbs asked, grinning down at her. He had a great smile, warm and inviting.

"Not quite what I expected, but definitely a lot of fun."

It wasn't anything she expected. She had an unfair preconceived notion of what she would be walking into. Massive amounts of drinking, and possibly drugs, loud metal music, and topless, maybe bottomless women scattered around the party. In her stereotypical assessment, she expected to catch a few sexually deviant acts.

Nothing surprised her more than seeing a bounce house in the yard by the main house. There were lots of people, and quite a few children running around. There was drinking, but nothing belligerent or out of control. The majority of women were dressed for a barbeque, though there was a lot more flesh than she was used to. It was exactly what she had been invited to—a barbeque.

Dobbs and the rest of the table laughed. "You want us to meet your expectations, babe, gotta come back tonight." Dobbs smirked, and his gaze perused her body giving her a small shiver and she shifted in her chair. Bailey spent most of her time alone, or in a town filled with people collecting social security. She couldn't remember the last time a man checked her out. *Except...*

"Dobbs!" Someone yelled from the main house and he retreated, keeping his gaze on Bailey until he turned. She watched him walking away. A group of women in short shorts passed by him, trying to get his attention. *Oh, they got it.* His eyes were aimed at their asses as he passed.

"You gonna come back tonight?"

Bailey turned to Meg, who was staring at her. Bailey widened her eyes and pointed to her chest. "Me?"

Meg laughed. "Of course, you. Hell, if I were your age and Dobbs asked me to come hang out, girl, I would find my sluttiest outfit, my highest heels, and be here." Meg winked. "I've heard things. The man is a good time."

"He's a man-whore," Macy said.

"He's single. He's allowed to be." Meg chuckled. "I'm not suggesting she marry him," Meg paused and smirked at Bailey. "Just take him for a ride."

Bailey's face burned.

Macy sat back in her seat and glanced around the open area where tables had been set up. "Saint's single, and he's not a whore."

Saint.

How just the sound of his name could hitch her breath and start her heart racing was beyond her. But it did. *Every time.* She didn't make eye contact with Macy. She knew the angle she was working. It seemed Bailey was not doing a great job at keeping her crush a secret.

Marissa elbowed Bailey in the arm and smiled. "No, Saint is a saint."

Bailey ignored the teasing twist of her lips. Although she never came out and admitted an interest in Saint, she had gotten pretty close to Marissa, and there wasn't a doubt she knew Bailey liked him. *From afar.*

Meg snorted. "Well, I wouldn't go that far, Riss. Not a man here is saint-worthy, but our Saint, he's definitely not a man whore, much to the dislike of most of the women who hang around here."

The statement gave Bailey small butterflies and got Macy's full-blown attention. She sat up, resting her elbows on the table, staring at Meg.

"So, he hasn't been with the hang arounds?"

Meg shrugged and gazed across the lot. "Not to my knowledge. Mick always said Saint was the internal opposite of every biker stereotype." She cocked a brow and turned back to the table. "Until you piss him off. The quietest ones are usually the deadliest."

What? Deadly was not appealing at all. However, she hadn't gotten a deadly killer vibe from Saint. Quiet, reserved, and mysterious? *Yes.* Gorgeous and sexy? *Hell yeah,* but dangerous? *No.* Then again, she wasn't the best judge of anyone's character. *Roll up those sleeves and let's see how good you are at detecting danger.* She pulled her shirt at her wrist, to cuff it around her palm.

"I'll get to the bottom of this." Macy sat up in her chair and waved to someone across the yard. All the women jerked around, including Bailey, to see Nadia smile and saunter toward them. Not walking, not strolling, the woman sauntered. And she did it effortlessly with her hips swaying.

"Get to the bottom of what?" Cheyenne asked.

Macy rolled her eyes. "If Saint is a closet man-whore, Nadia would know."

Bailey slouched in her seat. The other women seemed to be

amused by Macy's comment. Not her. Confirmation of him being like the others, mainly Dobbs, would have been disappointing.

"What's up, pretty girls?" Nadia smiled and glanced around the table.

"We need insider information." Macy leaned across the table and smirked. "On a member," she lowered her voice, "and his member." She wiggled her brows, evoking a burst of laughter from the entire table, this time, Bailey included. *I love her.*

Nadia raised her brows, clearly amused by Macy. "Who?"

"Saint." Macy paused, glancing over at Bailey then back to Nadia. "Is he a secret slut behind the clubhouse walls?"

Bailey watched Nadia's reaction. The corners of her mouth curved up, and she grinned, then licked her lips. Bailey noticed the teasing sparkle in her eyes. She was more than happy to play into Macy's antics.

"This stays between us."

Macy inched up. "Yeah, definitely. Now tell us."

Nadia glanced over her shoulder then slowly leaned closer to the group. Even Bailey shifted forward, waiting on her response. Nadia eyed all the women, one by one, ending with Bailey, who she stared at when she answered with a smile.

"No. Saint, to my knowledge, and trust me, I would know, has never, and I mean ever, dabbled with club pussy."

"Huh," Macy said, leaning back in her chair. "So, he's never showed interest in anyone around here?"

Nadia settled back on her feet. "Hmmm…showed any interest in a woman around here?" She slowly drifted her gaze to Bailey.

"I didn't say that." Nadia winked at Bailey and started back toward the clubhouse.

Bailey darted her gaze to the table and bowed her head slightly in hopes of shielding her face. The bright shade of pink on her cheeks would be impossible to hide. *Was Nadia referring to me?*

The subject quickly changed courtesy of Marissa, who asked about Cheyenne's new home and the shop. It was a perfect diversion.

As Bailey had told the residents, a bigger population would benefit the town. A few club members had bought property and were building. Others had renovated and moved into existing homes, which were on the verge of being condemned. Ghosttown was starting to emerge into a real town.

The businesses were also making a difference. Trax and Rourke had opened up a garage. The club was working on a parts store, Chey and Macy were almost ready for the grand opening of their shop. Main Street had gone from deserted to having most of the storefronts filled.

Bailey was half listening to Macy tease Cheyenne about something Trax did. Cheyenne simply rolled her eyes then laughed. Her sight behind her sunglasses was set on the only person who distracted her.

Saint was standing with Trax and Rourke in a circle. Whatever was being discussed seemed serious, not even the bikini-clad, fake breasted woman vying for Saint's attention all day could distract him. The knowledge he didn't randomly hook up with the club girls had Bailey a bit too relieved. Not that he'd ever take an interest in her. *Or did he?*

In the past few months, as the club settled into Ghosttown, she'd only seen him a handful of times. The most memorable was on Main Street when he'd come over during a verbal beatdown from Mr. Collins. She'd done her best to be friendly to the club as a whole, but there was a draw she had to Saint. She took any chance she got to interact with him. However, it was limited. And while he seemed to stare at her an awful lot, he didn't engage in conversation.

She crossed her legs, clasped her hands, and stared at Saint. He was too handsome. Bailey briefly heard one of the women say something about his eyes. She remained focused, staring at Saint. His dark hair was cut short, unlike the others, who always appeared in need of a haircut. She smiled, thinking of his eyes. His gaze went right through her that day on Main Street. It had been forever since she gotten revved up by just a look from a man.

Even Dobbs, as flirty as he was, was no match for Saint's silent gaze.

"His little girl has got em', too." Meg snickered. "Saint's in trouble with his daughter, a little stunner, and the sweetest." Meg turned her head, grabbing her beer. "Reminds me of our Bailey here. Soft-spoken, pretty smile, and too damn sweet."

What? Saint was a dad? She glanced over to him.

"Saint has a child?" Marissa asked in pure shock, similar to how Bailey was feeling.

"Mhmm…think she's eight or nine now. He doesn't bring her by much, and when he does, she's stuck to his side like glue. Though believe it or not, she's pretty tight with Kase. Kinda sweet to see Kase with a little girl. Reminds ya the hardass is human."

Bailey looked over at Cheyenne when she started laughing. "Just another thing to like about Saint, huh, Bailey?" Cheyenne winked. "Single dads are sexy, ask Riss."

"Very sexy," Marissa said, referencing her husband Caden.

Bailey tightened her lips at the teasing. It apparently was no secret to anyone, except maybe Meg, Bailey was harboring a little crush on Saint. A million questions raced through her mind, but she didn't have it in her to ask any of them. Thankfully, Marissa did.

"How long has he been divorced?"

Meg shook her head. "He's not, him and Tara never married. Decided to wait on the nuptials, which was good, 'cause things fizzled after Cia was born. Good friends though still, he spends the holidays with her family. She married Denny and they got two little boys. They've come to some barbeques in the past." She sat up and stretched her neck, then shouted, "Saint!"

Bailey jerked her head and saw Saint glance over his shoulder and then start their way, followed by Rourke. He was a few steps away from the table across from Bailey when he stopped. His gaze shifted to her, and she smiled. He dipped his chin. He always did that, rarely speaking to her though he seemed the same way with everyone.

"Just telling the girls about your baby, what is she eight, nine?"

"Turned nine last month."

Meg smiled. "You don't bring her around enough. Gotta get my fix spoiling some kids since these lazy bitches can't seem to get knocked up." Meg turned to Marissa. "Except you, Riss."

The group laughed, and Bailey joined in. Macy turned to Saint. "Got a picture?"

Saint didn't answer, and he seemed to hesitate before reaching for his back pocket and pulling out his phone. He must have pulled a picture because he turned the screen to Macy, who leaned in. She smiled and reached out, swiping the screen two more times and then looked at Saint. "Oh wow, she's beautiful, Saint."

"Let me see," Cheyenne said. When he angled the phone toward her, she grabbed it from his hands. His mouth tightened, but he didn't grab it back or say a word. He definitely wasn't happy with her move. She smiled and complimented her and then passed it to Meg.

Meg laughed. "You're screwed, Saint. She's a beauty, gonna be fighting off the boys in a few years." Meg turned and offered Bailey the phone. She could feel his eyes on her, and she wasn't sure if he would be happy if she took it. This would probably be the only opportunity she'd get to see his daughter, and it was too good to pass up.

She grabbed the phone with a shaky hand. Bailey's lips turned up, and she smiled. The little girl was beautiful. Dark long wavy hair, which was half in a ponytail and half out. Her nose scrunched up and she was laughing. Her eyes were squinting, but she could definitely make out the purple eyes just like Saint's.

"Bails, scroll to the one before, it's adorable," Macy said.

Bailey didn't even bother checking to see if it was okay, she slid her finger across the screen and her heart skipped then pumped hard. Someone must have taken it. It was Saint crouched down next to his daughter, her arms hugging him close around his shoulders. It was a sweet father and daughter picture. It wasn't the pose that had her mouth twitch and her belly warm. It was the smile. *His.* The one he shared with his little girl. She was a tiny beautiful version of Saint, and her smile was just as magnificent as his.

For all the times she'd seen him, watched him when he wasn't looking, she never saw his smile. It was worth the wait.

"A real beauty, right?" Marissa whispered next to her.

Bailey jerked almost forgetting she was sitting with a group which included Saint. She peered up, not at Marissa but Saint whose steely gaze was locked on her. If her heart pumped any faster, she might be concerned about a heart attack. She scooted her seat and rose up to her feet walking around Cheyenne and reached out to Saint, extending his phone.

"She's beautiful, especially her smile." Bailey licked her lips and then blurted out, "Just like yours."

His hand stopped in mid-reach and she swore she heard a rumble. A soft growl. Sexy as hell. She smiled, and he sucked in a harsh breath. She refused to look away. She couldn't. This was the most she'd ever gotten from him, and she wanted more.

With the worst timing ever, Kase shouted, "Saint, Rourke, let's go."

Both men jerked around. Rourke walked to Macy and kissed her. Saint tucked his phone in his pocket and followed Rourke. Everyone seemed to be stuck in silence. Bailey walked back to her seat, feeling the eyes of the women on her. She sat and peeked over at the house. The second she did, a small gasp passed through her lips. Saint stood at the door about to walk in, and he was staring at her. Even from far away she knew his heated gaze was on her and no one else.

She smiled.

A second passed before the corner of his mouth lifted at the same time as one brow. *Too sexy.* He disappeared into the clubhouse, and with a wave of disappointment, the small moment was over. She glanced back at the group who were openly gawking at her.

"What?" she said, feeling the heat rise from her chest to her face.

Macy burst out laughing. "What? You tell us. I almost felt like a voyeur watching the two of you." She grinned. "Hot as hell, though. When you bang him, I want details." Macy smirked and wiggled her brows. "Explicit details."

Cheyenne threw a napkin at Macy. "You're such an ass, leave her alone." Cheyenne turned to Bailey and giggled. "Can I be a bridesmaid when you guys get hitched?"

Bailey knew the teasing would continue. Whatever just happened between them did not go unnoticed. She shook her head trying to play it off. She was failing. The heat tingling her cheeks was a dead giveaway. She was blushing.

"Stop, the two of you. Ignore them, Bailey," Meg said.

Bailey glanced over and smiled.

"Forget what I said about Dobbs. Promise me you'll let me babysit when you and Saint make lots of babies."

All the women howled in laughter, and Bailey shrunk in her seat. Marissa reached out from next to her, patting her arm. It was meant to ease some of her embarrassment. It had been a long time since she'd been teased about a man. Knowing the whole table was privy to her blushing as a result of Saint was new territory. *This is what girlfriends do.*

This was another long time coming. Ghosttown's average age was fifty-five. Not exactly prime connections for a twenty-five-year-old. It provided the solitude she was so desperate for, a few years ago. Now, she realized it had left her out of touch with people her own age.

Fortunately, they spared her any more teasing and moved onto something new. It wasn't long after that they all began saying their goodbyes. Each woman gave her a hug and reminded her of a small get together at Cheyenne's new house next weekend. It seemed Bailey was being taken in the fold. They parted ways at the clubhouse entrance, and Bailey started out to the lot where everyone had parked.

The Saint

"Leaving, little Mayor?"

Bailey snickered, knowing the voice from behind. She stopped in front of her car and turned, watching Dobbs beeline for her. He stopped a foot away. He grinned and wiggled his brows.

"Coming back tonight?"

"Uh…" She fumbled her words. Tonight, as in for the real party? "I don't think so."

Dobbs stepped in closer. He really had a gorgeous face, very sexy. She'd never been partial to facial hair. On Dobbs, it worked. "Why not? It's gonna be fun, some dancing, we got a live band. You should come."

"I don't…" She didn't get a chance to finish. Dobbs softly gripped her waist, tugging her body against his. His head lowered, leaving just an inch between them.

Whoa! She had not seen it coming and braced her hands on his arms. She liked Dobbs. However, his approach seemed aggressive.

"I want you to come, Bailey." He lowered his lips and brushed them sweetly against hers. It felt nice and soft, and it triggered her heart to skip a beat. It had been so long since she'd been kissed. She stood frozen with her eyes wide, watching him. Dobbs pulled away and kept his hands on her waist.

"You'll come?" he asked.

Okay?

She merely nodded, still in a shocked state. He eyed her suspiciously with the corners of his mouth curling up slightly. He must have thought she was nuts. He nodded and let go of her, stepping back.

"Nine."

She nodded then forced herself to speak. "Okay." She licked her lips, turning away and unlocking her door. Bailey didn't look back at him again until she settled into her seat and started her car. He was at one of the tables with his arm wrapped around the shoulder of a woman. They were amongst a group of people.

Dobbs never shied away from a woman's affection when she'd seen him in the past.

What the hell just happened?

He was a flirt, she knew that, but kissing her seemed to be coming on a bit strong. Had she given him the wrong impression? Aside from light banter, she hadn't spent any time with him alone. Why did he kiss her? She glanced over again, catching his hand gripped dangerously low on the woman's hip. Had she been out of the game so long she didn't know the rules anymore? Was it customary to kiss one woman, and then walk away and immediately fondle another? Maybe it was.

She didn't have any interest in him romantically, but something about his offer to hang out intrigued her.

Dobbs would serve as a desperately needed distraction. Bailey had promised herself she wouldn't let Adam ruin her day. A promise she was able to keep until a minute ago. Between Adam's release, and receiving two letters in the past week, she was an anxious mess. Her stress level hit an all-time high yesterday when she received a call from him. It wasn't the first time he tried to reach out over the phone, though it had been awhile. She rolled her shoulders and breathed deeply. She turned her focus back to the present moment and made her decision.

Why shouldn't she go back tonight? She was a normal twenty-five-year-old, even though most days she felt older. It would be fun to have a drink, maybe listen to some music and flirt a little. She smirked with a sharp nod. "I'm going."

She pulled out of her spot and drove down the long drive. For once, she wouldn't overthink. She was coming back tonight. If anything, maybe Saint would be there, and she'd get her fill while hanging with the girls again.

It had been a long time coming. She was finally starting to feel like a normal twenty-five-year-old.

The Saint

THEIR MEETING HAD ENDED twenty minutes ago. Saint had stayed, working the details for the next delivery with Kase. As VP, he was on the planning end of this job. They had finally gone ninety-five percent legit. With the parts business, deliveries, and the extra income from the real estate, the club was sitting on a lot of cash, which was finally, after five long years, being distributed to the members.

Personally, Saint was almost a full-time resident of the small town. He'd finally be able to bring himself back to where it all started. As the heat grew a long while back, Saint separated himself a bit. Years ago, he even approached Kase with wanting out. It was a hard decision; it wasn't just about him. He had his little girl to think about. It took him years to grow up and see the big picture, which did not include a stint in prison and being separated from his daughter. Kase fought him on it. They'd been tight for years, and as Kase's most trusted brother, he didn't want anyone but Saint next to him.

Then the plan was born. Five years ago, Kase approached Saint with a vision. Together, unbeknownst to the brothers, they worked to have their vision become a reality. Saint didn't need any recognition for his part. He'd leave it for Kase. He was just happy to be on the straight and narrow.

Saint had enough claim to fame with his tattoo shops. Saint had hooked up with an old friend a few years back, opened a tattoo shop, and had tripled profits in the second year. They opened another and another until they had five well profiting shops. It was a fucking goldmine with Marco, his lead artist, at the helm. Saint's investment had been smart, and with him running everything behind the scenes, the money flowed in.

Kase pushed a document in front of Saint, and he glanced down. He shook his head and smiled. *He was out of his goddamn mind.*

"It'll never fly in Ghosttown, brother."

Kase lit his smoke and settled into his chair at the head of the table. "Why the fuck not? Townspeople gotta drink and eat, right?

Show me a man who doesn't like hot wings and cold beer while watching a pair of tits shaking in his face, and I'll show you a man with no balls."

Saint sat up and laughed. He reviewed the document. It was all in order, prepped for submittal. All it needed was to be signed off by the mayor.

The mayor.

Bailey had become a not-so-secret obsession of his since the moment she stumbled into the town meeting. Soft, long auburn hair flying in a mess around her creamy pale skin. Dark eyes that would have seemed bland on anyone else, but for him, they lit up. She was small, maybe five-three, and while thin, she had curves which would have any man stand up and take notice. In fact, he wasn't the only member of the club who had taken interest in the town mayor. She may not have shown skin like the usual women the club was surrounded by, but there was no denying her shape. *Fucking perfect.*

Her cover-up was strategic as he found out. Scars lined her body, though aside from her arm, he didn't know the full magnitude. He hadn't dug into her past until the club was enlightened to what had happened. Even thinking about it had him on edge and prepped to throttle the bastard through a fucking wall.

She had called it "the incident," according to Caden. She had shared her past with a support group a few months back. Then Caden had shared with the club. It was then they took an in-depth look into her past. A little digging and the club was exposed to her past. A previous boyfriend with anger issues had doused her with acid. *Psycho motherfucker.* Saint gritted his teeth and fisted his hands.

It changed everything. She stopped being just the Mayor of Ghosttown, and unknowingly fell under the protection of the club, mainly Saint. He had been biding his time before making his move to claim her. He was so close he could feel her.

"Saint."

He flicked his gaze to Kase, who was staring at him. He hadn't openly spoken to the club about his feelings for Bailey. A conversation with Rourke had him showing his cards to his brother. Kase, being as close to Saint as he was, knew without saying a word. Even Trax had caught his interest. He, too, remained silent on the subject.

"Bringing it up at the next meeting?"

Kase smirked and shrugged. "Yeah, unless you want to have a one on one with our mayor. Maybe put in a good word for the club."

Nice try, Kase. There was no way the first real interaction with Bailey would be him asking if a titty bar could come to Ghosttown. His brother was on his own with this little venture. Saint shook his head slowly, and Kase burst out laughing.

"Fine, I'll fucking do it." Kase stood, and Saint followed him out of the room and down the hall to the bar. The club was hosting another charter for the night, and from the looks of it, the party was already starting.

Saint walked past Kase and halted when he grabbed his arm. Saint glanced over his shoulder.

"Not staying?"

"Maybe."

"Just gonna scope out the guests, see who's still hanging out?" There was no denying the teasing in Kase's tone. Saint ignored him.

Saint walked through the room to the bar, grabbing a beer then heading outside. He noticed Cheyenne and Trax talking to a few people. The only reason he might stay was if Bailey was around. He assumed she was long gone at this point. He made his way out back and weaved through a group at the bonfire. As he rounded the building he stopped. A few yards away, he caught Bailey at her car. He balled his fists when he noticed the man backing away from her. *Fucking Dobbs.* As a brother, he loved him, and his flirting never bothered Saint in the past, until he turned it on with Bailey.

He'd watched them like a hawk earlier when Dobbs was at her

table. He also watched her, and her reaction was similar to most of the women. She smiled and laughed. He noticed she didn't blush, not like she did for him. That fact was the only thing saving Dobbs from Saint's wrath. Saint moved slowly, walking to the edge of the building, his focus on her. She seemed off. He watched as she retreated into her car, and after a few minutes, drove away.

It was his cue. He tossed his unfinished beer in the can out front and made his way to his bike in the lot.

"You leaving?" someone from behind shouted. The voice was familiar, but he couldn't be sure which brother it was. It didn't matter. He was done for the night. The club parties weren't his thing. Saint wasn't interested in meaningless sex and debauchery. There was only one woman he wanted, and she'd just left. No reason for him to stick around.

He mounted his bike and drove home.

Chapter 3

She stood next to her car for ten minutes contemplating whether or not she should go in. In the short time, she'd caught a topless drunk woman fall to her knees and start blowing a guy sitting at the fire. Another man dropped his pants and started pissing on the side of the building. She got a strong whiff of a familiar earthy scent reminiscent from her late teens.

The whole episode screamed, *go home, you don't belong here.*

She dismissed her inner voice and started up the stairs. She heard the music blasting before she opened the door. Her eardrums thumped as soon as she got inside. There were definitely more people now than earlier. She had a feeling all the children were long gone, and now the adult party was happening. She weaved her way through the crowd, unsure of where she'd end up. The interior was a lot different than the last time she was there for Caden and Marissa's wedding reception.

She hopped up on her toes. She must have been in the back of the large room because across the room a band was setting up on a small stage. Her body heaved forward when she was pushed from behind. She stumbled forward and was lucky to fall into a wall. She glanced up. *Scratch that, a wall of a man.* He glared down, and she backed up and circled a small group near the edge of the room.

She was out of her element. Forget being a normal, twenty-five-year-old woman. Sitting at home in her pajamas with a book was looking very appealing at the moment.

She decided unless she saw the girls in the next thirty seconds, she would backtrack and get the hell outta there. She was too busy scanning through the smoky room to see someone come up from behind her. When hands gripped her waist, she jumped, tossing her head back and nailing a hard surface.

"Shit."

Bailey spun around. She gasped when she realized it had been Macy who grabbed her. Macy's hands were covering her face.

"Oh my God, Macy, I'm so sorry."

She blinked quickly and started laughing while rubbing her nose. "No, my bad, shouldn't have grabbed ya. In a place like this, ya gotta watch your back." She laughed and clasped her hand, as they maneuvered through a large group of men. At the edge of the bar was Rourke. When he made eye contact, he seemed surprised to see her.

Bailey waved awkwardly. He lifted his chin but kept his strange look aimed at her.

"Dobbs invited me," she blurted as an explanation, which seemed to shock him even more as his eyebrows spiked to his hairline. Macy grinned at her.

"Really?"

She nodded with a smile.

"Very cool." Macy glanced around. "I saw him a while ago, maybe he's in the back, playing pool."

"Okay." She stayed where she was. She appreciated Dobbs inviting her, though she wasn't overly thrilled about hanging out with him. The kiss from earlier made it slightly awkward. She was hoping to hang out with the girls like this afternoon.

"So, we're heading out. I wish I knew you were coming."

She bit back her disappointment and shrugged. "Last minute decision. Why ya leaving?"

Macy leaned closer, screaming over the loud music. "I've got a conference call."

"Now?"

"At ten, from California." She rolled her eyes. "Won't get it done here with the noise, so we are gonna go stay at Caden's place."

"Why aren't you staying at your place?"

She rolled her eyes and huffed. "We just had the whole house painted, Trini's too, and the fumes are wretched. Can't stay at Chey's because they haven't gotten the furniture for the spare yet." Macy cocked her brow. "And I'm too damn old to sleep on the floor."

Bailey laughed and leaned toward her ear. "I've got a spare if you want to crash at my place."

"Really?"

"Yeah, it's on the first floor off the kitchen. Queen bed, it's all set up."

Macy eyed her with a grin. "You sure? 'Cause I would so much rather a five-minute drive than twenty to Cade's. Rourke's gotta be back early to help out Kase."

"Absolutely. Spare key is under the large blue planter on the back porch."

"You rock, girl." Macy pulled her in for hug.

Bailey noticed Rourke looking out over the crowd, then pointing down to her and Macy while staring at someone across the room. When Macy released her, she got the view of who Rourke was communicating with. She watched Kase nod and turn away.

What was that all about?

She spent another few minutes chatting with Macy before they started to leave. Before they did, Macy dragged her to the hallway, where only a few people filtered around.

"The pool room is down there." She pointed. "Make a right,

and it's at the end of the hall. No door so ya can't miss it. And a word of advice, if a door is closed, do not open it. I swear you'll be scarred for life." She chuckled, and Bailey laughed.

Before Bailey could say bye, Macy's face paled, and her mouth dropped open.

"What's wrong?"

Macy jerked her head. "I-I can't believe I just said….." Her lips clamped, and her cheeks turned a dark shade of pink.

Said what?

She played over in her head, Macy's words. *Ohhhhhhh, you'll be scarred for life.*

"I'm so sorry. I didn't mean it that way."

Bailey gripped her arms. "And I didn't take it that way. It's a figure of speech. You meant it to be funny." Bailey shook her playfully and grinned. "It was funny."

"I'm sorry."

Bailey rolled her eyes and gave her a push. "Stop apologizing. I'm not hurt, not offended. Now, go back to my place, make your call, and do scandalous things with your boyfriend in my spare room. My house needs to see some action."

The color finally came back to Macy's face, and she burst out laughing. She continued to laugh through the crowded room, and Bailey made her way down the hall. Maybe she could just hang out with Dobbs a bit, have a beer, do twenty-five-year-old things, and head home. There weren't many people in the hall as she made her way down, following Macy's directions. She heard loud moaning from her left. The door was half-opened, giving her an unobstructed view of three naked people having sex.

Three? Oh my God.

A man was lying flat on his back. She recognized him as a member but didn't know his name. A naked woman was between his legs on all fours blowing him. *It's like live porn.* She should have looked away. Aside from TV, she'd never seen people having sex. The man jerked his head up and reached over, grabbing a phone.

"Who is it?"

The graveled masculine voice came from deeper in the room and Bailey inched forward in the hall and angled her head. *Oh shit.* Behind the woman on her knees was a man fucking her from behind. The position didn't shock her as much as the man did.

Dobbs was thrusting forward against the woman as she moaned.

"It's Kase, Bailey's here, wants to know if you invited her."

She widened her eyes and raised her brows. She clamped her lips, biting back a laugh. His face became distorted, which was utterly comical. *Yeah, Dobbs, this is awkward.* Some women might be upset or angry. After all, he invited her and was now fucking another. Bailey just found his reaction amusing. She wasn't interested in Dobbs for anything other than hanging out and some easy flirting.

"Fuck." His voice was strangled, which got her attention more than Kase's message. "Let's finish up here."

Finish up? Bailey covered her mouth. If she had the balls, she'd poke her head inside and tell him to meet her at the bar when he was done. The whole scene was absurd. She wasn't sure how she could look at him with a straight face after knowing the back story here. She shook her head and chuckled. *Poor Dobbs.*

"You gonna ditch me for *her*?" the woman scoffed, glancing back at Dobbs and continued to bounce against his dick.

Her tone held a spark of nastiness, which had Bailey losing her smile.

Dobbs remained silent.

"Can you even get it up with her? God, those fucking scars, it's like the swamp thing, rippled, scaly skin." The woman shivered and twisted her lips. "Does she have them *all* over her body or what?"

Bailey staggered back a step. What did she say? *Swamp thing? Rippled, scaly skin?* Without thinking, she gripped her arm and pulled down her sleeve to the palm of her hand.

Dobbs slapped her ass, which seemed to get her off.

She moaned then angled her head again. "She's false advertising, ya know. Got a really pretty face which sucks you in. Then you're left trying to get your dick hard when ya catch a glimpse at her body. So gross, can't believe you get off on that."

Bailey's breath shallowed, and her stomach twisted into a horrible ache. She reached up, touching her cheek and slowly gliding her fingers down her neck on her smooth skin. Her fingers halted at the collar of her shirt. She knew what was underneath. Apparently, so did everyone else. She gulped and fought back against her tears.

Dobbs slapped her ass again. "Can you shut the fuck up so I can come?"

The woman laughed, dropping her head to the mattress. "See, just thinking about her is making it impossible to come. You better stay here with me, baby."

Bailey stepped back, staring at the door. Her breathing was labored, and an aching pain shot through her heart. Never in her life had she heard someone say such a vicious and cruel statement. *Swamp thing?* Her stomach turned and she felt the heat rise from her chest. *False advertising?* A cool brisk ice streamed through her blood and her head felt heavy. *Just thinking about her is making it impossible to come?* She stumbled away from the door and rushed her steps toward the main room. *I need to get out of here.* Her exit was very different from her entrance. She stormed forward, not even glancing around, and pushed through the crowds of people. When she finally made it to the door, she hurried to her car, with her only focus on getting the hell out of there.

SAINT SCANNED THE LIVING ROOM. He had boxes piled up and was in the process of unpacking. He'd set up Cia's room and his own last weekend Aside from furniture, he'd yet to unpack most of his belongings. He raked his hand over his head, surveying the clutter. He clutched the phone to his ear.

"Minka got a full schedule?"

Marco, his lead artist, and friend, scoffed. "She's slammed but ya won't hear her complain. She did a full sleeve last night, fucking perfection, Saint."

Saint smiled. He wouldn't expect anything less from her. Minka was equally as talented though she didn't get the notoriety as Marco received. Not yet. Her time would come; Saint would see to it. The two of them together set his shops to a higher level than others.

"Good to hear. How's Ace working out?" He'd hired and personally trained a new office manager in hopes he'd be able to fully settle in Ghosttown.

"Good, man. Everyone likes him. He knows his shit. It's a good fit."

It was exactly what he wanted to hear. With setting up the shops to run without him, it gave him the time to focus on the new location in Ghosttown, among other things, mainly setting up for his life in the small town. With Bailey and Cia.

His phone beeped, alerting him to another call.

"Gotta take this call. I'll be by next week."

"Sounds good, man. Have a good night." Marco hung up, and Saint switched calls.

"Yeah."

"Left too early, brother." Kase laughed.

"Too early for what?"

"It seems our mayor decided to come back for the after-party."

Saint stilled. Bailey was at the clubhouse? The last place she should be was there, without him. All the men received strict instructions that she was off-limits, however with a neighboring charter present, it was too many people to keep track of. Saint gripped his phone tightly, reaching for his jacket and stalking toward his back door.

"Guess, I'll be seeing your ass in a few." Kase laughed.

"I want eyes on her until I get there."

"How come none of you assholes follow orders? Said she was off-limits."

Saint clenched his jaw. Kase was fucking with him and knew damn well he didn't take orders from anyone. Especially when it came to Bailey. His friend was having a good time while Saint ripped through his yard. Saint hung up and shoved his phone in his pocket.

Chapter 4

In the dim light of her kitchen, Bailey sat at her table.

She'd slithered in about thirty minutes ago. She tiptoed around her house so as not to wake up Macy and Rourke. If ever there was a time she was regretting her hospitality, tonight was it. All she wanted was to be alone.

She should have been in bed trying to forget all the happenings from tonight, but her mind wouldn't settle. Other people's words and thoughts couldn't hurt her unless she let them. Unless she gave them worth and power. She couldn't combat it tonight. She was throwing in the towel and basically giving permission to succumb to the words of some woman she didn't even know, a woman who only saw her exterior.

It struck her as odd. This was the first time she had heard firsthand someone speak of her with cruelty and nastiness. She'd bore her scars for years but never heard the whispers. Is that what people thought when they looked at her? No amount of therapy could have prepared her for tonight.

When she went upstairs, she eyed her pajamas on the edge of the bed. It was her usual wardrobe for nighttime. A pair of lounge pants and a tank top. Usually, if she had guests, which was rare, she'd wear long sleeves. Not this time. *This is my house, and I will not hide.* After changing her clothes, she settled into the kitchen with a cup of tea in hopes it would relax her. It didn't. She was left in silence to hear the vicious words play over in her head on repeat. She stared down at the napkin holder as her eyes teared up.

"Bailey."

She hadn't even heard him walk into the kitchen, which was rare for her. She seemed to have gained superhuman hearing since the incident. It wasn't otherworldly. She was no superhero. Just a woman who had been caught off guard once and determined to never let it happen again. She glanced up through her damp lashes.

Rourke stood near the doorway from her guest room. It was directly off the kitchen. He seemed locked in his spot as his gaze traipsed over her body. His brows furrowed. She couldn't tell if he was shocked by her obvious departure from covering her scars or if he was disgusted by them. She'd allowed too many people to make her feel ashamed for one night. She certainly wouldn't allow it in her own house, her sanctuary. She drew in a breath and clasped her hands, resting her elbows on the table, glaring at him.

"Sorry, did I wake you?" she asked without an ounce of sincerity.

She had to give him credit. He didn't balk at her tone or cringe at the sight of her skin. In her small tank top, the scars trailing up her arm and over the left side of her chest were completely on display. Even with the low light, Rourke would be getting an eyeful.

"What's going on, Bailey?"

She shrugged, bringing attention to her arms again. Rourke stared straight at her. "Nothing. Just sitting in my kitchen in the dark at midnight." She sighed and twisted her lips.

"You been crying?" He stepped forward even though she could sense his hesitation. She didn't know Rourke well. Mainly her encounters with him were from her friendship with Macy.

There was a time when he stepped in or would have, had she needed it when she was having a hostile encounter with Mr. Collins. He and Saint had come over to make sure she was okay. *Saint.* Thinking of him and the small smile he donned earlier was turning her stomach. Was it pity for her? Was she a charity case to everyone around her? *Oh God, this sucks.*

"Want me to get Mace?" Rourke asked.

A lone tear fell down her cheek as she glanced up at him. This must have been ungodly awkward for him. In all the time she'd seen Rourke, he'd never seemed uncomfortable or even out of place. Even now, he didn't seem set to run. She tilted her head and stared back him. *He'll be honest.* She leaned forward on the table, stretching her arms out in front of her.

"Is it that bad, Rourke?"

His brows furrowed causing a harsh dent between his eyes. The lines on his forehead creased, and the corner of his eyes crinkled. He stepped forward, resting his hands on the back of the chair across from her. He remained silent. His gaze was inspecting. Not on her body, but her face. He was so intent on her eyes as if he was trying to read her.

"Is it?" she whispered through a shaky breath.

"I don't know what you mean. Is what so bad?"

She tilted her head, and the corners of her lips turned down. "Me."

The floor creaked behind him and he glanced over his shoulder. Bailey veered her gaze around him and saw Macy standing close to him. She was staring at Bailey. Rourke may have been confused by her question, but it was clear from the pale sorrow on Macy's face she understood what Bailey was asking. She hadn't heard her come in, but obviously, Macy had heard everything.

Macy stepped closer to Rourke, resting her hand onto his forearm and smiled sadly at Bailey. "No, Bailey." Her throat bobbed and Bailey figured Macy was seconds away from breaking down herself. "The answer is no."

Bailey smiled. Of course, Macy would say no, she was her

friend. "You have to say that, besides…" She trailed off, unsure if she could say the last part out loud. What she really wanted was the male perspective. Was she so ghastly a man wouldn't be able to get hard at the sight of her?

"Hey."

Bailey jerked her head toward the masculine voice snapping at her. Rourke straightened and folded his arms. She widened her eyes at his height and his hardened face. Rourke was not a typically handsome man. He was too hard and rough to ever be considered handsome. Sexy and brutish. Especially when he narrowed his gaze pinning her with his stare. "No."

Her bottom lip jutted out and trembled. It was sweet, for him. Apparently, he wasn't done.

"Got a lot of fucking scars on my own body. Ugly scars. And they don't mean shit, ya hear me?"

She nodded and sniffled back her impending tears. Macy had obviously decided she couldn't hold back anymore. She rounded the table and bent down next to Bailey. Her hand slid over her back in a soothing motion.

"I don't know what happened tonight, but you better hear me when I say this." Bailey slid her gaze to Macy. "You are beautiful and funny and sweet, and seriously, one of my most favorite people on this planet."

Bailey smiled, and Macy inched closer. "Ask Rourke, I hate almost everybody, but there's not one thing I don't love about you. You hear me?"

Tears rimmed her eyes, and she choked back her words and answered with a nod. It had been forever since she allowed herself to become overwhelmed with her past. Until now, until an ignorant woman decided to spread her nastiness.

The roaring knock on the back door startled all three of them. Bailey glanced over. It was after midnight.

While Macy stood, Rourke moved toward the door, sliding the curtain back then grabbing the knob. "Dobbs."

Her chest burned and she tightened her fists, dropping her

hands down to her lap. Her first instinct was to demand he not be let inside. Whatever he was going to say, she didn't want to hear it. She hadn't been upset with him until the woman had said all those awful things about her and he said nothing. *Nothing.* Not one word except telling her to shut up so he could get off. Her stomach churned.

She heard the soft whispering of greeting between the three of them and felt him move closer into the kitchen before the door closed.

"What's going on?" Dobbs said in a low tone.

Bailey remained silent and continued to stare at her placemats. She made a note they needed to be cleaned. She needed to focus on anything other than Dobbs at the moment.

"Bailey." Dobbs said. It was inevitable. She'd have to speak to him. She glanced up as he stood near Rourke staring down at her with concern.

She licked her lips. "Why are you here?"

He widened his eyes. "I was hanging in the back when I got a call from Kase saying you were there. By the time I got out to the bar, you were gone. Kase said you took off in a hurry, and I wanted to make sure you were good."

She snorted and squinted. "Why do you care?"

"What?"

The air in the room was tense, and she was making things harder than they had to be. She could have just made up an excuse and sent him on his way. She could have done the same with Macy and Rourke, giving them a sob story about it just being a bad night, and sent them back to their room. Then she'd be left alone, which was what she craved at the moment. But she couldn't do it. Not this time. She was tired. Tired of hiding and putting on a brave front. Tired of always smiling.

She aimed her stare at him and raised her brows. She purposefully spoke slowly. "Why do you care if I'm okay or not?"

Dobbs stared back at her in confusion. This was a side she

hadn't seen. The usual flirty and fun Dobbs shifted on his feet and glanced over at Rourke.

Macy moved closer. "Did something happen at the party?"

She curled her lip in disgust. "Yeah."

She noticed both men go rigid and tense. Rourke more so than Dobbs.

"What happened?" Macy asked. "Something in the back? Dammit, I shouldn't have left you by yourself."

Bailey shifted her gaze, locking eyes with Dobbs whose face paled, and he flinched slightly. "You were in the back?"

Bailey slowly nodded her head, never taking her eyes off of him. He was piecing it together though she figured he'd misjudge her reason for leaving. He rested his hands on his hips and bowed his head.

Rourke stepped forward. He was seething. He, too, was getting the wrong idea of what had upset her. "Did one of the guys do something? The girls? What, fucking tell me."

Bailey drew her gaze back to Dobbs, who was now staring at her again.

"I heard what she said." Bailey took a deep breath and finished, "About me."

He knew exactly what she was talking about. There wasn't a shred of confusion mearing his features. Only regret.

"She didn't say anything about you."

Son of a bitch! He was lying. She wasn't sure if he was protecting the girl or trying to save face. Or maybe he just thought she'd believe anything he said. *A scarred girl would buy any and all bullshit, right Dobbs?*

"Don't, please, just don't."

His lips strained down in a frown. "Bailey, I…"

Bailey slammed her hand on the table, surprising everyone in the room, including herself.

"She said she was better than the other one." Bailey pointed at her chest. "Me. I'm false advertising, right?" Bailey shook her head, completely disappointed. He was going the denial route. He should own his shit. *Be a man, Dobbs.* He became a blurry vision in her tear-filled eyes. "You couldn't be with me, right? How could something like this," she lifted her arms, "turn a man on?"

A sharp gasp to her left was a strong reminder she was doing this, all in front of an audience. Macy stepped closer to her side and squeezed her shoulder.

"It wasn't about you."

Bailey scoffed, and tears streamed down her face. "I'm scarred, Dobbs, not stupid. You and I know exactly who she was talking about." She rested her shaky hand over her chest. "Me."

There was a brief silence.

"Who was it, Bailey, describe her, and I'll make sure she can't speak for at least a fucking month."

"Doesn't matter who it was," she whispered then turned back to Dobbs. "Do you have any idea how deep her words cut me? Any clue?"

Dobbs stepped forward. He didn't get very far when Rourke moved in front of him. She could see his eyes trained on her over Rourke's shoulder. Remorse. *Too late.*

"Why invite me?" her voice was a mere whisper, yet everyone went silent and stared at her. "You kissed me then invited me to the party. And me being an idiot, I went and had a front-row seat to my very own roasting."

"I didn't think you were coming. I just figured you agreed to shut me up. If I knew you would be there, I never would have taken her in the back."

"God, you are such a fucking pig," Macy shouted, and Bailey jumped at the ferocious buzz she sent through the room.

"Macy," Rourke snapped.

Bailey gripped Macy's hand on her shoulder, giving her a tight squeeze. She appreciated her having her back, but this was Bailey's fight, and the last thing she wanted was bloodshed.

"You're missing the point here, Dobbs."

He tore his glare from Macy and softened his gaze.

"I'm not mad or upset because you were with another woman.

I didn't expect anything from you. I just thought we would hang out." She shrugged. It was true. She didn't have any feelings for Dobbs other than possible friendship. She was too busy pining over her infatuation with Saint to even consider Dobbs, really. But she did think she meant a little something to him. Her eyes burned, and her heart swelled. She teared up. "I thought you liked me, just a little, enough to be a friend."

"Of course, I like you." Dobbs' chest rose and fell rapidly.

"Not enough to stand up for me. When she called me the swamp thing, mocked me, saying I was gross and disgusting, you said nothing in my defense. You let her say all those awful things about me, and you kept fucking along like it was nothing." She scoffed. "False advertising, she said. My face will draw you in, but once you catch sight of my scars, you won't even be able to get hard. She said all those nasty things about me, and you said *nothing*." Bailey leaned in her chair, wanting him to really see the extent of her pain in her eyes. "I have never had a friend treat me as cruelly as you did tonight."

He winced as if he'd been slapped. She noticed Rourke's grip on his chest tighten. She'd gotten her point across, finally.

"Bailey." His voiced croaked when he called out her name.

She glanced up and saw the remorse and regret. Unfortunately, it was too late for her. The pity in his eyes only flamed her anger. Up until this point, she was more hurt than angry. Something triggered in her, and she squinted her eyes aimed solely at Dobbs. She stretched out her arms on the table and watched as his gaze dropped.

"I know what I look like. I know what people *see* when they look at my scars." She paused, waiting for him to look at her. His eyes were trained on the floor. "Knowing it and then hearing it? Just punch me in the face, Dobbs, I swear it won't hurt as much."

The sharp gasp from Macy had Bailey bowing her head. She shouldn't be doing this, not in front of all of them. She drew in a breath.

"Let's talk, just you and me."

She shook her head. "No, I just really need you to leave." She glanced up at Macy, who looked like she was ready to jump across the table and beat the shit out of Dobbs. "I need you all to leave."

Macy jerked her gaze to Bailey.

"Please." She scanned the room and nodded. "You took your call earlier, right?"

Reluctantly, she nodded without saying a word.

"I'm sure there's extra rooms at the clubhouse, you guys should go stay there."

Macy crouched down, putting them eye level and whispered, "I don't wanna leave you alone."

While she appreciated Macy's concern, all Bailey wanted was to be by herself.

"I've been alone for years. I'll be fine." She swallowed a breath, trying to calm her shaky voice. "I'm always fine."

She hated doing it this way. Macy had been only supportive of her and even proving to have her back. But Bailey needed to be alone. It was a shitty thing to do, renege on her offer for them to stay there. The thought alone had her rethinking what she had just said. Before she could change her mind, Rourke turned around to face them.

"Mace, let's go," Rourke said then glanced down at Bailey. "They got plenty of space at the clubhouse. Thanks for letting us come here, Bailey."

Bailey glanced up to see Macy glaring at her man. "I think we should stay."

"No, we're leaving." He glanced down at Bailey and nodded. "She wants us out. We get out. Now, go grab your shit and let's go."

"But…"

"No," Rourke said sternly. "This is Bailey's house…when she says you leave, you leave, ya hear me?"

Surprisingly, Macy left the room, disappearing into the guest room. Rourke's large frame separated her and Dobbs, and from the position Rourke had taken, she couldn't even see Dobbs. She glanced up at Rourke, whose gaze was aimed at the doorway.

Macy came through the door with her bag thrown over her shoulder. She went to stand in front of Bailey.

"You want me to come back, just call, okay?" She grabbed her hands and crouched in front of her. "Hell, you change your mind in ten minutes, you call me. Now, promise me, or I'm not leaving."

"I promise," Bailey whispered through the knot in her throat. Bailey had good friends back in her old life, but it had been a while since she truly felt someone had her back. Macy pulled her into a hug. When she released her, Macy turned and aimed her glare at Dobbs.

She pointed to the door. "You first, asshole."

"I'm not leaving." His words were directed toward Macy, with his eyes set on Bailey. *Oh, hell no.* He needed to go. She had said all she had to, and she wasn't up to listening to a word he had to say. Luckily, she didn't have to say anything. Macy had it covered.

"Yes, you are." Macy pushed forward. Thankfully, Rourke was quick enough to block her from getting closer to Dobbs. "Don't you have some chick to fuck back at the house?"

It was nasty and harsh, making Bailey cringe. Dobbs clenched his jaw and made no movement.

"Mace, outside, now." She whipped her head and glared at Rourke. Bailey raised her brows in surprise when Macy followed his orders.

He jerked his chin towards the door. "Let's go, man."

"Not leaving." His gaze locked on her.

Rourke leaned forward. "Yeah, you are. You decide how. Either on your own or me throwing your ass outta the fucking door."

Bailey flinched in her seat from Rourke's tone. She'd never heard him speak with such a feral tone. She couldn't turn away, watching both men chest to chest. Dobbs yanked his arm from Rourke's hold and stormed out the door. She released a breath she didn't even know she was holding. Rourke glanced over his shoulder.

"You good?" His voice was much softer than how he spoke to Dobbs.

Bailey nodded and clasped her trembling hands. She hadn't realized she was shaking. Rourke made his way to the door without saying a word. Here was this man she hardly knew, who carried out her demands for her. He walked through the door, grabbing the knob.

He turned back. "You'll call me or Macy if you want us to come back?"

She nodded.

His gaze scanned her body, and his face hardened. "You fucking listen to every word I'm about to say, you hear me?"

"Okay," she whispered.

His nostrils flared and his jaw squared. "You don't give what that fucking cunt said any headspace, you hear me? Not one fucking word, Bailey. She don't know shit about what a man, a real man, wants." He stepped closer. "She's nothing." He snapped and pointed to her. "You, you're something." He narrowed his gaze. "And to *somebody*, you're gonna be *his* fucking everything."

Her bottom lip trembled. It was one of the nicest things anyone had ever said to her. While it wasn't eloquent, it was perfect. It was exactly what she needed to hear at that moment. *I'm something.*

Bailey gulped with tears threatening at the rim of her eyes. She sniffled and brushed her hands against her cheeks. "You're a good guy, Rourke."

"No," he scoffed. "I'm not, but I'm honest." He backed up and turned to the door. "You remember what I said." He opened the door and walked through, closing it behind him.

And to somebody, you're gonna be his fucking everything.

SAINT PULLED in front of the clubhouse and parked. The first sight of the night was a guy on his knees in the grass puking. He rolled his eyes. He was too damn old for this shit. If not for Kase's call, he would have been asleep by now. He dismounted and caught a raging engine flying up the drive. *Great, now they were getting stupid.* He recognized the bike and the other coming up from behind. Though the second wasn't driving like an asshole.

Saint rested his helmet over his handlebars and started to the doors. He was a few feet from the steps when the screaming caught his attention. He stepped back and made his way to the side of the house.

"You piece of shit. If I knew he'd do it, I'd demand Rourke kick your ass. Since I know he won't, I'll do it."

Saint rushed over. *What the fuck?* Rourke had his arm wrapped around Macy's waist. She was flailing with her arms stretched out swinging. Dobbs stood a foot away, glaring at her.

"Rourke, fucking control her. Should have kept the ban on her ass!" Dobbs shouted.

Oh fuck. Saint moved closer as Rourke unraveled his hold and started to Dobbs. Saint moved a little quicker than usual and placed himself between his brothers. Fights were common at parties, but it was never good when it was brother pitted against brother.

Rourke halted. Saint knew if he moved, Rourke would take a shot at Dobbs.

Macy barreled into the right of her man and pointed at Dobbs, her hand shaking. "You should be banned. You are a vile piece of shit. You're not worthy to wear the patch."

Dobbs' face turned bright red, and Saint angled his body closer to him. He was raging, and the last thing he needed was a mouthy woman getting caught up in whatever was happening.

"Settle, brother." Saint lowered his voice, but Dobbs heard. He breathed heavily through his nose, his glare aimed at Macy.

"You don't make decisions in the club, sweetheart. Being Rourke's hole doesn't grant you a say."

Oh hell! Rourke pushed forward, grabbing Dobbs by the neck, and it took everything Saint had to muscle his way between them. He gripped Rourke's chest and pushed back, breaking contact with Dobbs. Saint gasped a breath, his own heart beating rashly. Whatever was happening he wanted a fucking answer. He usually kept himself out of the bitch bullshit between his brothers, unless it was necessary that he intervene.

"You ever call her a hole again, I'll fucking kill you!" Rourke shouted.

Dobbs swung out his hand. "She came at me with her fucking mouth, man. She needs to mind her own business."

Macy stepped forward, and Rourke grabbed a hold of the back of her shirt preventing her from getting closer. Macy, who he'd always thought of as sweet with a sarcastic tongue, was beyond livid. Her body was shaking in anger. He'd never seen her like this.

"Bailey is my business. And I'll say whatever I damn well please. You sure as hell did."

Her name immediately struck something in Saint. It was unnatural the way his chest tightened and blood rushed through his veins. He was prepared to demand answers. Macy saved him the trouble of asking.

"You invite her here, then fuck some random chick in the backroom who spews a bunch of vile bullshit." Macy face burned red, and her eyes darkened. "And you said nothing."

Saint had had enough.

"What the fuck is going on?" Saint snapped and looked at Rourke. He tore his gaze from Dobbs and took a breath. Rourke would be the best one to get answers from.

Rourke sighed, shaking his head. "Dobbs, over there," he lifted his chin past Saint's shoulder, "invited Bailey to the party. She came, apparently walked in on him fucking someone. Whoever the bitch was said some shit about her scars…"

"Made fun of her scars!" Macy shouted and pushed forward. "And that asshole said nothing. Just let her say Bailey was false advertising. Pretty face, but when ya got her clothes off, she's disgusting." Macy's voice shook. "Right, Dobbs? It's what she said, and you what, kept fucking her 'cause a hole is a hole? You and that bitch, you guys are the disgusting ones, not Bailey."

Saint's muscles tightened, and his blood chilled. He slowly turned facing Dobbs.

"Is that true?"

Dobbs' face paled slightly, and Saint was ready to rip his eyes out. He swallowed. "I told her to shut up." His words were a bitch excuse, and even Saint recognized Dobbs' shame.

"And yet ya still kept fucking her, huh? Aren't you a gentleman?"

Dobbs pushed forward, and Saint gripped his shoulder in a tight hold. "Shut the fuck up, Macy."

Macy lunged at Dobbs. "No, you shut the fuck up, you poor excuse for a man."

"Fuck." Rourke pulled Macy against his chest and lifted her off the ground. He walked down the drive with Macy protesting. When they were far enough away, Saint slowly turned to Dobbs. He opened his mouth, and Saint scowled.

"Don't. Speak."

Dobbs drew in a breath, clamped his lips, and followed his orders. For his own safety, Dobbs needed to remain quiet. Another word from his brother and Saint could not be held responsible for what he'd do. *Breathe.* His anger mounted as the story unfolded. Now, he was taking on Bailey's hurt and pain, which only amplified his rage. He could envision it, striking Dobbs' jaw, his head bolting back on his neck and him stumbling to the ground. Saint could see him trying to get up and his own foot kicking his face and sending him back to the ground. His boot shoved into Dobbs' throat while he gasped for breath.

"Everything okay here?" The soft feminine voice was the only thing saving Dobbs right now. If he was smart, he would thank Cheyenne the first chance he got.

Saint's glare remained locked on Dobbs, who appeared

nervous. *He should be.* Saint's reputation wasn't anything to take lightly. Saint stepped closer.

"I don't care who she is, who brought her, who fucked her." He slowly shook his head. "I want her out now, and she never shows her face here again. You feel me?"

Dobbs nodded. "Yeah. And I'm gonna go make it right with Bailey."

Her name on his lips was putting Saint over the edge. He snarled, lifting the top of his lip like a rabid dog. "You will stay away from Bailey."

"Saint…"

"You. Will. Stay. Away." He was eerily calm, which should have had Dobbs concerned for his own well-being. Saint wasn't done. "If you don't, the only way you'll be riding your bike is in a fucking sidecar. Not a threat, Dobbs, it's a promise."

Dobbs backed away. He watched Saint as he made his way around the back of the building. Saint didn't look away until he disappeared.

"What happened?" Cheyenne whispered from behind him. She was close. Too close not to have heard the exchange. He turned to find her standing a few feet away with Rourke and Macy.

"Mace," Cheyenne said.

Macy was focused solely on Saint when she answered her friend. "I'll tell ya later. It's about Bailey. He better not go back there, Saint. You didn't see her, she was destroyed, and the last thing she needs is him at her door tonight."

"He won't," Saint said.

Macy snorted with tears rimming her eyes. "She'll probably be up all night worried he will." Macy sniffled and wiped her cheek. When she moved toward Cheyenne, Rourke released her and turned to Saint.

"I always got a brother's back, Saint." He narrowed his gaze. "But tonight, seeing Bailey? I wanted to rip his fucking throat out."

Rourke was one of the most loyal brothers belonging to the club. His admission was confirmation of how bad it must have been. Saint straightened his back with a sharp nod. He walked to his bike, not saying another word to the small group. He mounted his bike, aware of them watching him. Saint didn't pay them any attention. There was only one place he needed to be right now.

Chapter 5

"Son of a bitch. Why can't this night just end already?"

She heard the engine idle in front of her house. It hadn't woken her. Sleep was not coming easy tonight. She forced herself to get in bed when her house had cleared out. What she needed was to close her eyes and forget, be whisked away into dead sleep. The sleep never came.

She glanced over at the clock. 1:37am. Bailey stared up at her ceiling fan, watching the blades swirl around. Maybe being mesmerized by the motion would send her into a relaxed state, ease her enough to fall asleep. She ignored the loud motor rumbling outside her window.

If he thought for one second he could come back after she specifically told him to leave, he was wrong. Majorly fucking wrong. She tightened her grip on the sheets, digging her nails into the soft fabric. After what he'd done tonight, humiliated her, and now he was sitting outside her house.

It was moments like this she wished she had neighbors. At least then someone could call and complain. She drew in a breath. Complain about what? Motorcycles were legal and allowed to be on the road. It was also legal to be parked in front of her house. She debated making her own call. Ghosttown didn't have a police department. They relied strictly on the State Police. It was rare they were called, but when they were, they showed up. *An hour later.*

She jerked her head on her pillow. The silence piqued her curiosity. Had he left? She hadn't heard the motorcycle rev its engine and take off down the road. Could he quietly stroll down her street without her hearing him? *Oh, please let the answer be yes.* She threw off her covers, kicking at the edge, and rolled out of bed. The room was basked in darkness except for a small nightlight from her hallway. She slowly moved to the side of the window and slid the drape aside a few inches.

"Dammit!"

The curtain fell from her fingertips, and she pressed her back against the wall parallel to the window. Why was he doing this to her? Why was he here?

She craned her neck and squinted her eyes for a better view. He remained seated on his bike, one foot on the ground, the other on his pedal. Bailey could see the silhouette of his body. He shifted forward, and she jumped against the wall but kept her sight on him. The last thing she needed was him coming to the door, which she was sure was his next move.

He didn't get off his bike. He simply removed his helmet, draped it over a steering bar and settled in, a little hunched over. A light glow from his hands caught her eye. She scrunched her nose and clamped her lips together in anger. The jerk was outside her house, keeping her up, and now he was playing on his phone?

"I've had it," she muttered and rushed to her phone on the nightstand. She waited a second, considering her options. If she did phone the police, it would take them well over an hour, and since he wasn't technically doing anything illegal, she wasn't sure they'd even bother sending someone out. She was left with only one other option. She scrolled through her contacts and hit call.

It rang three times, and she was sure it would go straight to voicemail.

"Yeah."

His gruff tone was usual, and from the music and ruckus in the background, she didn't think she woke him. His number wasn't one she used often. He made her a little uneasy. He'd never done anything to her, but his whole persona put Bailey on edge. Now she was calling him. She rubbed her forehead with the back of her hand.

"I'll give ya another second before I hang up." He paused, and she opened her mouth, but he interrupted. "Fucking speak, Bailey."

She blinked, tightening her grip on her phone. Did he have to be so damn demanding?

"I have a problem," she said then bit her bottom lip and waited.

"Okay."

She cleared her throat and paused, coming up with her wording before she spoke. Apparently, he wasn't sparing her any patience.

"You want me to fucking guess what it is?" He sighed and muttered under his breath. "Jesus Christ."

His lack of compassion for her having a problem in the first place, compounded with his impatience, fueled her fire for the man sitting outside her house. She'd always been respectful of the club. She was one of the few residents who had given them a chance and not assumed they were bad for their tiny town. Until tonight, she hadn't taken an issue with any of them. In fact, she'd gone out of her way to make them feel welcome, knowing they weren't getting any warmth from the rest of the town. *I went to a fucking club party!*

"All right, listen, this is..."

"No, you listen." She cut him off. "I have been nothing but nice and welcoming to you and your club. I've done everything in my little power to help the transition of your club into Ghosttown, I've even gone as far as to tell the residents, *who loathe you,* we need to be fair and accept you guys. So, don't tell *me* I have to listen to *you.*"

Her body shook in anger, and her breath skipped. Bailey couldn't recall the last time she'd been this infuriated. She paced around her room from wall to wall.

"Darlin'?"

"What?" she snapped, completely fed up with him and his club. And every single member. Guilt by association.

He chuckled, which only intensified her heated blood.

"You called me. Now, you gotta problem, just fucking say it. Otherwise, I'm gonna hang up 'cause as much as I appreciate you going to bat for the club?" His tone took an odd, eerily, quiet and fierce tone. "Never asked for it. Not giving out favors for you being fucking who you are. We don't owe you shit, Bailey. Ya get me?"

What an asshole! If she was a different person, she would hang up now and call all the residents of her town and form a lynching for this prick.

"You're an asshole, Kase. A gigantic, arrogant, undeniable jerk." She was feeding off anger, and her words were spilling out without any rational thought. She wasn't one to usually curse. However, he brought out her foul mouth. "You give bikers a bad name."

The rumbling through the phone was undoubtedly laughter. "I give bikers a bad name?" He coughed, and she heard the amusement in his voice. "That's a first."

This call needed to end before she did something stupid, like get out her bb gun and start shooting at Dobbs through her window.

"I'll give you five minutes to get him away from my house. If he's not gone in five, then I'm calling the police, and I will file a complaint of intimidation and harassment." She paused and balled her fist. "How well do you think you'll fare being on their radar, Kase?"

She had no plans of doing anything of the sort. Lying to get him to listen was a tactic she was willing to use. Anything to get Dobbs gone.

"Don't threaten me, Bailey." His tone was completely calm, yet sinister.

"It's no threat. If he's not gone, I'll do it. And since you insist on going back and forth with me, you now have four minutes. And yes, I'm timing it."

"Who the fuck are you talking about?"

"Your guy, in your cut, sitting on a motorcycle, in front of *my house*." She yelled the last two words.

"Who?" He barked.

"Dobbs. Get him outta here, now, Kase. Three minutes."

"What the fuck?" She heard him shuffling around and the feminine yelp. Great, he was probably having sex while she was ranting. She lowered her head and stared at her toes digging into the carpet.

"I don't know who the fuck you're talking about. I'm staring at Dobbs at the bar in the fucking clubhouse."

Her head spiked up. "What?"

"He's right here."

"But—" She rushed to the window. In the exact same spot as he was ten minutes ago, sat a man on his bike. He no longer held his phone. His gaze was directed to the vacant lot across the street from her house. "Then who is he?" She unnecessarily pointed. Kase couldn't see anyway.

"Fuck. I'll call you back." He hung up without another word.

Bailey moved closer to the window, watching the figure. *Who was it?* Rourke, maybe? It didn't make sense. Where was Macy then? He moved suddenly, dug into his pocket and brought his phone to his ear. Obviously, she couldn't hear what he was saying, but Kase must have known who he was. The call didn't last long, and it seemed like the minute he put his phone down, hers rang. She picked up before the first ring finished.

"It's Saint." He sounded extremely pissed off.

She leaned closer to her window, staring out at him.

"Saint? Why is he sitting out there?"

"You wanna know, go fucking ask him."

She gripped her phone. Why did Kase insist on being a jerk? And why was Saint sitting in front of her house in the middle of the night? She pulled back the curtain. *Still there.*

"Well, did you tell him to leave?"

Kase snorted in annoyance. "Listen, Bailey. It's been a long fucking night. You want him gone, get your ass outside and tell him. And good luck with that, Mayor. Haven't met a person Saint takes orders from, but have at it."

"Wait, you're his president, you can make him leave."

Kase laughed. "Yeah, you got a lot to learn about Saint." He hung up.

Shit. Now what? She moved slowly, getting in front of the window and peering down at the street. The only light was shining from her porch. He was back to staring at the lot across the road. She glanced over at the empty property. What was he looking at? More importantly, why was he sitting in front of her house at one-thirty in the morning?

She pulled back the curtain, giving her a full unobstructed view. She bit her lip with indecision. Half of her mind was screaming for her to get her ass outside. *Saint's here.* The other half was yelling for her to retreat and get back in bed. There was no way she'd fall asleep knowing he was outside. She drew in a breath and angled her head, getting a better view.

"He did smile at me earlier." Her tension eased a little. "Sort of." It was more of a half-smile, more than he'd given any of the other women at the barbeque. She stepped away, rushing to her dresser and grabbing a sweatshirt.

Decision made.

SAINT SCOPED the vacant lot across from Bailey's. It would require a lot of clearing, and he'd have to get the ground tested, but it was level. As far as he knew, no one from the club had claimed the property just yet.

When his phone rang, he glanced down and answered the expected call. "Yeah?"

"Brother, didn't know you made house calls?"

"A lot you don't know about me, Kase." Saint folded his hand under his arm. "What do ya need?"

"I *need* to get back to the tight slit who was sucking my dick when your little fucking pain in the ass started blowing up my phone."

Saint smirked. *Of course she did.* He knew damn well she thought he was Dobbs. What he didn't know was if she would come out to him and show forgiveness, or freak out and get pissed. He was pleasantly surprised with the outcome.

"I take it she's not happy."

He snorted. "Yeah, man, she's not happy considering she thinks it's fucking Dobbs stalking her ass. Brother, the girl had a fucked-up night, and it seems when our sweet mayor gets pissed, she turns vicious." Kase sounded exhausted and fed up. "Any chance I can get you to appease our threatening little mayor and leave?"

Saint smirked. "No."

"Ah, fuck me. Later." Kase hung up. Saint ended the call and shoved it in his pocket. He knew she was at the window watching. The only thing left was for her to follow through on her threats, which he assumed was calling in the cops or coming down to see him.

He settled into his seat. He was gonna risk it to see what she would do. He didn't have to wait as long as he thought. Five minutes later, the motion lights lit up her entire front yard. He stilled and heard the padded footsteps from behind him. When he felt her close, he glanced over his shoulder. She stood about five feet away, her head tilted gripping the sleeves of her sweatshirt. Her long red hair was on top of her head with a few stray strands framing her face. Her pale skin glowed in the moonlight without a trace of makeup. He caught her red-rimmed eyes, which heated his blood.

"Hi."

He lifted his chin. "Bailey."

Her eyes widened, and he watched the ball of her throat bob. He rarely spoke to anyone, including Bailey. He had tried to maintain distance until he was ready to move forward with her. *I'm ready.*

She glanced down her empty street then back at him. "What are you doing here?"

He didn't answer right away. He was struck at how beautiful she was bathed in the light. She was enveloped in a long sweatshirt which came down to her mid-thigh. She was tiny in stature. If he had to guess, he'd put her at just a bit over five feet. It was a huge contrast to his six-three height. He'd have to bend down or lift her up to kiss her. Either one was a viable option for him. Whatever he had to do. He glanced down her body. Her lounge pants fit loosely around her legs. She stepped closer, which he hadn't expected. She stopped a foot away from his bike. Her hands were clasped in front of her.

"Saint?" she whispered.

"Heard ya had a rough night." He stared at her watching the corners of her lips pin downward. "You told Dobbs to leave, and I'm just here to ensure he does what he was told."

She glanced down at her feet. "Guess you heard what happened, huh?"

He could have lied to spare her feelings. If she had been just any other woman, he might have done it. With Bailey, he would earn her trust, which meant he'd never lie to her.

"Yeah." Even in the dark, he caught her cheeks pinkening. He clenched his jaw and bit back his furious anger. She was embarrassed when she shouldn't be. The only people who should have regret and shame were the bitch who talked about her and Dobbs for allowing it to happen. "Look at me."

She peeked up through her lashes. Her dark eyes peered back at him.

"You got no reason to hang your head, sweetheart. You didn't do anything except overhear bullshit and lies from a jealous woman. You hear me?"

Her lips curled. He could tell whatever was said hit her hard.

"You came here to tell me that?"

He shrugged. "And to make sure you knew Dobbs wouldn't be coming back."

"Oh." Her brows knitted together. "Kase said he's at the clubhouse."

"I know, and he'll stay there."

She jolted her head in confusion. "If you know he'll stay, then why are you here?"

"*I* know he'll stay there." He pointed at her. "But *you* don't."

"So, you're here to make me feel comfortable?" The corner of her lips curled.

He lifted his brows and slowly nodded. Her gaze flickered to the ground, and her head bowed slightly. Even in the dark he caught the small smile playing on her lips. Some of the ease in her stance had mellowed. She was relaxing because of him. His chest opened with a deep breath. Bailey didn't know it yet, but he was going to ensure she always felt safe with him.

She tugged at the hem of her wrists, which had slid up. Shielding her scars was another thing he would address with her when the time was right. There would be no hiding from him. When he claimed her, he would claim all of her, her beauty and her imperfections.

"This is the most you've ever spoken to me." She tilted her head, glancing up through her lashes.

"Planning on changing that."

"Yeah?" The corners of her eyes crinkled. If not for his incredible self-control, he may have reached out and pulled her in for a kiss. In all the times he'd seen and spoken to her, she'd never looked more beautiful than with the glimmer of excitement in her eyes, standing in front of him now.

"Yeah."

She bit her lip, and he watched her chest rise. If ever he'd doubted Bailey would want to be with him, this was confirmation.

"Well, um…" She glanced over her shoulder and hooked her thumb toward the house. "Do you—" When she gulped, seemingly struggling with her words, Saint tightened his lips in a line to keep from smiling. "Do you wanna come in?"

Ah, fuck. He hadn't expected this. He knew their attraction was mutual, but he didn't expect her to act on it. More than anything, he wanted to go in. Bad timing.

"You need to get some sleep. It's late."

"Oh." Her face slanted, and he cursed himself. "Well, you should go, too. I'm fine, and I don't want you to have to stay here all night." She smiled through what he assumed was disappointment. "Like you said, it's late, and you need sleep too."

"You trust me when I tell ya Dobbs won't come by and bother you?"

"Yeah."

He nodded. "Then I'll head out when you get inside and lock up."

"Okay." She stepped back and turned, angling her head toward him. "Thanks, Saint."

He wasn't sure what came over him. His hand shot out, grasping her wrist. Under his calloused palm, her skin was silky and soft and warm. He swallowed a hard breath. "Bailey."

She turned quickly and glanced down at his hand. For a brief second, time stood still. Then she did the most unexpected thing. She stepped closer, twisting her wrist out from his hold and slid her hand into his. Her fingers folded over his knuckles, and he inhaled a sharp breath. His first real touch. It was better than anything he'd imagined. Another step had her a few inches away with a sweet smile playing on her lips.

"I'm out of town for the next few days and back Friday." He shrugged. "I'll bring breakfast over in the morning, sound good?"

Her smile faltered, and her brows knitted together. She slowly turned her head to her house then back to him. "You mean here? To my house?"

He flattened his lips, exercising great effort in not smiling. "Yes. Sound good?"

He watched her lips quirk. Ah, her fucking smile had him undone. She nodded.

He curled his lip. "See ya then, sweetheart."

Her eyes widened. He couldn't be exactly sure what provoked it. If he had to guess, it was the term of endearment. She needed to get used to it with him.

She smiled again and walked away, slowly releasing his hand. She bowed her head, crossing over the lawn and up her stairs. She glanced over her shoulder then closed the door behind her.

He waited for another fifteen minutes until her lights shut down, and he was sure she was settling in her bed. Her bed. He'd be there soon enough. Right now, he had to get to his own. He'd get only a few hours before getting on the road and heading out. He had scheduled a few days away to tie up any loose ends at his tattoo shops.

He'd spent the last few months training office managers, configuring a system which would allow him to monitor all the business remotely. In a week, he'd be officially back in Ghosttown permanently.

He took one last look at Bailey's house. He'd be back soon enough.

Chapter 6

Bailey pulled up the long driveway, up the embankment, and slowed down outside the house. She'd been there a few times and parked in her usual spot, right outside the gates, next to the big red truck. She glanced around the grounds. Caden's office was in the back, and usually there was more activity, especially on a weekday. It seemed almost deserted.

She was beyond excited for today. Marissa had asked her to paint a mural in the nursery. It was an honor, and she'd spent weeks perfecting the design. She had done a preliminary drawing to make sure Marissa liked it. It turned out she loved it. Of all the people she'd met since she moved to Ghosttown years ago, Marissa had become one of her closest friends. When she heard she was pregnant, no one was more thrilled than Bailey. *Well, maybe Rissa and Cade.*

She got out and made her way to her trunk, retrieving all her supplies. She had her head in the trunk when she heard the voices. Her heart plummeted to her stomach. A few days had passed, and she'd gotten over most of her humiliation. However, she didn't have any desire to see anyone from the club. Except one. *Saint would be a welcomed sight.* She peered around her bumper. *Oh shit!* Kase, Caden, Dobbs, and Gage were walking toward the gates. She jerked around giving the men her back. The voices grew louder, and she squeezed her eyes shut. *Please don't talk to me.*

"Hey, Bailey."

Dammit!

She grabbed her box under her arm and slammed the truck with too much force. She glanced over at the men who were about ten feet away. Maybe she was reading into it, but they appeared solemn, and she caught the pity glowering in their eyes. Dobbs started toward her, confirming he was the one who had called out to her.

"Hi," she shouted, noticing the small tremble in her voice.

"Wait, hold up," Dobbs said as she turned toward the path.

"Sorry, I can't, I'm running late. I'll talk to ya later." She quickly rushed up to the door.

She knocked harder than she intended. When she got no response, she banged against the door, causing the screen to shake. She wasn't sure if Dobbs had followed her onto the porch. She slammed her fist against the door.

"For Christ's sake." She recognized Jack's voice, and then the door ripped open.

He eyed her suspiciously, then the corner of his mouth curled. It was the same reaction she always got from Caden and Kase's father. He swung open the door. "Hey, darlin'."

Bailey smiled and rushed inside, watching as Jack closed the door. She sighed in relief.

"Hi, Jack." She leaned close to the window, watching the four men circle in the front of the house. "Shit," she muttered. The last thing she wanted was to see any of them, especially Dobbs.

"What's wrong?"

Bailey glanced over at Jack. He was scowling as he leaned forward to look out the window, then back to her.

"What the hell did he do?" Jack stepped closer, bending down and putting them at eye level. His wrinkled face tightened, and he searched her face. "It's Kase, right? You tell me what he did, and I'll set his ass straight."

Bailey shook her head. "He didn't do anything to me, Jack, I swear."

He squinted his eyes. "You sure, 'cause if he did, I will kick his sorry ass all over the back lot. I ain't too old to take on any of those fuckers who think to mess with you. Ya hear me?"

Bailey nodded fighting back her smile. "Really, I just um…" How was she supposed to explain to Jack that she was merely embarrassed and didn't have the balls to face anyone from the club?

"What?"

She drew in a breath. "I just don't wanna see anyone from the club is all. Maybe I should just leave." She was prepared for him to force her into telling him the reason. Surprisingly he didn't. He straightened his back, rising to full height and towering over Bailey. She watched him through her lashes. Whatever Jack was seeing on her expression was enough for him.

"You ain't going nowhere." He nodded and shifted around, walking to the door and turning the lock. He angled around and folded his arms over his chest. "Done. They can't come in."

Bailey's mouth fell open. *What? He was locking them out of the house?* Jack glanced over her shoulder.

"They ain't coming in."

Bailey turned around when she heard the faint female chuckle. Marissa was standing on the staircase, laughing. She held up her hands in surrender. "Fine by me, Jack." She walked over to Bailey, clasping her hand and guiding her toward the stairs. "We're going to start on the baby's room, c'mon up if ya get bored. But please, no fights, okay?"

Bailey shifted her gaze to Jack. He hadn't moved. "As long as those fuckers don't try to get in here, we don't got any problems."

Marissa smiled and shook her head. Bailey followed her up the stairs and down the hall. Beads of sweat lined her forehead.

She'd caused this mess. She waited until they got in the room and closed the door.

"I'm so sorry, Riss."

Marissa spun around. "For what?"

For what? How about for getting her old and sick father-in-law riled up and angry. Marissa had shared with her Jack's condition. The last thing the man need was more stress. Bailey's head throbbed with guilt.

"I upset Jack."

She snorted and waved her hand. "You didn't upset Jack, the club did, mainly Kase."

"Why?"

Marissa flattened her lips and remained silent.

"Because of me." She rested her hand on her chest, feeling the strumming of her pounding heart. This was an absolute mess, and she'd caused it.

Marissa furrowed her brows. "No, it's not, Bailey." She took a breath and glanced around the room with an uncomfortable silence. "Macy told me what happened Saturday night."

Bailey dropped her head and moaned. All she wanted to do was forget about it, and now it seemed everyone knew.

"Bails, stop. It's not your fault. Dobbs was a complete asshole. As president, Kase knows what his guys do falls on his lap. He should have reached out to you. It's what Cade said."

Her eyes widened. "Oh my God, Cade knows too?" She groaned. This was mortifying. "I really just wanna forget about it. It's not a big deal."

"Bailey," Marissa whispered.

She glanced up at Marissa. If ever there was a person, she felt most connected to, it was Marissa. "I'm embarrassed."

Marissa rushed forward, grabbing her hands. "Why? You didn't do anything wrong."

Bailey closed her eyes, seeking refuge in hiding. *Hiding.* It's was what she had done for the last few years. Hiding behind her long sleeve shirts, her soft smile, and her friendly persona. *I get to choose how people see me.* She'd been a fool to believe it.

"Bailey," The sympathetic tone was almost too much for her to take.

She blinked her eyes open, staring at her concerned friend. "I let myself forget who I really am." It was a painful admission. One she wished she hadn't shared.

"What?"

"No, it's stupid, just forget it."

Bailey shook her head, fighting back her tears. She was so over crying and feeling sorry for herself. She needed to let it go. Unfortunately, it had consumed her. Seeing Dobbs and the other members had brought her back to Saturday night, no matter how hard she tried to forget.

"Tell me," Marissa urged. "What do ya mean, you forgot who you really are?"

Bailey sighed and leaned back against the bare wall in the nursery. She was there to decorate, not unleash her ugly truth.

"Bailey."

Bailey pulled her hands out of Marissa's and shoved them in her pockets. She stared down at her shoes. Talking with even her therapist about her scars and how they affected her had been a challenge. Somehow, with Marissa, they shared a connection. *She'll understand.*

"I made the decision a long time ago to not let what happened to me ruin me." She made the promise to herself. "It was just gonna be something that happened, not something I'd let define me. It wouldn't be *who I am*." She scrunched up her shoulders, staring down at her dirty shoes. "Everybody has a past, right? And scars."

"Yeah, of course," Marissa whispered, and Bailey smiled, glancing up at her friend.

"When I look in the mirror, I don't see them, Riss. I really don't. I don't give them acknowledgment because they aren't who I am. I don't cover them up because I can't bear the sight of them. I do it because it bothers everyone else. It makes people uncomfortable. They see my scars, and I'm not me anymore, I'm the girl who had something really shitty happen to her. Everyone feels bad for me. I stop being me, and I'm left being a victim. I don't want their pity."

"Bailey, nobody pities you. I don't look at you and see scars. You know that, right?"

Her eyes welled, and she nodded. "I know you don't but it's not just that."

"What else?"

She wiped her cheeks, and her bottom lip trembled. "I forgot, Riss."

"Forgot what?"

"The truth. I blocked it for so long I forgot, Riss." Tears streamed down her cheeks. Her breath shook, and she gasped for air. "The girl, the one with Dobbs, she called me the swamp thing, said I was false advertising because I had a pretty face, but my body was gross." She sniffled. "Said he probably wouldn't be able to get hard when I took my clothes off. She said all that, and ya know what?" Bailey's hands began to shake, and she heaved a breath, losing control. "She's right. Everything she said, as cruel as it was. She's right."

Marissa gasped. "No, she's not, Bailey. You are beautiful."

"Yeah." Bailey motioned to her face. "Here and on the inside. But from the neck down, Riss, I'm not." She shook her head. Her vision blurred, and she covered her face with her hands. "It's ugly and gross, just like she said. What man would want this?" She pulled back her sleeves, and for the first time in years, she cringed at the sight of her scars. *This is who I am now.*

"Bailey," Marissa whispered, reaching out for her arms.

Bailey slumped against the wall for only a brief second feeling the weight of her own honesty weigh her down. It was painful and heart-wrenching, *because* it was the truth. She'd dismissed the idea of being intimate with anyone, and for a while it was okay. It had been on her terms. But she was seeing the reality now. No man would ever see beyond the scars. None, including the man who was bringing her breakfast in a few days. She heaved a breath and gasped for air.

A strong set of arms wrapped around her body in a tight hold, almost engulfing her into the point of pain. The hold was so tight she was scrunched into a tight ball. She pried her eyes open to see Marissa standing in front of her with tears streaming down her face. It hadn't sunk in. If Marissa was standing across from her, who the hell was holding her? She glanced to the side to see Jack.

Great. Not only had she yelled, screamed, cried, and lost her shit in front of one person, now she realized it had been two. Jack's hand caressed her back and his lips pressed against the top of her head. She closed her eyes. *So sweet.*

"I don't know who the fuck she is, but the cunt don't know shit. Ya hear me?" Jack shouted in her ear, and she jumped still locked in his embrace. He patted her back. "Eyes up here, darlin'."

Bailey glanced up, and Jack immediately wiped her tears from her cheeks. "You are beautiful. Ya hear me? Fucking, goddamn gorgeous, so what, ya got some scars, I got a fuck ton. Who gives shit?"

She drew in a deep breath and forced a smile. Leave it to Jack to somehow make it all okay. He rocked side to side with Bailey nestled in his arms.

"Thanks, Jack."

He unwrapped her from his hold and stepped back, keeping his gaze locked on her. When she sniffled, his glare hardened.

"I got my own set of rules. I can't break em'. God, I wish I could just this one time." He stopped in thought and grew silent. He shook his head. "No, I can't break it."

Bailey eyed Marissa, and she appeared just as confused by his statement.

"Gotta be a real son of a bitch to shoot a woman, even if the cunt deserves it. That I can't do." He sighed and straightened his back, glancing over to Marissa. "Where's my gun?"

Bailey gasped. *What the hell was he talking about? A gun?* Her heart raced against her chest.

"You're not killing anyone, Jack." Marissa narrowed her gaze and seemed extremely calm when she spoke, unlike Bailey who was on the verge of a panic attack.

"I ain't gonna kill no one. I'm just gonna shoot them, teach em' a lesson for bringing trash around Bailey." He pursed his lips. "Trust me. You remember your mistakes when ya got a gunshot scar to serve as a reminder."

"Oh, fuck me."

Bailey spun around to find Caden at the doorway.

"How'd you get in here?" Jack snapped.

Caden cocked his brow. "I have a key, remember, this is my house." He shook his head, and his gaze drifted to Bailey. She immediately glanced away. She wouldn't be surprised if Caden banned Bailey from ever stepping foot in his house again. She wouldn't be shocked if he forbid Marissa from hanging out with her, though, Marissa might make the decision on her own after this clusterfuck of a day.

"Pop, lunch is ready. Head down. We'll catch up."

Jack turned, not saying another word until he stood next to Caden at the door.

"Hey." Bailey whipped her head in his direction. He was apparently talking to her. He narrowed his eyes, and he pursed his lips. "Changed my mind. You want me to. I'll shoot the cunt. Break my rule for you."

Marissa burst out laughing, Caden rolled his eyes, and Jack remained fixated on her.

It had been the sweetest, most obscene offer she'd ever received. Bailey smiled. "No, Jack." A bubble of laughter built in her belly. This was the strangest conversation she'd ever had in her life. "I appreciate the offer, Jack, and thank you for being so kind to me."

He pointed at Bailey. "I'll do it for you, darlin', if you change your mind. You're a good one, Bailey, too damn pretty to be sad."

Jack simply nodded with a wink and left the room. Bailey avoided eye contact with Marissa and Caden. Her stomach turned with a harsh guilt. She had caused a chaos in their house when she was supposed to be painting a nursery. She gulped and glanced up to find them both looking at her. Neither one appeared angry. If anything, they seemed sympathetic. Bailey turned to Caden.

"I'm so sorry, Caden…" She stopped mid apology when Caden's hand lifted.

"You got nothing to be sorry for, Bailey." He was being sweet. "You didn't do anything wrong." He paused. "Pop is usually all crazy talk, but he's right. You're a good one." He smiled. "Too pretty to be sad."

Bailey curled her lip. The biggest take away from this shit show was the reminder that she had surrounded herself with good people.

"Why don't we do this some other time?" Marissa walked forward and smiled. "Let's have lunch or something."

Bailey furrowed her brows, and her shoulders sagged. She'd ruined everything. "You don't want me to do the mural?" Had she messed up so badly Marissa didn't want her help anymore?

Marissa flinched in surprise. "What? No, of course, I do."

Bailey drew in a breath and sighed in relief. "Then I want to do it. Today."

"You sure?"

"Yes."

Marissa clapped her hands. "I can't wait to see it."

Caden cleared his throat. "I got work to do. Holler if ya need something." He leaned over, kissing Marissa, and then turned to Bailey with a soft smile. "Thanks, Bailey. And you're staying for dinner."

"Oh, I don't…"

He narrowed his gaze. "Wasn't asking. You're eating dinner with us. Pop would probably shoot my ass if ya left here hungry. Consider it a thank you."

Good people.

"Okay."

He sighed and headed toward the door, then turned and rolled his eyes. "Gonna apologize for Trevor now. The kid can't help himself around pretty girls. He's gonna flirt with ya." Caden winked and left the room.

Bailey laughed, and somehow, the day had been saved.

SAINT HAD SCHEDULED the grand opening around Marco's schedule. His lead tattoo artist rotated around the five locations, giving him full access to all their shops. He wouldn't include the Ghosttown location on his routine schedule, but he would spend a week there during the grand opening, along with Minka. They were the best artists in the state and highly sought after. A few years ago, he offered to let Minka out of her contract and venture out on her own. She had enough clients that she probably would have made a killing. She declined, wanting to stay with him and Marco. She, like the rest of his employees, had become extended family.

"So, just a week?" Marco asked, sitting across from Saint's desk.

"Yeah, and I've got your accommodations set up. There aren't any hotels, but the club has a house available for you, Minka, and anyone else you might want to bring along."

Marco laughed. "Me and Gwen parted ways last week."

Saint had met his on-again, off-again girlfriend a few times. He hadn't been a fan. Saint had a keen sense on most people and didn't get a good vibe from Gwen. In true Saint fashion, he'd kept his opinion to himself.

He shrugged. "Wanted to travel with me, ya know, quit her job. She's good, got me thinking I might take her up on the offer. But I realized she might like my name and reputation a little more than she actually likes me. Too bad though."

Minka charged in the room, laughing. "Too bad, why? 'Cause she's a good lay?"

Marco laughed and raised his brows at Saint. "Pretty much."

Minka sneered. "You're all pigs." She settled into the chair next to Marco. "Except Saint."

Saint smirked and handed them the copies of their itinerary. They had both offered up their time for the new shop. Of all the artists he employed, he was closest to Marco and Minka. He was the one who gave each of them their first shot at tattooing. Best decision he ever made.

Minka glanced over the sheet and tossed it onto his desk. "I need to renegotiate my terms on this."

Saint looked up. "On what? Ghosttown?"

She nodded and clasped her hands, smiling. He was being more than generous with his offer. He'd pay their travel and food expenses, and put them up in the house. On top of their work, he added a healthy bonus, which both insisted wasn't necessary though he demanded they take it. What the hell more could she want? He eyed her suspiciously. He'd known Minka for years, and she'd always been fair, never demanding, or greedy.

"What else would you like?"

She arched her brow and side glanced Marco, who was watching her. She pursed her lips and stared at Saint with a glint in her eye. "I want to meet Bailey."

He sucked in a breath, watching her smile turn into a full grin. "And not some greeting of 'Minka, this is Bailey.'" She shook her head. "Uh-uh, Saint, I want to meet her, hang out with her, dinner, drinks, all of it."

Marco raised his hand, clearly amused. "I'd like to renegotiate for that too."

Saint had shared his feelings about Bailey to Marco. He was easy to confide in him since he didn't know her. It had been a long year of waiting for the right timing with Bailey, and he'd vented his frustration to Marco. On occasion, Minka was nearby. He wasn't surprised they'd want to meet her.

Minka lifted her finger. "Oh, and it's non-negotiable, Saint. If I can't meet her, I'm not going." She folded her arms over her chest.

Saint settled into his seat and clasped his hands on the desk, eyeing both tattoo artists—his friends who'd been traveling the same year with him on his wait for Bailey. "Then you'll meet Bailey."

"No shit?" Marco said, which was a dulled response compared to Minka, who shot up from her chair and leaned across his desk.

"You better not be pulling some shit, like when we get there, you renege."

Saint sighed, angling his head. "Have I ever reneged on an agreement?"

She leaned closer, squinting her eyes, which made him smirk. She smiled and hopped away from his desk, turning toward the door. She bounced in her step, which was utterly amusing. She turned back at the doorway and leaned on the frame.

"I'm so friggin' excited." She glanced at the ceiling. "Bailey Monroe. Has a nice ring to it, don't ya think?" Her teasing was in jest, and he could take it. However, she needed to reel it back in front of Bailey. The last thing he needed was anyone scaring her off.

He scowled. "Tread lightly, Minka. Remember who signs your paycheck."

She laughed. "I'm gonna have so much fun with this, Saint. Look at you, all sweet and in love with Bailey." She winked and skittered out the door.

Marco chuckled. "She's such a pain in the ass."

"Since the day we met her."

Marco sighed and tilted his head. "Gotta say, man, I'm stoked to meet Bailey."

Saint knew he would be.

His phone rang, and he glanced down to see Kase's name. He wasn't expecting a call.

"I got a client. We'll talk later." Marco walked out the door just as Saint answered the call.

"Yeah?"

"Call Cade."

Saint furrowed his brows.

"Why?"

"Call him."

This was unusual. While he had a fairly close relationship with Caden, this was a rare demand.

"Care to explain why you're telling me to call your brother?"

"'Cause I'm thinking ya don't wanna hear this shit second-hand, considering it's about Bailey."

His heart skipped. From Kase's words and his tone, this couldn't be anything good.

"What?"

"Call fucking Cade. Now."

Saint hung up and dialed Cade's number. He grabbed his jacket and stalked through the shop, ignoring the awkward glances. He threw open the door just as Cade answered.

"Hey, man."

"What's going on?"

"You got a minute to talk?"

The cool air hit his face as he ambled toward his bike. He was set to make the ride to Ghosttown if need be. "Cade, fucking tell me, is she okay?"

"Yeah, Saint, she's fine. Calm down, didn't Kase tell ya?"

"No, he said to call you, so fucking speak." His blood was racing through his body in a heated rush. He rarely used foul language. Unlike his brothers, he didn't find the need to incessantly curse. However, when he lost control, which wasn't very often, he did have an equally colorful vocabulary as his brothers.

"I swear, Saint, she's fine. She came over this morning. She's doing a mural in the baby's room. Anyway, I guess she saw the guys here, still embarrassed about how shit went down the other night. I didn't catch the whole conversation, and Marissa wouldn't go into detail saying it's private what Bailey shared with her." He sighed. "I was in the hall when she broke down crying, talking about how the bitch from the club said was right, some false advertising and swamp thing comment. Saying her scars were too ugly for any man to want to be with her."

Saint stopped dead in his tracks. His breath labored, and his nostrils flared. He'd heard about the comments relayed by Macy. For Bailey to be dwelling on them meant they struck her deep, and someone was going to pay.

"Anyway, she was crying, not making much sense to me, but she was wrecked, Saint. Bailey, man, we all got a soft spot for her, and seeing her like that?" Caden paused. "It ain't right. Not with Bailey."

He closed his eyes, wishing there was a way to take her pain away.

Caden chuckled, which seemed odd for the conversation. "Believe it or not, it was Jack who saved the day. He's a mean son of a bitch when it comes to us, but he's got a soft spot for the girls. Especially Bailey. Hugged your girl, telling her she was beautiful." Caden snorted. "Then the crazy bastard offers to start shooting people, mainly the bitch who said it."

For a brief moment, the mood had lightened. Saint smirked.

"Bailey declined the offer, 'cause ya know, she's sweet Bailey." He snickered. "Just thought you should know."

"How'd she leave?"

"Good man. Marissa wanted to hold off on the mural." He snorted. "Bailey wasn't having it. She worked for hours. Ya got come see it, fucking incredible. She's got a shit ton of talent. She stayed for dinner with us." He paused. "Trev flirted with her."

Saint rolled his eyes. Of course, Trevor would. He was seventeen going on manhood. Any interaction with a beautiful woman, he'd jump at the chance to flirt.

"She's good now, just wanted to give you the heads up."

"Thanks. Cade, need you or Riss to check on her. Won't be back for a few days."

"Yeah, Saint, we got her. Riss talks to her almost every day anyway. No worries, man. Later."

Saint hung up and shoved his phone in his back pocket. He had three more days of work piled on his desk before he could head back to Ghosttown. If he didn't finish, he'd have to come back. His own relief was knowing she was in good hands with Marissa and Caden.

And Jack.

Chapter 7

Saint Monroe.

"I can't believe he showed up," she muttered.

Bailey bit her lip, spying from the back door. She inched the curtain back slightly in hopes of going unnoticed. He was rounding the back of her house with a paper bag in his hand. She had heard the motorcycle pull in her driveway minutes ago. She couldn't believe he actually came over. Why was she surprised? He said he would Saturday night. Although a lot had happened in the last few days. Her outburst and breakdown had changed so much. She was sure Saint knew. They all knew. Her face heated, and she closed her eyes. *I need to let it go.* She'd spent almost a week harping over something beyond her control. Other people's opinions. *They only matter if you let them.* With all the therapy she'd invested in herself, she should have been able to move past it.

There was no way she could sit at her kitchen table with Saint and eat breakfast as if what happened hadn't affected her. It was impossible. Why had she said yes in the first place? *How could I not? It's Saint.* Her forehead broke out in a beaded sweat. *Think.* She twisted her lips and watched as he moved past her backyard flower bed.

Her car was in the garage. He might think she was out if she didn't answer the door. If she ran into him at a later time, she could just say she forgot. *Yeah, 'cause that's believable.* What woman would forget they were having breakfast with Saint? She drew in a breath.

Oh shit! She was a second too late to go unnoticed when she blinked and saw Saint strolling up her back steps, his eyes set on her through the sliver of the curtain. She jumped back from the door. *What now?* He knew she was inside, ignoring him was no longer an option. She stared at the door waiting for it to burst open or catch on fire. It didn't.

A soft singular knock sounded, and she drew in a breath, holding it tight. He'd seen her. She had to answer. *Breathe, idiot.* Bailey gasped for a breath and jerked back a step when he knocked again. It was strange. It wasn't hurried or demanding, no banging or pounding. A simple patient knock. It was as if he knew that eventually, she'd open the door.

While she didn't know Saint well, there was an air to him. Unrushed, stoic, and completely cool. As if he knew the outcome of every situation. Even last week, when things seemed extremely tense after the town meeting, Saint appeared collected and unfazed by the mounting tension with Kase and Coop. His title as VP had to hold some power, which she assumed meant when Saint spoke, people listened. When Saint gave an order, it was followed. *And when he knocks on your door, you answer.*

"Shit," she muttered.

She licked her lips and tapped her foot lightly. The internal struggle was twisting her stomach in knots. She was going over in her head how their interaction played out. He was prepared to sit on his bike all night just so she felt safe? Then, basically, he set up a date for breakfast. Her mind went straight to her default reasoning. Pity.

Everyone felt sorry for the girls with the scars.

He knocked again, replicating his first two attempts. How long would he do this? She glanced at the clock— 7:12am. She moved forward, grasping the knob and unlocking the door. She pulled it open wide. Her gaze set on the ground, hooked onto his beat-up, road dusted boots and blue jeans. They fit snug around his legs, probably because the man had thick, strong, muscular thighs. Her gaze traveled up to his chest. She couldn't be sure, but she assumed he had an amazing abs. He had his cut on. Her eyes skimmed over his patch—VP—and up his neck. His face was usually clean-shaven. This morning he was sporting a dark, five o'clock shadow. She bit her lip in indecision. She didn't know which she preferred. Both? *Ahhh, his face.* Strong, sharp features, cheekbones cut down to his jaw making his face harsh. His dark brows angled up in the center. Naturally she assumed, giving him a sexy sinister arch. The only light on his face were his eyes. Violet.

"Hi." Her breathy whisper made her face heat up. "I'm sorry, I was, uh…" *Freaking out?* She jerked her head to hide her blush and quickly scanned the kitchen, trying to conjure up a lie.

"Can I come in?"

She whipped her head and stared up at him. He was standing outside the door. There was nothing soft about Saint, but for some reason, he never frightened her. He was solid, almost sending the vibe that if he was in the room, it would be fine. She smiled. He remained stoic and staring.

"Uh, of course, c'mon in." She stepped aside and widened the door. Without an ounce of hesitation, Saint walked in. He passed by her, and she glanced up through her lashes and breathed in his scent. Fresh and clean with a hint of pine.

She released her breath and closed the door. She watched as Saint moved to the table, setting down a brown bag. For the next thirty seconds, she watched him amble around her kitchen, grabbing plates after two unsuccessful searches in her cabinets. He grabbed napkins from the counter before taking a seat at the table and reaching in the bag. He seemed very at home in her kitchen. Meanwhile, she stood near the door.

He glanced up with a small smile playing on his lips. "Are ya hungry?"

She cleared her throat but didn't respond. She slowly walked over to the seat next to him and remained standing. "Do you want anything to drink, coffee, or juice?"

"I'll take a cup of coffee if ya got extra."

She nodded and stumbled to the counter. *Calm down.* "Uh yeah, I got plenty." With her back facing Saint, she felt a slight relief. At least he wasn't witnessing her flushed cheeks. She grabbed the cream from the fridge and stopped halfway. *He takes milk in his coffee.* She turned around, putting it back and grabbing the milk. She poured a little, stirred and gave a splash more before adding two sugars.

She brought it to the table, placing it near his plate, and took her seat. She wiped her hands on her pajama bottoms as if there was something to wipe. There wasn't, but she wasn't quite ready to make eye contact.

"Ya know how I take my coffee."

She jerked her gaze, and his eyes burned into hers. She gulped. Unknowing to him, she'd watched him when he attended the town meetings, particularly when he was at the refreshment table. It was a safe time. He was busy making his coffee, unaware she was checking him out.

She gave an awkward chuckle. "Lucky guess."

His lips twitched as he continued to stare without saying a word. He must have thought she was weird. *Oh God, he thinks I'm some stalker chick.*

He raised his cup, taking a sip, his violet eyes glancing over the rim of the mug.

She tore her gaze from him and arranged her plate in front of her seat. The bag was on his left side so she would have to reach over him or just wait for him to offer a bagel. She waited. He placed his mug down.

"What kind do you want?"

"Umm... what do ya have?"

The Saint

"Sundried tomato, everything, and blueberry."

She smiled. "Damn, this is gonna be hard then, those are my three favorites."

He arched a brow. "I know."

He knows? How does he know?

"Whatever you grab is fine."

"Which one do you want?"

She shook her head. "It doesn't matter, really, I like them all."

He stared at her a bit longer and slowly shook his head, his brows coming down hard. "You get a choice, you always get a choice. You don't take what I give ya, you choose. Ya feel me, sweetheart?"

Oh. My. God. She wasn't feeling anything at the time, not a friggin' thing. Hell, she could barely feel her own breath. *Sweetheart?* Did Saint Monroe seriously just call her 'sweetheart'? Again. She'd never heard him use nicknames with anyone, always their proper names when he spoke to them. *But he just called me 'sweetheart,' for the second time.*

She stared back, knowing he was waiting on her response on her choice of bagel and if she felt him. She wasn't even sure what he meant. How was she supposed to answer?

"Uh...yeah, I feel ya." Her breath hitched, and she gulped. "Sundried tomato."

His lips twitched slightly, not enough to shake his stoic features, but giving her something she had seen before. She was amusing him. He dug in the bag, grabbing her bagel, and placed it on her plate. Before she could even ask for it, he reached over, grabbing the cream cheese and setting it down near her plate.

The corner of her mouth curled. "How do you know I don't use butter?" It was a small tease. She always used cream cheese. She could eat the stuff with a spoon.

He rested his elbows on the table. "The same way you know how I take my coffee, I assume."

She knew because she watched him. *Oh wow.* She averted her eyes from his penetrating gaze. She focused on her bagel. Her hand shook as she spread the cream cheese. *Calm down.* If Saint noticed her nervousness, he didn't mention it.

She bit into her bagel and moaned then clamped her mouth shut and chewed. She wiped her mouth. "This is so good, where'd ya get them?"

"Lawry."

"The mecca?" She smirked and raised her brows. Compared to Ghosttown, every place was a Mecca. It had become an inside joke because when the girls took the two-hour ride, they came back with a million bags.

"Yeah." He ate the last bite of his bagel, and she figured he would be leaving soon. For unknown reasons, it bothered her. She licked her lips and took another bite.

"Long drive just for bagels."

"Picked them up last night on my way home from seeing my girl."

She smiled, thinking of the little girl in the picture. "Cia?"

He nodded and watched her. There was something in the way he scanned her face, gauging her reaction. She wasn't exactly sure what he was looking for. She took another bite of her bagel and glanced back up to find his eyes on her.

"You like kids?"

She choked a little, completely caught off guard by his question. She swallowed the large chunk, forcing it down her throat. It took a few seconds to answer. She cleared her throat. "Uh, yeah, I like kids. I have two nieces and a nephew." She leaned closer and lowered her voice. "I'm kinda their favorite aunt." She snickered. "Probably 'cause we're about the same size. I swear, my nephew, who's six, thinks I'm one of the grandkids, too."

Saint's face transformed into a grin, and a low rumbling chuckle sounded from his chest.

"You have a big family?"

Bailey paused then glanced up at the ceiling. "I don't know if it would be considered big. My mom and dad. I have two older brothers and one younger."

Saint snorted. "That's big."

"Well, how about you?"

"My dad passed ten years ago, and my mom six. I have one brother."

"Oh wow, Saint, I'm sorry."

He nodded. She assumed talking about his parents was a subject she should stay away from. She took another bite from her bagel and chewed in silence.

"You close with your family?"

She nodded, finishing the last of her breakfast. "Yeah, I mean, sort of. I'm close with my mom and dad. My older brothers, not so much anymore. They have families now, and uh…." She let her voice trail off not wanting to give any more information. There was a reason she was no longer close with them. Discussing it with Saint was not an option. She sighed. "I'm close to Van, though, he's the youngest. Twenty-four, we're kinda like Irish twins." She smiled. "Most of my childhood memories include him." She paused. "What about you and your brother, you close?"

He nodded and tightened his lips. "Yeah, we're close. We're all we've got, which plays a part in our relationship. Don't necessarily see eye to eye on everything, but for the most part, Roman is a good guy." He cocked a brow. "When he's not being an asshole."

Bailey burst out laughing. She covered her mouth and watched as Saint gave her a full grin. His smile was amazing.

"Saint and Roman, huh?" Her lips twitched, trying her best to hold back her amusement.

Saint settled into his seat and folded his arms. "My mom was a diehard Catholic. Not a fan of the rules and commandments, but she showed up for Sunday mass. I think she figured if she gave her boys good Catholic names, she'd get a pass from the big guy upstairs. My mom was gonna need it." He chuckled with ease.

She was struck with her own ease. Long gone was the anxious energy from when he first arrived. The butterflies in her stomach were still running rampant. She could deal with it if it meant Saint was in her kitchen sharing his personal life. If he was willing to be open, maybe she could push the envelope. So much was unknown about him. Mainly the question weighing on her mind.

"Can I ask you something?"

His gaze flickered to her. "You can ask me anything."

Don't do it. She should have listened to her inner voice, but she had to know. She was aware he didn't mess with the club girls, but he could very well have someone he didn't bring around. Someone even Nadia didn't know about. This was a test. If he had a woman then it was confirmed. He was at her house eating bagels with her out of pity. If he didn't? Well, then…

"Do you have a girlfriend?"

He didn't even flinch, not a facial change or a reaction from his body. "Why?"

She shrugged. It was a yes or no question. She wasn't prepared to answer any herself. She glanced down at the table. "I don't know, just curious."

"Eyes up here, sweetheart." She responded immediately and looked at him. He rested his arms on the table, shifting his body closer to her. "No."

Her mouth went dry, and she reached for her coffee, spilling a little off the rim. *Pull it together.* She took a sip and settled back in her seat. "Yeah, I've never seen you with anyone." *Oh my God, shut up!* What was she doing? Too honest.

"Were ya watching me, Bailey?" His tone was low. His voice sent a shiver through her chest.

"A little bit," she whispered.

He smiled. Not a corner lifting or a tiny smirk. Saint gave her a heart-stopping, teeth gleaming, pleasured smile. Her face burned, and she tucked her chin into her chest, trying her best to keep her blush from showing. She wished she had moved her hands to her lap. There was a slight shake she couldn't seem to control.

His hand reached out, weaving his fingers through hers, leaving them palm to palm. *I'm holding Saint's hand.* Again, though this time, he initiated it. His thumb rubbed over her finger, and she felt her breath shallow. She peeked up through her lashes to find his gaze locked on her. His eyes darkened slightly, and she shifted in her chair, trying to release the pressure from her throbbing clit. Oh hell, she could never be with Saint. *I can barely make it through handholding without passing out.*

The corner of his mouth curled. "You okay?"

She nodded. *Don't you dare pass out.*

His hand tightened around hers, and he moved closer. Was he going to kiss her? "I have to get going."

No!

Her body deflated. She sunk into her seat and veered her gaze to the door. He released her hand, and she rested it over her lap. Her body still tingled from their connection.

The chair scraped the floor, and she watched as he got up. *It's over?* He was so tall and seemed double in size in her tiny kitchen. He fixed the cuffs of his shirt, and she was struck with a sudden pang of regret. She wished she could have spent more time with him. This was the most they'd ever spoken, and now it was over. He started to the back door and glanced over his shoulder. He was waiting on her.

She got up and rounded the table, stopping a few feet away. She was currently chewing on the inside of her mouth. It was the only distraction she had from making one of the biggest possible blunders in her life. *Don't do it, do not do it.*

"Do you wanna come over for dinner?" *Oh God, I actually did it.* The second she blurted it out, she regretted it. He turned slowly, glancing down at her. Now she put him in an awkward spot where he'd have to come up with some excuse. Leave it to her to take a perfectly great morning breakfast with Saint and ruin it at the very end.

"Ya know what? Um…forget it," she mumbled and gave a nervous laugh.

His lips parted, and the corners of his mouth jutted up. "You uninviting me now?"

She gasped. Now she was coming off not only flighty but rude. "No, I just…"

"When?"

She hadn't gotten that far in her thinking. She peeked up through her lashes at the ceiling as if a calendar would suddenly appear.

"Tonight?"

The door flew open and Saint stepped back with her following. He reached his hand behind his back, landing on her hip. It was a protective move. Macy barreled through the door and stopped mid-step, gawking at the scene in front of her.

"Hey, guys." Macy's grin and her glancing between them had Bailey shaking her head. *Please don't say anything embarrassing.* She was doing a great job by herself. She didn't need any help from Macy, who had a tendency to blurt things out at the wrong time.

"Hi, Mace."

Saint remained silent.

She raised her brows. "Am I interrupting?"

"No." Bailey cringed at her hurried response. It made her sound guilty.

Macy smirked. "Ya sure?" She glanced at the table and grinned. "You guys are having breakfast, huh?"

Oh hell, Macy, shut up. She needed to change the subject. "Didn't know you were stopping over."

Macy giggled. "Obviously."

Bailey closed her eyes and tried to shut down the heat racing toward her face without luck.

"You free for dinner tonight?"

"Oh…uh…" How was she supposed to answer Macy when she hadn't even gotten an excuse from Saint yet? She glanced up at him. He reached into his back pocket, retrieving his phone. She watched in silence as he punched the keypad then raised the cell to his ear. Bailey glanced at Macy who was watching her.

"Yeah, I'm out tonight." He paused. "No." He shifted his arm to rest on his chest, his hand tucked under his armpit. So damn sexy. "Yeah," he glanced down at Bailey. "It's more important."

Her bottom lip fell open, and his gaze dropped to her mouth. "Later." He clicked the phone, tucking it back into his pocket. "Seven?"

Bailey couldn't even speak, so she nodded and again his lips twitched. He grabbed the open door, nodded at Macy, and walked through, closing it behind him.

"Holy fuck, do you have a date with Saint tonight?" Macy shouted loud enough for Saint to hear through the door.

Bailey waved her hand and brought her finger to her lips.

"Oh my God, Bails." Macy rushed over, bouncing on her toes. "This is fucking awesome. So, tonight?"

Bailey nodded in a mind-numbing state. "I think at seven."

Macy's mouth dropped wide, and her eyes lit up. "Holy shit, holy fucking shit, Bails."

Bailey swatted Macy's arm. The more excited she was getting, the more anxious Bailey had gotten. "Stop or I'm gonna freak out."

"I think you are freaking out, girl." She laughed. "On the inside at least. Oh man, I cannot believe what I just witnessed. Chey's gonna be so jealous. Fucking Saint, as if I didn't respect the silent bastard already, I may have a bit of hero worship right now."

Hero worship? Why? Her excitement dwindled.

"Hey…" Bailey snapped. "It's not so far-fetched he'd want to have dinner with me, I mean, he brought me breakfast." Bailey pinched her lips and scrunched her nose. Macy was ruining her moment by being *too* shocked Saint would have dinner with her. "You're messing with my high here." She mumbled.

Macy jerked her head and furrowed her brows. "What? No, you don't get it." She stepped forward with her eyes lit bright. "Kase called everyone in for the run tonight. *Everyone*, no fucking exceptions. 'Your ass ain't on a bike, you answer to me' that's what he told the whole club, nomads, too."

"But Saint…"

Macy grinned, nodding her head wildly. "Yup, he just told his president, you," she pointed at Bailey, "were more important." Macy squealed.

No, there had to be something more to it.

"Maybe not everyone has to go."

Before she even finished her sentence, Macy was shaking her head. "You know Billy and Raina, they got married last year?"

"Uh...no."

Macy waved a hand in front of her face. "Ok, well it doesn't matter. Except, it's their anniversary today. Guess where Billy's ass will be? On a bike, not with his wife." Macy nodded, then got a devilish gleam in her eyes. "Saint's ass? In your fucking house. Holy shit!"

"No, that can't be right, maybe he wasn't scheduled to go."

"Everyone is going. You heard him on the phone, only one person he was talking to. Kase, who by the way, told all the members you were off-limits."

She blinked at the new piece of information. "What?"

Macy nodded. "Yeah, Rourke told me Kase made it clear you were off-limits to the guys." She wiggled her brows. "Guess Saint didn't get the memo." She laughed and grabbed Bailey's hand. "I'm so excited for you."

Bailey swayed on her feet. *I'm off-limits?* What did that even mean? And now Saint was blowing off a club thing to have dinner at her house? It made no sense.

"You okay?"

Bailey drew in a breath. "A little overwhelmed."

Macy smiled. "Let's go figure out what you are going to wear. Something sexy and easy to get off. God, if you two bang and you don't give me details, I'm gonna be so pissed at you." Bailey trailed behind Macy in a bit of a haze.

She had a date with Saint Monroe.

The Saint

SAINT PULLED up the long dirt drive and parked on the edge of the lot closest to the house. He could have just gone straight home, but he had some explaining to do. Kase deserved it and would be a relentless prick if he didn't. He dismounted and headed for the door when he heard his name being called.

Glancing over his shoulder, he watched Cheyenne saunter forward. Saunter, it was the only way the woman moved, all tits and ass swaying, not even realizing she was doing it. It amused the fuck outta him seeing his close friend lose his shit when she did it at club parties. Not a single guy with his eyes not glued onto Trax's old lady. Except Saint. He had eyes for only one woman.

She stopped two feet away and smiled. "Hey there."

He nodded. "Chey, how are you?"

She drew in a breath and grinned. "Good. The house is done, we moved in last week."

"I heard. Congratulations."

"Thanks." She bit her lip and shifted on her feet. "Still in the process of furnishing it. It's going to take time." He watched her draw in a deep breath. "You good?"

He nodded.

She clasped her hands and glanced around their immediate area. "Good."

He eyed her. She was stalling. She had something to say, and she was strategizing how to present it to him. Of all the women, Cheyenne was one of his favorites. She had come through for the club and been a saving grace for Mick when he took his last breath. He may not have expressed it often, but he was eternally grateful to her. Beyond club business, Trax loved her more than anything. Finally, his brother found a good woman he deserved.

She glanced up at him, and he raised his brows. *Yes?*

"So, um…well…" She smiled then chuckled and drove her hands through her hair. "Oh hell, Saint, I don't know how to do this right." She laughed again, which had his mouth twitch. She was nervous, though he didn't understand why. He usually kept his distance from the women. However, he made sure not to come across as intimidating with the old ladies.

"You could just say it," he offered.

"Just blurt it out?" She squinted her eyes, waiting on him.

He raised his brows and slowly nodded.

"Okay." She drew in a breath and smiled. "Okay, so I'll just say it then." She tightened her lips and stared at him. He folded his arms and stared back. At this rate, it would be a while before he made it inside to speak with Kase.

She nodded. "Ready?"

Saint arched a brow and cocked his head, slowly losing control of his chuckle. "Yes."

She sighed. "Make sure you're all in." She paused, gauging his reaction before she continued. "One hundred percent all in with Bailey."

Saint's jaw tightened, and his chest constricted. As much as he liked her, the topic of him and Bailey was strictly their business.

Chey held out her hand in front of her. "None of my business, I know, Saint." She paused, gathering herself. "I wasn't there last week when the shit with Dobbs went down. Macy filled me in on the details. Said she'd never seen anyone so destroyed. And I'm sure Dobbs didn't mean to hurt her, I know it wasn't intentional." She shrugged. "It doesn't make it hurt any less for Bailey." Cheyenne narrowed her gaze, and her lips tightened. "I don't want her hurt again." She folded her arms taking a stance against him.

He had to give her credit. Aside from her obvious nervous twitch at her temple and her rocking back on her heels, she seemed to be doing her best to convey a threatening pose. She was, of course, failing. He did enjoy the protective stance she was taking on Bailey's behalf. His woman needed to surround herself with other strong women.

She tossed her hands over her head, which made him smirk. "Oh fuck, Saint, just be all in or not at all with her."

He was a bit surprised from her outburst but could appreciate her passion when it came to Bailey. She loved her. All the women did. While Cheyenne's delivery may have sucked, her heart was in the right place.

He drew in a breath and watched as Cheyenne shrunk away. He leaned closer and lowered his voice.

"I'm all in, Chey."

Her lips curled up into a grin. "Yeah?"

"I'm all in."

"This makes me seriously so happy I could kiss you. But Trax would probably get pissed so I won't." She laughed. "You're one of the good ones, Saint." She winked and turned around, walking back from where she came.

He sighed with a smile and opened the door walking through. He caught the feminine shriek behind him as the door closed. He made his way through the quiet house, only a few brothers drinking at the bar, another two playing pool near the back. He gave a chin jerk greeting and walked the small hall to Kase's office at the back end of the compound.

He entered through the door, noticing Trax and Rourke sitting down with Gage, Kase, and Dobbs. He made his way to the empty seat at the end of the table and sat, not saying one word.

"'Bout fucking time," Kase sneered.

Saint stared back at him, settling into his chair. It wasn't a sanctioned meeting, but he knew Kase wanted to discuss the run for tonight.

"Where the fuck you been?"

"Out."

"Out? Care to fucking elaborate, brother?"

Saint smirked. "Considering you're not my keeper? No."

Kase sighed and shook his head. "At least a little fucking courtesy then, what's going on tonight? Thought I made myself clear, everyone rides, no exceptions. We need the numbers."

The run was backing Ghosttown Riders East. It was more for show, though there was a possibility of things turning another way.

"Got a better offer."

"A cute little redhead make the offer?" Trax asked. Saint caught his smile but didn't return it. *Christ, Cheyenne had a big mouth.* Or maybe he hadn't been as discreet with his attention as he had thought.

"You're blowing off the fucking run to hang with Bailey?" Kase raised his brows.

"What the fuck? My Bailey?" Dobbs shouted and slammed his hand on the table.

The heat immediately rose from his chest to his neck and he jerked his head to the left, aiming his glare on Dobbs. *His Bailey?* He clenched his jaw and demanded his body to not react. Every muscle in his body tightened.

"Oh fuck," Rourke whispered under his breath and stood.

Saint felt the heated rage course through his blood. He was seconds from grabbing Dobbs by the neck and throwing him against the wall. She was never *his* Bailey. Never would be.

Saint had done right by her, as hard as it was. He wasn't around the last year, and starting something with her wasn't fair to either of them. It also wasn't fair to stake claim on a woman he couldn't be there for. It didn't stop him from wanting her, though. Even when Kase labeled her as untouchable, it didn't do anything for Saint's desire. Nor did it mean shit. He wondered if Kase had knowingly marked her as off-limits for Saint's benefit. They'd been friends and brothers a long time. Kase, more than anyone, would know where Saint's mind was at.

"That's fucked, man," Dobbs spewed.

No, what was fucked was how Dobbs allowed Bailey to be treated by some skank. He sat back in his seat and folded his hands over his stomach, scowling at Dobbs. He needed to keep his usual cool. Hearing him refer to her as his was setting his anger in motion.

Dobbs narrowed his gaze at Saint. "Since when do we go after other brother's women, Saint?"

Motherfucker. Saint tightened his jaw, and from the corner of his eye, he watched Kase get up, and Gage veer toward Dobbs. The man, though a brother, was fucking with the wrong man. It seemed everyone in the room knew it, except Dobbs.

"Tell me, Dobbs, exactly when was she *your* Bailey? When you were balls deep in Kelsey? Or Rose? Or the goddamn cunt who disrespected her?" Saint shot up from his seat.

"Settle down, Saint," Kase said with an anxious hitch in his tone.

Saint ignored him and continued to glare at Dobbs. "I backed off for over a year, keeping away because I knew with me gone, that shit wasn't fair to her. You think I didn't wanna claim her? Make no mistake, brother, Bailey is mine."

Dobbs scoffed, testing him. It was a wrong move on his part. Saint may be the quietest of the group, but he was certainly the most dangerous.

"Guess the rules don't apply to you, huh, Saint? Kase told everyone she was off-limits."

Kase came between them. It was more for Dobbs' safety than anything else.

"Yeah, fucker, I did. You didn't seem to follow those orders, did ya?"

Dobbs furrowed his brows and held up his finger. "One fucking kiss."

Saint's blood completely boiled. This was news to him. He was under the impression Dobbs invited Bailey to the party but had no idea they had kissed. He shoved Trax out of his way, and Dobbs jumped up from his seat, skirting around the table. He held up his hands.

"Calm the fuck down, Saint."

Saint pointed across the table at Dobbs. "You will stay clear of Bailey."

Dobbs seemed to grow a set of balls with the table separating them. "If that's what she wants. Not you. Her."

It was taking every ounce of control Saint had not to jump across the table and punch him in his mouth. Bailey didn't want

Dobbs. It was evident from hours earlier, they shared a connection.

Trax moved forward. "C'mon, man, you don't want Bailey. Back off."

Dobbs shifted his eyes to Trax and advanced forward around the table. "How the fuck do you know?"

Kase stepped forward, pushing Dobbs back. It was a smart move. Dobbs was tough and a fighter. Still no match for Saint. The closer he got to him the easier it would be for Saint to make a move. Dobbs wouldn't stand a chance if Saint got to him, and Kase knew it. They all knew.

"Only get one warning," Saint said.

"Look at me," Kase demanded Dobbs' attention.

Dobbs glared at Saint, refusing to break his stare.

"You like her, fuck, we all like her, Dobbs, but you ain't feeling what Saint is."

Dobbs shifted his glare to Kase. "How the fuck do you know how I'm feeling?"

"In the last year, how many women you fucked? Twenty, thirty, a hundred?" He waited. When Dobbs didn't answer, Kase jerked his chin to Saint. "Ask him how many women he's had since Bailey came on the scene."

The room fell into complete silence.

"None," Saint said.

Chapter 8

Saint pulled into her driveway and parked near the front walkway.

He made his way to her front door and heard the distinct sound of scrambling when he knocked. It took her a minute before answering the door. When she did, it was well worth the wait.

Bailey stood in the doorway, wearing a tight pair of blue pants and a black shirt with a cutout above her breasts, showing a small amount of cleavage. Paired with a thick heel, she stood about two inches taller, which kept her well below his height. Fucking gorgeous with her hair flowing over her shoulders.

"Hi."

"Bailey."

She twisted her lips and stepped back, opening the door for his entry. It had been a while since he'd been on a date especially at a woman's home. Saint had always been selective with the women he chose to spend time with. Unlike his brothers, fucking random women wasn't his style.

He stepped through the door, carrying a twelve-pack of beer and two bottles of wine. As he made his way inside, he smirked. Until now, he had only seen her kitchen through the back entrance. Her place looked as if she lived there. The furniture was casual and comfortable with a few trinkets lining the shelves. She had a small desk tucked in the corner with a pile of papers. It was orderly enough, as was the entire living room. One thing obviously missing struck him as odd. She circled around him and waved for him to follow.

"Do you wanna put your beer in the fridge?"

He remained in her living room and glanced around.

"Is something wrong?"

He furrowed his brows. "You don't have a TV?"

She scoured her living room and shrugged. "In the bedrooms. Mine, upstairs with a spare, and then there's another one off the kitchen." She clasped her hands, and he was cursing himself for pointing it out. She released a nervous laugh. "My mom always said living rooms were meant for to people to visit." She shrugged. "Ya know, talk."

Saint smiled. "Makes sense."

"Did you wanna watch TV?"

Saint tightened his lips. "Are you inviting me up to your bedroom?"

She raised her brow, and her eyes widened. She didn't skirt around the question, as he expected. She glanced up at the ceiling and twitched her nose. "Would you say yes if I did?"

Ah, she was playing with fire. "Try me."

The little tease had proved too much for Bailey. The heat immediately rushed to her cheeks, and her smile was done through shaky lips. She didn't respond, but he had no doubt she was curious. Bailey ducked her head and walked through the small dining room into the kitchen. Saint followed. The house appeared larger from the outside. It was older, definitely, and original, with only minor updates. It was quaint and had a very warm homey vibe, much like Bailey herself.

Saint put the beer in the fridge, grabbing two, in case she preferred beer over wine. He stood off to the side while she worked around her kitchen in silence. The table was set, which made him smile. It wasn't fancy, but he noticed the unlit candles in the center. Her mind was exactly where his was. Their first date. She pulled out a large casserole bowl from the oven and closed the door turning to face Saint.

She scratched her head, veering her gaze around the room.

"Smells good," he said, recognizing her anxious stance across from him.

"I'm not the best cook. Probably should have warned you before I invited you. Um, it's just Shepard's pie." She shrugged and bit her lip. She was nervous. This was not how he wanted to spend their date, with her on edge. He walked over to the table and pulled out his seat and sat.

"I eat a lot of takeout, so anything home-cooked is gonna be great for me, sweetheart."

She smiled and turned to the oven. "My mom makes it all the time, reminds me of my childhood." She laughed. "This and SpaghettiOs."

Saint rested his elbows on the table with a sharp groan. It got her attention, and she glanced over her shoulder.

"You and Cia will get along great. She loves that crap."

Bailey grinned. "Well, then, your girl's got good taste, Saint."

The tension eased off a bit, and Saint settled into his chair, eyeing Bailey. A whole year of waiting, and here he was. With her.

She carried over the plates, setting his down first. He noticed her shaky hand.

She sank into her seat and draped the napkin over her lap and tossed her hair over her shoulder. He caught a small patch of rippled skin just below her collar bone. He glanced away before she caught him. The last thing the night needed was Bailey concerned with hiding her scars from him. She was already nervous enough.

He watched as she gazed up at the table then eyed him through her lashes. He held back his smile. He was reading her self-scolding of not lighting the candles before he arrived. It wasn't lost on him; the table and the candles were something

Bailey put effort into. He wouldn't have cared if they were eating take out on paper plates in the backyard, but Bailey did. He set his arm on the table and grasped her hand.

Her eyes glanced down then he met her stare.

"Don't smoke, no lighter on me. You have one or matches?"

The corner of her lip curled, and she slunk away, reaching into a drawer on his left. She walked over with a box of matches which he took from her. He lit the two candles centered on the middle of the table and dropped the box on surface.

He heard her giggle before glancing over to see her red cheeks and half-smile.

"It's corny, right?"

What? He cocked a brow, unsure of what she was referring to. Her chin lifted toward the center of the table.

"The candles."

He smiled. "No. Never had a candlelight dinner." He paused. "It's very sweet, Bailey." He glanced away and took a bite from his plate. The second it touched his lips, he knew it would become one of his favorite meals.

"This is good."

"Yeah? It's my Dad's favorite. He calls it the poor man's meal."

He snickered, taking another bite. He watched as she stared intently at her plate not taking a bite.

"So, um, Cia's nine?"

He nodded. "Yeah, last month."

Bailey stared back at him with a small lighting gleam in her eyes. "I bet you're a good dad."

He shrugged. He liked to think he was. He loved his girl more than anything and would do anything for her. She was still young enough she adored him, but his time was running out, he guessed. Before long, she'd be bringing boys home, and he'd be forced to scare the living hell out of them.

"Is she super girly or a tomboy?" Bailey took a bite of her food and watched him. She may not realize it, but he was falling harder for her every second she asked about his daughter. Most of the women he casually dated in the past weren't looking for anything serious, or maybe they were. It hadn't mattered. He was waiting for the right woman. He eyed Bailey. *Here she is, well worth the wait.*

"A little bit of both."

Bailey smiled. "I was like Cia when I was younger. I'd roughhouse with my brothers wearing my dress-up clothes and flower crown."

The rest of the meal was spent casually talking about Cia and her family. When he finished his meal, he drank a beer waiting on Bailey. She grabbed his plate and started cleaning up, which he helped along with.

He rested against the side of her fridge, watching her struggle with washing the pan. Each time her sleeve would get wet, she'd stop. She refused to pull up her sleeves, and Saint knew why. Exposing her scars was something Bailey didn't do. He understood why. People, even with good intentions, had a habit of staring.

He wouldn't come into her life and demand she change. Whatever worked for Bailey, he would deal with whether he agreed with it or not. *Except around me.* Hiding herself in his presence, he wouldn't allow. Setting it up now would prove easier for her in the future. He pushed off the fridge and rested his bottle on the table making his way to stand behind her.

"How 'bout I dry?"

She glanced over her shoulder, smiling. "You don't have to. I was going to set them in the dryer rack."

He curved his lip. "I don't mind."

He reached across the counter for the towel, and his chest grazed her back. He heard the small intake of breath then her hands pulled away from the faucet. The corner of her sleeve was soaked.

Saint tossed the towel on the counter and reached around her body, pressing his chest against her back. His hands clasped the cuffs of her sleeve, and he pulled them up to her elbows. He'd expected her response. She froze without saying a word, gasping a short breath. His fingers trailed down both arms, and she shivered against his touch. He knew it would be difficult, but covering up in front of him was not an option. Her hair brushed again his chin as she bowed her head.

"Does it bother you?"

The uncertainty in her voice was a knife through his heart.

"Yes." He sighed. "It bothers me."

Her head nodded, and she stepped closer to the sink breaking contact. He mirrored her move, and his chest sidled up against her back once more. He wasn't going to lie to her. He would be honest and give her everything he was feeling. He'd waited too long for her to take things slow when it came to her scars. He was prepared to put it all out there.

His fingers trailed down her arms again, circling over her scars. Her hands seemed shaky. "It bothers me knowing someone hurt you, bothers me I didn't know you back then, couldn't help you." His hand trailed over her skin, up her arm. He caressed across her shoulder up her neck before cupping her jaw and tilting her face toward his. He was struck by the uncertainty daunting her eyes. He angled closer, strumming his thumb lightly over her cheek. "It bothers me you suffered. You were in pain for a long time. No matter how much time has passed and how much you healed, you'll always have a reminder staring back at you. I'm glad you can move on, but it bothers me you'll never forget. And it bothers me that I can't do anything to make it better."

It may have been too heavy for their first date, but Saint was prepared to give her everything and not hold back. Her bottom lip fell open, and her brows spiked to her hairline. Maybe he should have waited. Her lips pressed together. If she wanted to say something, he wasn't sure she'd be able to get it out.

She gulped, keeping her gaze locked on his. He released her jaw, sliding his hands over her shoulders down to her arms again, and she glanced down at the sink.

He lowered his mouth to her ear. "Too much?"

She slowly shook her head, and he continued to caress both of her arms.

"What you just said? It's probably the sweetest thing any man has ever said to me." Her voice shook with a slight gasp. Her back shifted against his chest. "Thank you, Saint."

"Don't thank me for speaking my truth, sweetheart." His lips grazed over her head.

Her body, which had been completely on edge, relaxed against him as he continued touching her, never lingering, just a soft caress. Her scars didn't bother him, not the way she thought, and he was out to prove that point. He rested his chin on the top of her head.

"How about we do a fire in the back?"

She turned her head and smiled. "Yeah?"

He smirked. "You got marshmallows? 'Cause no self-respecting bonfire can happen without them."

Her nose scrunched, giving her an adorable innocent glow. "Didn't peg you as a roasting marshmallows kinda guy," she whispered.

He leaned closer. "Marshmallows, chocolate, and graham crackers are a staple in my house. Cia wouldn't have it any other way."

He pressed his lips against her head and shifted over, grabbing the towel and picking up a pan from the rack. Bailey continued washing dishes. He caught her peek up at him with a smile, which he gladly returned.

They were done within ten minutes before he headed out to the yard to start the fire. He took note Bailey hadn't moved her sleeves to cover her arm.

THE FIRE CRACKLED and popped from the pine. Fire was mesmerizing and calming. This wasn't the first time she'd sat by the fire, but having someone with her was new.

"You build a better fire than me."

His soft rumbling chuckle made her smile, and she glanced over at him. His stare was on the flames, legs extended straight, and leaning back into the chair, his hands clasped around the bottle resting on his stomach. *God, Saint is hot.*

"Thanks for coming over tonight." It was a lame excuse for conversation. The talking had ceased, and they were in a lull right now. He glanced over.

"Thank you for inviting me."

She smiled. She tried to put his admission into the back of her mind. If she thought too long, she'd probably freak out. Then more silence. *He'd leave soon, right?* She bit her lip. The last thing she wanted was for this night to end. She knew eventually it would, and she still wasn't convinced this had been a full-fledged date. *Of course, it's a date.* Maybe he was feeling pity for her after the whole Dobbs debacle. But to blow off the club run just to have dinner with her, it had to mean something. *Or not.* It seemed like a date. Wasn't this how dates went—dinner, conversation, hanging out, and ending the night with a kiss. A kiss? Was that even in the cards for them? He'd have to make the first move. There was no way she was leaning in and risking the rejection. She felt her face burn with the mental image playing over in her head. She'd lean in, rise on her toes because he's a foot taller, angle her head to the left, grasp his strong shoulders, and boom…. he'd turn away. Her stomach rolled in a painful twist.

"I'd never turn away, sweetheart."

Her heart stopped, her entire body ceased any movement, and her belly dropped. She wasn't even breathing. Did she just speak out loud? Her mouth opened, but nothing came out, no words, no breath, nothing. No, she imagined him saying that. She slowly lifted her gaze from the fire and peeked over at Saint, who was staring at her. *Oh my God. No!*

She did, she had said it out loud. Tears were threatening, the moisture building. Embarrassment had been a way of life for Bailey since she was a kid, but nothing, not one time had she ever felt the despair she had now. The need to run in the house, lock the doors, and hide in her bed forever was real. *Go, run, now!*

She planted her feet on the ground, prepping for her escape, still locked in a gaze with Saint.

"I-I..." She clamped her lips shut, knowing nothing comprehensible would come out.

Saint shifted forward, resting his beer on the ground and emerged from his chair, taking a step closer to her seat. He stopped staring down at her. Her heart was erratic, and if glanced down at her chest, he'd probably see it beating through her shirt.

"Been waiting on a kiss since I saw you stumble down the aisle at the town meeting, coming in with your head down, red hair flying around you, then you settle in, looked up, and I was done. Couldn't take my eyes off your face, those lips."

Her bottom lip fell open, and she stared in shock. She remembered very clearly their first meeting. She also remembered trying her best not to stare at the back of the room, bringing them unwanted attention. At the time, she was trying to be polite, as they stuck out like a sore thumb in the small town hall. It had taken effort once she'd gotten a glimpse of the man with the violet eyes. The same eyes staring down at her. *He'd been waiting a year for her? Is that what he was saying?* She swallowed the lump in her throat.

His jaw tensed, and his eyes darkened. "Then seeing you on the street, the old man screaming at you and knowing I was seconds from introducing my fist to his face if he took one step closer. He didn't. He left, you turned around, and again, same feeling. *I was done.*"

Oh my God.

"Now." he paused. "You're staring up at me, a sweet blush across your cheeks, a small glimmer in your eyes and again, those soft lips. A year of wanting. I'm done, Bailey."

Her heart raced and a tingling sensation coursed through her blood. She licked her lips, racking her brain for something to say. She had nothing. He'd left her speechless. *Stop thinking.* She rose from her chair, not thinking of blurting out anything, or her own embarrassment. She moved closer, trailing her hands up his chest. Even through the fabric of his shirt, she could feel him. Strong and masculine. She tipped up her chin and rose on her toes at the same time his head angled and dipped down. For as nervous as she was, nothing could keep her from kissing Saint. It certainly wasn't her first kiss. However, it had been a long time. Four years to be exact. Her introduction back with Saint was comparable to getting karate lessons from Bruce Lee. He was so out of her league. Her fingers trembled, and she cursed her nerves. She could probably blame it on the chill in the air if he asked. Saint wouldn't ask though.

His lips brushed against her, soft and slow. Nothing like what she expected. His mouth caressed hers. It wasn't passionate or a throwdown kind of kiss. If anything, it felt as though he may be holding back. She got up the nerve to rest her shaking hand over his heart and leaned into his chest. She was teetering on her toes and wasn't sure how much longer she could stay. Her lips skimmed over his as her heart pounded.

Saint took her weight, bracing her back and pulling her up against his body, leaving her feet dangling. Her immediate reaction was to grasp his shoulders, and when she did, it was like his button had been pushed. His kiss deepened, and she spread her lips, hoping he would take her cue. He didn't, and she was done waiting. She slipped her tongue past his lips, licking his thick bottom lip before swirling her tongue with his. His hand gripped her and crushed her against his chest.

She peeked her eyes open slightly to find his closed and immediately shut hers. *Closed eyes kissing.*

She caressed his neck with the pads of her fingers, digging into his skin. His lips were like silk sliding over hers.

He didn't break away even when he started moving and taking her with him. He was holding her in an iron tight grip, and her legs spread over his lap as he settled back into his seat. Her entire body was heating up from being so close to him. She was like a second skin over his chest and lap. She curled her hands over his shoulders while he caressed her back and slowly skittered over her ass.

She had obsessed over the prospect of kissing Saint, but not much of what would come after. Of course, he was a man who had available women whenever he wanted at the clubhouse. A simple kiss was not going to be enough for him. He'd want more, and by the bulge pressing against her, he was ready now. She gripped his shoulders and fought against wanting him inside her, and fear of getting naked in front of him.

She angled her head, wanting to get as close as possible to him. Her need was so great she swiveled her hips against his growing erection. Her desire was in battle with reality. She just wanted to be closer. She glided her tongue against his and moaned slightly. She gasped when his hands slid around to her waist, and he leaned back. She was straddling him, and as comfortable as she was, kissing was one thing, talking in her current position made her uneasy.

Saint lingered a soft kiss on her lips and kept his hands steady on her waist. Heat rose up her neck, and she refused to meet his stare. They were only inches apart when he settled into his seat.

She stared at his belt buckle and licked her bottom lip. Without looking at him, she could feel her skin tingle knowing his gaze was locked on her.

The heat from the fire was making her back hot. She reached around and tugged at the hem of her shirt, letting some air in. She refused to glance up, unsure of what she was doing. Her hand rubbed against his when she was adjusting her shirt. Saint released her waist and clasped his hand in hers, his thumb strumming over her knuckles in a very soothing, sweet gesture. She smiled slightly.

"This all right?" It wasn't a whisper. Saint had a low, calm voice. It was smooth, and he never hiccupped any words or got flustered.

"Uh-huh." It was all she could make out without letting her

voice crack or stutter. Oh, he must have thought she was a fool or a tease or so inexperienced, he was completely regretting ever agreeing to coming over tonight. His hand tightened around her.

"Are ya gonna look at me?" he asked.

She flickered her gaze up through her lashes to find Saint staring at her. Even in the dark with dim lighting, his purple eyes were amazing.

"I do something you didn't like?"

She furrowed her brows. Was he nuts? She loved every damn thing he'd said and done since he got there. Maybe it was a prelude to what he was thinking. Reverse psychology?

"Did I do something you didn't like?"

The corner of his mouth jutted softly. "I like everything you do, Bailey." He paused. "A little too much, I think." His brow perked up in a sinister arch. If not for his smile, she might have been nervous.

She licked her lips and cleared her throat. She didn't have the confidence or the ease that Saint had when he carried himself. She was a babbling idiot.

"Should I get up?"

"Not unless you want to." He wrapped one arm around her waist and hoisted his chest forward, which sent her leaning back. Had his arm not been locked around her, she might have fallen. *He wouldn't have let me.* She watched as he stretched out his free arm and grabbed his beer from the ground before settling back in his seat. The movement sent her rubbing against his erection.

It was a strange position to be in, sprawled over his lap. It was too intimate, and she wasn't sure where she should put her hands. She eyed the armrest to his left and reached out with a single hand. His grip around her waist didn't give, and she glanced up to find a small smile playing on his lips.

Without even realizing she was doing it, her lips curled, and she sighed. "You have a nice smile, Saint."

His eyes crinkled. "Yeah?"

She nodded. Then the silence. Another awkward moment of

her straddling him, which made her uneasy.

"I should get up. I'm probably crushing ya."

He snorted and lifted the bottle to his lips. She was mesmerized by the way his Adam's apple bobbed as he swallowed. Such an odd thing, though she found his extremely sexy. Then again, she had yet to find something on him she didn't find sexy and arousing. From his lips to his neck and knowing his toned chest and thick arms, she was shifting her weight and fighting against a throbbing clit. Her cheeks burned wondering if he could read her well enough to know she was wet.

"What did you do today?"

She blinked, focusing on his question. Hopefully, her libido would settle down with generic talk. If this conversation turned to sex, she might just orgasm, fully-clothed, on his lap.

"Dodging calls from Dobbs." She chuckled. It was an attempt to get her mind off anything other than her lingering sexual frustration. She wasn't prepared for his reaction.

All sense of ease drained from Saint's features, and his cheeks hollowed. A small tick plagued his jaw in a faint twitch. *Oh, this isn't good.* She shifted on his lap, pushing against his arm around her waist. Her breath hitched, and her heart pounded. Since the incident, any show of anger set something off inside her. Self-preservation, maybe. She gripped the armrest, keeping her stare on him. She needed to keep him in sight in case he was set off and came at her. She'd made that mistake once. It wouldn't happen again.

His brows dipped, and he scanned her face, down her body, and landed on her hand tightly wrapped around the chair. He sucked in a harsh breath loud enough for her to hear.

Truthfully, she didn't know Saint. She knew of him, knew how people talked of him with god-like status, knew the men respected him. She didn't really know Saint or what he might be capable of. She had no idea how he handled anger. Her breath shallowed. She was in the most vulnerable position, with a man she didn't really know.

He trailed his gaze up to meet her stare, and his eyes softened. Slowly, he unraveled his arm from her waist, and she noticed his fingers didn't touch her body. She was left merely sitting on him, free to get up.

"Whatever you're feeling, whatever has got ya wound up with fear, Bailey, you let it go when you're with me, sweetheart." His voice was low as usual, but she heard the restraint with each word. "I'd never hurt you." His chin lowered. "Never lay an unwanted hand on you. You hear me?"

"Okay." A simple word came out strangled. She cleared her throat and nodded.

"You get to choose, Bailey. Your choice has got no repercussions, do you understand?"

She didn't understand what choice he was referring to, and it seemed Saint could read her confusion.

"You want Dobbs. I won't say another word. Won't stand in the way." He drew in a breath, then released it slowly. "But you can't have us both. We're brothers, sweetheart, can't have you in the middle."

Couldn't have them both? Oh God, was that the impression she was giving? She liked Dobbs and could find forgiveness for him, but she didn't want to be with him.

"I don't want him." Her mind blurred for a brief second, and she spoke what should have remained in her thoughts. "I want you." The second she heard her own words, her eyes widened, and a trembling heat rippled over her skin. It was true. She did want him. However, she never meant to say it, have it lingering over her head and into his ears.

He moved forward, keeping a fair distance. There was a purposeful gap between them. It was for her benefit, she realized. Saint could be intimidating, and she was sure he knew it. It wasn't so much his height or build, or even appearance. His demeanor and his silence made others alarmingly cautious.

"Are you afraid of me, Bailey?"

How was she supposed to answer him when she didn't even know?

"No." She bit her lip. "I don't know." She pressed her hands against his chest. "I don't really know what just happened. I mentioned Dobbs, and it seemed to set something off in you." She scanned his face. "I don't know if you're mad at me, or Dobbs, or what."

The corner of his mouth curled softly. "Ah shit. I'm messing this up, Bailey."

He inhaled a breath and settled into his seat, putting more distance between them. She didn't like it. She wanted him closer. It may have been the answer to his question. If she was afraid, she wouldn't want to be near him.

"No, you're not, it's just..." Her voice cracked, and she clamped her lips.

"What?"

She released a breath in a short huff. "It was all going so well until I mentioned Dobbs." She bit her bottom lip. Under his stare, she was reeling from an unrelenting, desirable heat. "And I mean, I did just say I wanted you."

The corners of his eyes crinkled. "Oh, I heard it." Traces of amusement sounded in his tone. The mood was turning, lightening a bit. She lowered her hands onto his chest. One palm lay still over his heart which beat steadily.

"It's not fear I'm feeling."

"Good." He glanced down at her hands. "You don't know me, sweetheart, so I'll tell you. I'm capable of being with you, protecting you if you need me." He looked up from hooded lids. "I'm good at listening. Talking isn't a strong point. I'm willing to give it a try with you, Bailey."

She smiled at the sweetness of the statement and the sincerity of his tone. Her fingers dug into his shirt and she moved a bit closer. Saint remained where he was.

"I'm not capable of hurting you. I wouldn't, it's not who I am. Also not capable of sharing your affections with another man. If you give yourself to me, you're mine, and I'm not sharing." He smirked. "Probably have a hard time letting go too."

It wasn't just the words he spoke. It was how he said them. She found herself leaning closer, wanting to be near him, on him, with his arms back around her, holding her tightly against him.

Her heart raced, and her fingers dug into his chest. She hovered over his mouth, so close she could feel the warmth of his breath over her lips. "I want," she paused, "you."

She didn't wait for a reaction or response. Her lips pressed against his, and she enjoyed the tingling sensation coursing through her body. It was almost electric. She angled her head as she moved over his mouth, wanting to get closer. His chin lifted, and she spread her lips getting exactly what she wanted. His tongue slid into her mouth.

Ah, this man can kiss. She'd have to spend time thinking if she'd ever been kissed so passionately. It was highly doubtful. His teeth grazed over her bottom lip, sending a shivering tingle through her body and zoning in on her lower region. Her pussy ached as she ground herself against him. The only thing which would have made it better was if he was touching her. She quickly glanced down at his hands resting on the armrest.

He was being cautious with her. Had they been in any other position, she would have appreciated it, however, here and now she just wanted his hands on her. It became apparent he was letting her lead. She pulled away from his lips, dragging her mouth down to his neck. His head extended back against the chair, and a soft groan emitted from his lips. She melted against him, licking his neck up to his ear.

"Touch me, Saint." She barely finished her sentence before his hands wrapped around her waist, tugging her closer. It was confirmed he'd been holding back. It was her running this show, and he was following her lead. That notion made her want him even more. She found his lips again. Another kiss, another two or three, or forever, she just wanted to kiss him.

Ten minutes ago, she was wondering if she wanted to take it to another level, now she was practically crawling inside him. She wanted him everywhere. She draped her hand down his stomach. It was hard to wedge her hand between their bodies, but she was determined. She lifted her hip and slid down to the crotch of his pants. Her hand molded against his thick cock. He inhaled so deeply her breath was sucked from her chest.

It didn't even slow her down from kissing him, swirling her tongue with his and moaning into his mouth. His finger caressed over her back. Again, she could feel his restraint. He moved across her back, touching her everywhere except where she wanted those hands to be—between her legs, over her breasts, and on her ass. She tightened her grip over his cock, slowly jerking him. His hands shifted to her neck. His rough palms scraping against her skin sent shiver down her spine.

She was done and made her decision. She was so ready to be in bed with Saint Monroe and have him inside her. She tore her mouth from his.

"We could go," she caught her breath, "upstairs." Her hand gripped the outline of his cock and tightened her hold, making herself clear in her intent.

Saint angled her jaw and took her lips again, keeping her steady as he assaulted her mouth with his tongue.

They definitely needed to move inside. She may not have neighbors close by, but she didn't need anyone showing up and seeing her spread eagle on the dirt fucking Saint. If they didn't go inside now, that scenario wouldn't be farfetched. Despite the chilly night, she was prepared to strip down right here, right now.

Who the hell am I?

"Saint." She breathed against his lips and stroked him through his pants.

Saint let his head drop against the seat and reached for her neck, stroking his thumbs down the column of her throat. His breath was heavy, and he hadn't muttered a word. She leaned closer, her nose trailing lightly over his neck. She felt him shudder and she smiled.

Again, with his restraint. He needed more incentive. She dragged her fingers over his erection and looped her finger through his belt buckle. It would be difficult doing it one-handed. *Try!* She gripped his belt and pulled open the latch. It was as far as she got before his hand wrapped around her wrist. She glanced up at him.

"You don't want me to?"

He puffed out a laugh though he didn't seem amused. "There's nothing more I want than what you're doing right now." He closed his eyes. "Fuck," he whispered.

He was contradicting himself, leaving her confused. He was telling her he liked what she was doing, then cursing in frustration.

When she released his belt, he jerked open his eyes and aimed his focus on her. He sat up quickly and she scrambled to catch herself. She shouldn't have bothered. Saint wrapped his arms around her waist and sat up with her pressed against his chest. Her nipples beaded. It was the most contact they had gotten and were begging for more. She shifted her breasts against him and he smirked.

"You are making this hard, sweetheart." He shoved his face against her neck. "Trying to take my time here, and you are killing me."

"You could take your time with me," her fingers caressed over the back of his neck, "upstairs."

His hips shifted against her pussy, driving into her, and she moaned, letting her head fall back. He did it again, and she gripped his neck hard. She swiveled her hips, loving the sensation of riding against him. It felt so good.

"I want to take you up to your bed, lay you out, and feast on every inch of your body."

She drove her hips into him, grinding against his dick. "Yes."

"Bailey," he grunted, and his fingers dug into her skin.

"I want you, Saint."

His lips pressed against her neck and he tightened his grip on

The Saint

her body, keeping her steady and unable to further grind herself to orgasm. She raked her nails over his neck, up to his hair.

"Saying my name is cheating, sweetheart."

She stopped, unsure she heard him right. He lifted from her neck, putting them at eye level. His gaze was heated, and his face flushed. She wondered if she looked as affected as he did. He kissed her and then smiled.

"You say my name and I'll give you just about anything you want."

She brushed her lips against his. "I want you," she paused, "Saint."

He smirked.

"Don't you want me?"

His lips flattened. "Spent the last year wanting you, Bailey."

Her heart raced. A year wanting her? She curled against his chest.

"Then what's stopping you from taking me?"

He slid his hand over her chest, grazing her nipple, and she pushed her breast against his hand. *Oh, God it feels good.* "Let's go upstairs."

He palmed her breast and her lids lowered, loving the feel of his touch even through a thick shirt. His hand moved, and she felt the disappointment race through her body. He ran his finger over her cheek and across her bottom lip.

"I can't stay the night," he whispered. "Got Cia coming over tomorrow night and got a lot of work I got to get done beforehand.

His daughter's name caught her attention, tampering against her arousal. She flickered open her eyes to his smiling face.

"Oh." She understood, and it made sense. It did nothing to batten down her desire for him. She was on the verge of desperation mode. "You could leave after..." Her face flushed. *After what, Bailey, we fuck?* Just the insinuation was heating her up. She wasn't sure she'd ever said the words out loud. Sex, yes, intercourse, probably, making love, just once. But fucking, no.

"I get you in bed, Bailey, I'm not leaving." He kissed her softly. "You're not leaving." His lips brushed against her. "Gonna spend hours with you, and I'm gonna wake up with you. I know me, sweetheart. Not gonna be able to pull myself away from you."

No, he couldn't leave. Aside from being completely aroused, his sweet words were too much to let go.

"I could set my alarm."

He chuckled. Of course he was laughing. She sounded like a desperate woman looking to get laid. She needed to shut her mouth before she embarrassed herself even more.

"Sorry."

"Hey," he whispered and lifted her chin. "Everything you've got going on inside. You multiply it by ten, and it's how I'm feeling. Nothing more I want right now than to lay with you, naked and tangled up." He rested his forehead against hers and sighed. "Been waiting so long for you, it's almost painful to leave right now." His nose skimmed the tip of her nose. God, his words were getting her as hot as his actions.

"You and me got all the time in the world, okay?"

She nodded. She had two more options and rebuttals for him to stay. It was best to save face and not open her mouth.

"I'm gonna knock down the fire and get you settled inside."

She sat back. "I can do it. You don't have to..." He lifted his hand to her cheek, and she clamped her lips.

"I'm gonna do it, then help you clean up. Probably gonna spend another fifteen minutes kissing you and repeating my own words in my head about how I can't stay."

She chuckled. "I'm probably gonna suggest other options so you can." She glanced up at the sky. "Might even play dirty and say your name a few times."

For the first time since they had met, she heard him laugh. It was deep and hearty. She was pretty sure it had just become her new favorite sound. She had the distinct feeling this memory would be etched in her head forever. Looking up at the stars overhead with Saint's laugh ingrained in her mind.

He settled into the seat again, tightening his hold around her waist. "Come here."

She went. He cupped her jaw.

"My girl is spending the day and night. Dropping her off at school early. How 'bout I pick you after and take you out for breakfast?"

"On your motorcycle?" She perked up.

His brow arched. "Yeah, was planning on it. You up for taking a ride?"

"Yes," she answered too quickly.

"You ever been on a bike?"

"No, but I want to. You can be my first."

He snorted and kissed her. "And I'll be your last." He kissed her again and kept kissing her for well over thirty minutes.

She didn't have much time to mull over what he'd said. All her thoughts were on Saint, his lips, his body, and her desperate need for him not to leave. He did eventually, later than he had planned.

She slipped past her small hall and out to the living room, peeking through her blinds. She angled her head to get a better view of the driveway. She caught his shadow then watched him stop at his bike. God, he was so hot. She dragged her hands over her lips, which remained tingling even after their last kiss. Saint stood silently then lifted his head, staring up at the sky.

"What's he doing?" She crept to the door, lifting on her toes, and gasped when she saw him turn and head back to the yard.

She rushed to the back, and before she reached the door, she heard a soft knock. She grabbed the knob and pulled open the door.

"Hey."

His jaw tensed, and his brows arched with a small sexy scowl.

"Need you to set the alarm."

It was all he said before he stepped forward and grabbed her waist, tugging her chest against his, and his mouth dropped, meeting her lips.

Chapter 9

Her fingers threaded through his short hair, and her grip tightened around his neck. He tried, really fucking tried to walk away. He couldn't. He'd waited too long for her. Walking away was not an option. He lifted her against his chest and off the ground. He kicked the door closed and backed up, feeling for the lock without breaking the kiss.

Her hands were everywhere, on his neck, cupping his jaw, as if she couldn't get close enough to him. The feeling was mutual. His only regret was not knowing the layout of her house. *Where the fuck is her bed?* His lips caressed over hers, and her tongue swirled inside his mouth. If his erection grew any harder, his zipper would bust open. His hands traveled down her back, and he gripped her thighs, hoisting her around his hips.

She moaned and clutched her hands on his shoulders. Her hips swiveled, setting him on edge and he thrust forward, tearing his mouth from hers. She left him no choice, he wanted her and he needed to get her to the bed. Saint wasn't opposed to taking her on her kitchen table, or her counter. Hell, he was on the verge of taking her against the wall. *Find her bedroom.*

For their first time together, he wanted her laid out in front of him. He wanted her coming against his tongue before making her orgasm again while he was inside her. Bailey had no clue what was to come. Her body was going to be blissfully exhausted by the time he was through with her tonight.

"Where's your room?" he whispered.

She panted and he felt her hot breath against his neck. "My room or the closest bed?" she asked and licked his neck. He strained his neck, allowing her mouth to slide across. He gripped her ass tighter, unable to control himself. Ironic. He was a man always in control. With Bailey, he couldn't contain himself.

Her tongue circled his neck, and his heart pounded with his cock straining against the seam of his zipper.

"We are two feet away from my guest bedroom." She grazed her teeth over the lobe of his ear. "But I really want you in *my* bed, Saint." The pads of her fingers glided down his neck. "Tangled up in my sheets." Her lips skimmed his neck and she whispered, "All night."

Oh, fuck me. Bailey was full of seductress surprises. It seemed sweet little Bailey had a sexy side, and he was fucking loving it.

"Where?" He growled.

"Upstairs, first door on the right." She curled her hand around his jaw, angling his head and reached forward, taking his lips.

He stalked through her kitchen and into her living room, never breaking away from their fused connection. He slowed at the steps. He pulled away slightly and turned through the first doorway. A soft light from the bedside lamp had the room in a yellow glow. He hadn't given much thought to what her room would look like. He was happily surprised. It was all Bailey.

She wrapped her arms around his shoulders, hugging him against her body while her fingers dragged along the back of his neck. He needed her naked and under him before he lost complete control. His want and desire ended downstairs. He was now at the point of insatiable need.

He stalked to the bed, lowering her and reaching out onto the mattress. She fell back, but hung onto him, leaning closer and taking his lips again. Kissing Bailey had played over in his head for the past year. For all he imagined, nothing came close to how it felt. Her hands tucked under his arms and trailed over his back, ripping up the back of his shirt. They were both fully dressed, for now.

He pulled away, and Bailey rose. He'd been too quick. He straightened, taking off his cut and tossing it on the bed, then gripping the back collar of his gray t-shirt and pulling it over his head, and promptly dropped it to the floor. Her gaze perused his body with a heated glimmer. His breath evened watching her eyes travel over his chest. He knew what he looked like. He'd seen the appreciative glances from women. Seeing Bailey's eyes spark with desire, and want, had trumped any look he'd ever gotten from anyone. She reached over his stomach, and his breath hitched when the pads of her fingers draped over his skin. His body had never reacted to a woman's touch the way he did with Bailey. She seemed mesmerized by his abs as her fingers gently skated over his tattoos. He wasn't fully tatted, but there were more tattoos than bare skin. Her hands glided over his stomach, and she placed her hand over his heart.

"I love this," she said, peering up at him through her lashes.

He'd had it done nine years ago, a few days after Cia was born. Marco stilled referred to it as his masterpiece. She moved forward, sliding her hand down to his stomach and pressing her lips against his heart and Cia's tattoo. He threaded his hand through her hair. It was too much. Her mouth on his body, her sweet words, those fucking eyes… He had to have her before he exploded. He curled his hand over her shoulder, down to her waist. He gripped the hem of her shirt.

Then the air in the room shifted.

Her hand immediately grasped his wrists, halting him. He was willing to follow her lead. He sensed her hesitation wasn't from her lack of desire. It was something else. It was personal. She proved him right with her words.

"I wanna keep it on," she whispered and bowed her head. Saint was willing to take things at her pace without question.

Except this. He wouldn't allow her to hide from him. He wanted her. All of her.

"Bailey."

She refused to look at him. He cupped her jaw, forcing her to glance up. The uncertainty and shame struck him to his core, and he bit back the fury that some asshole had done this to her. His thumb slid over her cheek, then grazed her lips.

"Please." It was a plea. He'd give her anything. *Except this.* He leaned closer, bending over, leaving only an inch separating them.

"No, sweetheart, that's not gonna work for me." He kissed her temple, hovering over her body. She reached around his back and his skin electrified under her touch.

"Saint."

He propped his elbows on the mattress. "I want all of you. I wanna touch all of you. I don't want anything between us."

"It's not pretty." Her voice was so low, had he not been so close, he might not have heard her.

He pressed his lips against hers for a soft kiss. "You're beautiful, *all of you*." He kissed her neck, and she shivered before wrapping her arms around his bare shoulders. There was a hesitation in her touch, and it gripped his heart into a strangling hold.

"You're safe with me, Bailey," he whispered.

She snuggled into the crook of his neck, and her breath heated over his skin. "I feel it, Saint."

Slowly, the sharp ache of his heart eased. He pulled her up and holding her against his body. He caressed her jaw, and his lips grazed over hers before plummeting his tongue past her lips and receiving the sweetest moan.

He gripped the hem of her shirt and raised it above her head. Before she could further protest, he latched onto her lips. His hand skirted around her back, unclasping her bra. The strap fell down her shoulders, and he tore away the garment that separated them.

He pressed her down to the mattress and skimming his fingers over her stomach, making his way to palm her breast. He groaned in sync with her moan against his mouth. Her tongue lashed against his, curling around his tongue. He squeezed her breast and flicked his thumb over her nipple as he ground his cock against her pussy. They had too many clothes separating them. Bailey must have felt the same because she frantically ripped at his jean snap, yanking it open. He wasn't even aware she'd gotten his zipper down until her warm hand pressed against his pelvic bone and slipped into his pants, grasping his dick.

His hips shot forward against her hand, and he tore his lips away and groaned. "Fuck, Bailey."

"Take them off, Saint, I need you inside me." Her words had him dropping his mouth to her neck, grazing his teeth over her collar bone, and pinching her nipple until she gasped. He had visions of her coming on his tongue and screeching in pleasure, shouting out his name. That had been shot to shit when he realized his desperate need to be inside her. He sprung back off the mattress. He tore his jeans and underwear off. When he glanced up, her heated gaze only amplified his need for her. He leaned forward and gripped the hem of her pants, pulling them down her legs and tossing them onto the floor. Her eyes widened, and she reached for his cock. *Fuck.*

"Saint," she panted.

His need and desire were outweighing his common sense. He needed to wrap up. He had always carried condoms in his wallet since the age of seventeen. He wasn't sure if Bailey had them handy in her nightstand and didn't bother to ask. He pulled away, leaning over the bed and feeling for his wallet. It barely came out of his back pocket when he pulled out the square foiled packaging. He tore it open with his teeth as her hands grazed over his stomach. He stared down, focusing on her eyes. From his peripheral vision, he caught the marred skin. Her arm and upper left chest had taken the brunt of the attack. A small patch on her thigh and small scars across her stomach were lighter than the rest.

He sheathed himself and fell forward as she tightened her arms around his back. No guidance was necessary. His cock lined up with her pussy, and he slowly jerked his hips forward, spreading her lips and plummeting into her core. She was so wet for him that his cock glided in effortlessly, and they moaned in unison.

Her body trembled under his, and he gazed, finding her eyes closed and her lips parted. It was too much to resist. He pressed his mouth against hers and rocked into her body, fully seating himself into her pussy. Her hands trailed around his ribs and digging into his back.

"You feel so good."

His mouth brushed against her neck and trailed up to her ear, "No, sweetheart. You feel so good." He groaned as he shifted his weight. "I want to stay inside you for fucking ever." He rarely cursed unless the situation called for it. *This* called for it. The walls of her core tightened in a strangling grip, which forced him to pull out slightly before thrusting inside her again.

"Oh God, Saint." She panted. Her nails dug into his back. He wasn't going to last. He wanted her too much. His elbows collapsed on the mattress caging her in, and he dropped his mouth to her breast. Her beaded nipples were just inches from his lips. He tongued her nipple, and her chest arched giving him just what he needed to envelop her nipple between his lips. He drew strong pulls, and her hips swiveled setting his cock fully inside her. He wanted to take his time, but he was losing control. He drove deep, pounding through her walls while sucking her breast between his lips. He grazed his teeth lightly, getting the response he wanted.

"Ahhhh…" Her nails scraped into his back with a sharp, biting pain, but he concentrated solely on her harboring breath. She was close. His only desire was to make her come. He pulled out to the crown of his cock before gliding back into her with steady strokes. The bed knocked against the wall in rhythmic thumps, and he continued to tease her nipple until switching to her neglected breast. It seemed to charge her more, and she arched her back and moaned his name.

"Saint."

His name on her lips was too much. This woman was going to *own* him.

Her walls tightened around his dick. She gripped his back, and her entire body trembled against his before screaming out. It was exactly what he wanted to hear. He'd been so close to his own orgasm. He drove deep and steady inside her and thrust once, twice and… *fuck*. He came hard and long, his cock twitching until he was completely empty and spent.

He hesitated giving into his drained body. When Bailey wrapped her arms around his back, he released his weight and dropped his head to her neck. He'd spend the rest of his life reliving this moment.

OH. My. God.

His weight drew down against her body. He must have outweighed her by at least one hundred pounds. She didn't care. *If this is how it all ends, I'm fine with it.* She curled her arms over his tight, tense back.

It was almost surreal. She had thought about the first time she'd have a sexual encounter after the incident for years. Immediately after it happened, being intimate with anyone was the furthest thought from her mind. Her main focus at the time was getting better and healing, not just her body, her whole self. The incident took as much of a heavy toll on her mind as it did on her body. As time passed, she always looked forward to the future thinking one day she'd meet someone. She never took any steps to make it happen. *Now, look at me.*

I can't believe he's in my bed, on top of me, after the most explosive, exciting sex I've ever had in my life. His breath heated over her neck. His heartbeat began to steady while hers remained erratic.

"Are you gonna leave, or should I set the alarm?" She held her breath watching his eyes shift to down to her. She didn't want to come off as eager and expectant. *I really want him to stay.* He furrowed his brows and shifted on his side, propping himself on his elbow.

"Thought I explained myself, sweetheart. Once you let me in your bed," he leaned closer and whispered, "I'm not leaving." His lips grazed over her jaw, and she moved closer, wrapping her hands around his neck.

His lips pressed against her, and she melted into the soft mattress. His tongue glided against hers sending shivers over her skin. She couldn't be sure how long they kissed, minutes or hours, all she knew was when she finally succumbed to sleep, she was tucked against Saint's chest.

It was the same position she woke up in hours later when the alarm sounded. She stirred, burrowing her face into his side. He was warm and welcoming. It had been forever since she'd slept with another person. The intimate contact was something she missed, only realizing it now. When his arms tugged her waist, she crawled over his body, feeling his length against her bare pussy.

"Mornin'." His voice was gravelly and so damn sexy.

She jutted forward and, in the process, rubbed against his cock. He growled and cupped her jaw, lifting to take her in for a kiss. It wasn't as passionate and desperate as last night, yet somehow just as gratifying. His lips grazed against hers before dropping his head back on the pillow with the corner of his lips curling into a half-smile. She rested her palm over his chest and dropped her chin to lay over her knuckles, staring up at him.

Saint had been extremely open with her last night from the scars to the kiss. She wondered if his honesty would ring true now.

His finger traced over her forehead, down her temple, gliding over her cheek to her lips.

"All you have to do is ask, sweetheart."

She smiled. "Are you a mind reader?"

"I'm a Bailey reader. You have an expressive face." He chuckled.

"Why did you wait? With me?"

He drew in a breath. "Like I said last night, I was done the first time I set eyes on you." He paused. "Didn't have my life together back then. Wasn't living here, had my shops I spent the majority of my time at, and the other with Cia. Wasn't fair to make you wait around when I couldn't be here."

Damn. It was not the answer she expected.

"I would have waited, Saint." It was her own admission, which had her cheeks heating.

His finger tightened against her waist. When he pulled her forward, her face curled into his neck for a hug. She would have waited. He wouldn't allow it. God, he was almost too good to be true. They lay in silence for a while.

He kissed her head and whispered, "I have to get going."

She tightened her hold on him, not wanting him to leave. He returned the gesture. She held on a second longer before rising up. He'd been honest in telling her he had to leave. She just didn't want their date to end.

"You have a busy weekend?" he asked.

She did. She needed to set up the agenda for the meeting on Monday. There were a bunch of permit requests, mainly from club members. She had a few which were done and waiting to be delivered. The idea of seeing the members had her stomach roll in an uneasy twist. She eyed him carefully, and a thought clicked.

"Yeah, could you do me a favor?"

"What do you need?"

"I have the permits for the back-lot paving for Kase's shop. If I give them to you, will you pass them along?"

Saint eyed her suspiciously. She could understand his confusion. It would seem out of character for her to ask him to pass them along without presenting them herself. She valued her position as mayor and seldom used others to do her work. She took her position seriously. However, last week's events, then her meltdown at Caden and Marissa's left her feeling humiliated, vulnerable, and not wanting to come face to face with any member. *Except, Saint.*

"Yeah, I could do that." He eyed her, gliding his finger over her cheekbone. "Need me to drop anything off at Macy and Chey's place? They've got permits they're waiting on too."

So sweet.

"No, I can swing by their place tomorrow."

"But you can't swing across the street at the same time?"

Caught. Her lips tightened, and her cheeks flushed. Lying was never her thing, mainly because she didn't do it well. The truth was the best option. Though she couldn't reveal it while looking at him. She darted her gaze to his chest, staring down at his daughter's name over his heart.

"I'm embarrassed."

His thumb slid over her chin, and she nestled closer. "Why?"

She didn't want to talk about it. Not with Saint. She didn't want to be a whiny woman with him. She wanted to be sexy and beautiful. She tucked her head, but his grasp tightened, forcing her to look at him.

"You know what happened at Caden's?"

He nodded, and she dropped her face against his chest with a low groan.

His chest shook under her face. She was still getting used to Saint's laugh. She peeked up, and he smirked.

"You have nothing to be embarrassed about."

"I j-just..." How could she word it where she didn't come across weak? She licked her lips. "I overreacted." Before she finished her sentence, he was shaking his head.

"No, you didn't." His lips grazed against her forehead. "You were hurt. You have every right to be angry and pissed off." He lifted her chin and moved closer. "You don't get to be embarrassed. You didn't do anything to warrant it. You hear me?"

She heard him, though, she didn't necessarily agree.

"I had a meltdown."

"Not the first person to do it won't be the last."

She squinted her eyes. "I can't imagine you having a meltdown."

He smiled. "Would it make you feel better if I did?"

"Maybe."

He snickered and she settled against his bare chest.

She could have laid in bed with him all day. At his insistence, they got up. It was selfish of her. She knew he had things to do which included finishing his work before Cia arrived later that night. She was surprised when she offered him coffee to go. He chose to stay with her. She glanced at the clock knowing for every minute he stayed, he'd be behind schedule in getting his work done.

She settled in her chair next to him and sipped her coffee.

"You around tomorrow?"

She licked her lips, and she watched as his gaze darted down to her mouth. She nodded, holding back her smile.

"We'll stop by around two."

"We?"

"Cia and me. Want her to meet you."

Bailey gasped. "Um… isn't it a little soon?"

She'd never dated someone with kids. Surely there was a timeframe of waiting.

"No."

"Isn't there a waiting period or something?" She wiped her forehead with her shaky hand. "I mean, shouldn't you wait to see if you still like me in a couple months?"

Saint snorted and reached out, taking her hand. He pulled her arm, and she rose from her seat, walking to him. He pushed out his seat and guided her to his lap.

"Sweetheart, I liked you last month and the month before. In my mind, for the past year, you were mine. I don't see any reason to wait unless…" He paused searching her face. "You're unsure about me?"

His statement was comical though she didn't laugh. How

could he even think she was unsure? *Because our first date happened less than twelve hours ago.* She sighed and bit her lip. This man who she had obsessed over for the past few months wanted her to meet his daughter. Why was she stalling? She caught a small glimpse of her bare scarred arm in her view. She closed her eyes. What if Cia saw it? She'd obviously do as she'd always done and cover up. But what if by some freak chance she saw and then asked? How would she explain it? The truth was not an option, not for a nine-year-old.

He squeezed her hip, and she glanced up. His finger traced her bottom lip, and he stared down at her through hooded lids.

"I'm not unsure, Saint." She scanned his face and drew in a breath, prepping herself to give the same amount of truth he'd given her. "I wanna be with you." She couldn't bring herself to divulge her insecurities, though.

He smiled. "Two o'clock?"

She nodded. Her acknowledgment was a lie as excuses filtered her mind on ways to get out of meeting his daughter.

I'm an awful person.

Chapter 10

Saint stretched an arm over his head and cracked his neck to the sound of coffee percolating. This would be his third pot of the day. He was surviving on caffeine. He knew leaving Bailey's bed wouldn't be an easy task. However, he wasn't prepared for it to be nearly impossible. She set the alarm for seven. After hitting it three times, he turned the damn thing off, not wanting to hear the reminder, he'd be leaving soon. Instead, he chose to curl up next to her warm body. He noted she fit perfectly tucked into his chest. He sighed.

Bailey had been more obliging, offering him coffee to go. He couldn't resist another opportunity to sit at her table, gaze into her sleepy eyes, and stare at her messy, sex hair. There would be a time, hopefully soon, waking up with her would be a daily occurrence. Until then, he'd seize every chance he got. Bailey had a way of throwing off the always organized and responsible Saint. It wasn't her fault. All the blame lay on his shoulders for not leaving earlier. He spent the morning with her and headed home at about eleven. With the six hours of work he had piled up needing to be done before Cia arrived, resting was not an option.

He yawned and stared out the window. Leaves were falling early this year, which meant a cold winter. Hopefully, the snow wouldn't be so bad. He'd done some research. Their spot of Ghosttown was hit or miss. Some years they got off easy and were spared a few inches. Other times the residents were homebound for a day or two.

He grabbed a mug from the cabinet and prepared his coffee. A light, shimmering glow reflected from his kitchen window as Tara's minivan pulled into the driveway. Saint made his way to the front door, walking out to the porch and taking a seat on his steps. He smiled, watching through the van windows, the chaos erupting. If he had to guess, the vehicle was stocked with games, random toys, extra pairs of kid's clothes, and enough stale snacks between the seats on the floor to feed half of Ghosttown. His lips curled when he saw Tara crane her neck on the headrest.

The back door opened and out popped his girl. Her smile was huge, as it always was when she greeted him. Being closer and staying in one location would afford him more time with her. He'd always been strict with her weekends, never missing their time, but there were incidences where it made his work a million times harder.

She waved. *It was all worth it.*

"Hey, Daddy." Cia reached into the backseat, yanking the wedged bag with all her weight, and stumbled backward when it released. Saint snickered at the juice box, empty chips bag, and sock that flew to the ground near the door. Cia bent down, tossing the sock through the door, and grabbing the garbage in her hand. She slammed the door sending Tara into a mini-rant he couldn't hear. She shook her head, waved her hands, and her lips moved. Saint laughed.

He'd known Tara since he was eighteen, started dating her at twenty, and stayed tight off and on for five years. During an *on* time, she'd gotten pregnant. He'd never forget the dread he felt when she told him. He was too young, too immature, and independent. While he loved Tara, they'd both been drifting apart in their last year together. Being comfortable and familiar is what had them together for so long. They both knew it.

On the day he found out he was going to be a dad, he truly believed his life was over. Nine months later, he realized it was just beginning. Never would he have pegged himself for fatherhood, but he loved it, loved his little girl. He and Tara only lasted another year after Cia was born. It was done strictly out of obligation on both their parts. He was sure most people doubted they could still give Cia a normal and functional family life being separated. They proved everyone wrong. They made it work. It wasn't always easy, but they made an effort. A few years later, she married Denny. A good guy. Saint even attended their wedding and spent most holidays with them. Tara and Denny's boys referred to him as Uncle Saint. It may not have been conventional, but they did what they set out to do for Cia nine years ago. They gave her a family.

Cia dragged her bag along the grass, doing a speed walk, and spread her arms wide, taking him in for a hug. At nine, he knew his days were numbered with her affection. Eventually, the hugs and kisses would lessen, and instead of being cool, Saint would no doubt become embarrassing. The curse of a dad.

"Missed you." He hugged her close. The arrangement gave Saint two weekends a month. Tara had been lenient with it, though. If Saint planned something which didn't fall on his weekend, he was free to take her and vice versa.

She pulled away to stand in front of him. She was grinning. *She has a beautiful smile, just like yours.* With Bailey's words playing over in his head, he smiled back at his girl.

"We won the championships."

"Knew you would."

She twisted her lips in a cute pout. Much to Tara's dismay, Cia favored his side with her dark hair, high cheekbones, and violet eyes.

"How'd ya know?"

He reached out, tapping her nose, causing a sweet giggle. "'Cause I've seen ya dance."

She sat next to him, curling into his side, and he wrapped his arm over her shoulder. "It was really cool, we all got medals and flowers and stuff."

He pressed his lips to the top of her head. "Good job, baby."

Tara wandered up the walkway, her hair in a bun on her head. She was definitely sleep deprived. Even so, Tara was just as pretty as she was when he pulled up on his bike in front of her and a group of her friends. She stood out with her white-blonde hair and stunning green eyes. She had aged, like him, but kept her spark and her beauty. She remained the same sassy mouthed, inappropriate storytelling, big-hearted woman he fell in love with all those years ago.

"Hey, Saint."

He nodded. "T."

Cia angled up and pushed off the stairs, giving her mom a kiss and hug before dragging her things inside. "Gonna put my stuff away, then I'll tell ya about the comp. Mom took video." She disappeared inside, and he glanced back to Tara, who was leaning on the handrail.

"You look like shit." He smirked.

She lifted her hand and gave him the middle finger. "I feel like shit." She slumped back, putting her weight against the railing. "Seven hours." She sighed and emitted a soft agonizing groan. "Seven fucking hours, Saint."

He chuckled. "Including the car ride?" He knew it didn't.

She groaned, shaking her head. "Two fucking hours. Would have been shorter if I didn't have to stop every fifteen minutes to pee." She grunted and shook her head. "Pregnancy blows."

Tara was a few months along, adding another baby to her mix. She already had two boys with Denny. He knew his girl was hoping this time around she was getting her much-wanted baby sister.

"I would have taken her, T." He had offered initially. Tara insisted she wanted to do it. Besides, he wouldn't have fit in too well with the cheering squad of moms with posters. He'd attended all the local competitions he could for his daughter, usually opting to stand in the back.

"I know." She shrugged. "I bitch about it, but I do love watching our girl, Saint. Those girls kicked ass today." She snickered. "Besides, this is my thing with C. Hell, you got all the other stuff, I need something that's mine."

Cia was a sweet mix of girly and tomboy wrapped into a perfect well-rounded package. She may have loved the competitions, but she was as easily pleased climbing trees and going camping or on hikes.

"So?" Tara eyed him. "What did you want to talk to me about?"

He'd mentioned he needed to discuss something with her in a text. This was a long time coming. Last night had solidified what he had hoped for. He was making Bailey his, which meant, eventually, she would become all of theirs. He didn't doubt Tara would be happy for him, but he knew how much she enjoyed inserting herself into his life. She'd always been that way. It wasn't a bad thing, but for as wonderful as she could be, sometimes Tara could be overwhelming, especially for the quiet Bailey.

"Seeing someone and want her to bring her around C. Just wanted to give you the heads up." It was a mutual respect in telling her. He wasn't asking permission. Tara knew him well enough to know he wouldn't bring anyone around his girl he didn't deem worthy. That being the main reason he hadn't had a woman around since Cia was too small to remember.

He'd dated, of course, but nothing serious which would warrant meeting his daughter. Until now.

Saint sighed at her reaction. Her eyes widened, and her lips curled. She leaned forward. "You got a girlfriend?"

One date did not constitute a relationship in most people's eyes. After pining over her for a year and finally being with her last night, the word "girlfriend" didn't seem nearly as serious as the feelings he had for Bailey. *She's mine.*

"Yeah, her name is Bailey."

"Bailey?" she shrieked. "When do I get to meet her?" Saint wasn't surprised at her reaction. Tara had made it clear she wanted him to find someone. She was constantly on him about allowing her to set him up with someone. He declined every time. He didn't need anyone to find him a woman. He had no problem in that department. Women seemed to be attracted and intrigued by him. The issue rested solely on his shoulders. He didn't know what he wanted until a tiny, beautiful redhead stumbled through an old barn town hall. Then he knew.

"Gonna do a quick intro tomorrow. Then I was thinking of the two of them spending time together next weekend." He had previously asked to take her since his weekend was cut short from her competition. As usual, Tara obliged.

"Yeah? So, what's she like?"

"Twenty-five." He waited for a reaction. He usually dated women closer to his age, not ten years his junior.

Tara smirked and winked. "Good for you."

He chuckled. "She's sweet, good heart, you'll like her. Just don't scare her away."

Tara burst out laughing and reached forward, slapping his leg before settling against the railing. There weren't many people he joked with except those who knew him best. Tara was one of the few.

"Oh man, I'm happy for you, Saint. You've been alone too long." She paused. "Cia is gonna freak when she hears ya got a girlfriend." Tara smiled and tilted her head. "She worries about you being alone." Tara shrugged. "So do I."

"Maybe I like being alone." He actually didn't mind it.

"Or maybe ya just hadn't met the right woman until now."

"Christ, ya got me married off already, you haven't even met her yet." He smirked. "You could end up not liking her?" It didn't matter whether she liked Bailey or not, she was his woman, and she was there to stay.

"Pfft…" She dismissively waved her hand. "You have great taste in women. Present company included." She winked. "And the fact that you've never brought a woman around Cia…no, this one's gotta be special."

Saint swallowed the knot in his throat. "She is."

Tara beamed. "I can't wait to meet her." She leaned forward, kissing him on the cheek. She ambled down the stairs. "She needs to be at school by eight-fifteen, and don't let her pack her own lunch." She turned, narrowing her gaze. "Chips, fruit snacks, and a juice box does not constitute a lunch."

He nodded and pushed up from the steps, grabbing his coffee. He made his way inside. He'd planned a movie night with Cia then taking her to the diner in town for breakfast. She had hounded him to go see the new clubhouse, which he made arrangements with Kase earlier. If he was bringing Cia, he gave a heads up.

He stood at the bottom of the steps and glanced up. "Cia," he called. He heard her padded feet before she appeared at the top of the landing.

"Gonna start dinner, and then we watch a movie."

She smirked. "My choice?"

Oh hell. He sighed and raised his brows. She may be half tomboy. However, her movie selections usually strayed to the girly side.

"Yeah, you choose."

She grinned and turned. Cia stopped when he called her again. She turned back, staring down at him.

"Before we go see Uncle Kase tomorrow, we're gonna swing by a friend's house." He paused. "Want you to meet her?"

Her brows knitted together, and her lips curled. "A girl?"

"Yeah, her name is Bailey."

Cia's mouth fell open. "Is she your girlfriend?"

Saint sighed. *Again, with the girlfriend.* He nodded. "You want to meet her?"

Cia nearly bounced on her toes, and Saint took a step up, fearing her excitement might send her down the stairs. "Yeah."

Her eyes widened. "Invite her over now. She can do movie night with us."

"She's got plans. Tomorrow we'll stop by." He stepped back and pointed at her. "Need you to clean your room before dinner." Her shoulders sagged, and she dramatically dragged her feet to her room.

Saint continued with the night, making dinner and settling in for a movie marathon. Luckily, Cia had passed out with her head on his lap a quarter way through the second movie. He turned the tv off and lifted her in his arms, taking her upstairs to bed. The kid was a rock. Once she was down, there was no waking her.

He made his way downstairs to lock up and shut off the lights when he noticed the blinking of his phone. He grabbed it and smiled.

Bailey: Hi Saint

He typed on his phone and hit send.

Saint: Hey, sweetheart.

Bailey: Am I interrupting anything?

He walked to the kitchen, texting with one hand.

Saint: Just put Cia to bed. Thinking of you.

Bailey: ——blushing—— Thinking of you too.

Saint furrowed his brows and smiled. Her message was followed by three emojis. *So damn cute.* In the age of technology, Saint was fully capable, yet he refused to use pictures as a way to communicate.

Bailey: I'm so sorry to do this on short notice, but something came up tomorrow, and I won't be around. Next time you have her, let me know.

Fuck! He read through the lie. He should have seen this coming. She was extremely hesitant. If he thought she didn't have an interest in meeting his daughter, he'd have a true dilemma on his hands. It wasn't the case, he suspected. Bailey was scared. Calling her out would only intensify her stress and possibly push her away. He'd deal with it when he saw her, face to face.

Saint: All right.

Bailey: Will I still see you on Monday?

He stared down at the message. A simple sentence, yet he could read past it.

Saint: I'll pick you up after I drop Cia off
Bailey: I can't wait!
Bailey: And again, I'm sorry about tomorrow.

Saint drew in a breath. *So am I.* He could understand her nerves. Cia would have a harder time especially since he'd already mentioned it to her. From her excitement, this would be a letdown, something Saint tried not to do with his daughter ever.

Fuck.

BAILEY PRESSED her lips together and clasped her hands in front of her. A simple nod to appease him was seemingly backfiring as Arnett Collins' face burned two shades of red.

"Well," he snapped. "What are you going to do about it, *Mayor?*" His snarky overtone had Bailey drawing in a breath.

Arnett, aka the town crier, had put her phone on blast since six in the morning, demanding she check out the damages caused by the construction happening on Main Street. She assured him she would see to it. Her word didn't prove enough for him. He called every fifteen minutes until she arrived at half-past nine.

The so-called damages were a result of the work being done at Macy and Cheyenne's shop. There was a neat square of dirt. During a previous town meeting, their request to replace the existing tree was granted. Apparently, it wasn't done quickly enough for Mr. Collins' liking.

She had rushed around getting ready and made the call she dreaded. She had been looking forward to seeing Saint since he walked out of her house on Saturday morning. She waited until close to nine, not wanting to disrupt his time with his daughter when he dropped her off. In doing so, she was canceling last minute.

When she spoke to him and explained the situation, he understood without questioning her. The call was cut short when she got in her car. She tried to block the disappointment of him not trying to reschedule their date. *I should have said something.* She could have suggested meeting later on in the day, but she became flustered with her pending meeting. Arnett had held a vendetta and grudge ever since he lost the mayoral election to her. It came as a shock since she hadn't even run in the first place. Apparently, many of the townspeople had gotten together and decided she would be the best candidate. No one was more surprised than her when they announced Bailey as the new Mayor of Ghosttown.

"Do you see this?" he shouted, and Bailey jerked from the sharp edge of his tone. She should have been accustomed to him after all these years, but he still managed to get reaction from her.

"Yes, I see." She gulped. "Macy and Cheyenne assured the board they would be planting a new tree and shrubs once construction was completed." She glanced down at the dirt-filled square where the dying tree had since been removed. It was already an improvement, though she didn't voice her opinion to him. She smiled, which only seemed to ignite his fury. "They have shown us the plans, along with the exact tree they intend to plant. Mr. Collins, they are paying out of pocket, which technically isn't their responsibility, so we should be grateful and uh," she paused, "exercise patience."

Oh shit. Wrong answer. His lips twisted, and his eyes darkened into a menacing glare.

"You are allowing our town to be taken over," he shouted again. He inched closer, and Bailey didn't back away. He was all bark. "You are a disgrace as our leading official."

She tightened her lips. It could have been worse. Being called a disgrace was baby talk compared to some of the things he'd said to her in the past. She spread out her hands and attempted to reason with him again. She never got the chance.

"Back. Up." The low command sent chills down her spine.

She slowly craned her neck to find Saint standing a few feet away from them at the curb. She hadn't even heard his approach, yet there he was. His glare was trained over her head at Arnett. It was definitely bad timing, but her first thought was, *God, he is sexy*.

Saint stalked forward, and Arnett immediately retreated a few feet from her. Her gaze remained on Saint while his scowl hardened.

"I suggest you think long and hard about the next words to come out of your mouth." His tone was even, but Bailey could feel the menacing implication behind his demand.

His jaw squared, and she knew he was holding onto to his anger. She didn't know Saint well enough to know what would happen if Arnett became combative. If she had to guess, it wouldn't end well for Arnett.

"I am voicing a concern as a citizen of…"

His voice trailed as Saint stepped closer, right next to Bailey.

"You don't use that tone with her. Do you understand me?" Saint paused, and Bailey widened her eyes and shifted on her feet. The tension on the street was thick, and she was unsure how this would play out.

"I was j-just…" Arnett stammered his words, and Bailey jerked her head.

"I heard, and I'm telling you…" Saint's voice dropped. "Watch. Your. Tone."

She drew in a breath and prepped to insert herself back into the conversation. This was on the edge of getting out of hand. She knew what Arnett was capable of with his nasty tongue. She'd been front and center for the Phoebe incident, and she didn't want history to repeat itself. She inched toward Saint, who leveled Arnett with his glare. Before she could say a word, Arnett shuffled back on his feet and started down the sidewalk heading toward his car. They watched in silence as he got in and drove away, shooting a hateful glare in their direction as he passed.

She bit back a smile, noting this was the second time Saint had come to her rescue after a verbal attack from Arnett. He was focused on watching the car as she slipped closer and slid her hand into his palm. He tightened his grip and glanced down at her with his hardened scowl.

"He's an asshole."

Bailey chuckled, bowing her head. Saint tugged her closer, and she immediately fell into his side, resting her free hand on his stomach.

"He's difficult, yes."

Saint snorted and leaned closer. "You're too nice." His lips grazed her mouth, and she melted against him. She didn't give a single thought to who may be watching. Her mind was shadowed by Saint and his lips. She circled her hand around his waist to his back. If she had her way, they would be in a full-blown passionate kiss in less than two seconds. Unfortunately for her, Saint pulled away, leaving an inch gap separating their mouths.

She shook her head, and he cocked his brow in response. "No such thing as too nice, Saint."

His brows knitted together. "Bailey," he whispered in warning.

She knew what he was thinking. It was the same thing she'd been told over and over by the councilmen and other residents. If she didn't put Arnett in his place, he would continue to berate her.

She rested her chin on his chest and watched as his jaw retracted, and his tightened features eased slightly. The moment would have been perfect if not for the shouting call for Saint coming from across the street. She turned her head and pulled away slightly when she made eye contact with the voice.

Kase, Gage, and Rourke stood in front of their shop, staring at her and Saint. Her slight move was stopped when Saint tightened his hold on her waist.

"I gotta talk to Kase. Then I wanna take you on the ride I promised. Sound good?"

She nodded and scanned the street. Just a block away, his bike was parked near the corner. Saint pressed a kiss to the top of her head and moved forward. With their hands still intertwined, she

The Saint

was tugged forward. She dug her heels into the ground, and he turned back.

"I'll just wait for you by your bike, okay?" It was posed as a question, but it was more of a statement. She had zero desire to be around Kase and any member of the club right now. She didn't think any differently of them except Dobbs. Her embarrassment lingered, and she wanted to keep as much distance as possible.

Saint eyed her suspiciously before glancing over his shoulder at his brothers. His lips flattened, and he nodded, releasing her hand. "Just give me a minute."

She nodded and started down the street. She snuck a peek across the street to find Gage and Rourke staring at Saint, waiting on him. Not Kase, though. His eyes were trained on her as she made her way down the street. She jerked her gaze and bowed her head, continuing toward Saint's bike.

She'd never had an issue with any Ghosttown Rider before last week. She wasn't holding a grudge or upset with them as in guilt by association. She'd never do that. The members had always been welcoming and kind to her. This was on her, something she needed to work through before looking them in the eye.

The woman's words replayed in her head, sending doubt to who Bailey was, and she hated it. *Why can't I just let it go?* Her eyes teared briefly before she sucked in a deep breath to calm her nerves. Maybe it was time to reach out to her therapist again. It had been over a year since she'd seen her. Bailey thought she had finally put it all past her and moved on. It was proving to be a harder task than she anticipated. With Adam's impending release and the vile words spoken, old wounds flared, and she wasn't sure how to move on.

She paced around Saint's bike, smiling when she saw two helmets. *One of those is mine.*

She glanced up when she heard the heavy boots descend her way. Saint stalked forward. There was power in every step, a strong, confident stride. Visions of him naked had her rubbing her thighs together. *Am I seriously getting wet from this man walking?*

Yes, she was. As he moved closer, she caught a figure standing across the street. Gage and Rourke were walking back into the store, but Kase was standing at the curb, staring at Saint. *Or me?* She ducked her head.

Saint stopped and reached for her helmet, handing it to her, before taking his own. She put it on, and when he instructed her how to get on, she stepped on the pedal and swung her leg over the side. The seat was more comfortable than she imagined it would be. She nestled her butt against the cushion, leaving a small space between her and Saint. He glanced over his shoulder and smirked.

His arm reached around, pulling her into his back. She wrapped her arms around his waist and flinched as the engine roared. They had always been loud driving down the road. The sound was almost deafening, being so close. She didn't mind. She snuggled closer and felt his hand rest on hers.

"Where do you wanna go?"

"I don't care. I just wanna go for a ride. First time, remember?"

Under her palm, his chest rumbled. No doubt, he was laughing. His hand tightened on hers before releasing her and gripping the handlebars. One quick look to his left and they were off. She gasped and tightened her arms around his waist. Her stomach jumped and the excited energy strummed through her blood.

It was freeing in a sense, and slightly scary. He started down Main Street and turned right onto a country road. She knew Ghosttown well. Taking this road would only lead them to one place. She smiled with the wind beating against her face.

The river in Ghosttown was her favorite spot. Now, she was heading there with her favorite guy on her new favorite mode of transportation.

Perfect.

Chapter 11

Saint had been sitting in the back of the town hall for the past hour. Usually a member or two attended. Tonight, he was the only one. When he offered to go alone, all the brothers seemed relieved. The last meeting had been close to two hours.

He folded his arms and settled into his seat. He had an ulterior motive for being there. Spending the afternoon with her was not enough. He needed more time.

When he offered to come tonight, she tried to persuade him not to bother since it would be an Arnett show, as she called it. She nailed the description. The old man spoke for thirty minutes until he was cut off by another local wanting to change the subject and veer it toward a discussion on a town park.

Most people seemed relieved with the new topic. Especially his woman. She bounced slightly in her seat at the mention of a park. They talked about funds, which Arnett piped in complaining of the cost. He made a mental note to speak with Kase. Maybe the club could throw some money toward the financing of the park. They had a lot of connections he could utilize to save money for the town.

Once Bailey tapped the gavel, people filtered out. Saint remained seated, eyeing Arnett as he walked to the exit. The old man must have sensed him because he jerked his head in Saint's direction. He fumbled a bit from Saint's harsh glare and ducked out through the doors.

When Bailey started toward him, he stood. Her smile was bright and aimed directly at him.

"Hi."

Saint nodded. She seemed to rush toward him then abruptly stopped a foot away. She scanned their immediate area, then turned to him.

"What?"

She shrugged with a low giggle. "You don't seem like a PDA kind of guy."

He wasn't. Ever.

"I guess kissing you is out of the question, huh?"

He raised a brow. "Do you want to kiss me in front of the town?"

Her smile grew, and she stepped closer raising on her toes and swiping a tender kiss along his lips. It was a mere greeting, nothing scandalous.

"Gerry is doing clean up tonight, so I'm free to go." She licked her lips and stepping closer. "Do you want to come over to my place?" Her eyes widened, waiting on his answer.

It was sweet and cute, and a completely ridiculous question. Of course he wanted to be with her. He dropped his hand from her waist and intertwined his fingers through hers. She tightened her grip as he led them to the door. He caught a few stares, some whispers, and appreciative smiles aimed at Bailey.

They made their way through the parking lot. He walked toward her car, where his motorcycle was parked next to her. Her phone rang, and Bailey retrieved it with her open hand. The gravel crunched under his boots, echoing through the open lot. When she squeezed his hand, he glanced over. She seemed to be in a trance staring down at her phone with her brows knitted together. She hadn't answered the call.

"What's wrong?"

She jerked her head as if momentarily she'd forgotten he was beside her. She blinked and shook her head, shoving her phone back in her bag.

"Um—" She licked her lips nervously. "Nothing."

"Bailey."

Her lips were tight, and two fine lines indented between her brows. "Telemarketers," she blurted as if it was the first thought in her head. Saint simply nodded, not acknowledging her lie.

"If it's too late and you don't want to come over, I'll understand." He caught the disappointment in her tone.

He raised his brows. Something had changed and drastically. A few minutes earlier she'd been eager to get him back to her house. Before the phone call. When he remained silent, she nervously shifted on her feet.

"I just mean, I'm really tired." She waved her hand in a circular motion and stammered, "I probably won't be great company." She drew in a breath and glanced up at him through her lashes.

He wondered if he pushed about the call whether she would open up. Obviously, whoever it was, triggered something inside her. Forcing her hand on opening up to him was never the plan with Bailey. As much as he wanted to know who had called, it wasn't worth pushing her away. Saint had a strong idea who the caller might have been. He was well aware her ex had reached out to her. He just didn't know if she usually answered his calls.

He released her hand and wrapped his arm over her shoulder. Bailey curled into his embrace. "I'm pretty tired myself. You opposed to me coming over and sleeping with you?"

She slowed her steps, and the wariness he'd seen a minute ago had diminished. "You're willing to come over just to sleep?"

Saint snorted. "I'm *asking* to come over just to sleep." He stopped and turned, grabbing her face between his palms. "You in my arms sounds like a perfect way to fall asleep."

She smiled and rose up on her toes, pressing her lips against his. It was the answer he needed.

A half-hour later, they were snuggled in her bed. He was tempted to check her phone once she'd drifted off. He could get away with it, and she'd never know.

I would know. Trust was the foundation for every relationship. Saint wouldn't compromise his life with Bailey to appease his curiosity. When she was ready, she'd tell him. Until then, he'd respect her privacy.

Sleep came quick for him, feeling comfortable with her curved in his side. He wound up sleeping better in her bed than he did his own. Maybe it was because she was next to him.

When he woke hours later, he reveled in his cozy position with Bailey curled into his chest.

He could get used to spending the rest of his life this way. *With her.*

Bailey turned in his arms, still asleep, curling her face into his chest, and he smiled. She reached out, resting her arm over his waist. He hadn't taken a long look at her scars when she was watching him. Now, while she slept, he got an in-depth look at the torture some bastard had inflicted on her. His hand grazed slightly over her arm, feeling the red raised ripple skin under the pads of his fingers.

He wasn't turned off like he knew she suspected he would be. Instead, it made him want to be closer with her. Assure her the worst in her life was truly over. From here on out, with him, it would all be beautiful. His finger traced up her arm to her shoulder where the scars were most severe and slid over her chest. The scar stopped abruptly at her breast. He had noticed a few burn scars scattered on her stomach and a fairly large patch on the side of her thigh. He knew most people, and possibly Bailey herself would see them as horrific. He viewed them as badges of survival.

She curled into his chest and flickered open her eyes with a sleepy gaze. God, she was beautiful.

"Hi."

He smiled and leaned down, taking her lips. He couldn't resist. He was going to miss her the next few days. His tattoo shop was having most of the renovations done this week, which meant he'd be there long days and nights.

"Busy week for the shop. Gonna miss this all week."

She glanced up through sleepy eyes. "The weekend's not so far off."

Saint swiped her hair from her forehead. "Got Cia this weekend."

"Oh cool." She leaned up on her elbow. "You should take her by the river. They have a bunch of hiking trails. The views are amazing." Her eyes widened with excitement. "And go for pizza. They're opening on Friday. I'm telling you, it's so good. Something about the bread they use." She bit her lips, and he smiled. She was deep in thought. "We don't have too many things for kids. I really need to start my push for the town park." When she crinkled her nose, Saint smirked. *So damn cute.* "You should check out Turnersville, where Cade and Riss live. They've got a great park, and there are a few shops Cia might like." She snapped her fingers. "And hit the candy store there. I love that place." She giggled.

It sounded like a great plan with only one thing missing.

"What time will you be ready?"

She flickered her lashes. He'd caught her off guard.

"For what?"

"To come with us. T drops her off at ten on Saturday. We can swing by and get you about eleven."

Saint didn't like what he was seeing. Bailey's face paled. "Um," she paused, taking in a breath, "I don't think it's a good idea."

"Why?"

"Because isn't it too soon?" She pulled away from him,

another reaction he didn't like. "I think it's just too soon. Maybe in a month." She scanned the room. "Or two," she muttered.

"Bailey." He sighed. He hadn't expected this. She made a point of speaking about Cia, and so did he. He needed them both to meet. He was guessing her cancellation from the previous weekend would be a trend, and he was not happy about it.

"I'm not ready, and you can't push me on this, Saint." Her bottom lip trembled, and she whispered, "You can't."

Saint was realizing from her reaction, the fear she was dealing with about meeting his daughter was greater than he had thought. There wasn't a rush, except his own impatience of wanting them to all be together. If she needed a little more time, then he'd give it to her.

He reached out, grasping her arm and tugging her down to his chest. His lips glided across her forehead. "We'll wait, sweetheart."

She relaxed against his chest and sighed.

BAILEY GLANCED down at the dashboard. It was just after ten. She clucked her tongue. A little late for breakfast and too early for lunch. All her thoughts were on Saint. In the past month, she'd stopped by a few times with food. He'd been working tirelessly on his shop, and she wanted to help out any way she could. She had an ulterior motive. She wanted to see him.

The last four weeks together had been perfect. A few hitches, mainly her needing to wait on meeting his daughter. He mentioned when he had her and waited on her response, which was always a decline. Most recently, she was realizing her desire to meet Cia was slowly outweighing her own insecurities.

Progress.

She was just pulling up to an open spot on Main Street when her phone rang. She had planned on ignoring it until she saw the name pop up. Bailey put the car in park, smiled, and answered the call.

"I miss you, come home," she said, which was greeted with a loud giggle she'd missed in the past four months.

"Ahh, God, girl, you always know exactly what to say." Phoebe sighed. "A couple more months and I'll be raising hell in Ghosttown, don't you worry."

Bailey settled in her seat. "Everybody misses you. Town meetings just aren't the same without…"

"Inmate 76857890?" Phoebe laughed, which made Bailey smile. At least she could find the humor in the incident. Most residents could, and also saw the logic in what happened. She knew Phoebe well enough though to read past the humor. Her friend wasn't proud of what had happened.

"How are you?" Bailey asked.

"Same old, though I did get a contract for a six-month gig, which my bank account and shoe obsession are thoroughly grateful for."

Phoebe was a web designer. She'd set up the town website free of charge, though Bailey insisted on paying her. She declined, saying it was a form of community service.

"Congratulations, Feebs."

"Yeah, well, it helps with the court fees." There was an awkward pause. Bailey was about to ask what was wrong when Phoebe spoke. "Talked to Marley last night."

Bailey bit her lip and glanced down at the steering wheel, then closed her eyes and remained silent. She knew where this was going.

"When were you going to tell me, sweetie?"

Bailey slumped in her seat and sighed. "He's not out yet."

"Not yet, but soon. Very soon, Bails."

Phoebe's concern was coming from a good place. Her love for Bailey. She tapped her nails on the steering wheel, stalling. It was overwhelming at times when others expressed their worry and concern. It was also heartbreaking. Bailey hated the dark cloud looming overhead.

"I knew it was coming." Bailey scratched her head and wiped the small beads of sweat from her forehead. "I'm fine, Phoebe, I j-just..." She shook her head. "I don't want to talk about him. He's getting out, and there's nothing I can do about it, so I'm going to do what I always do and keep living my life."

"That's a fabulous plan, girl." When Phoebe chuckled, Bailey relaxed into her seat. Her friend had a way of easing her, and she adored Phoebe.

"Just promise me, if you find yourself *not good*, you call me. Doesn't matter when, you reach out."

She swallowed the knot in her throat. "I will."

"Okay. So what's going on there? What have I missed?"

The abrupt subject change was Phoebe giving her the out she needed. It was done with purpose. Yet, another thing she loved about the woman. Bailey bit her lip, weighing her options. She only had two close friends, Marissa and Phoebe, who she'd known longer. Should she mention it? *Hell yeah.*

"So, I'm kind of dating someone."

There was a slight pause, then a choking sound on the other end. "Phoebe?"

"Oh my God, I almost died choking on my coffee, which would have sucked because I wouldn't hear the rest of this. You got a man?"

Bailey chuckled. "Yep, sleeping with him and all." She had shared her concerns more with Phoebe than Rissa. It was hard to come out and say she was hesitant about being intimate because of her scars. During a late wine-drinking night, she had confided in Phoebe.

"Girl!" she screamed. "I'm so excited you'd think I was the one getting laid." She laughed. "Tell me everything. Don't leave anything out. Go."

"His name is Saint. He's uhhh, the vice-president of the Ghosttown Riders. He's...." She wasn't able to continue when she heard Phoebe squeal.

"You're banging a biker? Holy fuck, Bailey, I wanna be you when I grow up."

Bailey laughed, covering her face, which was turning red.

"Oh my God. That's awesome," she screeched, the excitement only adding to Bailey's. "And he's a good guy, right? I'm not gonna need another stint in jail over him?"

Bailey shook her head, smiling. "He is, Feebs, he's so great."

"Awww," Phoebe said. "I hear it in your voice, Bails. You're happy. I can't wait to meet him."

"You will if you ever come home."

Phoebe groaned. "Soon. The restraining order is up in two months."

"I told you, it doesn't restrict you from your home, Phoebe."

The small silence weighed on Bailey as she waited for a response.

"Time away is good for everybody. It's good for me, and it's better this way. But I'll be back, and when I am, I wanna meet this unworthy bastard who's got my girl all excited." Phoebe laughed. "I'll call ya soon, love."

"Bye, Feebs." She hung up and sighed. It would be good to have Phoebe back home in Ghosttown, where she belonged.

She got out of the car, making her way to the trunk.

There weren't many people her own age in town. It didn't matter much. Bailey could get along with anyone, but Phoebe and her had struck up a true friendship when Bailey first moved to town. She was pretty sure it was Phoebe who suggested to the town she be mayor, though she refused to admit it. The last four months had been hard with her not around. She missed seeing her. Phoebe hightailed it out of Ghosttown after an altercation with Arnett. *I miss her.* Why couldn't Arnett leave? Had it been a town vote, his ass would have been gone. Bailey chuckled.

Bailey opened up the trunk and grabbed her signs. They were

considering adding a park to the town, and she wanted as many people as she could get to vote on it at the impromptu meeting.

Time to get to it.

In the past few months, she hadn't bothered with posting signs for the town meeting. All the residents knew they were held on the first Monday of every month. This one was an exception. She decided on a special meeting after taking a vote on the interest of a playground off Main Street. It seemed everyone was on board. *Well, not everyone.*

"Just go in," she muttered, forcing the prongs from the poster board into the ground. There was always one which gave her problems.

Thankfully, there were only six signs. This being her last and most problematic. She stood, stretching her back to ease the tension in her shoulders.

"Need help?"

Bailey froze and scanned the area in front of her. The voice was coming from behind, and without looking, she knew who it was. She hadn't seen him in a few weeks which had been a blessing. For the most part, she tried to put the fiasco with Dobbs and her meltdown at Marissa's behind her. It was much easier to do when she wasn't forced to be in the presence of a reminder. It was all about to change.

Saint rarely brought up the club. She knew about a few missed parties at the clubhouse from Saint. He hadn't put any pressure on her to attend. He actually seemed content to hang out at her place, just the two of them.

"Can't fucking ignore me forever, Mayor."

She cringed. He had a point. She couldn't, no matter how hard she tried. Running into to him was inevitable. She was surprised they hadn't seen each other sooner. Who was she kidding? She had made it a mission to avoid any and all members. She drew in a breath and plastered on a smile. Bailey turned around, gripping the sign.

"Hi Kase, how are you?"

His usual scowl was locked in place though he lacked the glare.

He raised his brows and took a drag of his cigarette.

"How am I?" He shrugged and glanced around the empty street. "Be a lot better if you cut the cordial shit."

Oh hell. A confrontation on Main Street with the president of the Ghosttown Riders was the last thing she needed. *Feign ignorance.* She forced a shaky smile.

"Not sure what ya mean?"

He snorted. "Yeah, ya fucking do."

Damn. There was no good way to avoid it, seeing as how Kase seemed hellbent on discussing it.

Bailey hurried past him to her car. "I'm sorry, Kase. You've caught me at a bad time, I've got so much to do. Can we talk some other time?"

It was a stall tactic. Having any conversation with him was unsettling. Especially since the last conversation included her threatening the police on the club. *Shit, I forgot about that.*

"No." His tone was sharp. "We can't."

Bailey halted in mid-step and turned her head. He was intimidating and scary. She didn't have a fear he would hurt her, but he left her anxious. She wiped her forehead with the back of her hand.

"Okay," she whispered.

"Wanna make shit right here. Can't do that with you playing Wiley Fucking Coyote all over the place."

Play it off. She conjured up a laugh and waved her hand in front of her face.

"There's nothing to make right, we're fine."

"The fuck we are." He pointed down the street. "Either you're training for a fucking marathon, or I gotta think the way you disappear when a member shows up ten feet from ya, shit ain't fine."

She bit her lip. *New tactic. Anything to end this.*

She nodded with a smile. "Okay, I accept your apology."

Kase raised a brow. "Which would be great, if I fucking apologized. I didn't."

Why was he making this so difficult? Her shoulders sagged.

"Need you to tell me what we gotta do to make this shit right." He took a drag from his cigarette. "Let me lay it for ya, Mayor. You ain't right with the club? Saint ain't right with it. I'm thinking he's gonna be spending a fuck lot of time with you. And not with the club."

She blinked in confusion. One had nothing to do with the other.

"I don't see how me being with the club would affect Saint's relationship."

Kase furrowed his brows. "I know you don't, which is why I'm fucking standing here with you. You don't wanna be around the club. Then Saint won't be." He took another drag and shook his head. "He's been in and out with the club for years 'cause of the shops. Finally got the bastard living close, and he's still MI-fucking-A."

Was he blaming her? Was this somehow her fault?

"I wouldn't tell him not to go to the club or hang out with you," she said, taking her first step forward since the conversation began. Hearing Saint talk of the club and the brothers, she knew how important they were. The last thing she wanted was to come between them. "I'd never stand in the way of him and the club. I know how important you all are to him." She shook her head. "I wouldn't do that, Kase."

Kase watched her and sighed. The corner of his lip curled then he laughed. "How the fuck does anyone stay mad at you?" He laughed and glanced up at the sky.

"What?"

"You. I'm fucking trying to be pissed off, then ya give me the fucking sincerity and the puppy dog eyes. Fuck, maybe I'm just getting soft." He shook his head. "You do me a solid, Bailey. You come around with Saint. Ya show up, hang with the girls, have a drink at the bar, just fucking show up. The brothers miss Saint."

She gulped. "Okay."

"No, not okay." He stepped forward, towering over her. "What do I gotta do to make this right with you? 'Cause you show up like a prisoner, Saint's gonna read through that shit and not bring ya back. And if you ain't there, his ass will only show up when necessary. Don't want that."

"Okay," she muttered.

"Fuck!" he snapped. "No, fucking not okay."

She widened her eyes, and her frustration with him had finally reached her boiling point. Whatever she said, he was dismissing. She was trying to end this, and he wouldn't allow it.

"I'm embarrassed, Kase," she blurted, and immediately her eyes welled. She wasn't sad, just utterly irritated he forced her to say it.

"Why the fuck are you embarrassed?"

She whipped her head and glared. His lack of sensitivity was aggravating the hell out of her. Of course, she'd be embarrassed and humiliated the way the woman spoke of her, and Dobbs allowing it, then her meltdown, which she knew they were all privy to.

"I was the butt of a joke. She was laughing at me, mocking me."

He furrowed his brows. "The cunt from the club?" Kase scowled, glancing up at the sky. "You still pissed about that?"

She gasped. Of course she was still upset. How could he be so insensitive and dismissive about something which cut her to her core?

"You're an asshole." She pushed past him and managed to nudge his arm in the process. He had over a foot on her, and more than a hundred pounds, which made her feel even more triumphant when he staggered to his side.

"Oh fuck me." His voice was hushed until he appeared in front of her. She folded her arms and flattened her lips.

Kase stared for a brief second and stepped closer into the space. *Don't you dare back up.*

"Just tell me this, Bailey. Why the fuck do you care what some whore thinks of you? Hell, ya wanna know what some people have called me?" He snorted. "The bitch was thrown out on her ass the night it went down. Saint banned her ass from the club." He narrowed his gaze. "And I banned her from the town. Ya ain't never gonna hear her voice or see her face again." He raised his brows. "And if for some reason, she gets the idea to come back, not a single fucking member of the club is gonna let her back near us or you. Not one."

Oh. This was all a revelation she didn't know about. She licked her lips. "But everyone knows."

He scoffed. "Yeah, they do. They know some worthless piece of shit talked trash about a member's old lady. How do ya think it went over?" Kase sighed and folded his arms. "Ya got scars, Bailey. It ain't a fucking secret. How you got them, we all fucking know, and not one man in the club wouldn't give a fucking limb to get five minutes with the motherfucker who did it to ya."

She gasped.

His face softened slightly. "Nobody cares, Bailey. Not Saint, not the women, the brothers. Not me." He paused with a harsh scowl. "The only thing anyone gives a shit about is Saint and you ain't around." He drew in a breath and sighed. "So, fucking fix it, 'cause it's all in your hands, Mayor."

She was struck speechless. She had never heard Kase speak so much in her life. Everything he said was somehow honest, raw, rude at times, but overall, she understood exactly what he was saying. Without Bailey, they were losing a bit of Saint.

"Okay."

He clenched his jaw, and she figured he was ready to explode from her *okay*, again. She shook her head and raised her hands in front of her chest.

"No, I mean, okay, I get it. I promise we'll be there."

Kase seemed to relax slightly.

"I get what you're saying, and I understand it." She licked her lips stepping closer. "I don't want to come between Saint and the club. If it means I need to go to the clubhouse and hang out, then I'll do it." She shrugged. "I mean, I like most of the members, I do, especially the women."

He nodded and the corner of his lip curled. "And they fucking like you. We all do, Bailey." He lowered his voice, staring down at her. "We got ya. The whole club, we got ya. And I don't usually make guarantees, but I can make this one. What happened with you at the club will *never* fucking happen again."

For the first time in the past ten minutes, she drew in a breath which filled her lungs, and she was able to relax.

"Friday night?"

Bailey drew in a breath and nodded. "We'll be there."

He eyed her, searching her face. She raised her brows and grinned, which made him laugh. He lifted his hand and turned walking back to his bike.

It was strange to see him in a new light. Here was a man who, by all outward appearances, would strike the fear into anyone he encountered. Yet, he was a bit softer with her. She felt an odd bond with Kase which gave her the courage to ask a question that had weighed on her mind for weeks.

"Hey, Kase?"

He stopped and turned around, lighting another cigarette. He raised his brows. It was a Kase thing. It meant 'what the fuck do you want?' She clamped her lips, unsure how to word her question. Unfortunately, Kase lacked any patience.

"Fucking speak, Bails, I got shit to do." There was not an ounce of malice in his tone. In fact, her nickname on his lips made her smirk. It seemed so out of character for him, yet it easily rolled off his tongue.

"Did you tell the club I was off-limits?"

He brought the cigarette to his lips and scanned the road before taking a drag. It may have been a stall tactic, and she was prepared to call him out on his lie.

"Yeah."

She openly gaped at Kase. She expected him to deny it. "You did?" Her voice hitched and reached the highest octave.

"Yeah, made it clear my guys were to stay away." He said it matter of fact. An order, a rule. "Not gonna ask why?"

She shrugged.

"I figured you needed a good guy, family man, nine to five, on the right side of the law bullshit."

Been there, done that, got the scars to prove it.

"Yeah, well ya see how well that went." She snorted, trying to make a joke. Kase wasn't taking the bait. In fact, his jaw tightened, and he tossed his cigarette, taking long strides toward her.

"Didn't want anyone fucking with you, hurting ya. Didn't want you thinking you were gonna get some wholesome motherfucker, and instead ya got a biker who may or may not step out on you, or even fucking show up when he's supposed to."

She gulped. It was a bigger admission than she expected.

"You're not all like that, though. Trax and Rourke, they don't cheat." She paused, and her eyes widened. "Do they?"

He openly grinned and belted out a laugh. "No." He bent down, leaving them at eye level. "Some do though, like variety, not into settling down. Trying to spare ya any hurt. We see how that turned out." The last was a dig, not at her, but at himself, she guessed. *Dobbs.* Not Saint, though.

"How come you didn't warn Saint away from me?"

Kase straightened his back, folding his arms over his chest. "Told *everyone* you were off-limits."

She opened her mouth, but he interjected, "Everyone."

So, Saint had been told to stay away and defied his president's orders. *For me.*

"Did he get in trouble?"

Kase twisted his lips. "Saint doesn't get *in trouble*. He does what he wants, takes what he wants, and spends time with who he wants. Could have threatened the fucker with the end of my pistol, and he still would have bailed on the run, all because the sexy little mayor asked him over for dinner."

"Does Saint know you think I'm sexy?" she teased.

Kase winked and snorted. "Fucking smartass." He turned again, making his way to his bike. His departure halted, and he shuffled around and paced backward staring at her. "Saint's a good man, better than most."

"Yes, he is." It was a strange, natural admission. Saying it actually had a physical effect. Her stomach flipped.

Kase smirked. "The man's been waiting a long time for a good woman. Long fucking time. He deserves ya."

Chapter 12

Saint turned down the country road, headed toward the clubhouse. Not exactly where he wanted to spend his Friday night. He loved his brothers and the club, but it had been a long week, and all he wanted to do was spend time alone with Bailey. Her insistence on going to the party had left him with no doubt, Kase had gotten to her.

He was well aware of his president's unhappiness with him missing the run a few weeks ago, and now the party he originally had declined the offer on. He understood it. Of all the brothers, he was closest with Kase, and since moving, he knew he figured Saint would be around more often.

He eyed Bailey as she tugged down her denim skirt, currently riding up her gorgeous toned thighs.

"I like that," he said with a low growl.

She pressed her lips together and her nose crinkled. *God, she's beautiful.* Just staring at her with the moon lighting her face, he was tempted to make a U-turn and ditch the party. However, Bailey had been adamant on going. From the fidgeting she was doing, her nerves were on high alert. This was definitely a coerced decision.

Fucking Kase.

"Two hours max, then we're outta there," Saint said. The timeframe was not up for a debate unless she wanted to leave earlier, then he'd be more than happy to ditch the clubhouse. He rolled his shoulders and hoped to hell it was a tamer night than usual. Walking in finding a woman on her knees giving head to one of his brothers was a common occurrence which didn't faze him. Bailey, however, was in for an eye-opening experience.

He drove up the steep hill, gaging the number of bikes in the lot. It wasn't a huge party, but large enough to intimidate her. He parked his truck on the side of the clubhouse, turned off his ignition, and glanced over at Bailey, squirming in her seat.

"We can still leave?"

She whipped her head and widened her eyes. "Why would we?"

"Because you look like you're seconds from running and hitchhiking back home?"

She chuckled. "I'd never hitchhike, it's dangerous." She was trying to make light of the situation even though he knew she was nervous. He reached out, taking her shaky, clammy hand.

"I've known most of these men for fifteen years, some longer. You have nothing to worry about." When she opened her mouth to speak, he tightened his grip on her hand. "And nothing to be embarrassed about. The last thing any of my brothers want is for you to feel uncomfortable around them." The corner of his lip curled. "Probably gonna see most of them on their best behavior. You have nothing to worry about, you hear me?"

She nodded though he saw her hesitation. He got out of the truck and glanced through the back window as he rounded the bumper. She slowly got out and met him halfway. He gripped her hand and started toward the front. There were two members and a woman smoking and drinking by the entrance. When he felt her tug his hand, he glanced down over his shoulder.

"So, um—" She peeked past him, looking at the small group before gazing up. "Are there rules here? Should I stay with you the whole time, or do you need me to go away at some point so you can talk to Kase and them?"

He furrowed his brows. What the hell was she talking about?

"Or do the women hang out in a certain section?" She crinkled her nose and twisted her lips, obviously not happy with that scenario. Saint flattened his lips, doing his best to hold back his laughter.

"Bailey, it's just a house where we all hang out, some brothers live here. You've been here before."

"Not as your girl—" She stopped, and her cheeks blazed a beautiful shade of pink. "I'm mean, uh, friend."

He lowered his mouth to hers, grazing her lips for a soft kiss. He pulled away a mere inch. "Girlfriend, sweetheart. It's all one word." He cupped her jaw, raising her gaze. "No rules. You want to stay by my side the whole time, you won't get any objection from me." He cocked his brow. "If you want to hang out with the girls, you do it. If you want a drink, tell me, and I'll get it for you, or if you want, order it yourself." He watched as her features, which were tight, slowly eased. "The bathroom is down the end of the hall, I can show you when we get inside, or you can wander around and find it for yourself. My advice is if a door is closed," he winked, "unless you're looking for shock value, you keep walking past it."

She chuckled and moved closer.

"There are no rules, Bailey. I just have some requests." He paused. "Someone touches you; you tell me. Someone says something directed toward you that you don't like, you let me know. If someone does something, anything, that makes you uncomfortable, you come get me. If you can't find me, you tell Kase or Trax or Rourke, anyone who shares my patch. Okay?"

She bit her lip. "Okay," she whispered.

He headed toward the door lifting his chin at the two members. His greeting was usually silent, something all the brothers had come to expect. He noticed Danny stretch his neck and offer Bailey a welcoming smile. These men he chose as his brothers were all good. Not perfect, not always law-abiding, but good to the core whose focus was the club, and those in it which included the old ladies.

He pulled open the door and guided Bailey inside to the dark foyer. Two prospects were heading out as they passed. They did a quick chin lift in acknowledgment, and the newest prospect glanced over at Bailey. His gaze perused her body, and the corner of his mouth curled, eyeing her breasts. Saint's jaw locked, and he glared. It only took a second for him to realize his mistake. He flinched and moved closer to the wall, with his eyes dropping to the floor.

When Bailey chuckled, he scowled. He ignored her amusement. He would have to get used to it, he figured. Bailey was gorgeous, and men would look. He sighed as they walked into the main room. His calculations from the parking lot was off. There were more people than he anticipated. He stalked through the room, heading to the bar. As they got closer, Nadia glanced up and smiled, then her gaze drew past him, and she grinned. She moved down to the end of the bar where Saint was headed.

Nadia was an exception to the rule when it came to the club girls. Most of them were there for two reasons. One, to have a good time. And two, to become an old lady. Nadia, while she started out as just a good time girl, had grown closer to the club. Her loyalty and dedication were rare for a woman who didn't belong to a member. She was also very sweet, which set her apart from most of the club whores.

"Hey, Bailey." She smiled. Though he'd never confided in Nadia as they were not close, she spent a lot of time at the club, and he was sure she'd heard some of the whispers from the brothers about his interest in Bailey.

"Hi, Nadia." Bailey sidled up next to him when he took a seat on the stool. She remained standing, and Saint wrapped his hand around her waist, settling her in between his legs.

Nadia leaned her elbows on the bar. "I love your top."

Saint watched as Bailey gazed down. He didn't know shit

about woman's fashion. It didn't matter. Everything looked good on her.

"Thank you. I got it from a boutique in Lawry. They have some cute stuff and not too expensive." Bailey smiled and curled into Saint's chest. "Rissa and I make the drive once a month. Next time we go, I'll let ya know. You can come with us."

Nadia seemed taken aback by the comment, and her smile faltered. Bailey seemed to recognize it also.

"I mean, if you want," Bailey stammered.

Nadia grinned and nodded. "I'd love to. Thank you, Bailey."

Saint knew Nadia had a good relationship with most of the old ladies but didn't recall them ever offering to hang out with her outside of the club. Bailey might not realize it; this was big for Nadia.

"Drinks, Nad, I'm dying down here!" Gage shouted from the end of the bar. Saint laughed, and Nadia ignored him, focusing back on him and Bailey.

"What can I get you guys?"

"Beer," Saint said.

"Um, beer, I guess," Bailey said.

Nadia eyed her. "If ya don't like beer, I can whip you up a margarita?"

Saint watched Bailey shift, and her eyes lightened with a sharp nod. He'd make a mental note that his girl liked fruity shit. Her hand grazed his knee as she glanced around the room. The new clubhouse was doubled in size including the main room. The bar lining the outer wall was twice the size. When Nadia dropped off their drinks she pointed to the margarita.

"I got a whole pitcher in the fridge for you, so start drinking, girl."

Bailey laughed, leaning against his chest. Once Nadia walked to the end of the bar, Bailey glanced up.

"I've been told I'm a super fun drunk."

Saint snickered and lowered his lips to her ear. "Are you a horny drunk?" he teased.

She twisted her lips. "I guess we'll find out." She sipped her drink and side-eyed him.

BAILEY WAS WALKING down the hall from the bathroom when her phone pinged. She was sporting a light buzz and enjoying it. She pulled her phone from her bag and glanced down. She paused mid-step, and her breathing halted in an abrupt stop. She stumbled to the wall, reaching out with her free hand. Nothing was more sobering than the number in front of her with the listed contact. Department of Corrections.

She had known the day would come. Somehow, she figured, she'd be prepared for it. Five years was a long time, surely enough to heal.

"H-hello?"

"May I speak with Bailey Preston, please?"

Bailey cleared her throat. "This is her."

"This is Officer Brown. This is a notification call to inform you Adam Bollinger has been released."

Her reaction played out in slow motion. She slumped her shoulder against the wall. It was the only thing keeping her upright at the moment. The officer continued to speak. Her mind drifted, and while she could hear his voice, his words became incoherent.

He's been released.

She had been prepared for it. Her lawyer had reached out last month explaining what would happen upon his release. If it had been parole, she could have contested it. That wasn't the case for Adam. He'd served his time, been a model prisoner, and he had been released. She thought she had come to grips with it. Now that he was actually out, it had left an uneasy pit in her stomach.

She drew in a breath, trying to calm herself. Emotion was getting the best of her, and her eyes welled. All she needed was a deep cleansing breath. There was no need to panic. She was sure, seeing her was the last of Adam's priorities. She'd read all of the letters he'd sent through the years. His notes were never aggressive or angry. He apologized and begged her to write back. She hadn't. He talked a lot of remorse and what he was doing to better himself in jail. The only thing missing from his letters was why he had done what he did. Even in court, when he was convicted and sentenced, probed by her lawyers and the judge, he never had an answer as to why he'd done it.

She straightened her back and stepped away from the wall. It was her past. His release would have no bearing on how she lived. She'd make sure of it. *I'm the mayor of a town I love, surrounded by supportive, loving friends. And Saint. I've made a good life here, and I'm going to live it.*

She tucked her phone in her bag and started forward. She would not let this ruin her night with Saint. Bailey rolled her neck. When she glanced up from the floor, she stumbled a few steps. Kase stood a few feet away, staring at her suspiciously. She had to wonder how long he'd been watching her. The way he was eyeing her, she assumed long enough to catch the tears in her eyes. She wiggled her nose with a quick sniffle and plastered on a smile.

She raised her brows as she got closer. He was an imposing guy, tall, tatted, with a permanent scowl on his face. Intimidating was an understatement when it came to Kase Reilly. Had he relaxed more and allowed his handsome features to shine through, Kase would be gorgeous, she thought.

"Hello, Kase."

He squinted, aiming his gaze directly into her eyes. "Mayor."

Her assessment was correct. Kase was suspicious. *Ignore it.*

She stopped a few feet away from him and clasped her hands. "Kept my promise."

He nodded, but watched her carefully, making her slightly uncomfortable. She started past him, but when she got parallel, he stepped in front of her blocking her path.

"You okay?"

She tightened her lips and forced a smile with a sharp nod. She was obviously doing a horrible job at faking it, and there was no doubt, Kase wasn't buying into her lie. He folded his arms as the silence lingered between them. She shifted on her feet, scanning the hall. *Now, what?*

"Saint's waiting on me, so I'm going to head back to the bar now." She sidestepped and he matched her stance. She glanced up through her lashes to find Kase scowling at her.

"You're not okay. You tell Saint." He leaned closer, and she stepped back. "You can't tell Saint, you tell me, we fucking clear?"

She nodded, which seemed enough of an answer, and he moved, letting her pass by. She glanced over her shoulder to see Kase still watching her. She jerked her head around and slammed into a massive wall of flesh. She sprung back and widened her eyes when she realized exactly who she bumped into. *Ah, shit.* She was not drunk enough for this conversation.

"Hey, Bailey."

She smiled through her tense lips. "Hi, Dobbs." She veered her eyes to the woman holding onto his hips. She waved. "Hi, I'm Bailey."

The woman chuckled. "Saint's old lady, I know." She raised her brows and perused Bailey's body. Bailey braced herself for a rude comment. Instead, the woman's smile warmed. "He's a lucky guy."

Bailey let out a nervous chuckle. "Thank you."

Dobbs turned to the woman and jutted his chin down the hall. She seemed to take note and passed Bailey, not before glancing down her body again. *Is she checking me out?* Bailey turned her head and watched as the woman winked at her.

She turned back around to Dobbs and leaned closer, lowering her voice. She needed confirmation. "Was she checking me out?"

His lips curled, reminding her what a great, friendly smile he had. "Yeah, Rose swings both ways, and I'm thinking she'd prefer you to me right now."

Bailey's eyes widened, straightening her chest. It was a compliment. "Really?"

Dobbs laughed with a sharp nod. She smiled back and noticed his smile falter as he stared at her.

"I'm really sorry, Bailey."

She'd been blindsided by his sincere tone. It was heartfelt, she could feel it. He showed no signs of the easygoing Dobbs she'd always interacted with. She saw the remorse, and more prevalent, the guilt. He shoved his hands in his pockets and shifted on his feet.

"It's fine."

He shook his head. "No, it's not. You were right to call me out on the shit I pulled. I wasn't thinking of you. I was thinking of getting off. It was fucked up."

"Really, Dobbs, it's okay."

He stepped closer and lowered his voice. "You're a really good girl, Bailey." He glanced away from her and shook his head. "Probably the best woman I've ever met, and I should have had your back 'cause not many women consider me a friend." He glanced back as her bottom lip fell open. He seemed destroyed, unlike any expression she'd ever seen on him. "But you did, and I didn't see it until it was too late."

She couldn't help herself. Maybe it was the slight buzz or the heartfelt apology or a combination of them both. She reached out, catching Dobbs off guard and hugged him. Everyone made mistakes, including herself. She wasn't about to hold a grudge. It took a big person to admit their fault and it was genuine.

"I still consider you a friend, Dobbs."

She released him and patted his shoulder.

He grinned. "Yeah?"

She nodded.

"Not gonna let that shit happen again, Bailey." He cleared his throat. "I got ya."

And he did. Somehow, someway, she knew if there was ever a next time, Dobbs would have her back.

"Gotta get back to my man." She winked.

Yep, definitely still harboring a buzz. Dobbs stepped out of her way with a soft snicker, and she started down the hall. She clocked Saint at the end of the bar with his eyes set on her and a scowl threading through his brows. Not a doubt in her mind, he'd watched the little scene with her and Dobbs.

He was surrounded by a few members. She only recognized two. Gage and Trax both glanced over her at the same time and smiled. She gave them a short wave and ducked her head. Even though everyone had been welcoming, she felt out of her element amongst the club.

As she made her way through the swarms of people, she smiled at Saint, who cocked his brow. She glanced over at the bar.

"Nadia?"

She turned and smiled. "Yeah, babe?"

"Can I get another?"

Nadia chuckled with a wink. "Yes, you can."

She weaved in between two members and situated herself between Saint's legs, staring up at him.

"You good?"

"Yeah. Dobbs just wanted to apologize, which I accepted. Now, I'm ready for round three of margaritas." She leaned closer and whispered in his ear, "To see if I'm a horny drunk."

Saint curved his hand around her hips and kissed her neck, which she curled into. The drink appeared on the bar, and she was set to continue the night without thinking of the release of her ex. All thoughts would be set on Saint.

Chapter 13

It was confirmed. Bailey was a horny drunk, and he wasn't immune to her advances. For the first time in his life, Saint made out with a woman at the bar. He didn't have much restraint when it came to Bailey. She was definitely his weakness, and she seemed to be playing on it. He'd never shy away from her hands. When she melted into his chest and took his lips for a heated kiss, he'd been caught off guard.

He was seated at the bar with Bailey standing between his legs. Her hands curled over his neck, and her tongue swirled around his sending his cock into full erection. Just a fucking kiss and he was hard. His hand wrapped over around her waist, tightening his hold and keeping her close.

The party was pretty lively, but he didn't doubt they had eyes on them. This was not only a first for him, but a first his brothers were witnessing. Her lips angled over his mouth, deepening the kiss before pulling away slightly, grazing her teeth on his bottom lip. His hand tightened on her waist, digging his fingers into her flesh.

"No fucking at the bar, Saint."

She froze in his arms and pulled away, staring at him with

wide eyes. He glanced over her shoulder, knowing exactly who made the comment.

"Been waiting my whole fucking life to say that to you." Kase laughed and settled into the seat next to him. Bailey stepped away a foot before Saint pulled her into his chest. If she was going to hang out at the club, she would have to get used to it.

"Always the dick, Kase," Saint said, grabbing his beer with one hand and caressing her waist with the other.

Kase smirked and raised his brow. "You sound like Cade, asshole."

"Wanna another, pretty girl?" Nadia said.

Saint was shaking his head when Bailey answered, "Yes, please."

With Bailey's back to him, he mouthed to Nadia. *Last one*. He was slyly cutting her off much to the humor of Nadia, who was more than happy to see Bailey drunk and extremely friendly.

"Come on back here, Bailey."

Saint smiled, watching Bailey rush around him and Kase, heading behind the bar. He kept a close eye on her, seeing how friendly Nadia was getting. Watching them, he quickly realized, there was nothing sexual on either end. Bailey was sweet and friendly without judgment, and Nadia just enjoyed the friendship.

He watched as Nadia taught her how to make drinks and test them out on Gage. Nothing funnier than watching his brother taste Bailey's special concoction. The night couldn't have gone any better with Bailey letting her guard down, and Saint surrounded by his brothers.

"Our mayor is fucked up," Kase said, taking a drag from his cigarette.

Saint snorted with a nod.

"She's a good one, Saint. Fucking happy for ya, man." He sipped his beer. "Brothers are taking bets when we'll be throwing another fucking wedding here. I'm down for next month."

Saint turned. Kase was watching Bailey with a small smile playing on his lips. Of all the brothers, they were the closest having the most history together. A lot of people discounted Kase as a dick. For those who knew the true Kase Reilly, the side he didn't show many, Kase was a good man.

Bailey sauntered over, and he caught Kase watch as she made her way over. His scowl did nothing to discourage his closest brother. Kase side-eyed him. "She's sexy as hell. I'm fucking human, Saint. I'm gonna appreciate that shit."

Bailey slapped her hands on the bar. "I can make…" She paused. "A beer and a shot. It's all I got."

Kase burst out laughing, and Saint followed suit.

"Time to take you home, sweetheart," Saint said.

She raised her brows with a teasing smirk. "Oh yeah? Better make it worth my while, Saint."

Kase snorted, and Saint shook his head. Drunk Bailey was a bit sassy and wild. He couldn't wait to get her in his bed. He lifted his chin.

"C'mon."

She turned to Nadia, giving her a hug, and then proceeded to the end of the bar. He was watching her until he felt a soft hand on his forearm. He glanced up to see Nadia leaning closer. "I love her, and if you don't bring her back here, I'll kill you." She winked and tapped his arm.

It was the consensus, Bailey fit right in at the clubhouse. She'd be back, but right now, the only place she belonged was in his bed.

He slapped Kase on the arm and met a stumbling Bailey at the edge of the bar. He curled his arms over her shoulder and leaned closer, whispering in her ear, "Horny drunk?"

She curled her arms around his waist and glanced up. "Take me home and find out."

SHE COULD BARELY KEEP her hands off him during the ride. She snaked her fingers over his neck, down to his abs, however when she reached for his cock, he stopped her.

"The people of Ghosttown don't need an accident tonight."

She chuckled and continued her mouth assault on his neck. When the truck finally stopped, it took her a second to get her bearings. This was not her house. She glanced over the manicured lawn, and the cute cape tucked amongst the sprawling trees. She jerked her head to the driver's side.

"This is your house?"

Saint smiled, grasping her neck and taking her in for a kiss. She moved closer and tangled her legs over his thigh. He had only a few neighbors. Her inebriated mind wasn't thinking straight. Luckily, Saint was stone-cold sober. He nudged her back into her seat and got out of the truck. Her head felt light, and she rested back until the door came open with a welcomed cool breeze. She turned her head.

Saint squinted. "You about to pass out?"

She shook her head, shifting out of the truck and into his waiting arms. Instead of walking her into his house, he bent down, hooking one arm around her waist and the other under her knees. He stalked forward as she curled her arms over his shoulders.

She only caught a quick glimpse of his front entry and his living room. He took the stairs quickly and darted into a room on the left. She was dropped onto a soft mattress. She turned her head, taking in the scent of the sheets. Pine and fire, it was Saint's scent.

His hand gripped the edge of her skirt, hiking it up to her waist, and she felt the cool air drift over her pussy when he ripped her panties down her legs. There was no warning or prelude. He dropped to his knees, and his head disappeared between her legs. *Oh my God.* She jackknifed on the bed the second his lips grazed over her pussy.

"Saint." She gasped, driving her hand into his hair. Her eyes rolled into the back of her head.

Her head pressed down against the pillow as his fingers gripped her thighs in a binding hold, keeping her from wiggling away. Maybe it was the alcohol and her loss of inhibitions? Whatever it was, Bailey found herself grinding her hips against his mouth. The sensation and building pressure from his tongue flickering over her clit was too much and not enough. She gripped the short strands of his hair and tightened her fist.

"Feels too good, Saint." She moaned, arching her back, giving him better access. His mouth moved over her pussy, stroking her sensitive bead in a steady rhythm and sending a shiver through her entire body. The direct hit intensified, everything she was feeling. She ground her teeth, pressing her tongue against the roof of her mouth in hopes she'd control her urge to scream out his name.

"Right there." Her breath hitched, and she swiveled her hips against his mouth. Oh God, this man. *Had it always felt this good?* She released his hair and fisted the sheets between her fingers. It had been too long. Her vibrator had been an inadequate Plan B to the real thing. Until Saint. She clenched her jaw. *Right there.* His tongue caressed her clit, and she moaned, feeling the tremor course through her body in the most magnificent relief. *Yes!* Her knees clamped, and she gasped for a breath. Her body shivered, and her toes curled. *Yes!* It had been way too long. She panted heavily and closed her eyes, relaxing into his mattress. Her breath labored as her exhaustion set in.

She was mildly aware of the small kisses he planted on her inner thigh and stomach. She curled her lips and kept her eyes closed. She could envision him as his mouth spread over her breasts. His lips trailed up her neck, and she blindly curled her arms over his shoulders.

"I love you," she whispered.

His chest rumbled against her. His breath fanned her neck. "Is that the alcohol talking?"

She blinked her eyes open and turned her head, catching his gaze. "No. I really do love you, Saint."

His violet eyes darkened. He moved closer, taking her mouth for a hungry kiss. She could barely catch her breath, though she didn't care. All she wanted was him, his mouth, his touch, just Saint. He kissed her lips, trailing down her neck. He cupped her jaw and raised his gaze.

"Love you, too, Bailey."

Her heart pounded in her chest. *He loves me too.* She leaned closer, taking his lips and angling her legs to lock his hips against her. She wasn't thinking straight or responsibly. She just wanted him as close as possible. He pulled away, and she grasped his shoulders. Where was he going?

He reached across the bed, opening the drawer. At least one of them was being smart. She watched as he pulled back and put on the condom.

"No babies," she whispered with a smile.

His gaze flickered, and the corner of his mouth curled. He leaned over her.

"Not tonight." His chest rubbed against her breasts, tightening her nipples to sharp peaks. She was ready for orgasm number two. His mouth lowered to her ear. "I'm not ready to share you, just yet. But someday…" His voice trailed.

Someday. She pressed her face into the crook of neck. *Yes, someday.*

She felt the crown of his cock, nudge against her core. She grabbed his neck, digging the pads of her fingers into his skin.

Being this close and connected, only intensified her need. He sank inside her, and his low grunt sounded in her ear.

"Saint," she whispered.

His head stretched back, and the strained cords of his neck was all she saw. He moved slowly and methodically. Her internal walls gripped him, and he groaned. He was a vision. She stared up at him with his eyes hooded. She needed to see him, really see him in full view.

She hooked her foot around his ankle and pushed her weight against his body, sending him to curl onto his side. She heaved her body, keeping their connection, and climbed on top of him. Her fingers dug into his chest as she sat back over his cock.

His hands gripped her waist as she moved over him. She rode him slowly, loving the softs grunts he was emitting. His pleasure, it was all she wanted, though she was getting plenty on her end. She sank lower on his cock, taking him deeper into her body. She tightened her grip, digging into his chest.

"God, you feel so good." His words were hushed. She fell against his chest, and his hand splayed over her hips, down to her ass. This was different from any other experience he'd had. Maybe it was Saint. Maybe it was her. Most likely, it was *them*. Never in her life had she felt a closeness and bond like the one she felt with him. *Just us.* She gasped at the onset of her orgasm. Her mouth dropped to his neck, as he thrust inside her.

"There, Saint, right there," she whispered. He moaned, arching his back, just as he came.

Her erratic breath fanned over his neck, and his hands grazed over her ass, gliding up to her hips.

She released all her weight onto him and curled closer. She wasn't sure how long they lay together. She closed her eyes. She was completely done. *Perfectly spent.*

"God, I love you." His graveled voice rumbled in her ear.

"Is that the orgasm talking?" She giggled through her uneven breaths, and she felt his chest shake under her.

Saint grasped her hips and turned to his side, releasing her. She curled her hand under her chin and watched him get out of the bed and walk into the bathroom. She was enjoying the view of his sculpted body. The light flickered on, and she waited. She'd gotten her second wind. She should have been on the verge of passing out. Instead, she sat up and watched the door. When he emerged, she smiled. He came forward with his brow arched. *I love when he does that.* He dropped to the bed and pulled her into his chest.

"Let's eat snacks."

He furrowed his brows. "What?"

She wiggled out of his hold and sat back on her heels, staring at him, enjoying the heat lingering in his stare. She twisted her lips in a playful smirk. "I think we need to refuel."

His lips curled into a sexy half-smile. It took Saint longer to get out of bed than her. She drifted down the stairs giving her a peek at his place. She knew he'd gutted the old small home and rebuilt it, but never actually saw it once it was done. It was tastefully redone with new wood floors and a brand new fireplace. It wasn't huge, only slightly bigger than hers. When she moved to Ghosttown years back, she'd actually looked at the house. It needed too much work, so she passed on the deal.

She walked through the kitchen and stopped in the doorway. It was dim with only the counter lights on. *Holy shit!* It had obviously been completely remodeled, and while the house didn't seem overly extravagant, he'd paid special attention and a lot of cash on this room. The cabinets and countertop had been replaced, along with the appliances.

She was so caught up with looking at the kitchen that she hadn't realized he'd come downstairs until his arms wrapped around her waist. His lips grazed her temple. She curled into him, clasping his hands over her stomach. She glanced up to find him staring at her.

"I love your house."

"Good. You'll be spending a lot of time here. You should like it." He moved forward, forcing her to walk ahead of him with his hands remaining around her waist. On the opposite side of the room, next to the doorway to the mudroom, was another door. He stopped a foot away and reached past her, gripping the knob and pulling it open.

She gasped when the mystery door opened up to a fully stocked pantry. She scanned the shelves, filled with every snack imaginable, some healthy, some not.

"This is my childhood dream pantry. My mom was delusional and considered fruits and veggies a snack."

"I have those too. But I'm thinking you're not interested."

She shook her head.

He chuckled and released her. "Have at it."

She grabbed a bag of chips and a container of pistachio nuts.

"Beer, wine, soda, water, or juice?" Saint asked, and she turned to find him at the fridge.

"Water, please." She walked over. "We should just stay here all weekend and eat all your snacks and have sex."

He slowly cocked his head with a sexy smirk playing on his lips.

"Yeah?" He drew in a breath. "How about next weekend? I got Cia coming tomorrow."

"Oh right." She nodded. "I'll get outta here early then."

Saint's jaw squared. She'd seen the look before though never directed at her. He was leaning up against his counter with his hands clenched, gripping the edge. His whole body tightened, and his scowl intensified. Before she could ask what was wrong, he spoke.

"She asked if she could meet you this weekend, Bailey." His eyes darkened.

Her bottom lip trembled. Her face heated, and she flattened her lips. *His daughter is asking to meet me?* This added a whole new level of guilt.

"My daughter is everything, sweetheart."

She blinked in confusion. Did he think she didn't know that? "I know."

He jerked his chin to her and narrowed his gaze. "So are you."

She clamped her lips and stared back at him. She knew where this was going. If they were both important, he'd want them to all spend time together. It made sense, and there was a part of her that desperately wanted what Saint was offering. Meeting his daughter meant he saw a future with her. His admission alone was self-explanatory. She glanced down at the floor, fidgeting with her hands.

"Need those worlds to collide."

She sighed. "It's just too…"

Saint cut her off with a low firm answer. "No. It's not too soon." She expected him to make his way over to her. Instead, he remained across the room. "You keep stalling on something I need to happen. What are you afraid of?"

She jerked her gaze and knitted her brows. "I'm not afraid." *Liar.* She wasn't merely afraid. She was petrified.

"Bailey." He sighed. "You can't tell me…I can't help you."

Her shoulders sagged, and she rested against the wall. It was time to come clean. If she didn't, she was running the risk of losing him. She couldn't fault him either. "Is this a deal-breaker?"

He raised his brows and smirked. "Meeting Cia?"

She nodded.

"Well, considering I wanna spend the rest of my life with you, then yeah, it's imperative you meet her."

"No, I know eventually." She licked her lips and shrugged. "I'm not ready yet."

"Okay." He nodded. "Why?"

"Because…" She clamped her lips and let her gaze wander around the room, avoiding his stare.

Saint snickered. "That's your answer?"

Skating around her own insecurities was not working. Saint wasn't allowing it. If she wanted him to fully understand, she'd have to be honest. "What if she asks about my scars?"

All the humor faded from his features, and his lips leveled. "Then we tell her."

What? Her stomach plummeted, and her nostrils flared. She could actually feel the blood drain from her face. Tell his nine-year-old daughter what happened to her? Was he insane? Just the thought of giving anyone except those closest to her the background of her scars left her with a pit in her stomach. She'd gotten better with it over the years, but telling Cia was out of the question.

"No." Bailey snapped with an octave high enough to break glass. Her blurted response even shocked her.

Saint shifted forward.

She dropped the bags of chips on the table and backed away from him. "I'm not explaining to your nine-year-old daughter that some bastard poured acid on me because." Her heart raced in her chest. She was losing her breath in a wild panic. "I don't even know why." She screamed. Her body began to shake uncontrollably. She sidestepped his approach. "He wouldn't say it, Saint. He wouldn't even tell *me* what I did to deserve it," she screeched, which had Saint halt mid-step. She wiped her cheeks, only realizing now she'd started to cry. Her head felt so heavy on her shoulders with a blasting throb. "I need to go." She darted toward the doorway. She only got a few feet before Saint wrapped his arms around her body, pressing his chest into her back.

She'd never broken down in front of anyone. Not like this. She'd had her share of low moments, cried herself to sleep, asked herself "why me," and she'd done it alone. She purposely showed a brave face for everyone, even her family. *Especially my family.* She sobbed and remained in his arms where he held on tight, brushing his lips against her head.

"Saint, I'm so…"

"Shhhh…" He lifted her and carried her to his couch, setting her down before taking a seat next to her. "Need you to tell me what's going on in here." His finger lightly grazed over her temple, slipping her hair behind her ear. "Tell me what happened?"

She closed her eyes. She knew it was only a matter of time before he asked. She had a bit of blind hope she'd have more time. She was aware he knew about the incident. Small towns held no secrets. Him knowing wasn't the issue; it was the details he was seeking that bothered her. *I don't want to give him them.*

"Please."

She wiped her cheeks and tilted her head. "You already know, according to Kase."

Saint stared back at her, not answering immediately.

"I want to hear it from you."

Bailey tucked her feet under her butt and settled into the couch. The last topic she wanted to discuss with him was the incident. She had spent a lot of time in therapy working it all out, getting past it, or so she thought. Her relationship with Saint was bringing it back to the surface again.

Reliving it with him would set her back. He'd see her differently—no matter how hard he tried, he'd see her as a victim, and then he'd feel pity. There lay the truth. She wanted a normal relationship, not one with sympathy. Saint reached back and pulled down the blanket. When he opened it up, she thought he'd spread it across his own lap, but Saint draped it over her.

She drew in a breath and lowered her head to the cushion, staring at Saint. He remained silent. She knew he was waiting on her to speak. *To share.*

"I don't want you to feel sorry for me."

She was falling hard and fast. *I don't want to lose this.*

He nodded. "Tell me what you *do* want."

"I want us to be Bailey and Saint. I wanna go to inappropriate biker parties, drink too many margaritas, and come back your house." She curled her lips. "I want to raid your snack shack, sleep in your bed, and wake up with you wrapped around me." She felt a giddy bubble in her chest. She needed the mood to lighten. "I wanna hear you moan my name when you're inside me, and I want you to make me come while I'm screaming out yours." She smirked. "I really want that."

His finger grazed over her cheek and under her chin. "You have it, sweetheart."

Her smile faltered. "And I want to keep it."

"And telling me will change us?"

Yes.

"You'll look at me differently, Saint. I've seen pity in the eyes of everyone I know." She bowed her head and lowered her voice to a whisper. "I don't want to see it coming from you."

He reached over, clasping his hand on her leg and pulling her over his lap. She went willingly and untangled her legs from the blanket to straddle his hips. He drove his hands into the back of her hair and pulled her lips down to meet his.

"Nothing you tell me will ever change how I see you, Bailey."

She shook her head. "You say that…"

"No," he snapped. "I'll say it again, nothing you ever tell me will change how I see you." He grasped her hips and pulled her down over his chest. "I'm a selfish bastard. I want to know everything when it comes to you. I want all of you." He kissed her lips and angled her head. His tongue slipped past her lips, and her breasts jutted forward grazing his chest. It was the perfect distraction. Then it ended, and he pulled away from the kiss.

"You won't get pity from me, Bailey. All you'll get is love and respect and admiration of your strength. Never pity." He curled his hand around her jaw. "You told a room full of strangers, but you won't share with me?"

A room full of strangers? It took her a second. Her brows arched then her lower lip pouted. "Caden needs a lesson in confidentiality."

Saint smirked. "He did it because he wanted you safe."

Bailey climbed off his lap and sat next to him. She sagged in her seat. "It was different. At the meeting, we're all victims turned survivors. Everyone is on the same level." She turned her head. "I don't wanna be that to you."

"You won't."

There was no way around it. She sighed. She was resigned to telling him. Quick and fast, without diving into too much detail. She would tell it as if she was relaying how it happened to someone else and keep her emotions out of it.

She kept her gaze in front of her. "I met him in college. My first real boyfriend, I guess you could say. He was an upperclassman, and I was a freshman." She snorted. "My brother actually introduced us. So, you can imagine the guilt he harbors. I swear he could barely look at me after it happened." She stretched her neck and refused to look at Saint. "We dated for a year before getting an apartment off campus. I was just so in love with him." She sighed and sank into the couch, whispering, "I thought I was." Her first true love became her biggest nightmare. "I missed all the signs I should have seen. I just couldn't see it." She shook her head trying to stay on track. "It wasn't until after the incident I could finally see what was happening. He wanted me to spend all my time with him." She paused and fidgeted with her finger. "There were little things he would freak out about." She shrugged. "So, I just tried harder, ya know, to not do those things which would set him off. He never hit me. A little intentional shove now and then. I just let it go." She shook her head. *Why did I let it go?*

Saint spread his hand over her scarred arm. "What happened?"

She drew in a breath. "I went out with my study group." She laughed without humor. "Literally, we spent hours in the library working on a project. Then someone suggested we grab dinner. I was hungry, so I went. I texted, letting him know. Never got a response. By the time I got home, I knew he was there because I saw his car in the lot. But when I walked in, he wasn't around. Even after I announced I was home, I didn't get a response. I figured he was in the shower. So, I set up my computer at the little table we had in the kitchen. I needed to finish up a paper due the next day." She pursed her lips.

"I never even saw it coming, Saint" Her eyes teared, and she cupped her mouth. "One minute, I'm typing, and the next my skin is burning like it's on fire. I didn't even know what was happening. There was just pain, this horrible burn, so bad my vision went blurry, and I just started screaming and then choking, I couldn't breathe." She sniffled and wiped her cheek with her sleeve. "It's impossible to describe."

"Did you see him?"

She shook her head. "I didn't see anything. It was all black. I was consumed with the pain. God, it was…" She stopped. It had been so long since she'd really allowed herself to fully go back to the moment. Even with the group when she spoke, she hadn't dug as deep as she was now. For Saint.

She closed her eyes against her dampening lashes. "Apparently, I passed out. The doctor said the shock to the body forced unconsciousness." She snorted. "Thank God." She sniffled and wiped her face. "It didn't end there. Even hyped on as many drugs as my body would allow, there was still pain. It was constant, I didn't even have to move, and I felt it." She cringed in the memory. "I would be laying in my bed, and the breeze from someone opening the door would filter over my skin." The tears streamed down her cheeks. "It was tingling burn. God, it was awful."

"I'm sorry, Bailey."

She turned to Saint. "I wouldn't wish that pain on anyone." Her lips trembled. "Not even *him*, Saint."

His jaw clenched, and his fingers skimmed her cheeks, wiping away her tears. "It's not your fault. You did nothing to deserve it."

She sighed and forced a smile. "I know. It took a while, but I do know now. It wasn't my fault. And I learned a long time ago, if I was ever going to get past it and move on, I couldn't go back to the what-ifs. So, I don't. Usually." She sniffled. "Every once in a while." She choked on her breath. "I just wish I could have seen the signs. Or at least have some reasoning why." She sniffled and lowered her voice. "He never said why he did it, just that he was sorry."

He cupped her jaw with his hand. It may not have seemed like much to him but for her, at this moment? It was everything. She curled her face into his palm. For as hard as it was to relive the memory, this made it easier.

"You hear from him?"

"Yeah. The first letter came right after he was sentenced." She shrugged. "It was an apology." She snorted and wiped her sleeve against her eyes. "He writes at least once a month."

"Do you read them?"

She nodded. "Every single one."

"You ever write him back?"

She shook her head avoiding his stare. "No. His apology was more for him than it was for me." She bowed her head, staring at her lap. "I used to read them, two or three times. I was searching for the *why* in what happened." She glanced up. "It took a long time to realize, I'm never going to get an explanation." She shrugged. "I had to forgive him and move on."

His thumb strummed along her jaw. "You nervous about him getting out?"

She sighed.

"Bailey."

She picked at a string on her pants. "I got the call when we were at the clubhouse. He was released today."

"Why didn't you tell me?"

She glanced over. His body was tense and his jaw clenched as though he was grinding his teeth. It had been a long time since she'd been in a relationship, she was rusty. She should have mentioned it. She shrugged. "We were having such a good time." She smiled sadly. "I just wanted to be Bailey and Saint," she whispered, hoping he'd understand.

The corners of his mouth curled and his gaze softened.

She inched closer, leaning against his chest. "I just wanna leave it in the past." She gulped. "This, with you and me, this is what I want."

"Just us, sweetheart," he whispered.

Chapter 14

This is not what I need right now.

She had stopped into the diner to grab a dessert before heading to Saint's house.

Big mistake.

Bailey stood on Main Street, trying her best to be attentive to the older man. This was one of many heated interactions she'd had with him. Of course, the heat was always on his end. He babbled on, but she could barely concentrate. If she didn't leave soon, she'd be late getting to Saint's. She was meeting his brother and wanted desperately to get there on time. The odds were not in her favor. At this rate, Arnett would still be complaining a few days from now.

"If you can't handle the responsibility of the town, then maybe you should step down."

Oh, you would love that, wouldn't you, grumpy old man?

Bailey drew in a deep breath and forced her smile. It was all part of the job. This being the harder part.

"Mr. Collins, these are all issues which need to be presented to the town, not just me." She smiled, resisting the urge to stick her tongue out at him.

"Oh, I will. I got a lot of topics I need to bring to the table. Have you seen the goddamn traffic around here?"

Bailey tightened her lips. If by traffic he meant the ten extra cars on the road, then yes, she'd seen it, and couldn't be happier. More cars meant more people visiting their small town and the shops which had opened up. More importantly, it meant more revenue for the town, which should have made all the residents happy. The idea was lost on Arnett.

"We do need to stick to our agenda, so please send me an email with your concerns, and we'll address them."

"I don't have goddamn email." He threw out his hand, and the papers smacked against her face. "Take them," he barked.

Bailey gasped and retreated a step. She had always dealt with Arnett with complete control and calmness. He was the type of person who fed off getting a reaction from confrontation. With Bailey, she took the high road. Not this time. She rolled her shoulders and straightened her back. She was fully prepared to go up against him in the center of Main Street. *Enough was enough.*

She opened her mouth, finally prepared to stand up to Arnett.

"Problem?"

It wasn't the intrusion which had her angling her head around Arnett's large frame, it was the sinister growl which followed. She leaned to her right and saw a biker, tall with long brown hair tied back at his neck. She hadn't seen him before at the clubhouse and didn't recognize him as a Ghosttown Rider. *Though his eyes are eerily familiar.*

Arnett followed her lead and turned around, stepping back when he saw who interrupted his vent fest on Bailey.

The biker raised his brows. "Don't have all fucking day, man. Ya got a problem with her?"

Bailey's eyes widened. Who was this man?

"We were having a private conversation," Arnett barked, but she noticed he took a step back.

The biker stared at him. "Conversation is when more than one person talks. Didn't hear shit coming from her lips as you were ripping her apart for all of fucking Main Street to hear." He cracked his neck, sending a chill down Bailey's spine. "So, let me ask again, you got a fucking problem?"

Back down, Arnett, back down.

"Yes, I have a problem which has nothing to do with you."

She darted her eyes between the men.

He snorted. "If it has to do with *her*, then it's my problem too."

Bailey jerked her head and squinted, taking a better look at him. She would have remembered meeting him or at the very least seeing him at the clubhouse. *Who the hell was he?*

"And you are?"

"The man who's gonna beat the piss outta you, you ever yell at her again."

Bailey gasped. The biker, clearly fed up with Arnett, stepped closer. He wasn't much taller than Arnett, probably about six-two, but his muscular build would surely send the old man to the hospital. *Or the morgue.* She moved forward, placing her body between the men.

"I'm fine. Mr. Collins was just upset, and well, as mayor, it's my job."

"Your job is to have this guy shred you in front of the whole fucking town ''cause he's bitching like a pussy about property markers?" The man laughed and then his jaw tightened. He shook his head, and said, "No."

"I thought you were with the other one?"

Bailey jerked her head to Arnett, whose scowl was so deep she wasn't sure the lines in his forehead would ever ease.

"Excuse me?"

"The biker you been hanging around with, the one who comes to the meetings, sits in the back, doesn't say anything."

It was an accurate assessment. "Saint?"

He mockingly widened his eyes. "Any other biker fit that description? You got more than one suitor?" His comment was snarky, and his tone biting.

"Watch it, old man. I'm seconds away from grabbing my gun and pistol-whipping your ass for the whole fucking town to see."

Oh my God.

Arnett backed down, cowered away, and turned leaving altogether without another word. Now, she was left with the hostile biker.

The man peered down at her with humor in his eyes. What was she supposed to do now? She drew in a breath.

"I have to go." She turned, rushing to her car. She heard the steel-toed boots crunching under the gravel and she whipped around to face him. "Please don't follow me."

The corner of his mouth curled. "I scare ya?"

Yes! She grabbed her keys from her purse, angling one key between her fingers. It wasn't much of a weapon, but it was something. She squeezed the ring in her hand and steadied her stance.

"Please, leave me alone." Her breath hitched when he didn't back away, and she blurted. "My boyfriend is scarier than you, and unless you want to find out, I'd back up." The words slipped past her lips before she even realized what was happening.

The comment seemed to surprise him, and he snickered. His chin lifted, and she caught the teasing glow in his eyes.

"You think your boyfriend can take me?"

Oh my God, what am I doing? She was using Saint as a weapon. Her face heated. The damage was done. *Just go with it.* Hopefully, he'd back off if she showed confidence.

"I know he can so for your own safety, back up."

The comment only infused his laugh. *That backfired.*

"I'm serious."

"Don't doubt ya are, babe."

"Well, ya better go then before I call him."

He stopped and smiled, clearly still amused and reached in his pocket, grabbing his phone and dialing, then he brought it up to his ear with his eyes trained on Bailey.

"Got your girl here. Old man was fucking with her, stepped in, and now…" He smirked and extended the phone in her direction. "Wants you."

Bailey furrowed her brows and took the phone stepping away from the biker.

"Saint?"

"You okay?" It was his voice riddled with concern. "What happened?"

"Uh…" She eyed the biker who crossed his arms and stared back at her. His lips were flat, and if she had to guess he was holding back a smile. "Mr. Collins."

"I think it's time I had a talk with him."

"No, Saint, I'm mayor, it's my job to listen to complaints, I told you this."

"Listen, yes. Not get yelled at and ridiculed, that shit is not acceptable, Bailey."

She sighed and dragged her hand through her hair. "Well, it's over." She bowed her head and lowered her voice. "Is this guy a member of your club?"

"Hades?"

She glanced up. "If that's the big scary biker standing in front of me who seems quite amused, then yes."

Saint chuckled. "You just set his ego meter full throttle. The little prick gets off on scaring the shit outta people. Christ, been that way since we were kids."

"Kids?"

"Yeah. Hades is my little brother."

"What?" She widened her eyes. "Roman?"

Hades grinned with a slow nod.

"You look nothing alike." While they may have shared the same height, their build was different. Saint was muscular and lean. Hades was bulkier. His lighter hair was a contrast to Saint's dark. As she stared back at his brother, who was thoroughly amused, she saw the resemblance. It was hard to believe she missed it. Her lips curled beyond her control. "You have the same eyes."

Hades winked, and she averted her stare to the ground. *Don't look at him.*

"You on your way here?"

"Be there in five." She quickly gave Hades his phone, ignoring his amused gaze and spun around, making her to way to her car. This man was his brother? Saint had mentioned him once or twice. He'd left out the biker part. It shouldn't have come as a surprise.

She was at her driver's side door when she heard the crunching of the gravel, and she jerked her head over her shoulder. Hades stopped a few feet away, a smile playing on his lips. Saint was right. This man definitely got off on other people's nervousness. She straightened her shoulders.

The corner of his mouth curled. "No need to be scared, Bailey. I mean, we're practically family now."

"I'm not scared of you." She would have sounded more convincing without the hitch in her voice. A detail Hades noticed. His lips tightened, holding back what she assumed was a laugh.

"No?" He knitted his brows. "Not even a little."

"I have to go."

"Don't wanna get to know Saint's brother, huh?"

Oh hell, this was not going well.

"Okay, you scare me," she blurted, and immediately regretted it.

He chuckled. "I scare most people." He licked his lips and folded his arms. "And for most of them, it's with good reason."

Her hands trembled, and she reached out to clasp the door. The likelihood he would hurt her was slim to none. After all, she was with Saint and he was his brother.

"You really think I'd hurt you?" He raised his brows.

Did she? She shook her head.

"Like I said, Bailey, you and me are practically family. And no one fucks with my family." He slowly cocked his brow, and his stare turned sinister. "Ever."

She gulped. "Well, thanks."

He grinned. "Anytime." He walked away, and she watched as he mounted his bike. "I'll see you in a few."

SAINT HAD SPENT the last fifteen minutes listening to Bailey explain the confrontation on Main Street. She noticeably left out the part where Arnett was yelling at her and chose to focus on his brother aggressively coming at the old man.

"How Arnett didn't pee in his pants?" She shook her head and spread out her arms while shrugging. "I don't know. My heart was racing the whole time." She sighed.

He could imagine the interaction as he'd seen his brother go head to head with more men then he could count. Even when his opponent had a definite edge up on Hades, the bastard never backed down. He'd been that way forever. As kids, he got his ass kicked more often than not. That was when Saint would step in. If it was a fair fight, he'd let it be. *Sometimes you win, sometimes you don't.* But a few times, Hades unknowingly had been taken on by more than one boy. Saint had no problem explaining to those boys their mistake. With his fists.

Though once Hades hit his teens and well into adulthood, there weren't many losses under his belt.

"You're fine now?" Saint asked.

She nodded and sat in the chair at his kitchen table. She cocked her head to the side and stared. He was learning her small quirks and what they meant. She had something on her mind, most likely a question. Knowing Bailey, she was coming up with the right angle in her head.

"Just ask, sweetheart."

She glanced up through her lashes with a small smile playing on her lips. Her amusement had him intrigued.

"Do you think he really would have," she lifted her fingers, motioning air quotes, "beat the piss outta Arnett? And pistol-whipped his ass?"

Saint snorted. There wasn't a doubt in his mind Hades would have done exactly what he claimed. Too many people were eager to throw out idle threats. Hades was not one of them. If he was giving a warning, it was smart to heed to it. He folded his arms prepared to answer her honestly until he was interrupted.

Another trait his brother was known for was being abnormally quiet. Hades stood at the doorway with his shit-eating grin on display, leaving no doubt he'd heard Bailey's inquiry.

The short feminine gasp had Saint turning toward her. Hades sudden appearance had caught her off guard.

"Fuck yeah," he smiled, staring down at Bailey, "would be the answer."

Saint watched as her lips flattened, and she nodded her head. "Good to know."

Hades walked over to Saint, pulling him in for a hug, which he returned. It had been a few months since they'd crossed paths. Being in Ghosttown would put them geographically closer. It was good. For him, for them, for the family.

"Good to see you, man." He slapped Saint's back before stepping back. "Been too long."

"I'm closer now."

Hades nodded. "Yeah." He turned and walked over to the table, taking a seat across from Bailey. "Mayor, huh?"

"Yep."

He eyed her and took a sip of the beer Saint placed in front of him. He licked his lips and pointed the neck of the bottle at her. "You're too nice." Saint remained silent but internally agreed with his brother's assessment.

Bailey smiled with a soft chuckle. "So I've been told." She shifted in her seat. "He's old and a bit grumpy, but he's harmless."

"Don't like how he was talking to ya."

Bailey widened her eyes and turned to Saint. He walked over, sat next to Bailey, and stretched out his legs. "I don't like it either."

"Saint," she whispered.

Hades laughed and leaned his elbows on the table. "Aw, brother, this one is trouble."

Yes, she was. The best kind.

"I'm not trouble." Bailey furrowed her brows.

Hades snorted. "Fuck yeah, you are. You're gonna own this asshole, with the soft voice and your pretty, sweet face."

Hades called it, a little too late. She already owned him. Saint grabbed her hand resting on his leg and took a swig from his beer. He turned to Hades.

"What's going on?" Bailey had had enough for one day. It was time to turn the focus on his brother.

"Thinking about renting a place here."

"Yeah?" This was a first. It was hardly a place where he could envision his brother hanging out. However, the club would be a draw. Hades' club was about an hour away.

"Talk to Kase?"

"Not yet, figured you could get me the list. If they still got shit available."

"We do."

Bailey cleared her throat. "If you can't find anything, I can give you the number and contact for the McMillian property company."

Hades laughed and grabbed his beer. *Oh fuck me.*

"What? They own all the vacant land. I'm sure they'd have something for you."

Hades glanced up at Saint. "She doesn't know, does she?"

Saint sighed and turned his attention to Bailey who was staring at him with a confused stare. It hadn't been a secret since the club moved into Ghosttown. It also wasn't public knowledge. It was time to come clean, and he wasn't sure how she would take the news.

"The McMillian LLC? It's the club."

Her eyes widened.

"We've been buying up the property for the past few years under an LLC. Ghosttown Riders own three-quarters of the town."

Her jaw dropped, and her gaze skittered back and forth between him and Hades. "Why?"

He shrugged. "We wanted to make sure we had control."

Her back tensed and her eyes went wild. She was misunderstanding what he was saying. He tightened his grip on her hand. He needed to explain himself.

"We wanted a place to settle down. For the club. A safe place where the members and their families could plant roots. If we purchased all the land, we could control an outlaw element coming to the town. We have plans for it, Bailey. All good things." He leaned closer. "Got no intention of driving anyone out."

She nodded. He assumed there would be a lengthier discussion in their future. It was fine. He'd share everything.

"Except that old fucking asshole." Hades piped in. Even Saint had to agree. Arnett Collins would not be missed.

Bailey snorted. "Good luck. Even an assault couldn't scare him away."

"What?" Saint snapped. Assault? What the hell was she talking about?

He saw the slight panic in her face, and her cheeks flushed. She shook her head. "Nothing." She was back peddling. An assault? Saint opened his mouth, and Bailey lifted her hand.

"Don't ask, I'm not talking about it. All I'll say is," she glanced at the table and mumbled, "Arnett had it coming."

"Bailey." Saint wasn't ready to let it go, but she was. She darted her eyes around the room with a small shake of her head.

He tightened his grip on her hand. "If your safety is involved, I need to know."

She burst out laughing. "Then you definitely don't need to know, Saint. I'm in no danger, not even a smidge."

Hades chuckled. "Smidge?" He grabbed his bottle. "Too nice and too cute, Saint. She's fucking trouble."

Bailey rolled her eyes. "So, back to the properties. If the club owns everything…." She turned to Saint. "Then who is McMillian?"

His lips slowly curled into a smile. "Meg."

Her eyes turned the size of saucers. "What?"

"Meg McMillian, it's her maiden name. Needed someone we could trust."

She squinted her eyes and curled her lips. "Very smart."

"Yes."

Bailey asked a few more questions, which he openly answered. He wasn't trying to keep it from her. This was the first time since they'd been together it had been brought up. He trusted Bailey to keep the information to herself. He knew she would. Once the properties had been purchased, the secrecy wasn't necessary. As a club, they voted to remain silent. They didn't want the town to get the wrong impression of them coming in and trying to take over. It was never their intention.

The next few hours went more smoothly than he expected. It seemed Hades had taken an instant liking to Bailey. It shouldn't have surprised him. His brother just wanted the best for him, and vice-versa, though settling down wasn't on Hades' mind anytime soon. *Or is it?* His interest in taking up residency in Ghosttown had Saint wondering. It would be a discussion for another time. Right now, he was enjoying his brother and his woman sharing the same space.

Bailey wasn't completely comfortable, he noticed, though she tried. Hades had a presence which could be construed as overpowering. After dinner, they continued drinking and sat around the table. It had been forever since they'd done this as brothers. Saint missed it.

Their lives had taken them in different directions of sorts. While Saint couldn't wait to be rid of the illegal element, Hades thrived in it. Something had changed recently, though. He didn't know what, as Hades refused to share. There was definitely something happening that had Hades wanting distance from his own club. They were due for a talk. Now, was not the time, not in Bailey's presence.

He settled back into his chair and smiled as Bailey grilled him about Ghosttown East, the charter where Hades served as VP.

"Same club, different charter." Hades sipped his beer and settled in the chair across from her. "When we split ways years back, Saint went one way, and I went the other."

"That's good, right?" Bailey asked, peering between the two men. "Then you don't have to duke it out for who gets to be VP."

He glanced over at Hades, who had a similar reaction. Of course, Saint merely smiled while Hades snickered.

"Did she just say duke it out?"

Saint lifted his brow in amusement. *So cute.*

Hades smirked and turned to Bailey. "I think you're confusing us with a gang, babe."

Her cheeks turned a sweet shade of pink.

"It's a vote, sweetheart. Both of us were voted in by the club for the position. No fistfights," Saint explained.

"Well, that's good, right?"

Saint smiled.

"So, Bailey, if we had to *duke it out*? Who do you think would win?" Hades was teasing her.

Saint watched as Bailey twisted her lips in thought. She nailed Hades with her stare. "Saint."

That's my girl.

Hades scoffed. "You're biased."

Bailey laughed.

A warm rush heated his blood. He liked this scene. His brother and the woman he loved. He was exactly where he was meant to be.

They hung out together for the next hour before Bailey retreated into the living room while Saint grabbed another beer for himself. He grabbed the extra key off the hook and tossed it to Hades.

"This for tonight?"

Saint shrugged. "Keep it. You always got a place here. I'll reach out to Kase for the updated list of the properties."

Hades fisted the key in silence before he spoke. "I'm heading to the clubhouse now. I'll get it from him. Thanks, brother." Hades grabbed his cut and walked into the living room. When he veered right toward the couch, Saint moved to the doorway. Hades stopped in front of Bailey and held out his hand.

"Gimme your phone."

Her expression was adorably caught off guard, showing similar traits with a deer caught in headlights. Her bottom lip bobbed as though she was at a loss for words. He could have stepped in. Saint refrained. He knew exactly what Hades intentions were and wanted to watch the exchange. She would spend the rest of her life around his brother if he had it his way. She needed to grow accustomed to his abrupt attitude.

"What?" She sat up and straightened her back.

He cupped his hand, gesturing for her phone. "Give it to me."

Bailey slowly handed it to him and carefully watched. He knew Hades was putting in his number. He'd serve as a back-up for her if she ever needed something and couldn't get in touch with him. For as rough and dangerous as Hades was, family was his core, though he didn't let on to that little secret to any outsiders. He kept up a good front, but Saint knew him better than anyone. With Hades, his family came first, beyond anything else. And Bailey was family now.

Hades hit a button, and his own phone buzzed. He reached out, handing her phone back to her, which she took, watching him with suspicion.

"You got my number. Now I got yours. You ever need something, can't get ahold of Saint," he leaned closer, "you call me. Ya feel me?"

She tightened her lips with a slow nod. Then she glanced

down at her phone, and her brows knitted together. Saint watched as her lips curled and he heard a small giggle emit from her lips.

"Scary motherfucker?"

Hades laughed. "It fits, right?" He walked past her heading toward the door. He lifted his chin, smirking.

Saint smirked. *Welcome to the family, sweetheart.*

Chapter 15

He yawned, stretching his arms over his head. It had been a busy and exhausting weekend. After spending a few days with his brother and Bailey, his daughter arrived the following morning for his weekend with her. He'd made a point of making it an active two days. He was trying to make up for her disappointment when he explained she wouldn't be meeting Bailey this time. *Again.*

Saint heard the door creak from the counter at the kitchen. He glanced up at the stove catching the time. He should have had her pack up earlier, but they were too enthralled with binge-watching the zombie show. He sighed and waited for Tara.

"Hey." She sighed and slumped against the doorframe. Her hair was a mess and the bags under her eyes aged her a few years. She was still beautiful, always had been, but definitely in need of rest.

"How you feeling?"

She snorted. "Like I'm cooking up an alien with insomnia." She pushed off her shoulder and took a seat at the wooden table. "I hate the first trimester." She rested her clasped hands on her belly. "And I hate the bitches who say they love being pregnant." She curled her lip in disgust. "Liars, every single one of them."

Saint chuckled and took the seat across from her. "Thought you liked being pregnant?"

She scoffed. "Does this look fun to you? I like having babies, it's the incubation period that sucks." She smirked and eyed him quietly.

They'd spent many years together, and even after they separated, they remained close. Tara knew him well, and he knew her, which was how he knew she had something on her mind. He also knew she wouldn't come right out and say it if it was a sensitive subject. She'd slowly come at him. Which was exactly what she did.

"You *two* have a good time?" Her emphasis on two was not lost on Saint. He sipped his coffee then rested the mug on the table.

"Yeah, went hiking yesterday, took her to that place she likes to eat with the games, and then took her to Turnersville for a movie. We hit the diner for breakfast, then a ride to the water, and spent the afternoon binge-watching her show." He narrowed his gaze. "Still don't think she should be watching that shit."

Tara rolled her eyes and then sighed.

"So, no Bailey, huh?"

There it was…

Saint folded his arms and settled into his chair. "No, didn't work out this weekend."

Tara flattened her lips and nodded, glancing around the room. This was far from over. She was just planning her next move. Even with Tara, he never offered up more information than was asked. A trait which thoroughly annoyed her when they were together.

"Three times in a row, Saint."

There it was.

"I'm aware, Tara." He clenched his jaw. "Didn't mention meeting her this weekend." He purposely didn't. However, it was the first thing she asked when she arrived. He didn't miss the disappointment in her face when he said Bailey was busy.

"I know." She sighed loudly and twisted her lips. "She called me." She pointed to the ceiling, and he knew she was referring to Cia. "Last night before bed. She said you told her Bailey couldn't make it, but maybe next time."

He nodded. He knew his girl was disappointed. He hadn't known she reached out to Tara. That piece of information drove a stab through his heart.

"Look." She smiled, but it didn't reach her eyes. It was a cross between treading lightly with a sensitive subject to fed up. "I know Bailey is special to you, and I know our girl is the most important thing in your life. Balancing all of it isn't easy, I get it. Trust me, with Denny, I was forever wondering if I was giving more to one than the other. So, I get it, Saint." She paused and narrowed her gaze. "Cia doesn't." Her lips strained down. "If you wanna wait or she does on meeting Cia, fine. Then you wait. But you can't keep telling Cia one thing and then letting her down. She wants to meet Bailey so bad it's ridiculous, and she keeps getting disappointed. It's not fair to her."

"You don't think I know that?" Saint heard the anger rise in his tone. The last thing he wanted was his daughter upset.

Tara held up her hand.

"I'm not trying to start something here. I'm just saying you can't dangle something Cia wants, in her face, and then rip it away without hurting her. And her mind is going to self-blame, Saint." She raised her brows. "She asked if I thought maybe Bailey didn't like kids, and that's why she didn't want to meet her."

Goddammit!

"Fuck." Saint dragged his hand over the top of his head. "It's not that."

"It's what your daughter thinks. So, help me help you with this, okay? Why does she keep backing out?"

It was not his story to tell, and he certainly didn't want his ex privy to what Bailey had confided in him. But this was taking its toll on Cia, and he couldn't have that.

"She's scared to meet her."

Tara laughed, which pissed him off. He scowled.

"Saint, c'mon, scared of Cia? Our girl is the sweetest thing on the planet to begin with. Ya add her excitement of meeting Bailey? What does she have to be scared of?"

Saint licked his lips. It felt like a betrayal to Bailey to share it with Tara. His only other option was leaving his girl to think she was to blame for Bailey not coming over. He thought he had been convincing when he told her something came up. Obviously, he was wrong. Cia was a smart kid, and her mind went in the opposite direction.

"This stays between us. Need your word."

She furrowed her brows. "Of course."

Saint nodded and drew in a breath. Then he told her Bailey's story. He made sure to keep his voice low, so Cia didn't walk in unexpectedly and catch any of it. He told her about Bailey and her ex and relayed the story Bailey had told him. He added his take, which Bailey never came forth in saying. By alienating her from others, he was abusing her. Her ex may not have hit her, but shoving with aggression was very much physical abuse. Tara listened as he knew she would. Tara's reaction ranged from sympathy to sadness.

He was silent for a few seconds before he explained the last incident. It ripped him inside, knowing what that bastard had done to her, knowing all the pain she had endured. He kept his control while talking about her being doused in acid while she sat doing her schoolwork, her long and painful recovery, and the toll it had taken on her, not only physically but mentally. When Saint was through, the only reaction he saw from Tara was pure horror. She sat back in her chair and tears welled in the rim of her eyes.

"God, Saint." She covered her mouth with her hand as tears rolled down her cheeks.

"She's afraid of Cia seeing her scars, afraid of having to explain them, and what Cia will think." Saint drew in a breath. "She covers them, long sleeves."

Tara looked down at the table in silence. She was a good

woman, second only to Bailey and his own mother. She understood.

She peeked up through her lashes. "Does she cover the scars in front of you?"

She didn't. When they went out of the house, she did. When it was just the two of them, she didn't. He shook his head, and her lips curled up into a sad smile.

"Good, it means she trusts you."

"Yeah."

The creaking ceiling had both of them looking up. Cia was moving around, which meant she'd be down soon.

"Well, you tell Bailey to take whatever time she needs, okay? I'll help on my end and reassure Cia that it's got nothing to do with her. It'll be fine."

"Yeah." He hoped.

"Just make sure Bailey knows our kid is gonna love her. All of her." Tara winked and then wiped her cheeks and stood. She walked to the doorway and shouted up the steps. "Let's go, C."

Saint smiled. Tara may not have been the woman for him, but she was a damn good woman.

BAILEY WAS TUCKED on her couch when the phone rang. She glanced over and squeezed her eyes shut.

"Leave me alone," she muttered.

She didn't reach for the phone. Instead, she dropped her head back onto the cushion, trying to level her breathing. She thought for sure after the first time she answered, he would back off. It happened on Saturday morning. It was an unfamiliar number which usually she ignored. For some reason, she answered.

It was him.

She always wondered how she'd feel if she ever saw him again. It was strange. She never considered he'd reach out on the phone. The conversation was one-sided with Adam speaking. She remained silent as he apologized. She couldn't actually remember exactly what he'd said. She was shell shocked from the call. His voice brought back more than she was prepared for. When he was done speaking, she spoke.

"Don't ever call here again." Then she hung up.

For the next two days, he had called at least four times. She reached out to her lawyer, who suggested she didn't answer but adamantly forbid her from blocking his number. Apparently, they needed the proof he was harassing her if they ever needed to go forward.

The door creaked, and she angled her head over the couch, waiting on him. They had exchanged keys last week. It was an odd feeling. Yet, she just knew she wanted him to have access to her place and her to his. It just felt right.

"Hi."

He appeared in her doorway. *God, he's sexy*. She shifted in her seat on the couch as he made his way through the room. He sat next to her, leaning over and giving her a kiss.

"How was your day?"

"Good. Did some drawing and next week's agenda. I had a bunch of permits which were all approved." She winked. "And I got started on the plans for the park. Just need to take the official vote."

"Busy, huh?"

She nodded and curled into his side when he leaned back on the couch. "How about you?"

He sighed and covered his mouth as he yawned. "All day at the shop."

"On schedule?"

"Yeah. Forgot how time-consuming the tedious details are."

He circled his neck, and she heard the soft crack echo through the room.

"How was your weekend with Cia?"

He curled his hands over her hips, dropping his lips to hers for a soft kiss. "Good. Got her next week too, Tara and Denny are doing a weekend away, so I offered to take her. Tara's gonna drop her off around noon."

She drew in a breath. *Do it.*

"What are you guys gonna do?"

"Don't know yet. Why?"

She had spent a good part of the weekend wondering what Saint and Cia were doing. After her phone call with Adam, it triggered something in her to fully move forward.

"Just thought maybe I could come meet her."

"Yeah?" He seemed surprised and a bit hesitant. She could understand why. She had backed out enough times. If she was going to do it, she needed to commit,

"I'm ready. One hundred percent."

Saint wrapped his arms around her, pulling her over his body. As she kissed him, another thought from the weekend popped in her head. It had become routine for her to fall asleep to thoughts of her and Saint together when he wasn't with her. But there was one thing she had to leave to fantasy. Time to change that.

She slithered down his body, dropping her knees to the floor. It had been on her mind since the first night they'd spent together. His hands slid down her arms, and he eyed her. She reached for the snap in his jeans and lowered his zipper.

"I want to taste you."

His low growl echoed through the room. She tugged on the seam of his jeans, and he lifted allowing her to pull his pants down to his ankles. He was semi-erect and she slid her hands up his thighs, glancing up to see his eyes darkened and focused on her.

She hadn't had much experience with oral sex. She licked her lips.

She moved closer, and her hair draped over his thighs. She noticed the small tremble of his skin. She gripped his cock in her hand. Her thumb grazed over the crown of his cock, and he groaned.

"Teasing me, sweetheart," he whispered in a graveled tone.

"I'll be honest, Saint. I don't really know what I'm doing here."

The corner of his mouth curled. "Anything you do will be perfect."

It was just the vote of confidence she needed. She leaned closer, curving her tongue over the crown of his dick. Her lips covered his cock, and she took him down her throat. He was thicker and longer than the men in her past. She wasn't sure if she'd be able to take all of him. She fisted his length and spread her lips over him, getting the best reaction. His hand curled into her hair, brushing it away from her neck. Her tongue flicked down the root of his length. She started a steady even rhythm that had his breath hitching. Her hands slid up his chest, tracing over his sculpted muscles. Her tongue lashed against his cock and his body tensed.

She peeked up. His head was pressed against the cushion. His lids were lowered, staring down at her. He was watching her. She kept her gaze locked on him, driving her mouth over his hard erection.

"Fuck," he grunted.

His fingers threaded through her hair, massaging her scalp as his cock hardened between her lips. He was close.

"Pull back," he muttered.

No way. She wasn't lying when she said she wanted to taste him. She swallowed him down her throat, enjoying his gasping of breath.

"Bailey."

She quickened her speed, digging her fingers into his chest. It was mere seconds before he came. His hips jutted forward, and he swelled in her mouth. Perfect. He slowly relaxed against the couch. The low panting from his breath echoed through her living room as she made her way, crawling up his chest.

She licked her lips and the corner of his mouth curled.

"Hades was right," he breathed, wrapping his arms around her back. "You're trouble."

She dropped her head to his chest, smiling. Her hand reached out, circling the skull tattoo on his arm. It was done in black, and the shading made it stand out. His fingers trailed over her back as they lay in silence.

"I've always wanted a tattoo. Maybe I'll be one of your first customers here."

"Got a month-long waitlist."

She propped her head. "Really?"

He chuckled. "Yeah. Booked solid. If you want one, we'll have Marco do it when he comes in before the grand opening."

"Oh well, anyone can do it." Before she finished her statement, Saint was shaking his head.

"Marco does it. He's the best. You get the best working on you." He eyed her, and his lips curled. "You know what you want?"

"One of my drawings." She spread her hand over her left shoulder blade. "Right here."

"You gonna show me your drawings?"

She shrugged, feeling the heat flash over her cheeks. "If ya wanna see them."

"I do."

She smiled. "Now?"

He nodded.

She leaned across his body and opened the top drawer of her coffee table. She had several books of her drawings. She pulled out the top one and slid off of Saint, taking a seat next to him. He adjusted himself, pulling up his pants. It seemed an odd time to pull out her drawings, but Saint seemed interested, He grabbed the book from her hands.

She'd never been shy about sharing her drawings. As he flipped through the pages, she watched his reaction. She had a gift, she knew it. She could look at anything and draw it. His eyes seemed intent on each page, and he slowly turned the pages.

"These are amazing, Bailey."

She smiled. "You think so?"

He glanced up with a sharp nod, and then his attention was back to her book. "How long have you been drawing?"

She shrugged, curling closer to his side. "Since I was a kid. I mean, just for fun. You really think they're good?"

He turned and smiled. "Yes, I do. They're amazing."

She blushed and leaned forward, but she felt his stare on her. She flickered through the pages to a hummingbird and a flower. She pointed at the picture.

"Can Marco tattoo this one on me?"

When he didn't respond, she looked up. "You're very talented, sweetheart."

When it came to her drawings, she'd heard it most of her life. From her parents, friends, and teachers. Coming from Saint, it meant more to her.

"I'll call Marco tonight, set up the appointment."

She ducked her head against his chest and spent the next thirty minutes showing Saint the rest of her books at his request.

Chapter 16

She glanced down at the car clock for the fifth time in seven minutes. That was how long she'd been parked in Saint's driveway with the engine still running. With the phone in her hand, she stared down at the third rewritten text she'd done in the past four minutes. *Canceling last minute via text when I'm parked in his driveway?* She swiped the hair falling into her eyes and pulled at her scalp. She was angry with herself. It was ridiculous. This had been her decision. *Get your ass out of the car.*

She closed her eyes and sighed, fighting against her racing heart. Her nerves caused a swift shake of her fingers, and she dropped her cell in her lap. Her forehead broke out in a beaded sweat. *Get out of the car.*

The sharp knock on her window caught her off guard, and she jumped, jerking her head to the left and practically hopping into the passenger side seat.

She forced a jittery smile and rolled down the window.

"Hi."

Saint smirked and leaned down, resting his elbows on the door. His violet gaze narrowed.

"Hi." His tone was amused and playfully mocking. Saint never said "Hi."

"You got plans of coming inside, or do you want me to bring Cia out here?"

She gasped and shifted her gaze to the house then at Saint, then back to the house. *She's here. Oh my God, I'm gonna be sick.*

His hand swept over her cheek.

"Thought she was coming at one." She glanced at the clock. How long had she spent sitting there?

"They came early. Tara wants to meet you, hang for a bit."

"Tara, her mom, your ex?" Her skin tingled with heat, but not the good kind, the dreaded vomit-inducing, potentially passing out kind. "S-she wants to meet me? Like now?"

"Sweetheart, relax."

She shook her head. "Is it too late to change my mind?" She gripped the gear shift set to move to reverse. "Let's do it in a couple weeks or months. How about six months?"

His chest rumbled, the corners of his mouth curled, and the small lines near his eyes crinkled. Saint smiling was usually enough to ease her. She was too far gone. She couldn't do this. Before she realized it, his arm stretched in front of her, and he was shutting down her engine and taking her keys with him.

Oh no.

He settled back, and the door opened. She remained seated. He wouldn't possibly drag her out, right?

Wrong.

He leaned in, unbuckled her seatbelt, and grabbed her hand, guiding her out of the car. She stood in front of him with the door open, biting her lip. There was no way out unless she explained her anxiety and her nervous energy, which was sure to ruin the meeting. His child, who he adored, her mother who obviously wanted to inspect her—this was all too much.

"Saint, I-I can't do this, I really can't…"

He yanked her hand, and she fell forward into his chest. Both his hands slid up her arms, grasping her neck and tilting her head to meet his eyes. "Want me to lay it out for ya?"

She shook her head. "N-no, I think."

"No, stop thinking. Sweetheart, my girl has been waiting over a month for this. Been begging me to have you over, hell, two weeks ago, she Googled you to find your address."

"What?" Her voice was hushed in shock. Saint's daughter Googled her?

He raised his brows and nodded. "She said she was done waiting. And the only reason she was waiting was because I knew this would be a lot for you." His thumbs caressed under her ears. "Not me. Not Cia. Just you. My kid is a pain in the ass, only so long she's willing to wait."

This was all too much. Cia *wanted* to meet her? Her heart seized.

"She's waiting to meet me?"

He nodded.

"And Tara?"

Saint snorted. His face softened. "Another pain in the ass. Tara hears I got a woman. She wants to meet her."

"It makes sense, with me being around her daughter, she'd want to know I'm not some crazy lunatic."

Saint burst out laughing. "Sweetheart, that's got nothing to do with why she wants to meet you. She wants to see the woman who's got my heart."

His sweet words should have eased her anxiety. It didn't.

"I'm nervous."

"I know."

She bit her lip. "What if she hates me?"

Saint shook his head. "She won't."

"How do ya know, I mean she could."

"Bailey, stop." He caressed his thumbs over her jaw. "Caught her staring out the window, took a few minutes to realize she was watching you in the car. I was trying to give you time because I know you're nervous. I wanted to give you a minute. But Cia, she's too eager, she's been waiting on this. Meeting you."

That did something to her, and she melted closer to him.

"Now, we've been out here for five minutes going back and

forth, no doubt my girl's watching. You want her to think you don't wanna meet her?" He raised his brows, and Bailey's stomach dropped. She jerked her head to his front window. From the shadow of the porch, she couldn't tell if anyone was looking out.

"No. No, I want to meet her. Oh God, do you think she thinks that?"

He chuckled. "Sweetheart, gotta relax." His lips swept over hers.

"Don't kiss me, she could be watching."

Saint chuckled and wrapped his arm around her shoulders and led her to the porch. Before they made it to the landing, the front door opened, and a beautiful little replica of Saint stood in front of her.

"Hi." Her smile was just as Bailey had remembered from her picture.

Bailey smiled, stepping away from Saint. She didn't get very far. His hand slid down to her waist tugging her close. Bailey cleared her throat.

"Hi Cia."

"I have something for you," she blurted then spun so fast Bailey barely saw her disappear into the house.

"What the…" She moved forward when Saint nudged her through the door. She'd been in the house several times and usually felt comfortable. This was different. When she walked into the living room she halted. A pretty blonde sat on the couch. Tara.

Bailey smiled and drew in a breath. She'd never met an ex before, but read enough books and saw enough movies to know it rarely went smoothly.

"T, this is Bailey." Saint dropped something on the side table.

The woman stood up and made her way to Bailey. It occurred to her last minute that Bailey had yet to move or speak. Tara was probably thinking Bailey was the bitch. Fuck, she was messing this up.

"The infamous Bailey," she said and snickered. She stopped

and dropped her head back and held her hands in prayer. "Thank you, God." She giggled and looked back at Bailey with an amused grin. "If I had to go another two weeks hearing, 'Dad won't let me meet her. Do you think she likes popcorn, what kinda movies do ya think she likes?' And of course, my favorite, 'can we pass by her house, maybe she's outside.'" Tara burst out laughing and looked over Bailey's shoulder. "Hell, Saint, I think we might have a stalker on our hands." Tara leaned forward. "I feel for this kid's first boyfriend." She winked.

Bailey laughed, 'cause how could she not. Tara was funny.

"To say my girl has been dying to meet you would be an effing understatement." Tara stepped forward, extending her hand, which Bailey immediately shook. Her hand was warm and soft.

Bailey swallowed a breath and smiled. "It's nice to meet you, Tara."

"Same here, Bailey. I think—" She stopped mid-sentence when Cia came rushing down the stairs, barreling through the living room and halted directly in front of her. She glanced up, not far since Bailey only had about six inches on the girl anyway.

"Gimme your hand." Cia grabbed her hand before Bailey had time to oblige. She gripped her hand, pushing up her sleeve to the wrist. Bailey could sense the second Cia zoned in on her scar. This wasn't the first time someone had stared, though she couldn't recall a stranger being so up close and inspecting since…. Saint. Her heart skipped, and she watched his daughter's lip tug down into a frown. If she pushed her sleeve any further, she'd see the scar leading up past her elbow. *Please don't.* Her hand trembled slightly, and the room remained silent.

"Well, give it to her, Cia. It's all she's talked about for the last couple days, Bailey."

Bailey glanced up at Tara, who was smiling though it didn't quite reach her eyes. She knew the look, had gotten it so many times throughout the years. She'd recognize it a mile away. Sympathy.

Bailey felt Cia's hand over hers and gazed down. A multicolored beaded bracelet slipped through her hand, landing on her wrist. In the center was a red and black ladybug.

She stepped forward, practically leaning into Bailey. "Look, we have matching ones." She held up her bracelet, a smaller replica of the one Bailey wore. "Do you like it?"

Bailey was overcome with crazy emotions and on the verge of tears. This was new territory for her. She smiled at Cia, raising her hand against her heart.

"I love it, Cia. Thank you so much."

The little girl grinned at the same time she felt Saint at her back. His hands wrapped around her waist, and he leaned over her shoulder. Bailey held up her wrist, and his lips grazed her temple. "Where's mine?"

Cia giggled. "It's just for girls, Daddy."

The sound of her laugh had Bailey joining in, and relief spread throughout her body. Any anxiety she was carrying drifted away with a little feminine snicker. Here she was the adult, yet it was a nine-year-old putting her at ease.

"Come on, C, help me get drinks."

She jerked her head, and Saint smiled at her. Cia followed behind him, glancing over her shoulder with a toothy grin before slipping past the doorway. Now, she was left with his ex in a room alone. Tara seemed nice during their introduction. Now it was very awkward to be standing in silence.

She took a deep calming breath and faced Tara.

"I asked him to give us a minute."

Bailey's brows hiked up.

Tara waved her over to the couch and sat. Bailey slowly skirted past the table and took a seat at the opposite end. She clasped her hands on her lap.

Tara glanced at the kitchen and leaned forward. "Just wanted to have a little one on one with you."

"Oh." Was this where Tara threatened her if she ever hurt her child, she'd kill her? Or maybe she wasn't over Saint and wanted her to leave. From the description Saint gave her of his ex, these all seemed far-fetched, but it still worried her.

Tara leaned across the couch and grasped her folded hands, giving her a squeeze. "I'm just so happy to meet you, Bailey."

Not what she expected.

"Ya know, getting any info outta Saint is nearly impossible. Only gives ya what he wants, and he's keeping you all to himself." She released her hands and turned her body to face Bailey. "I just wanted to meet you, and hopefully, ya know, be friends."

"Oh." She shuddered at her inability to say more, but she was completely caught off guard. She cleared her throat and shifted around matching Tara's position. "Well, it's great to meet you. Saint talks about you, all good things."

Tara grinned and chuckled. "Well, he's leaving out a bunch then, since I can be a stark raving loon. You'll find out soon enough." She winked. "Denny says I can only hide my crazy so long before it comes raging out, usually around the holidays."

Bailey knew Denny was her husband, and although she didn't let on, Saint informed her of how nuts Tara got at Christmas. She kept that to herself.

"So, anyway, this is gonna sound strange, I just wanna put it out there."

Here it comes…don't mess with my kid or you're dead.

"You ever run into a problem with Cia, something you can't go to Saint with, you reach out to me and I'll get it sorted."

Bailey blinked in confusion. "Uh…what do ya mean?"

Tara snorted. "Cia's a great kid. Most of the time she's my favorite, though if you mention it in front of the other two, I'll deny I said it." She winked with a smirk. "But she's a kid, none of them are perfect, and sometimes, she gets sassy and snarky. I mean, she is my kid, so it's partially my fault. It happens, and I just want you know when it does, you have my permission to set her straight, and if she's not listening to you, you tell me."

"Shouldn't I tell Saint?"

"Yes, absolutely, but if for some reason, you couldn't or didn't want to have him in the middle, I'm here, and I'll make sure it works out."

This was strange, and she wasn't completely following Tara. The idea that the sweet girl who put her at ease would turn on her was making her a bit anxious again.

"Okay."

Tara smiled. "Good." She jerked her chin toward the kitchen. "Saint did that for me right after Denny and I got together. I appreciate that more than he'll ever know, of course, he doesn't know. Denny made me promise not to tell him I knew."

"Has Denny ever had to take him up on the offer?"

She shrugged. "Don't know. Denny never mentioned it. Marriage is hard enough, and in blended families, it can be harder." She snapped her fingers. "Another thing, we do holidays together, Christmas, Thanksgiving, her birthday, we usually get together at my house. It's a good time, but if you and Saint decide ya wanna do something on your own with Cia, that's fine too."

Bailey smirked. "You're completely ruining the stereotype of the bitter ex-wife."

Tara burst out laughing. She glanced over to Saint, who had come to the doorway. He looked confused as Tara howled again. Bailey smiled and shrugged. He shook his head and disappeared into the kitchen.

"Oh shit, we are gonna be best friends, I can feel it." She wiped her eyes and continued a steady chuckle.

"I appreciate you having this conversation with me, Tara. I didn't expect it, especially the first time meeting you, but thank you."

"I know it's weird, and you and Saint aren't walking down the aisle next week, but this thing you guys have?" She gave her a soft smile and nodded. "I've known Saint a very long time, and as much as it's hard to get anything outta him, I can see how he feels for you. You're the *one*. You're his like Denny is mine."

Bailey's heart raced against her chest. *I'm the one.* She was going to need a Xanax after this day was over. A roller coaster ride of emotions. Her heart couldn't take much more. She peeked up to see Cia race into the room and plop down on the couch near her mom, but her smile was aimed at Bailey. Her gaze flicked past the couch to see Saint standing at the edge of the room, staring at her with a soft gaze.

Her heart swelled. *I'm his.*

SAINT WAS BRINGING in the grill tools through the mudroom and stopped short at the kitchen doorway. Cia was sitting at the table with her legs swinging and staring up at the ceiling fan. He was thoroughly in tune with his kid. He had made a point of reading her since she was a baby. He didn't want anything to slip without him knowing.

She sighed heavily, and her shoulders sagged. He scanned the room. No sight of Bailey. They had pretty much stuck together for the last five hours since she arrived. Mostly it was Cia who stuck by Bailey's side. Had something happened when he was outside?

"C, you good?"

She jerked her head. "Yeah."

Something was on her mind, but she was holding it close. If he wanted her to let it out, he'd have to finagle it out of her. He walked toward the sink. "Where's Bailey?"

"Bathroom."

He lay the utensils in the sink and turned, leaning his back against the counter. She stared back at him, and he knew the look. She was reeling with indecision of wanting to talk.

"Talk to me."

She clasped her hands on her lap and squinted her eyes. She quickly glanced over her shoulder toward the empty doorway.

"Something happen with Bailey?"

"Uh-uh."

"You like her?"

Her face lit up, and she nodded. "Yeah, she's really nice and pretty. She said next time I come, she wants me to come over so I can see where she lives. Can we?"

"Yeah, we can."

Cia pursed her lips together. Something was eating at her, and she was having a hard time of it. Saint knew his girl, caught the long silent stare when she gave Bailey the bracelet and saw her scars.

"Proud of you." Saint smiled.

"For what?"

He shrugged, not wanting to make it a big deal, but knowing this conversation needed to happen to make things good for Cia.

"For not saying anything about Bailey's scars, playing it cool."

"Did I, 'cause I think I stared a little?" Her lips formed a deep frown, and she dropped her gaze to her feet.

"Hey."

When she looked up, Saint lifted his chin. "You didn't, C."

Her small body deflated a bit, and the tension eased on her forehead. She bit her lip, which made it obvious she had more going on in her mind.

"You wanna ask me something, just ask."

"Um..." She glanced toward the doorway then back at him. "Did something bad happen to Bailey?"

Oh fuck. How was he supposed to answer her? He'd always made a point to be truthful and honest with his daughter. But he knew Bailey's concerns about Cia knowing the details of what happened. He would have to handle it delicately, for both of them. Saint pushed off the counter and came to a stop in from of Cia, bending down to her level. He rested his elbows on his knees and gazed up at her.

"A few years ago, someone she trusted hurt her."

Cia's eyes widened. "Why would someone hurt Bailey?"

Saint ground his teeth together. "Because he was a bad guy. But he was punished, went to jail. He won't hurt her again."

"He gave her the scars on her arm?"

Saint nodded.

Cia's bottom lip trembled slightly. It was a lot for a nine-year-old to take in. She glanced up and raised her brows. "Did you tell her you'd never hurt her?"

Saint cupped her jaw and leaned in, kissing her cheek. "She knows, baby."

"Tell her anyway, Dad. Make sure she really knows."

"All right, I'll tell her."

"And tell her," she paused and gulped a breath, "tell her I won't hurt her either."

He pulled her in for a tight hug, and her fingers dug into his back. He and Tara may have made mistakes in the past; Cia was proof they'd done something right. He kissed her cheek and pulled away just as the sight of Bailey caught his eye. She slipped behind the doorway as to not be seen.

"Go pull out the chairs and set them up around the pit."

"Can we do s'mores with Bailey?"

"Yeah, go set up, and I'll wait for her." Cia jumped down from her chair and rushed out. He gave her a minute to get outside and when he heard the screen door close, he turned toward the doorway. Bailey peeked her head out and smiled shyly.

"She's a sweet one," she whispered and stared down at the floor.

"Yeah, she is."

Bailey peeked up, shifting on her feet. He hated the awkwardness between them. All he wanted was to walk over and take her in his arms. He just didn't know if it was what she needed right now.

The silence drug on as he stared back at her, and she avoided his gaze.

Fuck it.

He stalked over to her, and she jerked her head up and widened her eyes in surprise. He grasped his palm over her neck, kissing her softly. Bailey pulled away slightly, gazing down at his chest.

"You heard Cia?"

She clamped her lips and nodded.

He leaned closer, whispering in her ear and keeping his promise to his daughter. "Not gonna hurt ya, Bailey."

She glanced up through her lashes. "I know, Saint."

"And I'm not gonna let *anyone* hurt you." He angled her jaw, forcing her to meet his stare. "You believe me?"

"Yes." She teared up. "I know you had to tell her, and I don't want you to lie, I just wish…"

"Bailey," he whispered.

She wiped her face. "I just wish I didn't have a past like the one I have." She was shaking off the inevitable. Bailey was strong, stronger than most. She drew in a breath. He hugged her close.

"What can I do to make this better?"

She sniffled. "Get the marshmallows, chocolate, and graham crackers so I can have s'mores with your sweet daughter."

Saint couldn't resist. He loved this woman beyond anything in the world. He cupped her chin, making her looking up at him. She smiled though it was a front. The back of his hand grazed her wet cheek before his lips dropped down to hers. Bailey eased up on her toes and kissed him back, and then circled around him and headed outside.

He'd spend the rest of his life giving her so many good memories, she'd hopefully one day forget the bad. It wasn't plausible. Bailey would never forget. He was still going to try.

Saint made his way to the pantry, grabbing everything he needed and headed out to the back yard. He stopped at the edge of the steps. Bailey was bent down near the fire ring, stacking the wood with Cia standing next to her, shredding strips of old newspaper.

He'd obviously walked out in mid-conversation.

"And I told my mom, I'll share my room, too. I even know where we can put the crib if I move my bed by the window."

Saint smiled, inching closer. His little girl wanted a baby sister so badly. It would wreck her if Tara had another boy.

Bailey turned her head. "I always wanted a sister too. I hope you get yours."

"Mom says it's a fifty-fifty chance."

Bailey laughed and nodded her head. "Those are good odds." She winked and stood, reaching in her pocket.

Saint purposely waited while Bailey lit the fire. Watching the small bonding between these two was more than he thought his heart could take. Once the fire started, Bailey sat on the chair. He watched his daughter take the seat next to her.

"Do you like babies?"

Bailey jerked her head and smiled. "I love babies, especially girls."

Cia laughed. "I just really want a sister."

He watched Bailey's profile. Her features softened and she reached out, taking Cia's hand. "If I could have chosen a big sister, I would have chosen one just like you."

Cia turned, and Saint was struck by the view. The two of them smiling at each other. He was going to remember this moment for the rest of his life.

Chapter 17

"You're so full of shit. They are not real," Macy blurted.

Bailey choked on her margarita and quickly covered her mouth. She felt a hand pat her back, and she glanced over, catching Meg's amusement.

Just another Friday night at the Ghosttown Riders clubhouse.

She may have come in with Saint, but she was carted off to a table with Chey and Macy after ten minutes, and Meg joined a short while ago. They were seated in the pool room in the back. A neighboring club was visiting, as Saint explained. While he didn't stay by her side once the women gathered at the small table, she constantly felt his eyes on her.

"Nadia said they are," Cheyenne teased.

The current topic of conversation were Val's breasts. She was one of the club girls. Bailey had met most of them, who seemed sweet and friendly, with the exception of Val. She sneered in Bailey's direction any chance she got. Apparently, she loathed the girlfriends, according to Cheyenne, and Meg confirmed it. She noticed Macy's watchful eye when she sidled up to Rourke, who blatantly ignored her. Trax had done the same. Gage seemed happy to give her the attention she sought. Bailey found it odd she never engaged with Saint.

"How come she doesn't hit on Saint?" Bailey asked. She was basically thinking out loud.

Meg snorted. "The girls know better than to approach Saint. He's never given them any attention, even before you came around."

Bailey glanced over at Meg. "Never?"

She twisted her lips. "Some may have tried, but Saint shut it down. He was holding out for the real thing, I guess." Meg smirked. "Then you showed up."

She glanced over at Saint standing with Rourke. A cute brunette sauntered over to them. Bailey had met her earlier, and she seemed sweet. She leaned closer and Saint bent down, offering his ear. A heated burn filled her belly. What was she saying? Saint backed up and nodded. He didn't give her body a perusal as she'd seen a few other men do.

She had a sudden urge to go over there. Maybe it was her insecurity. *Who cares? Get over there.*

Too much time had been spent with her indecision.

"I'll be back."

"Okay, girl," Chey said.

Bailey moved past the pub tables and weaved through the small crowd by the darts. She leaned to the side, catching a glimpse of Saint with Rourke standing next to him and the cute brunette handing him a beer. She was wearing booty shorts and a bikini top. Her body was made for the outfit. Bailey halted and second-guessed her decision. Maybe she should just go back to the table with the girls. She trusted Saint. He'd never given her a reason not to. The woman leaned forward, not too close, and appeared to be shouting something to Rourke. He held up his bottle and shook his head. She smiled and turned, heading in Bailey's direction. Bailey stepped aside to let her pass, but she slowed down in front of her.

"I like your earrings, Bailey."

Her hand immediately went to her ear and tugged on the dangling silver. "Thanks."

"You need a drink?"

Bailey shook her head and forced a smile. "No, thank you."

She grinned and leaned closer, shouting over the loud music. "I swear, you are the politest person in here."

She winked and passed her. Bailey rounded a couple who seriously needed to get a room and walked over to Saint. He was facing Rourke with his back to her. She reached out to his hip, sliding her hand around to his stomach. His body tightened, and he jerked his head down at her.

"Hi."

His stomach unclenched under her hand, and he wrapped his arm over her shoulder, curling her into his side. She gripped his shirt and settled into his side, watching the pool game. She couldn't hear what Saint and Rourke were talking about over the music. It didn't matter. She just wanted to be close to him. His fingers trailed over her arm, and she glanced up. His lips were on her before she even realized what he was doing. His tongue poked past her lips, and she leaned in closer. Making out in public was new territory for her when she was sober. Surprisingly, she didn't care who was watching. She moved her hand up his chest to his neck when his lips trailed across her jaw and over to her ear.

"Don't do that again."

Do what? She flinched. *What did I do?* She tried to back up, but he held her tight.

"Watched you hesitate coming over here. Don't do it again. You want to be near me, talk to me, whatever, you come to me, don't care who I'm with, what I'm doing, you come to me. You understand, sweetheart?"

The warming in her belly had Bailey melting into his chest. Her hand clasped over his neck, and she whispered, "Yes."

He kissed the sensitive skin below her ear. "Good."

"Heard ya getting tatted up, Bailey?" Rourke said, breaking her out of her daze. She leaned over and smiled up at Rourke.

"Tomorrow." Saint's grand opening was on Saturday, but Marco and a few others were coming in a day early.

Rourke smirked and nodded, glancing back at the game of pool being played. "Watch yourself. Tattoos are addictive. After your first, you'll be itching for another." He gave her a side glance, the corner of his mouth curling, and he shifted his gaze to his arm. He had both arms sleeved.

"I already got something in mind for a second tattoo."

Rourke burst out laughing, turning to Saint. "Christ, you're gonna owe a shit ton of favors to Marco."

Saint snorted. "She could get both sleeves, and her back and Marco would still owe me."

"Well, ya got the best out there, Bailey. Marco did a few of mine. Since then, won't use anybody else. Need to make an appointment soon." He turned to Saint. "The wait still two months out?"

Saint lifted his beer, taking a swig before swallowing. "Three."

"Fuck, business must be good."

"It is." Saint lifted the bottle to his lips.

"And you got in the day before opening, huh?" Rourke rarely teased with anyone other than Macy, but he was clearly joking with her.

"Yep."

Rourke snickered, shaking his head.

She tugged on his arm, gaining Saint attention. "If Marco has a three-month waitlist, how'd you get me in so quick?"

Saint angled her closer, meshing her back to his chest and wrapping his arms around her waist. His hands locked over her stomach, and his nose ruffled her neck, closing in on her ear.

"Told Marco my girl wants a tattoo. He moved his schedule around to come in a day early."

"Why?" She turned her head and gazed up at him.

Saint smirked and whispered, "'Cause my girl wants a tat. You may not know Marco, but he knows you, sweetheart. Not many people I talk to, Marco is part of the select few. Last year, I talked."

He paused, and she let his statement sink in. "I tell him *Bailey* wants a tattoo? He comes early. He didn't even hesitate."

Her lips spread into a wide grin. "You talked about me? For a whole year?"

Saint smiled. She reared her ass against his crotch, and her hands gripped his arms around her. "We should leave soon." She raised her brows. "Very soon, Saint."

Saint smiled and lifted the bottle to his lips, and in three seconds, he finished his beer. He unraveled his arms, only to hook one over her shoulders and toss the bottle in the trash. He threw up his hand.

"Night, everyone."

Bailey said bye as they strolled out the door and through the parking lot toward his bike. This would be the longest ten minutes of her life.

THEY HAD BARELY MADE it through the door fully clothed. Public fucking was not his thing, but it might be if he didn't get her inside.

Thankfully, they had made it into his house, up the stairs, though their clothes were currently leaving a trail. He lifted her naked body against his and dropped her onto his bed. When she rolled on her side, Saint slipped in next to her.

Saint curled into her and grasped her hips, pulling her against his cock. Bailey pressed her ass against his throbbing length. *Fuck.* His hands drifted over her stomach as her arm reached back, tugging his neck closer to her. She hooked her leg over his thigh, giving him full access. His hand drifted over her ribs. Taking his time was not an option. He wanted her too much.

"I want you inside me.," she moaned.

He closed his eyes, fighting back the desire to fuck her hard. His fingers caressed up her chest, rounding over her breasts. Her nipples tightened against his palms, and he groaned softly. With her legs spread, he was lined up against her entrance. He was right there, feeling the moist heat from her pussy. Her. *Get a fucking condom.*

Her hand trailed up the back of his neck, and her hips arched. Her nails dug into his scalp. He squeezed her breast, and she moaned shifting her hips. *Fuck.* She felt too good.

"Gotta wrap it up, sweetheart."

She moaned and pressed her ass against him, sending the crown of his cock between her folds. His head dropped to the curve of her neck. She wasn't playing fair.

"Bailey," he growled, biting down on her neck.

"Saint." She moaned and pushed her hips back until he was fully seated inside her. He couldn't remember the last time he'd taken a woman bareback. He closed his eyes allowing her body to rock against his in slow precision.

He moved his hand between her legs, and she gasped. His finger caressed over her swollen bead, and her head dug into the curve of his neck. "Saint, right there, baby."

He groaned. His name, along with her calling him baby, was almost too much to take.

He shifted his hand away from her pussy, gripping her thigh and opening her up for him to thrust deep in her core. Her fingers clamped over his neck, and she moaned. The vibration of her voice had him thrusting harder, gripping her legs in a tight hold. Her walls clenched against his cock, and he groaned. She gripped his neck, digging her nails into his neck as she released a breathy moan.

He shifted, feeling the walls of her core grip him in a tight squeeze. *Pull out, motherfucker.* She felt too good to hold back. He was seconds from coming. He'd had sex a hundred times over, yet no woman had ever made him feel as alive as Bailey. *Her.* It was all her.

"Ahhhh…yeah, Saint." She mewled, and her body trembled under his hold. Her orgasm only rushed his own, and he pumped harder until his fingers dug into her hip. He pulled out, coming all over her hip. His body shivered as he spewed the long white strands over her skin. Her soft moan only enhanced his orgasm, and he gritted his teeth before falling back against the mattress. His breath was heavy. He hadn't ever come so hard and too fucking fast.

His arm, still hooked under her ribs, tugged her against his chest. She came willingly, curling herself into his chest. They'd clean up later. For now, he wanted her close.

Her lips grazed his skin, and he sighed.

"You didn't have to pull out." She whispered so low he almost didn't catch it. She curled into his chest with her fingers caressing over his abs.

"No?" he whispered.

"I'm on birth control."

For now.

Bailey gazed up through her lashes. He trailed his fingers over her jaw, caressing her pinkened cheek. Visions of her swollen belly with his child had him tightening his hold on her. He wanted everything with her. Everything and forever. They may not be ready just yet, but Saint would enjoy having nothing between them.

"Next time, I won't."

The corner of her mouth curled and she pressed her lips over his heart. This was all he wanted. Her with him. His daughter, a part of both their lives and someday, a child of their own making. He leaned closer and she extended her neck with their lips meeting.

"Love you," she whispered.

Saint drew in a breath. Sweetest words he'd ever heard came from her lips.

"And I love you, Bailey."

It had been a long night and sleep came fast for both of them. It seemed once he closed his eyes, his alarm was sounding. It was a struggle to pull away from the warmth of her body.

They showered separately, his choice not hers. Getting Bailey naked in the shower would guarantee she wouldn't make it to her appointment. When he came out from the bathroom fully dressed, she turned and pouted. *God, I love this woman.*

He'd gotten a text earlier from Marco. They'd arrived late in the night, opting to ditch the invite to the clubhouse and settle in. While the shop had been fully finished and stocked, each artist preferred to set up their stations. It would be a long day which was why he scheduled her appointment first thing in the morning.

At Bailey's insistence, they took the bike. One ride and she was hooked. Just confirming once again she was the perfect woman, aside from all her other attributes. He pulled in the back lot and parked next to the rental cars. Bailey immediately dismounted, taking off the helmet quickly.

She grinned. "I'm so excited."

Saint chuckled, getting off the bike while removing his own helmet. Along with her excitement he expected a bit of nervousness, which was common with a first tattoo. She showed no signs. He clasped her hand and walked in through the door, holding it open for her. They made their way down the small hall before Saint stopped and turned to her. A warning was only fair.

"What?"

He arched his brow. "Waited on you for a long time, sweetheart." His lips twitched knowing the reception Bailey was about to receive. He wanted her prepped and ready. An enthusiastic Minka held no boundaries. He hadn't been as open with her about Bailey, but she was always around, and he had his suspicions Marco mentioned some things.

"Marco and I are close, as I said yesterday. Shared with him."

She smiled and blushed. "Saint."

He scowled. "Gonna apologize now for Minka."

Her brows knitted together. "Minka?"

He grasped her hand and pulled her down the hall which opened up into the shop.

"Morning," he said, gaining the attention of two artists in the lobby. He caught a flash of jet-black hair with blue tips over one of the half cubicles. Her heels clicked and she appeared on the edge of the hall. It took her only a second to glance from him to Bailey and her mouth fell open.

The silence lasted less than two seconds, which was longer than he anticipated.

"Oh, my fucking God. It's fucking Bailey!" Minka's screech had Bailey tighten her grip and Saint rolling his eyes. He glared as Minka approached. She was too fixated on Bailey to notice or even care. She stalked forward with a wide grin. She was much taller than Bailey. He could only imagine what Bailey was thinking. Without any warning she grabbed Bailey and tugged her into a hug bouncing on her toes. Saint released her hand and smirked.

At least Bailey would know she was welcome. Minka stepped back holding Bailey's arms in a tight squeeze. "I thought for sure, it was some bullshit when he said we were going to get to meet you." Minka laughed. "But here you are."

Bailey giggled, her cheeks pinkening. "It's so great to meet you, Minka."

"Oh my God." Minka pulled her in for another hug. "You're so friggin' cute I can't take it."

"Try, Minka." Saint sighed and pushed gently on Minka's shoulder encouraging her to release Bailey. He scowled, though Minka could read through it, he assumed. She laughed and slapped his arm. She finally let go of Bailey, stepping back and shaking her head.

"I can't believe you're here." She spread out her hands then jerked her head over her shoulder. "Marco, fucking Bailey is here."

She really needed to hold back her excitement. While he enjoyed her enthusiasm and making Bailey feel welcome, putting her on the spot and on display might be uncomfortable for her.

Saint growled and inched forward. A soft familiar hand rested on his chest. He glanced down to seeing Bailey laughing. She shook her head. He would take her lead which meant allowing Minka to go bat shit crazy with excitement.

"You are so friggin' adorable, I can't even."

Saint rolled his eyes again and glared down at Minka.

Marco poked his head out from his cubicle. He didn't even look at Saint, his stare was glued on Bailey as they started forward. He hopped up from his seat and waited as they approached. His gaze flickered to Saint. He nodded and reached out his hand to Bailey.

"Been a long time coming, Bailey. It's good to finally meet ya."

She leaned closer and took his hand. "Nice to meet you. Saint talks about you all the time." She winked. "Only good things."

Marco grinned with a nod, keeping his attention on Bailey.

"Well, let me just say, I'm honored to be doing your first tat."

Minka inserted herself between them with a grin. "Can I do your second?"

Saint drew in a breath. "Minka." It was meant to be a firm warning, instead she ignored him, waiting on Bailey.

"Um, sure."

Minka jumped on her feet again, twirling around. Marco shook his head while Bailey laughed. At least they could appreciate Minka. Saint shook his head and grasped Bailey's hand leading her into Marco's room. The cubicles were set up with half walls. It left the shop with an open feel. It gave the artist enough privacy without them feeling boxed in. In the back of the shop, there were two separate rooms for tattoos which required privacy.

Marco dropped in his seat and had everything set up for Bailey. Saint had left Bailey's drawing so he'd be set to go when they came in.

"Have a seat, Bailey. I've got the drawing so I'll place it and then we'll start, sound good?"

She nodded and curled her sweater around her stomach. This would be the hardest part. He had given Marco a rundown about her scars. He trusted his friend to be nonchalant. When he'd spoken of Bailey, he'd given Marco full disclosure. Minka knew as well. But he knew it would be hard for Bailey.

Saint reached for her sweater and she allowed him to slide it down her arms and pull it off. When Marco turned, he smiled at Bailey, not making any eye contact with her arm or chest.

Minka appeared at Saint's side. "You wanna hold my hand. I heard it helps for first timers."

Saint glanced down at Minka who slipped past him and sat next to Bailey, grabbing her hand.

Marco rolled his seat over. "Bailey, it's totally fine to tell Minka to get the hell outta here. Trust me, it wouldn't be the first time."

"Shut up, asshole. She likes me." She turned to Bailey. "And if Marco fucks up your tattoo, I'll fix it, so don't worry."

Bailey laughed.

Marco slid the strap of her cami down her arm and transferred the sketch. He was a perfectionist, and angled his stance to make sure it was perfectly set.

"We good?" he asked Saint.

Saint moved closer and nodded. He walked around to face Bailey and sat on the rolling chair, sliding it in front of her.

"Ready?"

"It's like getting laid for the first time. It hurts like hell, but if you're lucky, you're left with a good memory," Minka said, and Saint shook his head.

Bailey giggled, clearly amused by Minka. "Is that what yours was like?"

Minka sighed. "No. Mine was like getting an STD on prom night. My ex was an amateur tattoo artist. It was so fucked up; the asshole tatted his friggin' name on my hip." She shook her head. "And he even misspelled it. How the fuck do you misspell your own name?"

Saint was privy to the story. Bailey had a similar reaction as he did the first time he heard it.

Her jaw dropped and she gasped. "Oh my God, what did you do?"

Minka shrugged. "I broke his nose, ditched his ass and walked into Saint's first shop, and Marco fixed it."

Marco chuckled as the tattoo gun sounded. "True story, Bailey." He rested his free hand
on her back. "You ready?"

Bailey nodded. Saint knew the second the needle made contact with her skin. She flinched.

For the next thirty minutes, Minka distracted her with tales of past boyfriends and other regrettable tattoos.

"I'd give you instructions on the aftercare but I'm sure Saint will cover that with ya."

"No sweat, so no doggystyle, Saint."

"Christ sake, Minka. Tell me again why I haven't fired your ass?" Saint snapped.

She winked. "'Cause I'm a fucking genius when it comes to tattoos." She peered over Bailey's shoulder. "It's gorgeous, Bailey. It's absolutely perfect on you."

That's why I haven't fired her. That sweet fucking heart of hers.

Marco handed him a mirror and Saint angled it for Bailey to see. Her bottom lip fell open. "It's so beautiful."

Marco snorted. "The props go to you, Bailey, it's your creation. I want to see your drawings, by the way. Saint's been bragging on you."

She turned and glanced up with her cheeks turning a soft shade of pink. Seeing the look on her face, he wanted nothing more than to take her home and get her back in his bed.

Minka and Marco had other plans.

Once Marco wrapped her shoulder, the whole staff walked down the street, taking over three tables at the pizzeria and enjoyed their dinner. Saint and Bailey were the first to leave. With the opening tomorrow, he wanted to get in at seven.

He held the door open and Bailey slid past him. They started down the street back to the shop where he was parked. Her hand grasped his and she threaded her fingers through.

"I like your people, Saint." She curled closer to him and he released her hand to wrap his arm over her shoulder.

"And they love you, especially Minka."

"She's fabulous."

He flattened his lips. "Not the word I was going to use, but she's definitely one of a kind."

She giggled as he unlocked the door and started through the shop out to the back. He scanned the area and his chest expanded. This one would be his best. It would keep him grounded in one location. Keep him close to everything important. He started forward to find Bailey waiting by the back door, smiling at him.

All I need.

Chapter 18

Saint cracked his neck and rolled his shoulders. It had been a long day, and he was eager to close up shop and head back to his place, make a fire in the yard, and settle in with a beer. And Bailey.

The grand opening had been more successful than he'd originally hoped for. A few brothers had scheduled time with Marco and Minka. A few others even tested out some of the new talent. So far, there hadn't been any complaints. He wasn't surprised. Saint had always been meticulous in his business, including who he hired. There was a lot of traffic through the better part of the day, which meant Saint was working and not with Bailey or Cia.

He'd caught them hanging out on the couches in the waiting area for a while, then Bailey brought her over to the diner for lunch, and they stopped in Macy and Chey's place. There weren't many sights which melted a man like Saint. Watching Bailey come into his shop holding his daughter's hand was one of them. Cia had taken to Bailey as he knew she would. His relationship with Tara and Denny had helped with co-parenting in the best interest of Cia. Tara had stopped by with the boys who were over the moon to get tattoos from Minka. Non-permanent, of course.

His phone vibrated in his pocket. He reached back and glanced down at the screen before bringing it up to his ear.

"Yeah."

"Not gonna make it."

"Okay."

"Sorry, man, got held up here. How'd it go? Good turnout?"

Saint tucked his free hand under his arm and straightened his back. "Better than I expected. Marco's been at it all day, same with Minka."

"Fuck, man, can't believe I'm missing Minka too."

Saint rolled his eyes. Though he refused to hear any details, he was well aware of the common hookups between his brother and his artist. They were both consenting adults with the same outlook on sex. Strictly fun without commitment.

"They meet Bailey?"

Saint smiled. "Yesterday. Marco did her first tat, came out incredible and." He sighed. "Minka lost her shit when we walked through the door."

Hades drew in a breath, assumingly taking a drag from his cigarette. "You surprised? Fucking Minka is a freak. Hot as hell though. Anyway, just wanted to reach out. Be there next time, man."

"I know you will. Appreciate it." Saint assumed the call was ending and was about to say bye when Hades spoke.

"You hear anything from Decker?"

"Not yet. I'll give it a few days then I'll reach out."

"Sounds good, you need me, you call me, Saint."

"I will." Saint ended the call, tossing his phone on the desk.

They hadn't always had the most amicable relationship, but Saint and his brother were tight. They chose similar, yet opposite paths, and always remained loyal to one another. His move to Ghosttown would put them closer in proximity. From the sound of Hades' intentions, even closer if he settled in town.

The sharp knock at his office door was followed by an abundance of pounding when he didn't answer right away. Saint headed toward the door. It flew open before he got there. Tara's boys rushed in, pushing against each other to get to Saint first. He glanced up to see Bailey's crinkled nose and squinting eyes. His guess would be she hadn't been exposed to many boys, especially rowdy ones like Tara and Denny's.

"They wanted to show you their new tattoos."

Simultaneously the boys threw up their arms and Saint bent down, dropping onto one knee putting them eye level. He grasped their hands and looked closely, inspecting the work. His mouth curved.

"It looks good. When are you two coming back to get the sleeves done?"

"Oh hell, bite your tongue, Saint."

He snickered and stood, meeting the gaze of his ex, standing closely with Bailey. Tara threw her arm over Bailey's shoulder and laughed. It was comfortable and familiar, and he noticed how at ease Bailey was with her.

"We gotta run. Cia's pissed she can't stay, but she's got the comp early tomorrow morning." Tara sighed as Saint made his way over to her.

"Thanks for coming. Denny like his tat?"

Tara raised her brows. "Yeah, the tattoo and the price, kinda hard to beat. How the hell ya expect to make any money if ya don't charge people, Saint?"

"You're not people, you're family. And my family doesn't pay."

She rolled her eyes and leaned in, kissing him on the cheek, and repeated the same with Bailey. Saint watched as she gathered her brood. Those boys were running reckless all over the place, reminding him so much of him and his brother, at their age.

Cia raced toward him from down the hall. He braced himself and bent down, wrapping his arm around his girl. She was growing up too fast. Soon, she wouldn't be so eager for her kiss and hug goodbye.

"Bye, Dad. I love you."

"Love you too. Good luck tomorrow. Call me when it's over and let me know how you did."

"Okay." She unraveled her arms and turned to Bailey for a hug. Unlike Saint, Bailey was short enough not to have to bend down. He watched as they embraced and Bailey kissed the top of Cia's head.

"You're gonna kill it tomorrow, I know it."

Cia laughed and stepped back. "Thanks, Bailey. I'll see you next week, right?"

Bailey nodded.

"Okay, love you." Cia raced back down the hall and out the door.

Bailey eyed him. "Was she talking to me or you?"

"Pretty sure that was for you."

Bailey smiled.

"BAILEY, THESE ARE REALLY GOOD."

She glanced over his shoulder as he flipped through the pages. Her cheeks heated from his praise. Marco was an incredible artist, and for him to think her work was good, it meant something. She'd been hesitant to show him but he'd been insistent.

"All freehand?"

"Yeah."

"You should tattoo."

Bailey laughed. When he glanced over his shoulder, she realized he wasn't joking, he was completely serious.

"No, I just draw for fun, I mean, I can't tattoo."

He swiveled in his seat and beamed up at her. "Why not? Drawing on paper is the start to every tattoo and you got talent." He glanced down at her book, flipping another page. "A lot of talent."

She drew in a breath and smiled. The idea was absurd. When he slammed her book closed, she jumped back, startled.

"You're doing a tattoo, I'll teach ya."

Bailey widened her eyes. "What? No, I can't."

"Can't what?" Minka walked into the cubicle and glanced between her and Marco.

Marco kept his smile on Bailey and jutted his chin. "Gonna show Bailey how to tat."

She expected Minka to laugh at the absurdity. Instead she whipped her head to Bailey and bounced on her feet, clapping her hand. "Yes! Tattoo me."

"What? Oh my God, no. I don't know how to do it." Bailey shook her head. Were they insane? From the eagerness from both of them she'd say yes, they were nuts.

"Marco will teach you, I'm not afraid."

"But I am." She shook her head and Minka pouted.

Marco rolled his chair over to Bailey, taking her hand. "You got too much talent to keep it hidden." He held up her book with his free hand. "You got a whole book here, and if I put it out on the table, I bet you I'd get a lot of people asking for one of your drawings on their body." He wiggled his brows. "We're doing this."

She was overwhelmed by his compliment. So much so, for a brief second, she considered it. *What?* She shook her head.

"It's permanent, what if I mess up?"

Minka snorted. "You won't."

"What if I do?"

"Then I can fix it," Marco said.

She bit her lip. Could she tattoo? *No!*

"There, it's settled, you're doing it," Minka said and glanced over Bailey's shoulder. "And since you refuse to tattoo me, we just have to find someone else." She smiled but not at Bailey.

Bailey laughed. "See, you'll never find anyone who's willing to be my first tattoo." Of course, they wouldn't. Minka, though wonderful and sweet, was obviously a little crazy for offering it up. No sane person would willingly offer their body as a canvas for her to tattoo.

Marco smirked. "We got a taker." He pushed the chair and it

glided over to the table. Bailey spun around and gasped. Saint was standing behind her, gripping the hem of his shirt. She watched as he lifted it over his head, exposing his perfect chest and fully displaying his tattoos.

Then it clicked. *No. No. No.*

"Saint," she whispered as he stalked toward her with a smirk. "No."

"Here, man." Marco tossed Bailey's drawing book over to him which he caught with one hand. Bailey had to step back to make room for Saint to slide past her, and he sat on the chair, and opened up her book.

Minka pushed past her. "Don't start, I gotta get my phone, I wanna take a picture of Bailey's first tattoo."

Bailey's head whipped around the room following all the chaos. Actually, everyone seemed completely at ease, expect for Minka, who was overly excited. Marco was prepping his station, and Saint was flipping through her book. She surged forward and he looked up.

"I can't tattoo you."

Saint smiled. "Yes, you can."

"No." What the hell was wrong with him? "I can't do this, Saint. What if I mess up? What if I get nervous? My hands will shake and you'll have swiggly lines all over your body. It's gonna look like you let a two-year-old tattoo you."

Marco chuckled and she ignored him, focusing on Saint. She moved closer and his hand circled around her waist. With him sitting down, they were eye level.

"I'm gonna pick a drawing and you're going to tattoo it on my body. I want your mark, permanently, on my body, Bailey," he whispered.

How did this man, always know the perfect thing to say?

She lowered her head, taking him for a kiss. It was soft and lingering at first but any time she kissed him, she found herself getting carried away. His tongue glided across her bottom lip and she opened to him. She grasped his neck and sank against his bare chest.

"Forget about the picture of the tattoo, I want one of these two making out."

Bailey froze and pulled back from his lips. She turned to Minka who gave her a devilish smile.

"You two are sexy together."

Saint's hand glided down her ass to her thigh. He leaned in and kissed her neck before continuing his perusal of the book. She bit her lip, watching and waiting. Her drawings usually veered toward the feminine side.

Saint's brows knitted together and he brought the book closer to his face. He looked intently at the page and she stretched her neck to see which one he was looking at. From her view, she couldn't make it out. She stepped closer and Minka bustled behind her.

Saint turned his head, his eyes softening. He turned the book to face her. "This is your hand."

She smiled. "Yeah. I like hands. They're very delicate. I practice using my own as a model." She shrugged. "It's silly, there's just something personal about a hand."

Saint stared and the corner of his mouth curled.

Marco stepped forward. "You decide?"

Saint nodded keeping his stare on her while he handed the book to Marco. "This one."

She leaned over and caught a glimpse of what Saint had chosen.

My hand.

Chapter 19

Bailey finished off her coffee as she glanced down at her phone. It was later than she expected. She tossed a five on the counter and shimmied off of the barstool.

"Bailey," Carla warned.

She kept her head down and buttoned up her jacket. Facing off against the head waitress was a feat in itself, one she rarely chose to do. She reached over grabbing her bag. Before she could take it, Carla grabbed the strap.

Bailey straightened her shoulders. "You can't tell me what do with my money." She bit back her laugh when Carla squinted.

"Coffee is a dollar, twenty-five." Carla glanced down at the five-dollar bill on the counter. "You sit at the counter, I walk two steps to serve ya."

"And I think it deserves a tip."

"A three hundred percent tip?"

Bailey shrugged. "Like I said, it's my money."

Carla grabbed the money and shook her head. Bailey darted out the door and bundled up her jacket. It was cooler than predicted today, and there had been talk of possible flurries overnight. It had been all Cia talked about when she spent the weekend. Bailey smiled. *Snow days are the best days.*

She crossed the street, making her way to Cheyenne and Macy's store.

Another topic of discussion over the weekend had been Cia's request for scented candles in her room and Saint's flat out refusal. Bailey understood his concerns. An open flame in a nine-year-old's room was a recipe for disaster. She had suggested a diffuser and oils which had both Cia and Saint appeased.

She was a few feet from the store when she heard her name.

"Bailey." The voice was low, and cracked with a small hitch on the last syllable. It was eerily familiar.

She glanced behind her, scanning the area. No one. A cool shiver spread over her skin, tingling up into her scalp. It could have been her imagination. She slowly turned around, eyeing the three short blocks of Main Street.

Aside from a few cars lining the street and the bikes in front of the parts store, the street was empty. She could have sworn she heard someone call her name. The echo of faint footsteps from the side street had her slowly backing up and peeking around the corner.

Oh God.

Every bone in her body tightened, and her hands slowly curled, forming tight fists. Her nails bit into her palms. It seemed as though the next few seconds passed in slow motion. Her breath shallowed as her heart raced erratically. It was as though all she could hear was a thumping beat in her eardrums.

"Hey."

His smile was shaky, and he made no move to come forward. Thank God, because, at that moment, she wasn't sure she was capable of moving. A sharp pain shot through her temple. She blinked in an effort to relieve some of the pressure building in her head. *What's wrong with me?*

She watched his hand as it shifted over his head. It was shorter than she remembered. She'd always loved the color of his hair, a very dark blond which curled around his ears.

"You're here," she mumbled in disbelief. His presence had immobilized her into a frozen state.

The corners of his lips curled. She tilted her head. *Why is he smiling?* A smile she once loved.

She squinted, trying to find the appeal now. She couldn't. His eyes stared back her. A soft hazel rimmed with a gold lining. When they'd first met, she remembered being struck by the softness in his eyes. *Now?* They were just eyes. She sucked in a breath. *I trusted those eyes.*

"It's been a while," he said.

God, five years. It seemed so long ago, yet not much had changed except the length of his hair. She inspected him carefully, looking for signs, the ones she'd missed five years ago.

"You look the same." He smiled, and Bailey followed the curve of his lips.

I look the same? Her breathing grew heavy. *I look the same?* Heat coursed through her veins, and her blood boiled under skin.

Her brows knitted together. "No, I don't." Five years ago, her body wasn't riddled with scars. Daily reminders of all the pain he'd inflicted on her.

His face flushed, and he clenched his jaw. *I remember that.* When he was frustrated, his jaw squared, and he ground his teeth. It was either followed by him snapping at her or ignoring her. Her heart kept an odd steady pace. How was he here? Ghosttown was her home, her safe place and yet, there he stood. *Telling me, I look the same.*

"What are *you* doing here?"

He stepped forward, and she immediately stepped backward, fumbling on her feet.

He froze, holding up his hands. "You don't have to be afraid, Bailey." He dragged his hand through his hair. "I'm better now."

"Why are you here?"

"To apologize."

"You already did, on the phone." She gulped. "I told you not to call me again." She licked her lips. "And here you are."

He smiled. "You left me no choice."

He did have a choice. He could have respected her wishes and left her alone.

"Adam." She sighed, unsure of what she was going to say.

"Look, I'm sorry for what happened. My mind, I just wasn't right back then." He lifted his chin. "I did my time."

She wasn't sure what she had expected if she ever crossed paths with him again, but this certainly wasn't it. He did his time? As if somehow his prison sentence would erase what he'd done to her? *What about my time?* The life sentence in a body he left mangled and scarred. This was surreal.

"Why are you here, Adam?" she snapped.

He shrugged. "To make amends. My sister, Elle, just moved out here a year ago to Lawry. She offered for me to stay with her while I get reacquainted with life outside, ya know."

He lived in her state now. Only a few hours away.

"Yeah, anyway, heard you moved this way, and I figured I needed to come see you. Ya know, face my past, what've I've done." He shrugged. "You keep dodging my calls, so I figured, face to face would have to do. The prison psych doctor said it would be good for me."

She snorted. "Good for you?"

He nodded. "Yeah."

She couldn't wrap her head around what was happening. He was here to make amends, which would be good for him? Nothing he said or did could make up for what he'd done to her. An apology wouldn't erase her past, her nightmares, and trauma, the pain she endured, all the hospitals stays, infections, the agonizing pain. Nothing he could say would take away the years of healing, the setbacks. *It won't regenerate new skin to take place of my scars.*

His apology would change nothing, except make him feel better. Her stomach rolled in an aching twist.

"Come have lunch with me, we can talk, get shit squared away."

She gasped and widened her eyes. "No." What the hell was he talking about? She wouldn't go anywhere with him, let alone share a meal.

The rumbling engines had her jerking her gaze over her shoulder. She saw three members getting on their bikes and a fourth making his way out of the store. She drew in a breath and watched. She wasn't sure if he'd felt the weight of her stare or if it had been pure luck. Gage stopped at his bike and glanced over at her. He squinted his eyes, blocking the sun, then raised his hand, and the corner of his mouth curled.

Her breathing labored, and she stood statuesque, never taking her eyes off Gage. All she had to do was call for him, and he'd rush over. Gage would make it to her before anything could happen. She could, but she didn't. *I got this.*

She turned to Adam and drew in a breath. "You need to leave and don't come back."

"Bailey, listen to me…" There was a sharp command in his tone.

"No," she said, keeping her control intact and her fear at bay. She never saw it coming when he attacked her. It was a harsh regret she lived with. She wasn't going to let it happen again. She straightened her shoulders. "I don't have to listen to anything you say. I don't want to see you or eat with you. I don't owe you anything."

His nostrils flared, and he glared. "I just want to…"

"I don't care what you want, Adam." She stepped closer and tugged up her sleeve. His eyes immediately drew down to her scars, and his lips twisted. "I didn't want these."

He reached out, and her hand shot out, slapping his arm away. "Don't you dare touch me. Now, get in your car and leave, and do not come back. If you do, I will have your ass thrown back in jail, you hear me?"

He clenched his jaw and his face flushed. She remembered. For all her brazenness, she realized she may have been in over her head. His hardened face and the shadowing of his eyes reminded her of the past. She stepped away and kept her eyes on him. He seemed to hesitate as his scowl hardened. *Oh hell.* Her heart raced against her chest, and she was strategizing her escape from the vacant street.

"Fine." He turned and made his way to his car.

She moved forward, stepping slowly as he got in his car. He was leaving. She watched as he drove down the road. A wave of relief coursed through her, and her tense muscles relaxed. *I made him leave.* It was a small feat, but she basked in it. She'd spent a long time being a victim. A slow smile crept. It was empowering. She had faced off against Adam, and this time, she won.

When she turned, she slammed into a hard mass of flesh.

"Who's the guy?" Gage asked, grabbing her waist to keep her from moving away. His gaze was set on Adam's car as he drove away. *Oh shit.* He was not happy.

"No one."

He glanced down at her and furrowed his brows. "Who is he, Bailey?"

She shrugged. "Just some guy." She was well aware, all the members of the club were privy to her past. This would not sit well with any of them, especially Saint. She moved around him, but Gage fell in line with her steps.

"Saint know him?"

She chewed on her lips. She had every intention of telling Saint about her encounter. When the time was right. He would be livid. She knew this. She'd have to broach the subject delicately. *For him.* As for Bailey, she was damn proud of herself. She'd gone head to head with Adam.

"No."

"Who is he?" Gage growled.

"I handled him, Gage." Just saying it had Bailey straightening her shoulders. She took in a breath feeling a burst of pride. She had handled her first run in, fearlessly and on her own. It was a triumph. She had doubted her ability to stand strong, but she did it. She faced her fear, and he was the one walking away, not her running.

Gage was not on the same page. His scowl deepened. "Handled who?"

Be proud. "Adam."

Gage's reaction didn't mesh with her high. His jaw clenched, and his scowl grew harsh as his cheeks burned. "That was the motherfucker?" Bailey flinched then scanned the street. No doubt, everyone within a half-mile radius would have heard him.

"Calm down."

Her statement only proved to incense him even more. He stalked closer, towering over her and aiming his sharp glare at her. "Why didn't you call for me? I was right fucking here, you saw me, Bailey."

She winced. "I handled it, Gage. He left." She pointed to her chest. "I made him leave." She scanned his face, waiting on understanding to filter through his features. It didn't.

He shook his head and turned around, giving her his back. That was when she caught sight of Kase crossing the street flanked by Rourke and Trax. *Oh God.* If this was the reaction she got from Gage, she could only imagine how Kase would overreact.

And then there's Saint. *Shit.*

She rushed closer to Gage who furrowed his brows when she leaned close to him. "Can you not tell Saint?"

Gage's mouth dropped open, solidifying his nonverbal answer.

"Please." She forced a smile. She had every intention of telling him. *Next week, next month, ten years from now.*

"What's going on?"

Bailey whipped around. Oh hell, this was the last thing she needed right now. If Gage, the most laidback of them all, had been upset, the others would not handle it well. Bailey grinned. "Hey, guys."

Kase eyed her and glanced up to Gage. "What the fuck, I heard you from inside?"

Bailey snorted, doing her best to play it off. "We were just talking."

Kase didn't even glance her way. Instead he was fixated over her shoulder. Bailey turned to find Gage with one arm crossed over his chest, and his phone lifted to his ear.

"Saint, get over here. We're on Main."

"Gage, no," she whispered and tugged his arm. He flicked his glare at her and continued.

"I'm with Bailey. Guess who just showed up here?"

He paused and sighed.

"Didn't see him until he was driving away, but he had her cornered."

Bailey crossed her arms. "No, he didn't. And I handled it." She stepped closer pointing at the phone. "Tell him that I took care of it. He's gone."

Gage ended the call and glared at her. "Saint's on his way."

"What the fuck is going on here? Who cornered you?" Kase was standing a foot from her.

"No one," she said simultaneously as Gage said, "Adam."

From the looks on their faces, they were all familiar with his name. It came as no surprise to Bailey.

"I handled it. It's my issue, and I dealt with it." They were missing the big picture. This was something to be celebrated. She had gone up against Adam and won. Why couldn't they see it?

"Why the fuck didn't you call us?" Kase snapped, taking a step closer and towering over her.

Bailey squinted. "I took care of it, Kase. I didn't need any help." She straightened her shoulders. "I told him to leave and not to come back." She drew in a breath. "And he left. See, it's over?" She smiled at Kase. His jaw clenched as his temple pulsed. She'd never seen his face darken to that shade of red. She furrowed her brows.

"Saint's gonna fucking lose his mind." His brows knitted together, and his sharp glare was aimed directly on her.

"Lose?" Gage scoffed. "He fucking lost it."

Bailey groaned and closed her eyes. They were overreacting and missing a huge detail. "How many times do I have to say it before it actually sinks in with you guys?" She scanned their faces. Rourke and Trax, who had remained silent seemed just as angry as Gage and Kase. "He's not coming back. He didn't hurt me or corner me. I had the situation completely in my control. I was never in any danger."

"Bailey." Kase's voice shook with anger. He was losing his patience. He widened his eyes, then jerked his head up. "I wanna fucking strangle you right now."

"You are blowing this out of proportion." She snapped as her own frustration mounted.

"Really?" Kase barked. "Showing me your fucking arm, Bailey. Then tell me you aren't in any danger with this motherfucker."

Bailey flinched, and her bottom lip fell open. It was for shock value, she knew it. Kase wanted her scared. It was a shitty way to go about doing it. She gritted her teeth and squinted her eyes. His own glare never wavered.

Fuck you.

Bailey eyed the men and threw her hands up. "I'm leaving."

"The fuck you are," Kase said.

She shook her head and started toward her car, parked a few spots away.

"Bailey." Kase growled. "Get your ass back here. Now."

Bailey paused and glanced over her shoulder. "No." She continued walking and was prepped for Kase to block her. Much to her surprise, he didn't. She got in her car and drove home. She was supposed to meet Saint at his house, but a little time apart might be best. She had all intentions of telling him, just not on Main Street surrounded by the members.

When she pulled in her drive, she heard the rumbling engine come down the street. She recognized Trax's bike as he pulled in front of her house. He didn't even glance her way even when she made her way closer.

She stopped at her walkway. "Trax, you don't have to stand guard."

He slowly turned his head, glaring back at her. She held up her hands up in defeat. Insisting he go away wouldn't make a difference, and she'd had enough confrontation for one day. *I'm done.*

He remained on his bike in front of her house until she got inside. Even then, he sat waiting.

Bailey knew exactly *who* he was waiting on.

SAINT HAD PRIDED himself of being a master of self-control. There weren't many times he'd allowed himself to let anger and fury get the best of him. Currently, his boundaries were being tested. He couldn't recall a time he'd ever been so livid to the point of destruction.

He'd gotten the call from Gage when he was home. It took him less than ten minutes to get to Main Street, just to find out Bailey had left. Kase had tried to settle him down, insisting he gave it a few minutes before storming to her house. It was one of few times Kase had been the one calming Saint down. Usually, he was the voice of reason and patience. Not this time.

He pulled in her driveway, not bothering to acknowledge Trax parked in front of her house. He double-stepped the stairs and ripped the door open so hard he may have loosened the hinges. He barreled in, and Bailey sat crossed-legged on the couch, staring up at him.

She spread her hands. "I handled it, Saint."

He needed to gain control of his anger. He stood silent and still, with his gaze locked on her. She was reading him, and from her uneasy shift, she was getting the full understanding of his fury.

"Why didn't you call me?" He spoke through gritted teeth.

She was one of the last people in the world he'd want to unleash on, but he was teetering on the edge.

"I was going to." She licked her lips. "When I got home." She shrugged and averted her gaze. "Gage beat me to it."

His jaw locked, and he ground his teeth. She was lying.

"You're lying."

Her eyes widened, and she clamped her lips. They were in a staredown. She was the first to avert her gaze. Because she was lying.

"Bailey."

Her shoulders sagged and she peeked up through her lashes. "Okay, so maybe I was going to wait a few days, a week tops before I mentioned it."

He balled his fists.

"B-but, I was going to tell you." She swallowed her breath and hoisted herself forward, sitting on the edge of the couch. "I didn't want you to get mad, Saint. Or worried. I planned on waiting for the right time." She paused and tilted her head. "I was going to tell you, I promise."

His pounding heart remained beating viciously against his chest. He was mentally rationalizing her position, gaining a bit of control. He kept his breath steady.

"It's over now, Saint."

Her inability to see the truth was his breaking point.

"For Christ's sake, Bailey." He dragged his hand over his head. "It's not over. This is just the beginning for this sick fucking bastard. He came to where you live, Bailey. How can you not see the danger in this situation?"

"I do."

"Clearly, you don't," he barked.

"Why is it so hard for you or anybody else to see, I handled it." She folded her arms. "Five years ago, I didn't." Her breath hitched, and her eyes welled. "Today, I did."

It took a moment for it all to soak in. Her handling the situation was a milestone for her. As much as it pissed him off, she needed this, and he wouldn't take it away. However, he couldn't let it go. Her safety was everything to him.

"Bailey, you've *handled* enough." He stepped forward and narrowed his eyes. "You shouldn't have to *handle* anything from him."

She sighed. "What would you like me to do, Saint? Should I go into hiding? Should I run?" She tossed a pillow onto the couch and rose. "Tell me. I figured if I ignored his calls, he'd go away. I didn't think he'd actually come here," she shouted.

What the fuck?

His blood instantly heated. "He's calling you, and you didn't think to share with me?"

She clasped her hands, twisted her fingers. "I didn't want you to get upset." She waved her hand in his direction. "More upset."

He understood where she was coming from, but it was unacceptable.

"Is this how you want our life to go? We keep things from each other to spare each other's feelings and concerns?"

She pouted and dropped her gaze to the carpet. "No, of course not."

"Then you tell me everything, Bailey. No secrets."

She nodded. "Okay, I promise."

He spread his palm over his forehead and dug his pinky and thumb into his temples.

"Do you still want me to come over tonight?"

He furrowed his brows. She was set about ten feet from where he was standing, awkwardly fidgeting and swaying on her feet.

He stalked forward, grabbing her waist and yanking her against his chest. "What happened changes nothing about our plans. Not for tonight, tomorrow, or fifty years from now, Bailey." He cupped her jaw. "This will be the first of many arguments in our future, I'm sure."

The corner of her lip curled. "'Cause I'm trouble?"

The tension in his shoulders eased slightly. Yes, she was trouble. *But worth it.*

Chapter 20

Bailey took a deep breath and walked onto the porch. She sidled up near the column, opposite of where Saint stood watching his daughter mope across the grass. The usual, enthusiastic, and happy Cia looked as though she was having the worst day ever. Bailey glanced over at Saint and caught the flash of concern marring his features.

After their first fight yesterday, she was hoping for a fun and light weekend with Cia. While things between Saint and Bailey had been resolved, a small tension lingered. She knew it stemmed from his fear for her safety. It was coming from a good place. *His heart.* Still, she didn't like it. Cia's presence was a much-needed distraction from the Adam situation. Her energy was contagious.

Except at the moment.

"Not gonna even say bye to your mother?" Tara shouted with a smirk on her face. Cia didn't even spare her mom a glance. She continued up to the house, her head hanging low, clearly upset by something Tara was amused by.

Cia dragged her feet on the steps. She expected her to go directly to Saint's side. Instead she veered toward Bailey. It caught her off guard, and she quickly unclasped her hands when she realized Cia was coming in for a hug. Bailey wrapped her hands around her numb body and hugged her into her chest. "Hey sweetie, you all right?"

"No." It was a pouty reply. Bailey tightened her lips and glanced over at Saint. He smiled but not at her. *At us.* He liked this, her close to his daughter. So did she.

Bailey rubbed her back. "Can it be solved with junk food, pizza, and manicures?"

She shrugged. "We can try."

Bailey held back a giggle and leaned over, kissing her head before releasing her. Cia continued her sad walk and fell into Saint's side. He reached out, tugging her close for a hug she didn't return.

"Hey, baby."

"Hi, Daddy." Her tone was low and mumbled as she stared down at the ground with a sad frown.

"Not gonna see Mom for a couple days. Wanna say bye?"

Cia lifted her hand with a short wave, and a muttered, "Bye."

Tara smiled, shaking her head and walked up to the porch carrying Cia's bag. She plopped it on the ground and sighed dramatically. Bailey smiled. She liked Tara, enjoyed being around her, loved the only connection she wanted with Saint was friendship and co-parenting. Bailey was thankful Tara was kind and inviting, and most of all, she liked Bailey and what she and Saint had.

"Well," she announced, placing her hands on her rounded pregnant belly. "It's another boy for the Dillon clan."

Bailey's heart sank, and her eyes darted over to Cia. Saint's girl was really hoping for a little sister. She spent hours talking with Bailey about what she was going to do with her little sister, even offering to share her room. Bailey drew in a breath and smiled.

"Congratulations, Tara, boys are awesome."

Tara smiled. "Thanks, Bailey, I think so too."

"Happy for you guys, T," Saint said, curling Cia into his side as if some way he could take the disappointment from her. *God, I love this man.*

"Another boy," Cia mumbled.

Bailey covered her mouth, and Tara rolled her eyes. "Baby, I can't control the gender. Trust me, If I could have, I would give you a baby sister."

"You said this one would be a girl," Cia muttered.

Tara lifted her finger, shaking her head. "No, I said there was a chance, baby."

"Now, you're quitting, and I'll never get a sister," Cia said, curling closer into Saint's side.

"Oh Lord, help me." Tara jerked her head toward the sky.

"What am I missing?" Saint asked. She was glad he did because Bailey was just as confused with Cia's statement. *Quitting what?*

Tara sighed, resting her hands on her hips. "Denny and I have decided baby number three is gonna be our last. Gonna get my tubes tied this time. I'm too old to be getting knocked up."

Bailey burst out laughing. Tara had no filter, something Saint said she was like even as a kid. She wasn't the only one amused. She heard the masculine rumble and saw Saint smiling down at Tara.

"Not fair."

Tara threw her hands above her head. "Baby, this isn't my fault. Let's blame Denny, okay?" Again, Bailey found herself laughing at Tara's eagerness to throw her husband under the bus. Motherhood was rough. Sometimes a mom had to pass the buck and spare herself some guilt. "He only makes boys, and I told you, it's the man who determines the sex of the baby. See, it's Denny's fault."

"Tara," Saint warned.

She shrugged, then her eyes landed on Saint, then Bailey, and she smirked. Bailey suspected the conversation was about to make an abrupt turn.

Oh no, don't you dare.

"Denny only makes boys, but your daddy makes girls, baby."

Oh, hell she did it!

Cia's head popped up and eagerly smiled at her dad. "Dad, you should have a baby with Bailey. It'll definitely be a girl. Oh please, Dad." Cia bounced on her toes. Had it been anyone else in the scenario, Bailey would have laughed. A nine-year-old girl begging her dad to knock up his girlfriend? Hilarious.

"Baby," Saint said, and then huffed a breath scowling at Tara.

"Oh, please, Dad? You love Bailey, I hear ya tell her all the time, and I hear her say it back." She planted her hands on Saint's stomach. "And we have an extra room here." She whipped her head to Bailey. "And you said you like babies, remember?"

Bailey pressed her lips and smiled with a slow nod. "I do like babies." She flicked her eyes to Saint, and the corner of his mouth curled slightly. She couldn't tear her gaze away from the warmth of his eyes. Until Cia continued.

"See, Daddy."

Tara burst out laughing and Bailey followed. She couldn't help herself, it was a hysterical conversation being led by a nine-year-old. Saint shook his head and sighed.

"No more talking about babies. Go say bye to your mom and get your stuff to your room. Club barbeque in an hour."

"Awesome!" Cia shouted and ran down the steps embracing Tara. She grabbed her bag and raced inside. Saint waited until they no longer heard her footsteps and turned his heated glare on Tara.

"Not cool, T."

"Oh hell, lighten up, Saint."

"Lighten up? You just told her when Bailey has my baby it'll be a girl. What if it's a boy, T? Now ya gonna have my girl hating me?"

Tara scoffed and rolled her eyes. "Christ sake, Saint, no, she won't. Hell, Cia thinks you walk on water. Loves her daddy more than anything else in the world." She gazed over at Bailey. "And you? Non-stop talking, Bailey this, Bailey that."

Ohhhh. "I'm sorry."

Tara furrowed her brows. "Why the hell are ya sorry? She loves you, and I want her to love you, Bailey. Hell, I'm half in love with ya." Tara winked. "That's all I want, all of us, you guys, me and Denny, our boys, Cia, and hopefully your babies, all one big fucking family."

Aw….that sounds nice.

Tara chuckled and shook her head. "I just need her not to *hate me* for this. She's not a baby anymore. Now, one day she hates me, the other she loves me." Tara sighed and her shoulders sagged. "Just take this one for me, Saint?"

Bailey smirked as Saint glared at his ex. "I'll take it."

"Thank you, and well, if ya have a girl, everyone wins. Besides, your eyes on Bailey's beautiful face." She burst out laughing. "You need to start stocking double ammo for the boys who are gonna come calling for Cia and your girls."

Tara continued laughing across the yard, but halted and turned back. "Almost forgot. Christmas. My folks are coming and Denny's sister and the kids. I'll give you first dibs on the basement if ya want?"

Saint shook his head. "We'll get a room."

Tara winked. "Good. Start making that baby sister for Cia."

"Tara," he warned with a growl.

She waved her hand dismissing him which made Bailey chuckle.

"Bailey, you make anything special?"

"Cookies?"

"Girl after my own heart. Saint, you're in charge of beer, Bailey with the cookies. Have a good weekend."

Saint walked over hugging Bailey into his chest and she curved her back settling in as they waved to Tara.

"I try to picture you two as a couple, but I just can't."

"Sweetheart, there's a reason we only lasted a few years."

Bailey giggled, resting her head back, onto his chest. "Can I tell you something crazy?"

His lips grazed her ear. "What?"

The heat rose from her neck to her cheeks. "I think about what our babies would look like."

She angled her head to look up at him. His brows arched and he searched her face.

"You mean, what they *will* look like." His lips skimmed hers causing a heated tingling rush to course through her body. "They'll be beautiful, just like their mom."

"They're probably going to be a little bit of trouble." She smirked brushing her nose against his jaw. His chest rumbled against her back.

"Oh, they'll definitely be trouble." He cupped her jaw and she angled her head, staring back into his eyes. "Strong and beautiful hellraisers."

SAINT WALKED DOWN THE STAIRS, veering into the kitchen. He stopped in the doorway, appreciating the view. Bailey was at the sink with her back to him. Her tight jeans hugged her ass in a way which had him adjusting his stance. It was a tease. He knew he couldn't have her. It was her rule, not his. If Saint was the deciding factor, Bailey would be in his bed tonight.

"Staying the night?" He watched her hair slide across her back as she shook her head. He smirked. It was worth a shot, no shame in asking.

He walked through the kitchen, coming up behind Bailey and gripping her hips, pressing his growing erection against her ass. She swiveled her hips, and he dropped his mouth to her neck.

"No," she whispered. He assumed she was trying to be firm but it came out more of a purr. He chuckled and planted a kiss on her neck before stepping away and making his way to the fridge. He grabbed the handle, but stopped to read the list on the outer door.

Bailey and Cia had made her Christmas list after dinner. It was a sight which hit him hard. They'd spent an hour writing it, mostly laughing. Nothing made him happier than knowing his daughter loved Bailey as much as he did. Almost. He didn't think a person alive could feel more for Bailey than he did.

He opened the door, grabbing a water before turning back to Bailey. He loved the idea of her spending the holidays with them. Being a month away, he hadn't thought to mention it until Tara did. He'd been waiting all day to bring it up but didn't want Cia to be around when he did.

"Not going home for Christmas?"

She halted at his question then glanced over her shoulder. "Ghosttown is my home."

"You know what I mean, to your parents'?"

She shrugged, turning back and grabbed the towel drying off her hands. She was purposely avoiding eye contact. Saint watched as she quietly worked around his kitchen. She walked to the fridge, opening the door and remained silent.

"Sweetheart." It was obviously a touchy subject, though he wasn't sure why. Bailey had mentioned her family with ease. She didn't share much. From what she did, it seemed as though she had a good relationship with them.

She closed the door, keeping her hand on the handle of the fridge. He noticed the tension in her tight brows.

"I go back east every other year. I went last year." She raised her brows. "This is my year off."

Saint was leaning against the door frame with his arms folded. "Year off?" He chuckled. "You make it sound like a community service."

She snorted. "It's complicated."

"Thought you got along with your family?"

She released the door and grasped her hands in front of her. It was obvious she was not enjoying the conversation. *Why?*

"I do."

Maybe he was reading this from the wrong angle. Could Bailey be tight lipped about her family in fear they wouldn't approve of him? Saint never gave much thought to how others perceived him. However, if it was a concern for her, then it would be an issue for him.

"You think Mom and Dad will approve?" he asked.

She whipped around and pointed. "Of you?"

He cocked a brow and nodded. The corners of her mouth curled.

"Oh yeah, my mom is going to love you. Seriously, she might even flirt with you, but don't freak out, she's like that with everyone." She gave a bright smile, the first since the topic had come up. "And my dad has watched every biker documentary on tv so he'll spend hours picking your brain and probably ask for you to divulge secrets." She raised her hands. "Of course, I know you won't. Just giving you a heads up." She chuckled. "My brothers, especially Van, will seriously love you, Saint. Cia too."

The information should have put him at ease. It didn't. He was left wondering what she was holding back.

Her smile faltered. "Did you think you were the reason I wasn't going for Christmas?"

He shrugged, remaining silent. He wanted her to open up without having to push her.

She rested her hand on her chest. "It's me, Saint, not you, I promise."

He lifted his chin. "What do you mean, it's you?"

She drew in a breath then gulped and inhaled another breath. "I love my family." She sighed and scrunched her nose. "This is going to sound bad."

Saint smirked. "Tell me."

"Promise not to hold it against me?"

He nodded.

"They drive me nuts."

Saint chuckled. "Why?"

Bailey rolled her eyes. "I love them."

"You said that." He held back his amusement.

She folded her arms. "Ever since the incident with Adam, they've become increasingly overbearing and overprotective." She

The Saint

widened her eyes which made him chuckle. "Except my youngest brother, Van, who also moved a thousand miles away from my family, so it's not just me." She winked then her humor faded.

"When it happened," she jerked her chin toward her arms and didn't elaborate on the *it*, "my family rallied around me, of course. My mom spent nights at the hospital, can't remember a day when my dad wasn't there, same with my brothers. Everyone just wanted to help me." She paused. "And they did." She smiled. "I really don't think I could have gotten through it without them."

His chest tightened. It may not have been him, but she had her people with her. "Sounds like good people, Bailey."

"They are. They all stood by me during my recovery and the trial. I couldn't ask for a better support system." She dragged her hand down her face. "This is going to sound so bad."

"Tell me."

She dropped her hand from her face. She was struggling with her honesty.

"Tell me, sweetheart."

She sighed. "It changed them. I could feel the anxious air when I'd walk in a room, they walked on eggshells around me. Everyone was so guarded with what they said and how they spoke to me. Even my older brothers, who had made it their life's mission to tease and torture me throughout our childhood." She snorted. "They were so damn polite and kind and different with me." She stared at the floor and whispered. "I can't believe how much I missed being mocked and ridiculed by them." She sighed. "I just wanted everything to be normal. It took me a while to realize, *this was* the new normal. And unless I changed it, this would be my life." She rolled her shoulder and lowered her voice. "And theirs, too."

It was an eye opener seeing all the damage Adam had cost Bailey. Damage beyond the naked eye. His actions hadn't only scarred Bailey but her family too.

"So you moved and became Mayor of Ghosttown?"

She laughed and glanced up. "Pretty much." Her cheeks

turned a dark shade of pink. "I just needed space from them and their constant coddling. And they needed it too, though they'd never admit it. It sounds worse than it is, I swear." She glanced down, fiddling with a string on her shirt. "It was a good move for my family as a whole."

"How'd they feel about the move?"

She groaned. "They hated it, but my dad reasoned with my mom, and she finally stopped giving me a guilt trip every time I spoke to her." She pursed her lips. "Oddly enough, the distance brought back some normalcy. I still limit my visits." She twisted her lips. "My family is wonderful, in small doses."

"They visit often?"

She nodded. "Mom and Dad twice a year, and my youngest brother, Van, comes for a week in the summer." She smirked. "You'll like him, reminds me a lot of Gage."

Just what we need, another Gage. He snickered. "I look forward to meeting them all."

She squinted her eyes. "You don't think it's wrong? Me keeping distance with my family?"

Saint shook his head. "I wouldn't tell you what to do, I don't walk in your shoes, Bailey." He pushed off the wall and started toward her. There was no hesitation when he got close to her. She reached out, resting her hands on his chest. "It's your choice how you handle it."

The corner of her lips curled. "I always have a choice. It's what you said to me on our first date."

"Always." He leaned in kissing her lips. "Just like now, you have a choice to stay the night."

She pulled back and rolled her eyes. He could see the humor glimmering in her gaze. "I'm not sleeping over with Cia here."

"Just sleeping, sweetheart."

She snorted and poked his chest. "You're a bad liar, Saint."

He chuckled and released her from his arms. If she wasn't staying, then he didn't want her out driving too late. She seemed to be on the same page as she grabbed her sweater and bag from his table.

"I'm going to get some groceries before I stop over in the morning." She started out the door and he followed. He'd heard her mentioning to Cia about baking something. The two of them had planned out the next two days since Cia had off on Monday and would be spending it with them.

She turned at her car and he ambled closer, sending her back against the door. He cupped her jaw, grazing her cheeks with his thumbs.

"I love you," he whispered.

Bailey leaned closer for a kiss, mumbling. "Hearing those words, never gets old." Her lips spread and her tongue slid against his lower lip. *Kissing Bailey never gets old.* Her hands drifted around his back. She slowed the kiss which was a good idea. Another few minutes of kissing her and he'd be taking away her choice of staying the night. His lips grazed her mouth.

"I love you too." She smiled and leaned in for a quick kiss. He stepped away, opening her door and allowing her the space to slide in.

He waited until she turned out of the driveway.

Saint was making his way up the back steps when his phone rang. He glanced down and quickly answered. He'd been waiting to hear from Decker, knowing he'd only call when he had information.

"Yeah."

"Saint, how's it going?"

"Good. How about you?"

Decker laughed. "All's good here. So, I pulled up everything I could. It was a bitch getting the phone records. Had to call in a fuck ton of favors for that one." He paused. He didn't need to go on, Saint understood what he was insinuating with his silence. Saint would owe Decker.

"Let me know what ya need."

"I will. But back to you. You already know he's shacking up

with his sister. Got a factory job, third shift. Had a guy tail him last week. Nothing out the ordinary."

"Where does he spend his time?"

Decker laughed. "Where do most ex-cons spend their free time, Saint? Titty bars."

Saint rolled his eyes. "Phone records?"

"Yeah." He inhaled a deep breath which Saint could hear through the receiver. "On average, he makes four calls daily to your woman."

Saint gripped the phone, feeling the rush of ice stream through his veins. "Does she take them?"

"Only a few, for about five seconds. I figure just enough time to tell him to fuck off then hang up. From what I can tell with the time stamp, he mostly hangs up before leaving a message."

"Son of a bitch."

"I take it she hasn't shared that with you, huh?"

She had withheld in her sharing. Bailey had mentioned his calls, but not four times a day.

Saint tightened his lips. "Is it a registered phone?"

"Yeah." He chuckled. "Dumb fuck, if ya ask me. You stalk a woman, you use a burner, not something that can be traced back to ya."

It was reckless, which made Adam more dangerous.

"Okay. Send me over his employment address and a copy of the phone records."

"I'll send it over now. You let me know ya need anything else."

Saint hung up and swung open the door. The new information had him on edge. Usually, he could formulate a plan immediately. This was cutting too close. He dialed the phone and waited as it rang.

"What's going on?" Hades asked.

"Need you to come up tomorrow."

"Tell me."

It was nothing which could be discussed over the phone.

"When you get here."

His brother cursed. "I got Allie, man. Reach out to Meg for me?"

Meg had always been their go-to person to watch the kids. However, she wasn't needed this time.

"Bailey will be here."

"Okay, then I'll see you tomorrow."

Saint hung up and tossed his phone on the table. He'd wait until he got the call from Bailey that she arrived home safe. He should have insisted she stay. The new information of his incessant calls changed things. Until they knew where Adam's mind was at, she wasn't safe. But leaving Cia home alone wasn't an option either. He'd had the prospects making routine drive-by's her house since Adam had made an appearance. This new information called for more.

"Fuck."

He grabbed his phone and pulled up the contacts. It was a given, any one of his brothers would step in and have his back. He searched his contacts and called the number. Two rings.

"What's up, man?" The noise in the background gave away his location. From the loud music at the clubhouse, he was definitely in the middle of a party.

"Need eyes on Bailey's place. I got Cia here, I can't leave."

The small silence had Saint shifting on his feet. The background noise was muted and he heard a door slam.

"Done. Getting my keys now, I'll be at her place in ten minutes."

Saint nodded his head and sighed in relief. "Thanks, Gage."

"Anything for our mayor, brother." Gage laughed. "You're a lucky bastard, Saint. I would have called dibs on her had ya not claimed her."

Saint smiled. Bailey was a prize and every brother knew it. Unfortunately, for them, she was Saint's.

Chapter 21

It was just past ten when she pulled into Saint's driveway. She stopped mid-way up the double drive, parking next to an unfamiliar pickup. He hadn't mentioned having anyone over. She got out and grabbed the bags from the trunk and started toward the backyard.

"Hi Bailey," Cia shouted from the swings. She pointed to the swing next to her with a little girl. "This is Allie."

Bailey smiled and waved. "Hi Allie."

The little girl couldn't have been more than four, and not as successful as Cia when it came to the swings. Her tiny legs flailed in opposite directions. She was going half the height of Cia. She kept her hands tightly wrapped on the straps, and wiggled her fingers in a wave.

Bailey made her way up the back steps, glancing over her shoulder at Cia and little Allie. This would be another conversation later. Bailey smiled and opened the door, walking through the tiny mudroom into the kitchen. Saint turned when she cleared her throat.

"Please tell me she's not stealing random neighborhood kids to prove how good she would be at having a little sister."

Saint furrowed his brows then his lips curled and he laughed.

He turned toward her and jerked his chin over her head. "I see ya met Allie."

Bailey smirked. "Oh good, so you know the little cutie?"

He chuckled and nodded. "Yeah."

"Do her parents know she's here?" She stepped forward, no longer caring for the joking banter. All she wanted was a kiss. She was growing addicted to Saint. She wrapped her hands around his waist, resting her chin on his chest. "Where's my kiss?" she whispered.

In their time together, Bailey had gotten more brazen, and Saint seemed to enjoy it, though he still seemed slightly amused. His head bent but a slow seduction was not what she wanted. She lifted on her toes and kissed him.

His lips. *Soft.* She angled her neck to deepen the kiss, holding herself steady on his hips. With her body meshed against his, there was no denying the erection butting into her stomach. It was almost torturous knowing they'd have to wait. His hands grasped her neck and through her shivers she opened for him, dipping her tongue between his lips. Kissing Saint would never grow old, she guessed. She moaned softly against his mouth. His only response was to tighten his grip on her neck. The thought of stopping because it may have been getting out of hand was fleeting. She pulled him closer, grazing her teeth on his bottom lip and gliding her tongue along the outline. It was a little move, she discovered Saint liked. A lot. Her hand unraveled from his waist and drifted lower.

A little fooling around, a mere tease in the kitchen while the kids were outside couldn't hurt. She only got as far as the edge of his pants when he grabbed her wrist halting her. Stunned, she pulled back and found his heated stare slightly amused and corner of his mouth curled.

"Oh, this is fucking great." A deep voice riddled with sarcasm jolted her away from Saint. His hand on her neck kept her from getting too far. She jerked her stare over her shoulder to see Hades standing in the doorframe, arms crossed and a harsh scowl.

The Saint

Her bottom lip fell open. *How long had he been standing there?*

Hades glared at Saint. "You do that shit in front of my kid, I'll be fucking pissed, Saint. Not looking forward to giving her the fucking talk, period." He shook his head then turned on Bailey. "Not giving it to her at four, ya get me?"

She didn't get him, in fact, she could barely comprehend what he was saying. She was still focused on how long he'd been standing there watching them. Bailey gazed down at the floor. A little heads up from Saint about Hades being there would have been nice. She shot a look to Saint, but his eyes were drawn to Hades.

"Allie's fine, relax, Roman."

Wait a minute. She jerked her head and stared back at Hades. Allie was his?

"You have a daughter?" Her tone was clearly shocked. A little detail Hades did not miss.

"That hard to believe, Bailey?" Hades narrowed his gaze.

Yes!

"No," she blurted.

Hades snorted, obviously not believing her lie. His gaze lingered between Saint and Bailey, landing on her, and he smirked, shaking his head.

"It's always the quiet ones."

"Hades." Saint's tone was stern with an obvious warning Bailey didn't miss, and neither did Hades.

When she glanced back at Hades, he was smirking. Then he mouthed, "Trouble."

His teasing halted and he turned his head toward the door just as the girls came barreling in hand in hand. Then something amazing happened. Hades smiled, a true genuine sign of happiness, and it was set on the little girl trailing behind Cia.

"Can we have lunch now?" Cia asked.

The room was silent and Bailey had her sole focus on Hades. He was a dad? To a little girl? She hadn't realized she was staring until he glanced at her and raised his brows. She shifted her gaze and realized everyone was staring at her, waiting on her.

"So, can we Bailey?" Cia asked, clasping her hand and winding her fingers through hers.

"Oh, uh…" She turned to Saint and smiled. Why was she asking her?

He sighed. "Hades needs help with something at the clubhouse, asked if I'd come along." He seemed uneasy, which was completely out of character for Saint. "Wondering if you could watch the girls tonight."

She widened her eyes and nodded. "Sure."

"Yeah?" he asked as though he was trying to gage her answer. This was odd.

"Yeah, no problem." She squeezed Cia's hand gaining her attention. "Why don't you and Allie go watch some TV while I make you sandwiches, sound good?"

"Yeah. Can we have chips too?"

"Uh, yeah, as long as it's good with your dads." She glanced over at Saint whose face had softened.

"Whatever ya wanna give them, Bailey."

"C'mon," Hades said, and she watched his hand reach for Allie's, and she rushed over putting her tiny hand in his. They walked toward the living room, followed by Cia.

She jerked her gaze to Saint and snickered. "Hades is a dad, huh?"

Saint snickered, obviously understanding her surprise. "Damn good one, too." He hooked his arm around her waist. He lowered his voice and she angled her head. "You okay with this?"

"Yeah."

His brows furrowed together. "Was gonna ask, sweetheart. Cia came in before I got the chance. You don't have to. I can call Meg or one of the girls."

She pulled away slightly. "Wait, why would you call someone else?"

"Just don't want you to feel like I'm pawning my shit on you."

"Don't you trust me?"

It was Saint's turn to look confused. "What?"

She shrugged. "I don't have crazy experience with kids, but I mean, I can watch them and feed them and make sure nothing happens." The more she spoke the more anxious she was getting. "Cia seems really comfortable around me, I mean, I'm pretty sure she likes me. I can take care of them, Saint."

"Sweetheart, look at me."

She glanced up and saw a small smile playing on his lips. "I know you can. Wouldn't have asked if I didn't. Cia doesn't like ya, Bailey, she loves you. Half the reason she wants to come here is you." His hands slid up her chest and neck landing on her jaw. He angled her head and reached down, pressing a soft kiss to her lips before straightening. "Just wanna make sure you're okay with staying with them. Don't want you to feel like I'm asking you to take on my responsibility."

"I want to though."

Saint smiled, kissing her again. This time she leaned closer, opening her mouth and taking his kiss deeper.

"Christ, Saint." The booming voice behind her jolted Bailey into Saint. His chest rumbled and she glanced up to see him holding back a grin. *Caught again.*

SAINT SETTLED into his seat and glanced down at his phone. It was after midnight, he needed to head out soon if he wanted to be there by four. Starting time for that motherfucker. He shoved his phone in his pocket and noticed Hades watching him instead of the club whores.

"Everything good?" he asked.

Saint nodded. He had checked in with Bailey a few hours ago. She was settling into bed. Not alone. Apparently, the girls insisted on a movie in his master, and all three were snuggled up watching a movie. They were in safe hands. And so was Bailey. He had a prospect watching the house.

Saint shifted in his seat. "Gonna head out. I'll see you tomorrow."

"Where the fuck are you going?" Kase snapped.

Saint drew in a breath. He'd mentioned the Adam situation to Hades, but decided to handle it on his own. Unbeknownst to Hades, of course. And his brothers. Or so he thought.

Kase slammed his beer on the table and leaned forward. "Not fucking alone, brother."

It was one of the downfalls of knowing each other so well. Kase knew exactly where he was headed. Saint stood and adjusted his cut.

"What the fuck, Saint?" Hades asked then glanced over at Kase, who was glaring at him.

"I can handle him alone."

Kase narrowed his gaze. "Not how we do things and you fucking know it."

He did. Had it been for another brother, he would have insisted on going himself, along with a few more brothers. It was how the club worked. When Rourke had his issue with Macy's attacker, they all stood together and handled it.

Hades shifted in his seat and eyed Saint. "This is why ya gave her the story about us at the club for the night." He shook his head. "Motherfucker. You just gonna go at it alone?"

Kase cleared his throat. "Time we paid the motherfucker a visit, brother."

It was.

"I need to get inside his head, see where he's at."

Kase laughed, and Saint glared back at him. Kase and Hades were one at the same.

"Need to take him out," Kase said.

"Talking with Hades, I see."

Kase shrugged. "Only way to guarantee her safety."

"Yeah, and where does murder fall into your going legit plan, Kase?"

"There's always an exception." He shrugged his shoulder. "This time it's Bailey."

Saint's hands weren't completely clean when it came to illegal activities in the past few years. With one exception. *Mick.*

His blood brother stood and finished off his beer before slamming the glass on the table. "Let's go."

"Not your business, Hades." It was bullshit and even Saint knew it.

"The fuck it isn't. This asshole thinks he can fuck with my brother's woman and get away with it? Yeah, it is my fucking business. You and her, my business."

Saint was aware of the small gathering around the table. Rourke and Trax rounded his side with Gage making a close entry from the back. Even Dobbs stepped closer to the mix. Not how he wanted to handle it.

"What's going on?" Trax asked.

Kase narrowed his gaze at Saint and dipped his chin, gesturing to Saint. "Your asshole VP thinks his business ain't ours. Thinks he needs to handle shit with Bailey without the club backing him."

"What the fuck, Saint?" Rourke snapped.

Saint eyed Kase and shook his head.

He smirked, leaning forward. "Your girl." He raised his brows. "She's one of mine, now, and if you think for a fucking second I don't wanna piece of that motherfucker, then you don't know me as well as ya think you do, brother."

Saint tensed his shoulders and straightened his back. "Just a warning, it's all I'm doing."

"And you do it with your brothers at your back," Kase said through gritted teeth.

"Gimme ten, I gotta get Macy home," Rourke said. Trax followed behind and he assumed he'd be doing the same with Cheyenne.

Saint eyed his brothers. All of them. Those in brotherhood and one in blood.

Thirty minutes later, they were on the road. They made good time, not one brother needing to stop, and they made it in a little over than three hours. They pulled into the gas station across from the factory Adam had recently been hired to. It was still dark, but from their location, Saint could see everyone who arrived at work. He kept his gaze trained on the parking lot.

"What's your plan?"

"Just a warning," he said.

Hades scoffed. "Getting fucking soft on me, brother?"

Saint didn't respond. He wasn't even close to soft. This wasn't about him. This was for Bailey.

"We should kill him," Hades said without a trace of humor.

He was probably right. For what he'd done to Bailey, he deserved to die. Saint drew in a breath as he caught sight of Adam's car turning into the lot. His whole body tensed as he lifted off his bike. This would be a warning he'd be smart to heed. As he started across the street, the brothers flanked his back. He would take the lead and they would follow.

He would end this for her. Tonight.

Chapter 22

Bailey yawned, covering her free hand over her mouth. Her other was curled around Allie who had become attached to her hip since last night.

She had a newfound respect for moms. She couldn't remember ever being so tired. After lunch, riding their bikes, playing dress-up, seven rounds of checkers, a craft which she was still trying to figure out how to get rid of all the damn glitter, dinner, and two movies, she had tucked the girls in bed in Cia's room. When she finally dropped onto the bed, she was seconds from sleep when Allie poked her the stomach. She had turned her head to find the wide-eyed cutie staring back at her.

"You okay?"

"Can I sleep with you?"

Bailey pushed up off the mattress. "Um…" *What was the right protocol?* She was weighing her options when Allie tossed her stuffed dog on the bed and crawled over to Saint's side, slinking under the covers. Decision made.

She turned and tucked the covers around Allie and lay back down, closing her eyes. She was just losing consciousness when she felt a warm breath fan her face. She opened her eyes to find Allie inches from her face.

"You have freckles."

Bailey nodded with a tight smile. From the looks of it, Allie wasn't nearly as tired as she was.

Allie titled her head. "How come?"

One little question, was followed by a hundred more. By the time she'd actually fallen asleep, Cia was at her bedside waking her up. Bailey staggered out of bed giving a glance over her shoulder at Allie, who was fast asleep and would be for the next four hours.

So, this is motherhood.

After making breakfast, two times, they all showered and got ready for their day. After painting toenails. Twice for Allie who couldn't seem to sit still long enough to allow them to dry, they played in the yard, made beaded necklaces, played a few rounds of I Spy on the front porch, and rode their bikes which ended in a small disaster when Allie fell off skinning her knee on the gravel. After twenty minutes cleaning it out through tears and seven different Band-Aids they were settled into the living room watching a movie. Cia brought out tons of pillows making a fort for them, but ten minutes into the movie, Allie grabbed her stuffed dog and climbed up on the couch, tucking herself into Bailey's side.

Saint and Hades came back hours later. When they walked in Cia barely acknowledged them unable to tear herself away from the best part of the movie. Bailey giggled since it was the third time she declared the statement in the last thirty minutes.

"How'd it go?"

Saint nodded giving her a small smile while taking in the scene playing out in front of him. Allie had made herself completely comfortable in the nook of her arm and laid her head on Bailey's chest, barely lifting it when they came in.

"Everything go good here?"

"Yeah, we ate, we played, even did our nails," Bailey said, then smiled when Allie kicked her feet from underneath the blanket and wiggled her toes.

"Looks pretty, Als," Saint said.

"My knee is broken, see?" Allie leaned forward whipping the blanket off her legs, exposing the colorful array of Band-Aids.

She heard his boots clamor down on the hardwood and caught his growl before she heard his whispered, "What?"

Bailey sat up and angled her head toward Hades who was wearing his signature scowl. "She fell off her bike, but I cleaned it out, got all the gravel, and disinfected it. The bandaging was Cia's work. I assure you most of them are for decoration." She laughed nervously.

Hades ignored Bailey and bent down bringing him eye level with his daughter. "You all right, baby?"

She nodded. "Uh huh, Bailey fixed it. Then I got two," she held up her fingers, "ice pops 'cause I'm brave." Allie glanced up at Bailey. "Right?"

Bailey hugged her into her side and smiled. "Super brave." She laughed then glanced up at Hades who was staring at her. Allie wiggled off the couch to get her bag from the floor, packing up her dog, baby dolls and all her stuff.

"Thanks," Hades said.

"No problem. I'm sorry she got hurt." She lowered her voice. "She was trying to keep up with Cia."

Hades turned and his featured softened. "Happens. Appreciate you taking care of her. She doesn't get that a lot."

It seemed like such a strange comment. "Get what?"

"A woman fussing over her. Her mom is shit, so when she gets it from a female, she eats it up." He cocked a brow. "Gets an extra ice pop and shit." He smirked.

"You saying she played me?"

He shrugged. "Probably."

Saint laughed, hooking his arms around her waist with her back against his chest. She clasped her hands over his. Hades gaze dropped to where Saint held onto to her. There was a calm silence. He straightened his shoulders and glanced back up. Not at her, at Saint. Bailey watched but couldn't read his expression. When

Hades' chin dipped, it felt as though he was giving some sort of approval. She couldn't be sure.

"Uh, Hades?"

He glanced up, remaining silent. Bailey shrugged and glanced down at Allie. "If you ever need someone to keep an eye on Allie, let me know. I work from home, so I'm always available." He continued to watch her without saying a word. She shifted against Saint. "Ya know if you ever need someone." Her words tapered into a whisper.

His eyes squinted, and the corner of his mouth curled. "I appreciate it, Bailey." He nodded. "Don't have many people I trust with her beside Saint, so yeah, I'll do that."

She widened her eyes caught off guard by his admission he trusted her. She smiled. He turned toward the living room.

"Let's go, Al," Hades said.

Cia got up and hugged her little cousin. Saint unraveled his hold and bent down, wrapping his arms around Allie. She turned her head, giving him a kiss on his cheek, which for some odd reason hit Bailey hard. It was so sweet especially seeing a big man like Saint melt over a little girl. Hades grabbed Allie's pink backpack, and she bit back her giggle. The only thing odder than Saint with Allie was Hades holding a pink bag.

"Bye Bailey." She felt a tug on her pants and glanced down to find Allie looking up at her. She bent down to her eye level. She was so cute.

"It's Aunt Bailey." Cia garnered everyone's attention. She glanced at her Dad then uncle. "Well, if Dad is her uncle, then Bailey is her aunt, right?"

Bailey licked her lips. It was extremely awkward with the adults in the room silent. Allie seemed unfazed. She threw her arms around Bailey's shoulders, which made her smile, then leaned back and pressed her tiny lips on Bailey's cheeks for a kiss.

"Bye, Aunt Bailey." She turned, making her way to Hades and clasping his hand.

Bailey straightened and clamped her lips.

"We're outta here." Hades opened the door and glanced over his shoulder. "See ya guys next week." His gaze shifted to Bailey, and he smirked. "Later, Aunt Bailey." He winked and closed the door behind him.

What the hell just happened?

HE FINALLY HAD HER ALONE.

She glanced over her shoulder, and the corner of her lip curled. "You hungry?" She bent over the counter, and the edge of her skirt inched up on her thighs. It was a tease. He eyed the hem of her skirt. It rose just high enough to catch a glimpse of her ass cheek.

He stalked forward. He grasped her hips, pulling her against his cock, which was hard just from his view. She jutted up, pressing her back against his chest and winding her hand up his neck. Just from a touch he was risking losing control with her. His fingers grazed her stomach and caught the hitch in her breath as she pressed her ass against his hardened cock, again. Fuck. She swiveled her hips.

He heard the bike pull into his driveway. Kase's was louder than all of the brothers. Bailey moaned in frustration. *Bad fucking timing, brother.*

"It's Kase."

She dug her nails into his skin. "Make him go away."

He nestled his face against her neck. "I can lock the door, but he's a stubborn bastard. He'll ring the bell until I answer."

When the engine shut off, he backed away from Bailey, noticing her small pout as she walked out of the room. He adjusted his pants and turned to the back door.

Kase appeared, scanning the room. "Where's the mayor?"

He jerked his head toward the doorway.

"Need to talk to her."

"About?"

Kase smirked. Bailey came into the room and stopped at the doorway. She must have heard Kase. Her gaze flicked between him and Kase. She may have pulled herself together, but Saint could see the residual heat in her eyes when she looked at him. *Fuck, Kase.*

"Hi, Kase. Need a permit?" She raised her brows.

"No." Kase chuckled. "Just need to talk to you."

Bailey arched her brow. "You want to hire me as the new bartender?" she teased, and Saint laughed.

"Need a favor."

Bailey's eyes widened, and she moved into the room, taking a seat at the table across from Kase. Saint was oddly surprised and relieved she showed not an ounce of uneasiness around him.

"Sure, what do ya need?"

Kase pulled out the chair from across the table. "You know the owner of the property next door to the clubhouse? Shaw?"

Saint handed him a glass of bourbon and watched Bailey's reaction. Long before they moved to Ghosttown, the club had been trying to obtain the property next door. They'd been unsuccessful. There hadn't been much talk since the last offer was declined. Saint figured Kase had given up.

Bailey smiled and nodded. "Yeah, I know Phoebe. We're actually pretty close friends. She's awesome."

Kase halted in mid-sip of his drink and stared at her over the rim of his glass. Saint bit back his smile. This would be fun to watch, he assumed. He'd known Kase for a long time and was well aware of his brother's intentions with the adjacent property.

"You want me to introduce you? You guys will like her. She mostly keeps to herself. She's very friendly and easy-going. If ya think she'll give you trouble, she won't. You won't have to win her over like some of the other residents."

Saint snorted, and she turned to him. He had his focus on Kase. *Give it a shot, brother.*

Kase cleared his throat, settling back into his chair. "I wanna buy her property. Had our people reach out. She declined." He sighed. "All six times. Need you to talk to her."

Bailey straightened her back. "You want me to try and get her to sell?"

Kase raised his brows and nodded.

"No."

"Why the fuck not?"

"'Cause it's her home. If Phoebe doesn't want to sell, I'm not going to try and force her to. Besides, I don't want her to leave."

Of course, Bailey wouldn't. Saint sipped his drink, enjoying the exchange between them.

"Look, let me lay it for ya. We need the property if we want to expand and keep shit close to us. She's got four acres of untouched land and a small shack just taking up space. She can find a better place for what I'm offering her. She'll make bank. We get the property. Everyone fucking wins. You hear me?"

Bailey bit her lips, eyeing Saint. "Yeah."

She didn't have to say another word. Saint was so in sync with her. He knew what her response would be. However, Kase didn't.

Kase sighed. "So, you'll talk to her?"

Bailey clamped her lips then slowly shook her head. Kase may reign king over the Ghosttown Riders, but Bailey wasn't bowing down. *That's my girl.*

"You're starting to piss me off." His lip twitched.

"I know." She smirked.

Saint chuckled. There was a lot Bailey was willing to do for the club, but convincing Phoebe to move wasn't one of them. She hadn't mentioned her much, but if she was resisting, they must have been close. Saint wouldn't play a part in this. This was Kase's fight.

Chapter 23

Bailey dried off her hands at the sound of her bell. It seemed odd since visitors rarely used the front door. She stopped at the living room hall catching the tall shadow through the curtains on her door. She groaned softly, dropping her head.

This could only be one person. She couldn't believe Arnett had the nerve to show up at her house. Saint was right. She needed to set ground rules of some sort. Why not call? Showing up at her house past nine was completely unacceptable. She drew in a breath and marched to the door fully prepared to lay it all out for him. She had been nice for too long. She clicked open the lock and yanked the door wide.

Oh my God.

Oh.

My.

God.

Her chest tightened, and her gaze seemed off, almost fuzzy. The only sound blasting through her ears was the erratic thump of her own heartbeat. It was frantic. For as heavy as her heart beat, her body had an adverse reaction, cold and numbing, as if the blood was draining from her body and her stomach twisted.

It wasn't over.

"You call off your dogs, ya hear me, Bailey?"

Adam stood two feet away, yet he sounded so far away, the way his voice echoed as if he was in a valley. But he wasn't far away. He was standing here, in front of her, staring back at her with a blazing glare. *He's at my house.* She stepped back in a stumble, her head felt so heavy, and a wave of dizziness washed over her. If not for her harsh grip on the door handle, she may have fallen to the ground.

I handled this.

"Bailey," he snapped, and she winced, gasping for breath. It was as if her throat was closing. She gasped again, needing the air to fill her lungs. She blinked incessantly, the room closing in on her. *Oh hell.* She was going to pass out and be unconscious with him in her house.

"Jesus Christ."

Her body was frozen with fear, only stabilizing her more when his hands gripped her forearms tight, and her feet left the ground. She shook her head and opened her mouth. Nothing came out until her back hit the couch, seemingly knocking her back into life. She choked out a cough gasping for as much air as her lungs could take. Her eyes teared up and her skin prickled then shivered.

"Still a fucking mess, I see." His tone was nasty and condescending. It seemed not much had changed in the last five years. She glanced up through her lashes. Adam was standing in the middle of her living room. The man who had scarred her and changed her life forever was standing in her house, insulting her.

She swallowed a harsh breath. "Get out."

He shook his head. "You tell them to back the fuck down."

He wasn't making sense. "Who?"

His nostrils flared, and he moved toward her. She scurried into the couch, shifting her gaze around the room, desperate for an escape path. She was fucked. He had over a hundred pounds on

The Saint

her, and by the looks of him now, he'd spent the majority of his sentence working out. *Oh, I'm so fucked.*

"The fucking pussy squad who showed up at my work threatening me. How ya think my boss takes it when those fuckers rolled up on their bikes and started spewing their bullshit? I just got the job, and I'm on fucking probation, you stupid cunt. They show up again, and I'm fired." He leaned in close and curled his upper lip. He always did that, coiling like a snake before he snapped. "You fix this shit, bitch, or I'll fix you. *Again.*"

She didn't know what came over her. She balled her fist and swung forward, cracking against his jaw. His head jerked back, and she gasped. *Oh my God, I did it.* Her small victory was short-lived. He spun, burning rage filtering through his glare.

Bailey bolted toward the edge of the couch, fully prepared to throw herself over the back and run out the back door. She was desperate, and while she wasn't sure if she'd get away, she had to try. His hand gripped her ankle, yanking on her leg. She twisted around and heaved back and kicked with as much power as she had. He wasn't prepared and let go of her leg. She scrambled up, her foot slipping out from under her, and tripped into her bookcase. The sharp edge stabbed into her hip bone. Her slip up gave him the time he needed to recover. She coiled around the small end table and could see the back door. *Run!*

She was just at the kitchen table when his hand gripped the back of her head, weaving into her hair and yanking her backward. Pain ripped through her scalp, and she tried to grasp at his hands, but her body spun, and she flew through the air, landing on the hard floor back in the living room. Her head bounced against the hardwood, and her gaze shifted. Bright white spots made it impossible to see where he was until she caught the sound of his boots. It echoed, like a dysfunctional march—loud, hard, hurried steps pounding from all around her. Then they stopped.

A simultaneous click, a familiar sound, though she couldn't place it. *Again, and again, and again.* She blinked, trying to gain back her sight. The room went from a chaotic rampage to eerily dead silence. *What the hell was happening?* She moved onto her side, heaving her body up to a seated position and glanced up. It was still fuzzy. Adam stood in front of her with his gaze locked overhead. Beyond his shoulder, she could make out a large man. She leaned to her side and widened her eyes. Rourke, with Trax next to him stood side by side, both aiming a gun at the back of Adam's head.

She swiveled around and gasped, her bottom lip falling open at the sight of the front of her living room. Kase and Saint mimicking their brothers, guns loaded and aimed at her ex.

"Saint," she whispered, her voice groggy and timid.

She'd seen a stoic, unemotional Saint before, but nothing like this. This was deadly.

A pair of boots moved forward. "Take him out back and wait for us," Kase said.

She pushed off the ground feeling the aches and bruises setting in, and she dropped her head, trying to find her strength. Her arms were shaking, making it even harder to get up. She felt him near before she saw him and felt his touch.

"Easy, sweetheart."

There it was, the only voice she wanted to hear. She glanced up, and Saint gently wrapped his arm around her waist, lifting her against his chest and hooking his other arm under her legs. She threw her arms around his neck and completely lost it. With her fear subsiding, reality struck of what could have happened if he hadn't shown up. She sobbed heavily, squeezing him harder. He moved them to the couch, seating himself and holding her close to his chest.

His hands drew circles over her back, and his mouth grazed her ear. "I'm here, sweetheart. Nothing's gonna hurt you, I promise, Bailey."

"He came to my house, Saint." Her chest heaved. "I didn't handle it."

For all the pride she felt in holding her own with Adam, it meant nothing. *He came for me.*

"Yes," Saint whispered in her ear. "You did, sweetheart."

She shook her head and cried into his neck. She hadn't. He showed up at her house. She hadn't handled shit with him.

"This is on me, Bailey. Found out where he was, stopped in to make sure he knew to stay away, and what would happen if he didn't. Didn't think he'd come back again after I threatened him. This on me, sweetheart." His voice was strained as he hugged her closer. "I'm sorry, so fucking sorry."

She wouldn't allow Saint to take this on. He was only trying to keep her safe. "It's not your fault." She tightened her grip around his neck. His hand circled her back in a soothing motion.

I need this to end. She could almost envision her future with Saint with the threat of Adam lingering over them. She wasn't sure how long he'd sat with her, cuddled into his arms. It could have been minutes, hours, possibly days. Whatever the time frame, when she finally pulled away and glanced up at him, she felt a safe security wash over her.

"Rourke and Trax are gonna stay here with you, okay? I'll be back soon, and then I'm taking you home with me. Need you to pack some stuff for a few days, okay, sweetheart?"

What, no? He couldn't leave her; she needed him.

"No, I'll go with you."

He shook his head. "You can't." He gazed over her shoulder. "The guys are gonna be here, and nothing is gonna happen."

She glanced over her shoulder to see Trax and Rourke taking a protective stance in her living room.

"But I want. No…I *need* you to stay with me." She was on the verge of losing her shit. He was the only person keeping her calm right now. His hands grasped her jaw, bringing his face an inch from hers.

"Need you to stay with Rourke and Trax." His voice was low and gentle. He was making it clear this was not up for debate. She sniffled, and her chest shook.

"Hey, Bails, I can get Macy or Chey over here if ya want?" She recognized Trax's low voice from behind her. She closed her eyes. It was a sweet offer. Unfortunately, only Saint would do at the moment.

"You want the girls to come over? Would you feel better if they were here?" Saint asked.

She shook her head. "Feel better if you stayed." Even through her glassy stare, she caught his tiny sad smile. He leaned in and kissed her head, resting his lips on her forehead.

"I'll be back soon, I promise." He kissed her again, tugging her into his chest as his mouth glided over her ear. "Love you, sweetheart, and I'm coming back. Just need to handle this."

She squeezed his shoulders and hugged him into her body.

She lingered for a minute, and he let her. Whatever he needed to do would wait until she let go. Then she did. She slid off his lap and onto the couch, tucking her feet underneath her and wrapping her arms around her waist. Saint drove his hand softly through her locks and planted a kiss on her head before getting up and walking to the kitchen.

She heard the whispers but couldn't make out what they were saying. The door closed, and she heard footsteps.

"I can call Macy. She can be here in fifteen minutes?" Rourke's voice had been softer than usual.

She shook her head, keeping her gaze on the floor. She only wanted Saint. No other substitute would do.

"All right, if you change your mind, I'll get her up here for you."

She sniffled and glanced up through her glassy eyes. "Thanks, Rourke."

He nodded and drew in a breath. "It doesn't feel like it now, Bailey, but the worst is over, I promise."

She nodded.

Was it?

THE DRIVE to the secluded site took over an hour. This would happen, but not in their backyard, and nowhere close enough to link it to Bailey. If it came down to it, he would take it all, but it wouldn't, and he knew it. This was not the first time he'd play a part in the removal of trash however it was the first time it'd be personal, which meant he wouldn't have hands-on. Saint ground his teeth. Him laying hands on Adam would mean going up against Kase, and even more so, Hades. It was a rule from years back; if it was personal, the brother was a mere spectator. He'd strongly enforced the rule more times than he could count. He understood, the true retribution wasn't doing the damage; it was watching and appreciating the pain. He drew in a breath and stared out the window. Nothing but darkness stared back at him.

"Look for a marker, orange flag. He said it's the third on the left." Kase slowed down the truck.

He caught sight of the flag and jerked his chin, not uttering a word. Kase continued on the road, making a left at the barely seen driveway. It was overgrown with dense weeds. *Seclusion.*

Kase veered down the path past the three bikes, and the SUV parked out front. He circled the house, parking next to the van. They emerged from the truck and were greeted by two of Hades' brothers.

"He's inside," the biker said then turned to the truck. "We got him in the basement."

Saint hesitated and eyed the two bikers he'd known for years. Blade and Roan. They weren't his brothers, but there was a certain respect they granted being their Vice President's brother and a certain fear from knowing what Saint was capable of.

"No mistakes."

Blade nodded. "My word, brother."

Saint started toward the house with Kase following behind. He hadn't been here before and didn't know who the old farmhouse belonged to originally. If this was a safe house for Hades, then he was definitely the new property owner. He opened the screen door and made his way down the long hall, which opened up into the living room. Not one piece of furniture. The place had obviously been abandoned.

"Boys," Hades said, bringing a cigarette to his mouth for a drag. He lifted his chin to the open door leading down to the basement.

"Everything set?" Kase asked.

Hades blew out the smoke and his lips curled in a nasty smile. Saint was well versed in Hades and his devious mind. He lifted his brows. "Care to share?"

Hades' grin was menacing. "Eye for an eye." He took another drag, shrugging his shoulders. "Then I got some fun shit planned." Hades laughed. "Gonna make this last."

It was more than fair. This man maimed, scarred, and put his woman through excruciating, gut-wrenching pain, which lasted far longer than what he'd have to endure. But he would suffer.

"Let's go then." Kase followed Hades, and he passed Saint. Saint grabbed his arm halting him, gaining both men's attention.

Saint knew how this worked. Somehow, being a mere spectator wasn't going to work for him. "He's mine."

Hades straightened his back. Saint knew his brother would have his back. Kase, on the other hand, shook his head. There was a reason behind it, and Kase wasn't backing down. "Not the way we do things."

Saint growled. "Make an exception."

"No."

Saint could feel his anger rise.

"He's. Mine," Saint snapped, taking a step to Kase who didn't back away.

Hades brothers, Blade and Roan, had fallen in behind them, yet no one uttered a word. Ghosttown East handled retribution differently. They wouldn't understand.

Kase ambled forward and gripped Saint's shoulder. "The hands you touch your woman with will not be smeared with the blood of this piece of shit." It was a hard rule, one Saint had stood by, and one Kase wasn't willing to let him forget. "You feel me, brother?"

Saint nodded sharply. There was a reason behind this rule. His own anger was clouding it. Kase nodded and started down the steps as Saint followed, along with Hades, Blade, and Roan.

The dark, dank basement was exactly what he expected. He could smell the fear even before he descended. It was cliché, but it served its purpose. Adam was seated in the center of the room with Hades' men circled a few feet away. No escape.

His eyes were wild with fear.

Saint purposefully stepped slowly toward him. Sometimes the fear of the unknown was far greater than knowing one's fate. He would suffer physically and mentally. Just as Bailey had.

"Look." His breaths were uneven, as though he'd just finished a marathon. Sweat beaded his forehead, dripping down the side of his face. "I'm sorry, I made a mistake, but I wasn't gonna hurt her."

"You tossed her across the fucking room when we walked in," Kase growled and darted forward. Saint stopped him. With nothing more than Saint's arm blocking him, Kase halted.

Saint glared back at Adam. No words.

Hades stepped next to Saint, and his maniacal laugh barked through the room. "I'm gonna enjoy watching you suffer, motherfucker."

Adam jolted in his seat.

"N-no wait..." His heavy breath echoed through the barren room. "I j-just..."

Saint was not willing to listen to anything he said. The idea he could somehow justify seeking Bailey out and then going to her home had Saint burning with rage. He was notorious for his restraint. Adam's words were testing his control.

Saint stepped closer, and Adam's eyes watched his every move. "I made myself clear. It was a warning, not a threat." His brows embedded into a scowl. His tone was calm but lethal. "I gave you a chance. You chose not to take it."

"I'll never see her again."

Saint lifted his chin, his harsh glare aimed at Adam. "No, you won't."

Hades snorted. "In fact, you won't be *seeing* anyone ever again." The room erupted in laughter, everyone but Saint and Kase.

"What are ya gonna do, kill me? You don't think I got people who are gonna come looking for me? You won't get away with this." He shouted his threat and struggled against his restraints. His shaky tone only exposed his own doubt of what he was saying.

Saint stalked forward. "You tell anyone where you were going tonight?"

Adam drew in a breath and blurted. "Yes."

Saint smirked. "Liar."

"I did," he countered. Saint could see through it.

Saint cocked his brow. "I was going to let you live. I gave you fair warning, and you went against me." Saint walked toward him noticing his body tremor with fear. He leaned down bringing himself eye level with Adam. "Now, you die, slowly, painfully, but ultimately, you will die."

Saint straightened and stepped back, turning around silently. No one spoke another word. The only sound resonating through the cool, damp basement was a whimpering whine of a man whose fate had been sealed. *And he knows it.* When Saint reached the stairs, Blade nodded and stepped aside, clearing the path for his mandatory exit. If given the choice, Saint would have no issue with killing Adam with his bare hands.

Violence was never something Saint enjoyed. If the situation called for it, he acted. However, finding a resolution without violence had always been his priority. In most cases, it suited him. Not this time.

Saint walked up the stairs and through the old living room. The floors were weathered and thin, most had planks missing. He grasped the door but didn't halt when he heard the gut-wrenching shriek from down below. He walked outside and folded his arms, basking in the retribution from below.

Adam's wailing died down until it became muted. He must have passed out. Just as Bailey had when she was attacked. Saint drew in a deep breath, scanning the remote, desolate area. Without street or city lights, the area was drowning in darkness, with only the moonlight casting a soft glow.

Saint steadied his breath, combatting his fury into even breaths. Storming back into the house wouldn't change the outcome. Hades and Kase wouldn't allow him to partake with Adam. Just as he wouldn't allow it with other members in the past. Saint was forced to stand by the rule he himself set in place.

He remained fixated on the open field in front of him when the door from behind opened. An echoing scream for help vibrated over the wood under his feet. The desperation and agony in Adam's gurgling pleas had Saint closing his eyes. While he had no regrets seeking revenge for Bailey, he had an unexpected reaction.

In his mind, it was a soft, sweet cry, begging for help. It was Bailey.

"You good?" Kase asked.

"I will be when it's over."

Kase snorted. "Won't be much longer."

Saint inhaled, smelling a cigarette, and turned to Kase, who was watching him.

Kase jutted his chin. "You have second thoughts?"

Not one.

"I warned him to stay away from her." Saint drew in a breath. "I gave him a fair chance to walk away. Even with all the suffering he caused her, I gave him an out. All he had to do was take it." He paused. "He's getting exactly what he deserves, and we're getting a front-row view of the pain that Bailey must have gone through." *Eye for any eye, Hades said.* He gritted his teeth, fighting against his natural instinct to barrel through the door, storm down the steps, and kill Adam with his bare hands.

"It ends tonight, Saint."

Saint slowly shook his head. "Not for Bailey. The bastard will live forever in her past."

"And you'll be her future, brother."

Saint would be, along with Cia and the club.

They stood in silence. It had become eerily quiet which Saint assumed, meant Adam had passed out once again, or if they were lucky, he was dead. It wasn't an especially long suffering but it had certainly been a painful and torturous one. Saint had always been a man of few words, unlike his best friend beside him. It was odd standing next to a silent Kase. Quiet was never good. Saint glanced to his brother.

Kase stared back at him for a split second before smiling. He lifted his chin. "First time we met her, the town meeting. Fuck, man." Kase shook his head with a chuckle. "Came tripping into town hall like a baby giraffe."

For the first time all night, Saint smiled, remembering the first time he'd laid eyes on her. Then her voice, soft and sweet. And her smile.

"It was a fucking shit show. The whole fucking thing. Way too fucking Mayberry for us. Knew they wouldn't warm up to us. All the plans we made would fall to hell because the town wouldn't let themselves accept us. Not that it mattered, we were coming home, and wasn't a damn thing anyone could do." Kase shrugged. "Then Bailey happened. No fucking hesitation. Fucking shook our hands, brother. Friendly, welcoming, and I called bullshit on it." Kase turned, lifting the cigarette to his mouth. "No one's that fucking nice, right?"

Saint snickered. He didn't share Kase's thoughts when he'd met Bailey. For a man like Kase, who trusted only those close to him, he could understand his skepticism. Most people they'd met seemed to deal with the club with caution. Not Bailey.

"Took a few more meetings for me to see it. Your woman, all genuine, no agenda, good to the fucking core with a past that should have fucked her up, made her bitter as hell." He snorted, taking a drag. "And she's yours, Saint."

Yes, she is. He'd make it his life goal to make her happy and keep her past where it belonged. He eyed Kase. They'd known each other for so long, Saint was in-tune with what his friend had done. Kase created a distraction, focusing on the purpose of tonight being Bailey.

Saint smirked. "Regret making her off-limits?"

Kase knitted his brows and the corner of his mouth curled. "I don't deserve a woman like Bailey." Kase paused. "But you do, brother."

Kase was wrong. He did deserve a good woman. Someone who could see past his hard exterior and see the real Kase. A good man. It was on the tip of his tongue to tell him so. He never got the chance.

The echo shot sounded through the open field, jolting the wood under his feet. One shot was all it would take. It was done. He expected to feel a weight off his shoulders. He didn't. That would come when he had Bailey in his arms. He drew in a deep breath, releasing it slowly.

"Let's go." He started down the stairs with Kase next to his side.

Chapter 24

She heard the engines roll up her street. She had feigned being tired an hour ago. She knew they meant well, but she needed to be alone. Rourke had offered calling Macy several times. It was with the best intentions. The same with Trax when he suggested he call Marissa. She adamantly declined. This was her mess, and having her pregnant friend drive out to sit with her was not an option.

She'd spent the first hour with Rourke standing silently next to the couch. She had told him he didn't need to stand there, but he insisted. He vowed nobody would hurt her, and she believed him. Trax was equally protective, making her soup and sitting down next to her while she had a few bites. Even Gage, who sat quietly across from her, made her feel safe. *Saint's brothers, all there for me.*

Any stereotype she may have heard about rough and threatening bikers went out the door with these three. At one point she broke down, wanting to know what was happening. Trax curled her into his chest and soothed her. *Well, he tried.* He whispered, "Saint's gonna make this go away, Bailey. Trust him, okay?"

She simply nodded.

She had eventually retreated to her room. She was given the time to think. Possibly too much. When she heard the whispers from downstairs, she sat on her bed, hugging her knees into her chest.

Minutes later, her door creaked open, and Saint walked in. She scanned his body. She wasn't sure what happened tonight, but she needed to know he was okay.

He closed the door but didn't move farther into the room. She stared at him, waiting for him to speak. He shoved his hands in his pockets and stared back at her.

"He won't bother you ever again, sweetheart."

Maybe she should have asked what he meant. Maybe she should have been concerned about Adam's fate. She wasn't. All that mattered was Saint was standing across the room from her, not making any effort to come closer. He was keeping his distance when all she wanted was for him to hold her.

"I hate that you waited a year," she whispered, tears pooling in her eyes.

He furrowed his brows and stepped forward, but halted when she shook her head.

"Last year? I was a better version of myself. I had it all together. I could have given you the best of me." She rested her hand over her chest. "No baggage, just me."

"Not true, sweetheart."

It was. Before Adam's impending release, she was different. Without his dark cloud looming over her, she was just Bailey.

"It's how I feel. A year ago, I could have shared on my terms. I was stronger, Saint."

Saint drew in a breath and slowly made his way to her bed. He reached out, wiping her tears. She curled her face into the palm of his hand.

"I don't want a version of you, sweetheart. I just want you."

She lowered her head, curling into a ball on her bed. The mattress shifted, and she glanced up to see Saint sitting down staring at her.

"First time I saw you I was done. Remember?"

She nodded, remembering their first date and his admission.

"The woman stumbling into the town hall? There is no better version."

No, he was wrong. She covered her face with her hands, not wanting him to see her. Not the real her, with all the baggage and flaws and regrets.

His hand rested on head, weaving his finger through her hair.

"I don't want a version of you. Or you from five years ago? That's not the woman I fell in love with." His voice hovered over her ear. "This girl, the one who talks sweet to me, curls in next to me and sleeps in my arms, loves my daughter as if she were her own, the one who embraces my club, the one whose mark is permanently on my body, that's her, Bailey. You." His lips grazed her head. "I just want you, Bailey."

HE RESTED AGAINST HER HEADBOARD. It had taken an hour before she finally drifted and succumbed to her exhaustion. This wasn't over, not by a long shot. It would take time; he knew it. There would be questions, and he wasn't sure how he would go about answering them. All he knew was his future was with her, and he'd do whatever it took to keep her.

She curled into his chest as he rubbed her back. There was no going back from tonight. He may not have handed Adam his final blow, but he'd played a part. A major part. He tried to rouse an ounce of guilt, but he was left empty. He'd given Adam fair warning to stay away. He chose not to. Saint glanced down. Even through the dim light, he could see the raised bruise on her cheek and, as his gaze lowered, to her bottom split lip. A man like Adam would continue to abuse women. If not Bailey, some other poor woman.

His phone pinged, and he reached over to the nightstand, grabbing his phone.

"Yeah."

"It's done," Hades said.

It was the only way to guarantee her safety.

"You do it clean?"

It was imperative it couldn't be traced back to them, especially Bailey. It ended for her tonight.

"Yeah. Made sure nothing will ever touch Bailey. Won't touch any of us."

"Thanks."

Hades snorted. "Don't, man. She's family. You don't ever fucking thank me for family shit." He sighed. "How is she?"

Saint peered down at Bailey. She was fast asleep, and for the time being, she was good.

"She's good."

"Keep her that way. Talk to ya soon, brother." The phone clicked, and Saint ended the call.

Bailey stirred in his arms, and he caressed her back. She pried her eyes open.

"Who was that?"

"Hades."

She scrunched her nose, curling closer into his chest. "I am good, Saint," she whispered. "But I don't wanna know now."

"Okay."

"Not now. Someday I might want to."

"And if you do, I'll tell you."

She glanced up. "You will?"

His hand grazed her chin. "No secrets between us. You want to know, I'll tell you. If you don't? I won't bring it up." He cupped her jaw. "Need you to know, whatever did happen? All the men involved did it to keep you safe. They'd do it again."

The corner of her mouth curled as she stared up at him

"Can I change the subject?"

He nodded.

She heaved her body closer, leaving her lips inches away from his and her eyes staring back at him with a small smile playing on her lips.

"When we have children together? I hope they get your eyes."

Saint smiled.

"And your smile."

He shook his head. "As much as I'd like to give you everything you want? I want them to have your smile and your eyes, all your beauty and strength."

She chuckled, curling her face into his neck. "No, your eyes, Saint. I want those eyes looking back at me from everyone I love. You, Cia, and our babies."

Chapter 25

"Hey sweets, get me a beer?"

Bailey jerked her head and glanced up at the extremely tall, gruff man peering down at her. He must have been a member of the visiting club since she didn't recognize him. After spending the last few months with the Ghosttown Riders, she knew them all. She eyed his tatted arms, his belly poking out hanging over his belt, and his long silver-lined beard. He was standing with another man who she didn't know and was watching her with an amused grin.

"Hey."

Bailey shifted her gaze.

"Beer, anything on tap."

She flinched and widened her eyes. *Who the hell was this man? Hey sweets, get me a beer,* was not going to cut it.

"I'm not a waitress. If you want a beer, you'll have to get it yourself." She pointed behind him. "The bar is over there."

His friend laughed, but he didn't see the humor in her statement. His brows arched.

"Get me a fucking beer. Now."

Bailey snorted. "No." She turned away and crashed into a hard wall of flesh. She flattened her hands on his chest. The force was too hard, and her nose smashed into his leather. Large hands gripped her arms to steady her.

Her first instinct was to push him away.

"Hey, Grain, problem?"

Bailey glanced up at Dobbs, who was smiling, though it appeared forced. His jaw was tight, and his hooded eyes were aimed directly over her head. She slowly turned in his arms. He released her, and he remained close enough for their arms to touch.

"Won't be one if she gets me a beer like I fucking told her."

Dobbs snorted. "You told her to get you a beer?"

"Yeah." His tone was growing increasingly angry.

Dobbs laughed, which seemed out of place with the tense exchange. He pointed at Bailey. "Her. You told *her* to get you a beer?"

Grain stepped closer, and Bailey immediately retreated. The man seemed to be on the edge of losing his patience, and she didn't want to be in the crosshairs when it happened. She gripped Dobbs' arm, tugging him lightly. She was hoping to get his attention and have them both walk away. He didn't budge.

"I fucking told the cunt to get me a beer." He was only a foot away from Dobbs.

She peered up at Dobbs, who was smirking. What the hell was he doing? She saw nothing funny about this situation.

Dobbs lifted his hand. "Okay, I just wanna make sure I'm getting it a hundred percent. You," he pointed to Grain. "Are ordering her," his thumb hooked over his shoulder, gesturing to Bailey, then paused. "*Saint's old lady*, to get you a beer. Is that what's happening?"

"Oh, fuck." The hushed curse caught her attention, and she looked at the man who was standing with Grain. His face paled, and he was staring at the ceiling. She shifted her gaze to Grain, who was staring down at her. He'd lost his scowl, which was replaced by what she assumed was fear.

Dobbs laughed and slapped the man on his chest. "Yeah, fucker."

"I didn't fucking know." He eyed her. "Why didn't you say something?"

She shrugged. "You didn't ask me. Besides, it shouldn't matter who I'm with. You shouldn't order any of the women around."

Dobbs snickered. "She's got a point, man."

"Fuck." Grain drove his hand through his long greasy hair.

Dobbs stepped closer to him. "Turn around, walk your fat ass over to the bar, and get a beer, man."

Grain drew in a deep breath, not even fazed by the dig on his weight. His only concern seemed to be with her. He looked over at Bailey and nodded his chin before turning and disappearing into the crowd. Dobbs angled his arm around her shoulder and walked her through the door to the yard, where she was originally headed before the confrontation.

Once they got outside, Bailey stepped out of his hold and turned. "Thanks."

Dobbs shrugged. "Believe it or not, he's not a bad guy. You gonna mention this to Saint?"

"Should I?"

"Not unless ya wanna see Grain get his ass beat all over the parking lot."

The last thing she wanted to see was a physical altercation.

She shook her head. "No."

Dobbs laughed. "Didn't think so. Doesn't mean I'm gonna share that with Grain, though. Let the asshole sweat all day, watching his back for Saint."

Bailey laughed and started down toward the table where the women were seated. The club had a family barbeques once a month. For the past two, Cia had joined them. If she wasn't with Bailey, she was glued to Saint's side. As she moved closer, she noticed her other little sidekick sitting in her seat.

Allie wiggled off the seat when Bailey got closer.

"The big kids are on the trampoline in the back. You want to go play?" she asked Allie. She knew the answer before she asked. Allie was like an extra limb when Bailey was around.

"No, I'm tired."

Bailey sat, and before she was fully settled, Allie was climbing on her lap.

Hades had taken Bailey up on her offer to watch Allie occasionally, and as his work took him out of town, Saint and Bailey became his go-to sitters, which neither of them minded, especially Bailey. She curled her arms around Allie.

"You need to get one of those of your own." Meg chuckled, gesturing to Allie.

Bailey smirked. "I'm working on it." *Liar.*

Macy slapped the table. "I knew it." She winked. "You owe us details."

Bailey snorted. "Are you gonna give up details on Rourke?" It was a counter.

Cheyenne moaned and held up her hand. "She will, so don't ask."

The women laughed and continued their banter. Bailey had a feeling the reason Macy wasn't currently sharing had something to do with the four-year-old nestled in her lap. *Thank God for Allie.*

"How's Riss?"

Bailey curled her arms around Allie and rested her chin on her head. It took less than five minutes for her to fall asleep.

"Ready to pop."

"We need more babies around here," Meg said, downing the remainder of her beer. Bailey noticed Macy eye Cheyenne with a small smirk. Though it hadn't been formally announced, she could read through the exchange between the best friends. Bailey smiled.

Looks like Meg is gonna get her wish.

"God, he's sexy," Meg whispered with her gaze over her shoulder. She turned her head to catch Saint and Hades walking toward them.

Bailey giggled. "Yes, he is."

The Saint

Meg glanced over at Bailey and laughed. "I was talking about Hades, but yeah, your man is hot, Bails."

She felt his hands on her shoulders. "Ready to head home."

She was. As much as she enjoyed the barbeques, she was equally, if not more happy staying at home. Either house, as they had yet to spend a night apart from each other. It had become an issue in the past two months. When Saint brought up the idea of moving in together, she jumped at the chance until where they would live became topic.

The most sensible choice would be his place. His house was updated, and been completely renovated. He had four bedrooms and large enough property to build on. He'd just acquired the two vacant properties next to his, which meant he could build a separate garage. Cia was also working on him to put in a pool. His place made sense.

Yet, she couldn't bring herself to sell her own house. It was small, and not on the best piece of land. But it held her memories.

Saint squeezed her shoulders, and she moved to the edge of the chair, hoisting Allie closer. She stood, saying goodbye to the women before turning toward Hades and Saint.

"Thanks for watching her," Hades said, reaching out and taking Allie. Bailey rested her hand on Allie's back, and she grumbled but settled in against Hades wrapping her arms around his neck and her legs around his waist.

"She give you any trouble?"

Bailey rolled her eyes. "Never."

Hades snickered.

Saint curled his arm around her waist. "How are you feeling?" he whispered in her ear.

Like Cheyenne, it was too early to share their news with everyone. She was only a month along. They had only shared with one person and swore her to secrecy.

"Tired." She reached up, taking his lips for a quick kiss. "Where's Cia?"

"Kase." Saint smirked. "I came to get you while she finished kicking his ass in darts in front of the brothers."

Bailey laughed.

They made their way through the clubhouse barroom and down the hall. She grasped Saint's hand as they entered the back room. There were quite a few brothers scattered around the room. At one of the pub tables, Cia sat with Kase, Trax, Rourke, Gage, and Dobbs while a few others were gathered.

When they walked in, the room was drowned in silence, and each of the men turned toward them. Bailey furrowed her brows. She was accustomed to a friendly greeting from the men, including Kase, but this was off. They were all smiling, pure joy shining on each one of these rough and dangerous men's faces.

She glanced up at Saint, who was sending a sharp stare to the middle of the group. She followed his gaze to Cia, who was centered between the brothers. She was smiling with a tinge of guilt flashing over her features.

"Cia," Saint said sternly.

She shrugged her shoulder. "Sorry, I'm just really excited."

Bailey's shoulders sagged. She felt the giddy bubble fester in her stomach and the rise of her laughter. *This is what ya get when you share a secret with a nine-year-old.*

Bailey squeezed his hand, gaining Saint's attention. He glanced down at her, and his scowl eased, and the corner of his lip curled.

She turned to the group. "Well, who's gonna make the first toast?"

The room erupted in laughter. Kase was the first to raise his glass.

Saint cleared his throat and glanced down at Cia. Bailey watched the silent warning. Whatever Kase was about to say had to be PG-rated. Kase glanced down at Cia and lifted his chin to her glass of soda. She grabbed it, striking her hand in the air and smiling back at Bailey.

Kase continued. "To the next Ghosttown Rider…"

Cia hopped off her seat and turning to him. "Uncle Kase, no. We want a girl."

Bailey giggled at the same time Saint snickered as he pulled her into his chest.

"Right." Kase nodded, then glanced up at Saint, raising his glass. "May you continue to be surrounded by beautiful, sweet girls, my brother."

The roar from the brothers was more than she could take. She may have wanted to wait on telling everyone, but hearing the excitement was well worth Cia's sharing their secret.

"What's going on?"

Bailey turned to find Macy, Cheyenne, Meg, and Nadia standing at the door, glancing around the room in obvious confusion. Keeping their secrets from the ladies wouldn't be possible now. She knew they'd share in her excitement. Her belly swirled as she opened her mouth. Unfortunately, Cia beat her to the announcement.

"We're having a baby!" Cia blurted out, and Bailey laughed. She loved how she said, *we are having a baby*. It was true. This baby would be just as much Cia's as it would be Bailey and Saint's. She felt his arm wrap around her stomach with Saint's hand resting on her belly. His breath fanned over her ear.

"Next baby, we aren't telling her until we announce it, I promise."

She turned her head and leaned up to kiss him. "I don't care, as long as I get to have more babies with you."

"As many as you want, sweetheart." Saint kissed her again, but it was cut short from the squeals in the room. He unhooked his hold over her as the women made a beeline for her.

Macy got to her first, hugging her and kissing her cheek. "Oh my God, I'm gonna make the best aunt, I promise."

She would. She didn't get to relay that fact because Meg had wedged herself in between them. She pulled Bailey in for hug and whispered in her ear, "I'm gonna spoil this baby, just a warning." She released her and walked to Saint. They were only a foot apart when she heard Meg whisper, "Mick is looking down, smiling on you, Saint." She kissed his cheek then cupped his jaw. "He is toasting a cold one up there for you."

Saint nodded, and Bailey could see a slight break in his usual solid stoic demeanor. She knew who Mick was and what he meant to the club. *What he meant to Saint.*

Hands gripped her waist, and she turned to find Cheyenne with tears in her eyes.

"I'm so happy for you, Bailey." She hugged her closer, and Bailey whispered, "And when you announce it, I'm going to be this happy for you, Chey." Cheyenne hugged her tighter, and when she pulled away, she grasped her hands and lowered her voice. "They'll either be best friends, or they'll date." Cheyenne winked and released her.

The outpouring of excitement had Bailey regretting they had waited. She turned and watched as the women and men circled around Saint offering their congratulations. She realized how much not only they were loved, but this baby was. She rested her hand on her belly and sighed.

A soft hand grazed her shoulder and she turned to find Nadia with tears in her eyes.

"Congratulations, Bailey." She sniffled. "I'm so happy for you guys."

"Aw, Nadia." Bailey wrapped her arms around her shoulders. "Thank you."

"You and Saint are just gonna make the best parents." She tightened her grip. "And I'm available for babysitting any time." She laughed.

Bailey pulled away and tilted her head. She reached out, wiping her cheek. "You better be, *Aunt Nadia.*"

Nadia's smile faltered, and her eyes teared again. "Bailey," she whispered. Bailey couldn't be sure exactly what she was seeing from Nadia, but whatever it was, it warmed her heart. This woman was just as much a part of their lives as any member of the club. Bailey saw them all as being a part of her life, Saint's life, and their babies'.

Nadia sucked in a breath and shook her head while wiping her eyes. "We don't have champagne, but we got tequila, I'm gonna get a round of shots." The room cheered and she turned glancing over her shoulder. "And a shot of orange juice for the mama-to-be." She winked and sauntered out the door.

Once I have the baby, I'm definitely gonna get her to teach me how she does that walk.

She was lost in thought when she felt his arms wrap around her waist. She turned and reached out, wrapping her arms over his shoulders and pulling him down for a kiss. Her lips glided over his. She wanted nothing more than to deepen the kiss, but the time and place was not now.

"Who would have thought, you, me, and a baby," she teased.

"The mayor and the biker," he whispered.

She peered up through her lashes. "And they lived happily ever after."

The End

About the Author

Amelia Shea writes contemporary romance. She released her debut novel in 2015 and has followed her passion for series romance ever since. Her writing style includes a little sweet, a little sassy, and lots of steam. She loves building stories with settings that become comfortable and familiar, and developing characters who feel real, and though they may be flawed, they learn and grow, and finally deserve a happy ending.

Born and raised a Jersey girl, she has settled down in the South with her amazingly supportive husband, her fabulous (most days) children, and her loyal, four-legged, furry sidekick, Bob.

Website: AmeliaShea.net

- facebook.com/AsheaWrites
- twitter.com/AsheaWrites
- instagram.com/Author_amelia_shea
- amazon.com/Author/Amelia-Shea
- goodreads.com/Amelia_Shea
- bookbub.com/authors/amelia-shea

Printed in Great Britain
by Amazon